EXPEDITION!

* WAGONS WEST *
THE FRONTIER TRILOGY
VOLUME II

EXPEDITION!

DANA FULLER ROSS

G·K·Hall&Co.

Boston, Massachusetts
1993

**This Large Print Book carries the
Seal of Approval of N.A.V.H.**

Published in Large Print by arrangement with
Book Creations, Inc.

G.K. Hall Large Print Book Series.

World rights courtesy of Book Creations.

Printed on acid free paper in the United States of America.

Set in 16 pt. Plantin.

Library of Congress Cataloging-in-Publication Data

Ross, Dana Fuller
    Expedition! / Dana Fuller Ross.
        p. cm. — (Wagons west, the frontier trilogy ; v. 2)
    (G.K. Hall large print book series)
        ISBN 0-8161-5514-3 (alk. paper). — ISBN 0-8161-5515-1
    (pbk. : alk. paper)
        1. Large type books. I. Title. II. Series.
    [PS3513.E8679W47 1993]
    813'.54—dc20   92-30415

Also published in Large Print from G.K. Hall by Dana Fuller Ross:

Wagons West
Independence!
Nebraska!
Wyoming!
Oregon!
Texas!
California!
Colorado!
Nevada!
Washington!
Montana!
Dakota!
Utah!
Idaho!
Missouri!
Mississippi!
Louisiana!
Tennessee!
Illinois!
Wisconsin!
Kentucky!
Arizona!
New Mexico!
Oklahoma!

EXPEDITION!

Part I

This town is finely situated on both banks of the Muskingum, at the confluence of that river with the Ohio. It is principally built on the left bank, where there are ninety-seven houses, including a court-house, a market-house, an academy, and a post-office. There are about thirty houses on the opposite bank, the former scite (sic) of Fort Harmar, which was a United States garrison during the Indian wars, but of which no vestige now remains. Some of the houses are of brick, some of stone, but they are chiefly of wood, many of them large, and having a certain air of taste. There are two rope walks, and there were on the stocks two ships, two brigs, and a schooner. A bank is established here, which began to issue notes on the 20th inst. Its capital is one hundred thousand dollars, in one thousand shares: Mr. Rufus Putnam is the president.

The land on which Marietta is built, was purchased during the Indian war, from the United States, by some New England land speculators, who named themselves the Ohio Company. They chose the land facing the Ohio, with a depth from the river of only from twenty to thirty miles to the northward, thinking the proximity of the river would add to its value, but since the state of Ohio has began (sic) to be generally settled, the rich levels in the interior have been preferred, but not before the company had made large sales, particularly to settlers from New England, notwithstanding the greatest part of the tract was broken and hilly, and the hills mostly poor, compared with those farther to the westward, on both sides of the river.

—Fortescue Cuming
"Sketches of a Tour to the
Western Country"
The tour having been made in 1807–1809,
publication from a Pittsburgh press, 1810

I

God had made prettier country than the Ohio River valley, Jefferson Holt thought as he guided his horse down a road that ran alongside a stream. He had seen quite a bit of it, particularly those majestic peaks that formed the spine of the continent. Some called them the Rockies; to the Indians who lived there, as well as to men like Jeff Holt, they were the Shining Mountains.

But the rolling hills of Ohio, lush and green with the arrival of spring of 1809, were beautiful, too. To Jeff they represented home.

That was a beautiful word, Jeff thought. *Home* . . .

He was in his prime, twenty-four years old, with the strength and vitality that sprang from a frontier heritage and a vigorous outdoor life. He rode straight in the saddle, his keen brown eyes scanning the terrain ahead and to either side of him. A black felt hat was cuffed back on his head, revealing a shock of curly, sandy-blond hair. He wore a homespun shirt, laced at the throat with a rawhide thong, and fringed buckskin trousers tucked into high black boots. He carried a flintlock pistol under his broad black belt, which also supported a sheathed hunting knife. Balanced on the pommel of his saddle was a long-barreled .54 caliber flintlock rifle with brass straps, buttplate, and patchbox on the polished wooden stock, a product of the Harper's Ferry armory in Virginia. Slung over his shoulder were a powder horn and shot pouch.

Once Jeff had been a farmer. Now, however, he had the look of exactly what he was: a frontiersman. He had spent the past two years trapping beaver in the great western mountains with his older brother, Clay. The previous fall Jeff had voyaged down the Missouri River to St. Louis, along with a boatload of pelts belonging to the man who employed the Holt brothers, the shrewd fur trader Manuel Lisa. After waiting out the harsh winter in St. Louis, Jeff had struck out for Marietta, Ohio, which had, some twenty years earlier, been the first white settlement in what was then known as the Northwest Territory. The Holt family homestead was near Marietta.

Jeff frowned as bitter memories flooded his mind. He and Clay had left Marietta under a cloud, after an outbreak of violence that had resulted in several deaths, including those of their parents, Bartholomew and Norah Holt. Jeff intended to pay a visit to the family farm while he was there, but that was not the real reason he had come back.

He was there for Melissa.

Melissa . . . his wife, his love, the beautiful young woman he had been forced to leave behind when he and Clay headed west. Not a single day had passed during those two years when Jeff had not missed her terribly. Now that he was nearing Marietta, he felt his excitement build. Soon he would be holding Melissa in his arms again. After all this time, it was hard to wait.

He turned the horse away from the main road toward a path that ultimately led to the Holt farm. His primary destination, however, was another farm on the same path. It belonged to his father-in-law, Melissa's father, Charles Merrivale.

Would Melissa be surprised to see him? He had written her from St. Louis, but mail service was undependable, especially west of the Appalachians. It was entirely possible the letter had been lost or delayed so that Jeff would arrive before his message did. He almost hoped that would be the case; he would enjoy seeing the look on Melissa's face when he rode up, called her name, then swept her into his arms when she came running to him.

As that pleasant fantasy played itself out in his mind, he urged the horse on to a faster pace.

Soon the Merrivale farmhouse came into view. One of the most impressive structures in the area, it was built of planed and finished logs, which gave it a more sophisticated appearance than the crude cabins that were so common. The roof was covered with wooden shingles, and the windows had panes of glass in them, glass that Charles Merrivale had paid dearly to have transported from the East. Only the best for his family, he had been heard to say many times, only the best.

That had not included Jefferson Holt as a husband for Merrivale's daughter, his only child. But ultimately he had not been the one to make that decision. Jeff and Melissa were in love, and they had been married with her father's grudging acceptance, if not his blessing.

His heart pounding rapidly, Jeff reined the horse to a stop in front of the house. He could see no movement from inside or from the barn out back, and except for a few cows, the fields were deserted. Everyone must be inside, he figured. It was about midday; Melissa and her parents were probably sitting down to dinner.

He was swinging down from his saddle when from out of the corner of his eye he saw the black snout of a musket emerge from a hole cut into the wall near the door for defense. Shocked by the sight, he froze.

The musket blasted. Instincts honed by his life in the mountains took over, and Jeff grabbed his rifle and flung himself off the horse as the musket ball sliced through the air where he had been an instant before. He landed hard, then rolled over, and the impact sent his own rifle slipping from his fingers. He rolled again and came up into a crouch, reaching for the pistol tucked under his belt. A second shot from the cabin whipped past Jeff's ear, making him dive forward. He sprawled on the ground, sheltered by a watering trough with thick wooden sides.

"Hold your fire!" he shouted without lifting his head. "It's me, Jeff!" Maybe Charles Merrivale had not recognized him, had perhaps taken him for a thief. Jeff knew his appearance had changed in the two years he had been gone. He was leaner, tougher, harder-looking now.

Or maybe Merrivale had recognized him after all. The man had never liked him. But would he try to kill him?

"It's Jeff, blast it!" he called again. "Jeff Holt!"

An unfamiliar voice shouted, "I don't know no Jeff Holt! Come on out of there with your hands up, stranger, and maybe I won't kill you!"

Who the devil . . . Jeff did not know whether to believe the man or not. If he stood, he might end up with a musket ball through him.

On the other hand, he could not lie there in the dirt all day. He had ridden hundreds of miles to see his wife, perhaps even to take Melissa back west with him, and he was damned if he was going to let some lunatic with a gun keep him away from her.

"All right," he replied, raising his voice but keeping his head low. "I'll stand up, but go easy on that trigger, mister. I don't mean anybody any harm."

"We'll see about that. Get up slow and easy, and you'd best not be holding a gun when you do."

7

Jeff slipped his pistol under his belt, took as deep a breath as he could lying on the ground, and pushed himself up onto his knees. Carefully he got to his feet.

After he had raised his hands, palms open to show he was unarmed, the door of the cabin opened, and a man stepped out, a musket clutched tightly in his hands. He trained the weapon on Jeff, who could see that it was cocked.

"Who the hell are you?" the man demanded suspiciously. He was tall, rawboned, and balding. "I don't like folks sneaking around my place. Now speak up, or I won't fire another warning shot."

Neither of the first two shots had been meant as warnings, Jeff thought grimly. They had come altogether too close to his head. But Jeff was not going to argue with him, not under the circumstances.

"I told you, my name is Jefferson Holt. I'm looking for the Merrivales. Are they here?"

"This is my place," the man snapped. "It don't belong to nobody named Merrivale."

Now that he'd had a chance to get a better look at the house, Jeff noticed some changes in it. The window glass of which Charles Merrivale had been so proud was dirty, with at least several months' worth of grime accumulated on it. Some of the wooden shingles on the roof had come off and not been replaced, and one of the puncheons that formed the porch stuck up at an angle. Jeff glanced at the barn and saw that it was in dis-

8

repair, too. Charles Merrivale never would have allowed such deterioration to go unchecked.

That realization sent Jeff's heart plummeting. Charles and Hermione—and Melissa, too—were gone. He would have seen that right away had he not been so excited and full of anticipation when he'd ridden up to the house. And he had been too busy dodging musket balls since then to see what was now so obvious.

"Listen," he said urgently to the man holding the musket. "I'm not looking for trouble. Some people named Merrivale used to live here. Please, do you know anything about them? If you do, just tell me and I'll leave peacefully."

"You'll leave peacefully if'n I don't tell you nothing."

"Wait, Walter!" came a voice from inside the house. A woman leaned out the doorway. "Don't hurt the boy. He doesn't mean any harm."

"Get back in the house, Katey!" the man ordered without turning around. "I told you to stay in there with the young'uns, where it's safe."

"It's safe enough here," the woman said, stepping into view on the porch. "Mr. Holt's not going to hurt anyone."

"No, ma'am. I'm surely not."

The woman had the plain, hard-used features of most frontier wives, but as long as she was telling her husband not to shoot him, Jeff thought she was beautiful. Several children clustered around her, hiding behind her skirts.

"Look, I bought this place fair and square,"

9

Walter said, still pointing the musket at Jeff's chest. "We been here now for more than a year. I done paid my taxes. This farm is mine!"

"Nobody said it isn't." Jeff tried to remain calm and hoped Walter would do the same. "I'm not interested in your farm. My family has a place of its own, on up the road about a mile. The Holt homestead? Maybe you've heard of it."

The woman called Katey said, "I've heard of the Holts. Thought they'd all moved away, though."

"We have, ma'am," Jeff told her. "But I've come back for a visit, to make sure the place is all right and see that the taxes are paid on it. And to see my wife. I thought I'd find her here."

Walter shook his head. "Told you we don't know nothing about the Merrivales. Now I'll thank you to git."

"I swear, Walter, I've never known you to be so unsociable!" Katey exclaimed. "Now put that gun down. We might as well be civil to this young man. He looks as though he's ridden a long way."

"From the Rocky Mountains, ma'am," Jeff warmly informed her. "And I'd surely admire to put my arms down without having to worry about your husband blasting me with that blunderbuss."

"Aw, hell." Walter lowered the musket. "I reckon you ain't no thief after all. But don't try nothing, or I will shoot you, sure as anything."

Grateful, Jeff lowered his arms. "Thanks, but you don't have to worry, Mr. . . . ."

"Seeger," Walter replied, still surly and suspicious. "Walter Seeger. This's my wife, Katey, and our young'uns."

Jeff tugged his hat off and nodded to the woman. "Pleased to meet you, Mrs. Seeger. I'm sorry if I've upset your family by showing up like this today. Like I said, I just want to find my wife."

It was taking quite an effort of will for Jeff to keep his voice calm and his words polite. Panic was scrabbling around in his mind like a crazed animal. *Where could Melissa and her parents have gotten to?*

"Why don't you come inside, Mr. Holt?" Katey Seeger asked. "We were just about to sit down at the table, and you're welcome to join us."

From the look on Walter's face, Jeff could tell that he was not happy about the invitation his wife had just issued, but he was bound by the code of hospitality that frontier folks lived by: No stranger was turned away from the table as long as he was peaceable.

Jeff tied his horse to a post beside the watering trough, then turned toward the house. Walter kept his musket tucked under his arm as he followed Jeff, Katey, and the Seeger children into the cabin. As he entered and looked around, Jeff saw that the expensive furnishings he remembered from his visits to the Merrivales were gone, replaced by rough-hewn tables and chairs that had probably been built by Walter. The floor was bare; no sign remained of the woven

11

rugs in which Hermione Merrivale had taken such pride.

There were four Seeger children, three girls and a boy, all under the age of ten. They watched him shyly as he sat down at the table with their father.

The farmer placed the musket on the bench beside him, looked at Jeff shrewdly, and asked, "You say you used to live around here?"

"That's right. My father was Bartholomew Holt. My mother's name was Norah," Jeff replied. "My family's lived in these parts since after the Revolution, when the government paid off some of the soldiers with land in the Ohio Valley."

"I wasn't in the war," Walter said. "Not old enough. Would've fought the damned British if I could have, though."

"That was before my time, I'm afraid," Jeff said. "I heard my father talk about it some. He had a great admiration for Mr. Thomas Jefferson. That's how I came to have the name."

"Jefferson"— Walter made a face. "Nothing but a dandified whoremonger, if you ask me."

"Walter!" Katey exclaimed. "Think of the children and watch what you say!"

Grumpily Walter said, "Sure, sure. I just don't have no use for any of them politicians, Jefferson included."

Jeff made no comment. He had never met Thomas Jefferson and knew little of the man's personal life, but he held some admiration for the former president anyway. It was Thomas Jefferson who had sent Captain Meriwether Lewis and Captain William Clark on their already legendary journey of exploration to the Pacific several years earlier. Jeff's own brother Clay had been part of the Corps of Discovery led by Lewis and Clark, and that experience had led Clay to return to the Rocky Mountains as a fur trapper, taking Jeff along with him.

Katey stirred the pot of stew simmering over low flames in the fireplace.

"Holt," she mused. "Seems like I do remember hearing talk in Marietta about a family named Holt. There was some sort of trouble a few years back, wasn't there?"

"Yes, ma'am," Jeff said, his features grim. "There sure was. My ma and pa were killed when their cabin was burned down."

"Oh, my!" Katey raised a hand to her mouth. "I'm sorry, Mr. Holt. I didn't mean to bring up any bad memories."

"That's all right," Jeff told her kindly. "It's all a long time in the past now. What I'm really worried about is finding the Merrivales."

Walter rubbed his stubbled jaw and said slowly, "I been thinking about that. I reckon I did hear something about them, after all. Took me a few minutes to recollect."

Jeff leaned forward, trying not to let his eagerness get out of hand. "What have you heard?"

"Just talk in Steakley's store, you understand. Seems they pulled up stakes and headed back East. Merrivale must've been a fool if he was willing to give up a piece of prime land like this," Walter added. "Either that, or he purely hated living out here."

"Some of both, I imagine," Jeff said. "Mr. Merrivale never was very comfortable as a farmer. He was a businessman from the East somewhere."

"Then I reckon that's what he went back to."

That made sense, Jeff thought. It had been a mistake for a man like Charles Merrivale to try to live the life of a gentleman farmer on the frontier. Jeff would not be surprised in the slightest if Merrivale had decided to return to his former home and go back into business. Hermione would have accompanied him, of course, and Jeff was sure, knowing Charles Merrivale as he did, that the man would have insisted Melissa go, too, even though she was married. Merrivale was used to running roughshod over the members of his family, and Melissa had a tendency to give in to her father's demands. Jeff had to admit that about his wife, no matter how much he loved her.

"You didn't hear anything specific about where they might have gone?" he asked.

"Nope. Or if I did, I've forgot it by this time. Been quite a while since I heard anything about the Merrivales, you understand."

Katey carried a wooden bowl full of the steaming, aromatic stew to where Jeff sat and placed it in front of him.

"We could try to find out, if you'd like," she offered.

"No, ma'am, but thank you, anyway. You've

14

done enough, just showing me your hospitality like this." *And keeping your husband from shooting me,* Jeff added to himself. "I reckon Mr. Steakley at the store still remembers me. He'll know where the Merrivales went, if anybody around here does."

"You're right," Walter said. "Ol' Steakley usually winds up knowing just about everything there is to know about folks in these parts."

Katey gave Jeff a hunk of bread torn from a loaf that was warming on the hearth, then filled a mug with fresh milk from a pitcher before serving the meal to the rest of her family. The food was good, although at that time of year the stew was heavy on venison and light on vegetables. Jeff had little appetite, however, and ate without really tasting the food. He was too busy thinking about the unexpected development that fate had thrown his way.

For months now—years really, ever since he had left Ohio for the first time—he had been anticipating his reunion with Melissa. He had played out the scene countless times in his mind. But never in the wildest stretch of his imagination had he thought that she would not be there. Originally, she was supposed to go to Pittsburgh with Edward, Susan, and Jonathan Holt, his younger siblings. When he was in St. Louis, waiting with Clay for the fur-trapping expedition to head up the Missouri, Jeff had received a letter from Melissa explaining how she had decided to stay in Ohio with her parents. Jeff had accepted

15

that, although he would have preferred her sticking to their original plan. But to get back to Ohio and then find her gone . . .

"Mr. Holt?"

Katey Seeger's voice interrupted Jeff's brooding thoughts. He looked up.

"Something wrong with the stew?"

He realized he had stopped eating and was just sitting there with a spoon in one hand and the hunk of bread in the other.

Smiling, he said, "It's all delicious. I was just thinking."

"About them Merrivales, I reckon," Walter said. He spooned stew into his mouth, chewed, and swallowed. "I wish we could be of more help, but there's just no telling where they went. Ain't you got no idea?"

Jeff had already begun casting his mind back over every conversation he could recall with all three Merrivales, not just Melissa. Had any of them ever told him exactly where they had lived before coming to Ohio? Jeff had never spoken much with Charles Merrivale, due to the tension between them, and although Hermione had been friendly enough to him, she had a tendency to ramble rather aimlessly when she was talking. His conversations with Melissa had usually centered around the present or the future, rather than the past. Besides, any time they had been alone, there had not been a great deal of talking going on.

"Back East" was the most precise answer Jeff

16

could come up with to the question now plaguing him. And it was not much of an answer.

During the rest of the meal, he forced himself to be polite and pleasant to the Seegers, although impatience was building inside him again. They were curious about the Rocky Mountains, and he answered their questions about his life as a fur trapper. Since the Seeger youngsters were also listening avidly, he deliberately glossed over some of the more bloody and dangerous events—like Indian attacks, knife fights with other trappers, and a murderous Frenchman named Duquesne who had nearly plunged the whole frontier into chaos.

"You say your brother is married to a Sioux woman?" Katey asked eagerly, her eyes shining. People on the frontier were always hungry for a story, even one that had no real connection to them.

"Yes, ma'am. Her name's Shining Moon. She's mighty pretty, and I don't reckon we'd have made it out there without her and her brother, a young man called Proud Wolf. They are from the Hunkpapa tribe, part of the Teton Sioux. They've been helping us out right along."

"That's remarkable," Katey breathed.

"You trust them Injuns?" Walter asked with a scowl.

"Some of them I'd trust with my life," Jeff declared. "I've done just that, in fact. Shining Moon's people, the Hunkpapa, have always gotten along real well with the whites. The Black-

17

foot, now, they're a different story, and so are the Arikara and the Crow. We steer clear of them whenever we can."

Walter shook his head. "With all the stories I've heard about them savages, I wouldn't trust a one of them, not even them Sioux. That brother of your'n'll wake up one mornin' with his throat cut by that squaw."

Jeff said nothing. Shining Moon was about the prettiest, bravest, most gentle woman he had ever met—except for Melissa, of course—and he was sure Clay had nothing to worry about except being deserving of such a mate. But sitting there and arguing with Walter Seeger would not serve any purpose.

When he had finished the food, Jeff thanked Katey again and then reached for his hat. "I'll ride on into the settlement," he said. "I appreciate the help. And thanks for not shooting me, Walter. I know it wasn't for lack of trying."

Walter grunted. He looked a bit sheepish. "Sorry, Holt. A man's got to protect his family out here, though. Can't be too careful."

"That's right." Jeff said good-bye to the children, tipped his hat one more time to Katey, then went outside and mounted up. The Seeger family watched him from the porch as he rode away.

Nice folks, Jeff thought, although Walter was a mite on the unfriendly side.

Jeff kicked his horse into a fast trot toward the river road. When he reached it, he swung toward

Marietta. Seeing his family's homestead would have to wait until he found out Melissa's whereabouts.

The settlement was laid out on the northwest shore of the Ohio River, opposite the site of Fort Harmar, which had been established by General Rufus Putnam following the end of the American Revolution. At first, Marietta had been known as Campus Martius. Over the years it had grown into an attractive community, with several wharves built into the river and warehouses nearby. There were businesses, churches, and even a school. It represented civilization, picked up bodily and carried into what had been wilderness only a few years earlier.

The center of town, at least from the standpoint of community activities, was Steakley's Trading Post, a large, stout structure of logs with a porch that ran around three sides. It did a brisk business. If one was looking for someone in the Marietta area, Steakley's was the place to wait. Almost everyone went there sooner or later.

The establishment was busy as usual that afternoon, Jeff saw from the number of horses, wagons, and buggies tied up at the long hitching rail in front of the building. He found a place for his horse, flipped the reins around the rail, then climbed the three steps onto the porch. As he headed toward the main doors, one of them opened, and a man stepped out with a bag of sugar balanced on his shoulder.

"Jeff Holt!" the man exclaimed in surprise.

"Hello, Mr. Steakley," Jeff replied. "I'll wager you never expected to see me again."

"Hell, no, boy." The storekeeper grinned. He was a balding middle-aged man with stooped shoulders. "We heard that you'd likely gone west to the mountains, but most folks around here figured you'd get your hair lifted by some of those red heathens. What in blazes are you doing back in Marietta?"

"I came to pay the taxes on the farm, to make sure it stays in the family." Jeff paused, then went on, "And to get Melissa. But I'm told she and her parents don't live here anymore."

Rathburn Steakley pursed his lips. "Let me put this sugar on Hank Bradford's wagon, and then I'll tell you what I know. But I warn you, it's not much."

"Anything will help."

Several customers passed Jeff on the porch while Steakley loaded the bag of sugar onto one of the wagons in front of the store. Some of them looked at Jeff curiously, as if they almost recognized him but not quite, while others paid little or no attention to him. In the two years Jeff had been gone, Marietta had grown, and a lot of the people were strangers to him.

Steakley approached him and put a hand on his arm. "Come on inside. We'll go into the office to talk."

Jeff let Steakley lead him through the long room crowded with counters, shelves, and customers. Two young men wearing the white aprons of clerks were behind the main counter in the back of the store. Steakley's business had also expanded, Jeff noticed. He could remember when the man had run the trading post by himself.

Steakley opened a door behind the rear counter and led Jeff into a small office dominated by a desk covered with papers. There were two chairs, and as Steakley waved Jeff into one of them, he sank into the other with a sigh.

"It's not like the old days," the storekeeper said. "Bills of lading, ledger books, account books. . . . I recollect when folks would pick up what they needed and pay me with a nice fat pig or a couple of good roasting pullets. I never wrote down a thing in those days. Now it seems as if all I do is write things down." He shook his head and then looked at Jeff. "What have you been doing with yourself for the last two years, son?"

"Like you said, I've been out West. With Clay."

Steakley plucked at his bottom lip with his blunt fingers.

"Maybe you'd better not tell me anything about that brother of yours," he said after a moment. "Jasper Sutcliffe'd still like to talk to him about Pete Garwood getting killed."

Jeff was not surprised to hear that Marietta's constable had not lost interest in the Holt-Garwood feud. Those tragic times had taken not only the lives of Bartholomew and Norah Holt, but also those of Luther and Pete Garwood. The whole countryside had been talking about it, and Sutcliffe probably would have charged Clay with

21

Pete Garwood's murder if he could have caught up with Clay—even though Pete had met his death in a fair fight.

"I didn't come back to hash all of that out," Jeff told Steakley now. "What I really want is Melissa."

The man's hound-doglike features lengthened even more.

"She's gone, Jeff," he said quietly. "Her and her folks, too."

"I know. I stopped by their place and talked to the Seegers. They didn't know anything about where Melissa and her parents might have gone."

"They wouldn't; I don't reckon anybody does. Ol' Merrivale just up and hired him some wagons and drivers one day, loaded up all that fancy stuff from his house, and left, heading upriver."

"He didn't say where they were going?"

Steakley leaned back in his chair, clasped his hands together over his paunch, and frowned in concentration.

"Let me think," he said. "I don't remember anything right off, but you never know."

"Melissa didn't say anything to you before they left?" Jeff asked, anguish creeping into his voice. He could imagine Melissa giving in to her father's bullying and leaving Marietta, but he could not believe she had failed to leave a letter or some sort of message for him. "Did she give you anything to hold for me?"

Steakley shook his head decisively. "Now that part, I'm sure of. I didn't speak to her or even

22

see her before she and her folks left. Merrivale came in for a few provisions, I seem to recall, and he said . . . I think he said something about heading for New York!" Steakley's voice rose as the memory came back to him. "That's it. I'm sure that's what he said."

Jeff sat back and blinked, stunned. *New York?* It was a long way to New York, and it was a hell of a big place. How was he supposed to find her with nothing more to go on?

The storekeeper must have read the signs of confusion and frustration on Jeff's face because he said, "I know this has really hit you hard, Jeff. If you want my advice, youll go back to the mountains and forget about Melissa Merrivale. Her pa's probably got her married off to somebody else by now."

"No!" Jeff was out of his chair before he realized it, and he found himself standing over Steakley, his left hand grasping the front of the man's apron, his right clenched into a fist and cocked for a blow. Steakley gasped in fear as Jeff lifted him half out of the chair.

"Take it easy!" Steakley pleaded. "Take it easy, goddamn it!"

Drawing a deep, ragged breath, Jeff released the storekeeper's apron and let him sag back into the chair.

"Sorry," Jeff said without looking at the man. "Didn't mean to jump you that way. But her name's Melissa Holt now, and she's not married to anybody else. She can't be."

"Sure, sure, I know that," Steakley said quickly, pale with fear of the reaction he had unwittingly provoked. "Don't know what I was thinking, Jeff. I'm the one who's sorry."

Jeff closed his eyes and massaged his temples. "I never figured . . . never even dreamed—"

"I know, son. The news has to come as a mighty bad shock. If there's anything I can do to help—"

"No, thanks." Jeff opened his eyes and squared his shoulders. "I'll ride over to the farm and stay there for a while, give myself some time to figure this out. Suppose I'll need some supplies."

"Whatever you want, it's yours. Be glad to put it on account for you."

"I've got cash money, but thanks, anyway."

"Jeff, the cabin wasn't ever rebuilt after—well, you know."

"After Zach and Pete Garwood burned it down and killed my parents, you mean?" Jeff smiled coldly. "Doesn't matter. I've spent a lot more nights outdoors in the past two years than I have under a roof. Besides, there's the cabin where Melissa and I lived."

"You're right." Steakley stood up and extended a hand to him. "Welcome back to Marietta, Jeff, and no hard feelings."

"Thanks." Jeff shook hands with him. "Reckon I'll pick up those supplies now."

His thoughts were a blur as he bought flour, sugar, salt, and bacon. One of Steakley's clerks put the things in a bag for him, and Jeff went out to his horse with the parcel slung over his shoulder. Sort of like the possibles bag he'd used back in the mountains, he thought.

And as he mounted up, still numb from the shocking news, he wished he was back in those mountains right now.

New York . . . God! How would he ever find Melissa?

"Arrogant young son of a bitch!" Steakley muttered under his breath as he watched Jeff Holt ride away. The Holts had always been a violent bunch, he thought, but Jeff's time in the mountains had turned him into little more than a savage himself.

Steakley turned and stalked back through the store to his office. He shut the door behind him, sat down, and leaned back in the chair. He could have told Jefferson Holt a thing or two if he had wanted to, yes, sir!

Like the fact that Melissa had indeed left a letter there for him, a letter that had no doubt told exactly where the Merrivales were going when they left Ohio. She would never go off without letting Jeff know where he could find her. The only problem was that Charles Merrivale had anticipated his daughter's actions, and he had visited the store after Melissa. He had been generous, too, paying Steakley well for that letter and a promise from the storekeeper to keep his mouth shut about where they were going.

Merrivale hated Jeff Holt, hated him with a

passion, and so did Steakley. Maybe he *was* almost old enough to be Melissa's father, Steakley thought; that did not mean he would not have been a good husband to her. Every time he had started to hint around about that, however, Melissa had made it clear she did not have any romantic interest in him. She only had had eyes for Jeff Holt.

Well, that was over good and proper now. Melissa was thousands of miles away, and Holt would never find her. *Never.*

Steakley picked up one of his account books. He might not have Melissa, but he had a thriving business, and when the need got too great, he could always go see Josie Garwood. Josie was always glad to see him and his money. He had a pretty good life, Steakley decided.

But Jeff Holt, now . . . he had nothing.

II

The Indians could not brook the intrusion of the whites on the hunting grounds and navigable waters which they had been in habits of considering as their own property from time immemorial.

—Fortescue Cuming
"Sketches of a Tour to the Western Country"

The paddle in Clay Holt's hands bit smoothly

into the waters of the Yellowstone River, sending the birchbark canoe gliding over the placid surface. The Yellowstone ran narrow and fast in places, but here it was wide and peaceful, sparkling with a blue and white shimmer in the midday sun.

Spring was Clay's favorite time of year in the mountains. The sun was warm during the day, and the nights were still cool enough for a man to sleep well, rolled up in a buffalo robe—especially when that robe was shared with a woman like Shining Moon.

Clay looked back at her, sitting in the rear of the canoe and lending her efforts with a paddle to his. Her dark eyes met his, and his expression softened. With his lean, hard features and the rumpled thatch of black hair under a coonskin cap, he could often appear rather grim, but Shining Moon nearly always was able to draw a smile out of him. A man could search the whole world over, he had thought more than once, and never find a better, more beautiful wife.

They made an impressive-looking couple as they paddled along the clear mountain stream that ran through a thickly wooded valley between rugged, snowcapped heights. Clay was dressed in a buckskin shirt and trousers, along with high-topped fringed moccasins and a coonskin cap, its ringed tail dangling on his right shoulder. He had tucked a brace of .54 caliber North and Cheney flintlock pistols under his belt, and he carried two knives, one in a fringed sheath on his belt, the other sheathed and strapped to the calf under his right moccasin. Resting against his left hip were his powder horn and shot pouch, hung from a strap that crossed his broad chest and right shoulder. His Harper's Ferry rifle, identical to the one he had given his brother Jeff, lay at his feet in the bottom of the canoe, where it would be easy to reach in case of trouble.

Shining Moon, a young Hunkpapa Sioux woman of twenty summers, also wore buckskins, but her dress was decorated with porcupine quills painted different colors and arranged in elaborate patterns on the garment. In addition, a band of brightly colored cloth was tied around her forehead to keep her long, raven-dark hair from falling in front of her eyes. She wore a hunting knife and, like her husband, had placed a rifle at her feet. She was not as expert a marksman as Clay Holt, but she could outshoot most male members of her tribe, who had only recently become proficient in the use of firearms. And none of the Hunkpapa, male or female, were as good at tracking and reading sign as Shining Moon. She had been invaluable on the journey, leading Clay and his companions unerringly to creeks and smaller rivers teeming with beaver.

As a result, Clay's canoe was heavily loaded with beaver pelts—plews, as the mountain men called them—as was the canoe being paddled by Proud Wolf, Shining Moon's brother, and Aaron Garwood, the fourth member of this partnership. Their canoe was directly behind the one occupied by Clay and Shining Moon.

Though it was still early in spring, Clay and the others had trapped enough beaver to require a visit to the fort established by Manuel Lisa at the junction of the Yellowstone and Big Horn rivers, where they could sell the pelts. The previous year, Clay and Jeff had worked for the Spaniard; this year, Clay had decided to go it alone except for his wife, her brother, and their friend Aaron. Instead of using equipment and provisions supplied by Lisa, they were responsible for outfitting themselves; but Lisa would provide a market for the furs, and Clay and his companions would keep the profits they realized, rather than work for wages. In the long run, Clay thought, they would make more money, though they would also have more at stake.

Clay wondered how Jeff was doing and if his brother had reached Ohio by now. Would he bring Melissa back to the frontier with him when he returned? Clay and Jeff had talked about that, but Clay had no idea what decision Melissa would come to. There were worse places to live than these mountains, Clay thought.

The past six months since he and Shining Moon were married in a Teton Sioux ceremony had been like an extended honeymoon. Jeff might choose to remain in so-called civilization, but not Clay. This was his home now, and he would be happy to spend the rest of his life in the Shining Mountains.

29

It was about time to stop for the noon meal, so he gestured to Proud Wolf and Aaron to head for shore. Proud Wolf, sitting in the front of the second canoe, nodded his understanding.

Suddenly the sound of gunfire came floating to their ears, followed an instant later by blood-curdling cries.

"What in blazes!" Clay twisted around to look at Shining Moon.

"I do not know," she said. "It comes from up-stream."

Clay could tell from the anxious expressions on the faces of Proud Wolf and Aaron that they also heard the ominous noises. He pointed to the shore again, more urgency in his gesture.

The prow of Clay's canoe struck the grassy bank, and he jumped out, rifle in one hand, and after Shining Moon had stepped out, he reached back to haul the canoe onto dry land. A few feet away Proud Wolf and Aaron beached their canoe and joined Clay and Shining Moon.

The gunfire from upstream continued, sporadic blasts punctuated by shouts and cries. A battle was going on, no more than a few hundred yards away.

"What do you reckon that's about, Clay?" Aaron asked as he gripped his rifle. He was a slender young man with brown hair and a beard that did not totally disguise the surprisingly gentle cast of his features. He had been in the mountains less than a year and was not totally at home yet; given his nature, he might never be, in such

30

rugged surroundings. His left arm was thinner and weaker than his right, the result of its having been broken in a fight with Clay back in Ohio, when the Garwoods and the Holts were feuding. Those days were in the past now, and Aaron looked on Clay with a mixture of friendship and admiration.

Clay shook his head in reply to the young man's question. "Don't know, but I intend to find out before we go any farther. You and Shining Moon stay here, Aaron. Proud Wolf and I will go have a look."

Proud Wolf's chest swelled, and he smiled broadly. At sixteen the Hunkpapa Sioux was still young and his body was undersized, but he had a warrior's heart and spirit. He admired no one more than his brother-in-law, Clay Holt, and to accompany Clay on what might be a dangerous chore appealed to him.

"You should take me," Shining Moon said quietly. She had never been one meekly to accept a decision with which she disagreed, even if it came from her husband. "I can move as silently as the wind and without the exuberance of youth."

"You are only four summers older than me, sister," Proud Wolf reminded her.

"Four summers can sometimes be a great deal of time."

"Proud Wolf goes with me," Clay said. "He can keep quiet enough when he wants to, and I want you and Aaron covering our back trail, Shining Moon."

31

She nodded, realizing that Clay's decision had been based on logic rather than his feelings for her. He knew all too well that nothing got her dander up quicker than sensing that he was trying to be overprotective of her.

A fresh flurry of shooting exploded upriver. Somebody was burning a hell of a lot of powder, Clay thought as he and Proud Wolf made their way along the shore. Thick brush thronged the bank, growing in some places all the way to the river, and Clay was grateful for the cover it provided.

Behind them, Shining Moon and Aaron Garwood crouched at the edge of the growth, rifles held ready in case of trouble from an unexpected direction.

The river had been running straight, but as Clay and Proud Wolf made their way along it, they entered a stretch of twists and bends. With the thick growth on the banks, it was difficult to see past some of the turns, and Clay and Proud Wolf were almost on top of the battle before they got sight of the conflict. The gunshots were louder now, and as Clay parted the screen of brush to peer through it, he saw that some of the combatants were less than fifty yards away.

In the middle of the river was an island, little more than a sandbar, really, with a few trees and bushes growing on it. On that island, their backs to the shore where Clay and Proud Wolf crouched, were some two dozen white men, trying to fight off a band of hostile Blackfoot war-

32

riors on the far bank. Clay recognized the Black-foot markings by the beadwork on their mocca-sins—a design ending in three prongs, which designated the three tribes that comprised the Blackfoot: the Siksika, the Blood, and the Piegan. The warriors were raking the island with arrows and musket fire, and as Clay and Proud Wolf watched, one of the white men crumpled, bend-ing almost double over the arrow that had been driven through his midsection. Several more lay motionless on the sandy island.

"Damn!" Clay swore. "Those pilgrims are in a bad way."

"They have more guns, but the Blackfoot are many. They will attack the island, I think."

Clay agreed with Proud Wolf. The island was separated from the far shore only by a narrow strip of shallow water. The Blackfoot would wait, content to thin the ranks of the island's de-fenders before charging across those shallows to overrun the white men. Clay searched for any sign of canoes but did not see them. The white men must have been on foot; when theyd been jumped by the Blackfoot, they must have retreated onto the island, pinning themselves down.

"What will we do?" Proud Wolf asked quietly.

Clay looked over at him and saw that the young man was almost jumping out of his skin with eagerness to join the fight. The Sioux and the Blackfoot were ancient enemies, and Clay knew that Proud Wolf would like nothing better than to spill Blackfoot blood. Clay had no love for the Blackfoot, either. He had first clashed with them during the Lewis and Clark journey, and he knew them to be a treacherous, horse-stealing bunch.

But when you got right down to it, this was not his fight, and he hated to risk the lives of his wife, brother-in-law, and friend to help a group of men who had blundered into a bad situation. A man had to take care of his own troubles on the frontier, and if he could not, he went under. It was as simple as that.

At least that was what Clay tried to convince himself of for all of ten or fifteen seconds. Then he said, "I reckon we'll pitch in and do what we can to help. The way the river bends here, I think we can get our canoes up to this side of the island almost before the Blackfoot see us coming."

Silently, Clay and Proud Wolf retreated through the brush until they reached Shining Moon and Aaron Garwood. Clay explained tersely what they had witnessed.

Aaron said, "Were going to help those folks, arent we?"

"I don't see as we've got much choice," Clay replied. "Don't reckon I could live with myself if we went off and left them there to die."

"Nor could I," Shining Moon said, "not at the hands of the Blackfoot." Her eyes were aflame with the same ancestral hatred of the Blackfoot that her brother possessed.

Quickly Clay outlined a simple plan. They would approach the island from the deeper channel of the river and throw their four flintlocks into the battle on the side of the whites. There were too many people on the island for Clay and his companions to rescue; if only three or four had been in the party, the canoes would have had room enough to carry them away.

Shining Moon got into the canoe while Clay pushed it into deeper water. Likewise, Proud Wolf shoved off from the bank in the other canoe with Aaron. They made sure their rifles were primed and loaded, then took up the paddles and propelled the canoes toward the bend.

They could not waste any time, Clay knew. The arrows of the Blackfoot would probably not be able to reach them as long as they were in the stream, but musket fire was a different story altogether. They would have to cover over fifty yards of open water before they reached the shelter of the island itself. And since the river narrowed as it passed the sandbar, the current was liable to be stronger there, and paddling against it would slow them down. Still, they could do nothing else.

Hunched forward in the bow of the canoe, Clay dipped the paddle deep into the water, the corded muscles in his arms and shoulders working smoothly. Shining Moon was also strong, and together their efforts sent the canoe shooting through the current. Proud Wolf and Aaron followed behind them as best they could.

As they rounded the bend, the island came into view. A haze of black-powder smoke hung in the air over it and along the shore. Flintlocks still boomed, and arrows hummed in the air. Clay bent his back even more to the task of paddling, sparing only a brief glance toward the bank. Although he could see only a few Blackfoot warriors, he figured they outnumbered the defenders on the island two to one.

Four more rifles would not make a great difference, or at least one would not think so. But Clay had confidence in his own marksmanship, along with that of Shining Moon, Proud Wolf, and Aaron. If they could reach the island and make every shot count, the Blackfoot might decide the price they would have to pay to continue the attack was too high.

Ten yards slid under the canoes, then twenty, then thirty. They were more than halfway there, and so far the Blackfoot had paid no attention to them. That changed abruptly, however. Over the gunfire and the splashing of the paddles, Clay heard a sudden cry of alarm, echoed seconds later by other warriors. He saw a splash just ahead to the right and knew it was a musket ball hitting the water. As long as the aim of the Blackfoot stayed that far off, he was not worried.

More musket balls peppered the surface of the river near the canoes. Clay ignored them and kept paddling. A few seconds later, the sandbar loomed ahead to the right, between the canoes and the far shore where the Blackfoot hid in the trees. Clay dug down with the paddle and sent the canoe grating onto the sandy beach. He and

Shining Moon leapt out with their rifles as Proud Wolf and Aaron safely arrived nearby.

Some of the island's defenders had seen them coming. Buckskin-clad bearded men jumped up and ran toward the newcomers. They would have been better off fighting the Blackfoot than greeting the reinforcements, Clay thought.

Then he realized that a greeting was the last thing these men had in mind. Without slowing down, one of them slammed into Clay, knocking him off-balance. Clay caught himself before he fell but had no chance to regain solid footing before another man slashed at him with a rifle butt. Clay blocked the blow, but this time he went down under the impact. A few feet away Shining Moon cried out in surprise and alarm as another man knocked her roughly aside and sprang into the canoe.

"Hey!" Aaron yelled as he and Proud Wolf were the victims of a similar assault. "What the hell are you doing?"

One of the bearded men paused long enough to throw him a hideous grin. "Getting out of here, sonny!"

Clay got to his knees and saw at least half a dozen men trying to pile into each of the canoes, fighting one another for space. They were making a desperate attempt to escape, abandoning the others to their fate. Clay's instincts cried out for him to put a shot in the middle of the ungrateful lot of them, but from the corner of his eye, he saw one of the Blackfoot emerge from the shelter of a deadfall on the shore—and train his musket on the fleeing men.

Throwing himself down on his belly, Clay brought his rifle to his shoulder, thumbed back the cock on the flintlock, and settled the sight on the chest of the Blackfoot warrior. He fired at the same instant as the Blackfoot. There was no way of knowing where the ball from the Indian's musket went, but Clay's shot caught the warrior in the chest and sent him sprawling backward.

Clay glanced over his shoulder and saw that both canoes were in the river now, riding low in the water with too many passengers. They were not even trying to paddle but were content to let the current carry them downstream.

A smaller band of Blackfoot detached themselves from the main party and raced along the shoreline, firing arrows and muskets toward the canoes. The men who were trying to escape soon discovered they had left the sparse shelter of the island for something even worse. A couple of them toppled from each canoe, arrows protruding from their bodies. Others sagged, wounded by musket fire, but managed to stay aboard.

The crude boats were awash within moments, however, perforated by balls from Blackfoot muskets. From the island, Clay saw the canoes sinking and uttered a heartfelt curse. He knew that when they went down, they would take all the supplies and a season's worth of pelts to the bottom of the river.

And he could do nothing about it, he realized.

Supplies and pelts meant nothing if he and the others were killed. Clay helped Shining Moon to her feet, and together they ran toward a clump of small trees where several defenders were clustered. Aaron and Proud Wolf ran to a thicket nearby.

Clay and Shining Moon threw themselves to the ground beside the other defenders. Musket fire still rattled and popped around them. Clay's eyes widened in shock as he realized that one of the whites was a woman. A young woman, at that, with strawberry-blond hair underneath a hooded cloak. An older, round-faced man hovered beside her, one arm over her protectively. Neither of them seemed to be armed, but the men with them, all buckskin-clad frontiersmen, were firing toward the shore with pistols and rifles.

Debris was clumped at the base of the trees, and Clay guessed it had caught there during the spring floods, when the river had run higher. The driftwood and brush provided some shelter from the Blackfoot attack; it was unlikely to stop a musket ball, but it would prevent many arrows from getting through.

With fast, practiced ease, Clay reloaded, then rose up to get a bead on one of the Indians. The Blackfoot was showing only a few inches of shoulder behind a tree, but that was enough. Clay's rifle roared, and the warrior went staggering, his right arm dangling uselessly from a shattered shoulder.

"Good Lord!" cried the round-faced man sheltering the young woman. "That's quite some shooting!"

Clay put the rifle on the ground and jerked out his pistols. They did not have the range of the long gun, but in his hands they were accurate enough to down a couple more Blackfoot. Beside him, Shining Moon fired her rifle and sent another attacker spinning to the ground. From the nearby clump of brush, Proud Wolf and Aaron added their firepower to the efforts of the defenders, spacing their shots so that they would be firing while the others were reloading.

As he crouched down and reloaded the rifle and pistols, Clay glanced toward the river and saw that both canoes had sunk, leaving the would-be escapees floundering in the water. Some were floating facedown; others struggled back toward the island. The current was too strong for any of them to reach the far shore and escape that way.

Clay swallowed the revulsion he felt for those men. There would be time later to deal with them—if he came out of this mess alive.

His weapons reloaded, he fired again. This time one of the pistol shots missed, but the other one and the ball from the rifle hit their targets. Another Blackfoot died, and one more staggered away badly wounded. Clay had put five of the warriors out of the fight already; Shining Moon, Proud Wolf, and Aaron Garwood were taking an impressive toll with their fire, too.

"Pour it into them!" Clay shouted, his voice booming out over the island. "Keep firing!"

40

Leading by example as well as words, Clay rallied the defenders over the next few minutes, and although two more were killed by the attackers, the casualties suffered by the Blackfoot were much greater. Rifle fire raked the shoreline, the defenders shooting in volleys rather than offering the scattered, disorganized resistance they had before Clay's arrival. He was not surprised when the attackers suddenly broke and ran.

A cheer went up from the men on the island as they saw the Indians retreating, but Clay stood up and shouted, "Give them a hot send-off, boys!" He had his pistols in his hands, and he fired both guns after the fleeing Blackfoot. The others followed his lead, sending more balls whining through the forest after the Indians.

One man let out an exuberant whoop, slapped Clay on the shoulder, and cried, "We showed 'em, didn't we? We really taught them redskinned bastards a lesson!"

Clay looked over at the man, saw that his buckskins were soaking wet, and savagely backhanded him. Only the fact that Clay had tucked away the pistol he had been holding in that hand saved the man from a cracked skull. As it was, he staggered back a few steps, tripped, and fell heavily to the ground.

"Touch me again and I'll kill you," Clay said coldly.

The man's face twisted with rage, and he scrambled to his feet, his hand reaching for the knife sheathed at his waist. He stopped short as

41

he saw Shining Moon, Proud Wolf, and Aaron positioning themselves beside Clay.

"Here now, there's no need for fighting among ourselves!" exclaimed the heavyset, middle-aged man who had been hovering over the young woman. He pushed himself to his feet, helped the girl up, and said, "We've just saved ourselves from those savages. We should be celebrating."

Clay did not look at the man who had just spoken but nodded toward the buckskin-clad man on the ground. "No thanks to this son of a bitch and the others like him who tried to save their own skins. They stole my canoes and ran out on the rest of you."

"The hell we did!" flared the man in the wet buckskins. "We were just—just tryin' to get around behind those redskins so that we could catch them in a cross fire." He folded his arms across his chest and glared at Clay. "That's what we were doing."

"Sure," Clay said, his voice filled with contempt. He turned to the older man, who seemed to be in charge of this group. "Name's Clay Holt. This is my wife, Shining Moon; her brother, Proud Wolf; and our friend Aaron Garwood."

"I'm exceedingly pleased to meet you, Mr. Holt. I am Professor Donald Elwood Franklin, and this is my daughter, Miss Lucy Franklin. We're from Cambridge, Massachusetts. Harvard, you know. I'm an instructor in botany there."

Clay greeted this announcement with some surprise. What the hell was a botany professor

42

from Harvard doing in the middle of the wilderness, especially dragging his daughter along with him?

"Let's get off this island," he said. Explanations would have to wait.

III

They made camp in a clearing not far from the island. The men who had been dumped in the river were miserable in their wet buckskins, and although Clay felt no sympathy for them, he built a fire so they could dry out. For the time being, he was stuck with this bunch; he might as well make the best of it, he decided.

Franklin was a talkative sort, and Clay could easily believe he was a professor. He seemed to be full of knowledge about anything and everything—except how to survive on the frontier. He wore a dusty dark suit, a silk cravat, a white shirt, and a beaver hat that Clay thought looked faintly ridiculous. His ruddy features were those of a fleshy, middle-aged cherub, and his cheerful expression caused his eyes to twinkle with amusement, even though as far as Clay could tell, he did not have much to be happy about in the present situation.

Lucy Franklin was not taking things so well. She was pale, and her green eyes remained wide and haunted with terror from the Indian attack. She said little and seemed content to huddle near the fire.

The professor brought out a pipe and a pouch of tobacco and was soon puffing away as he sat on a fallen log near his daughter.

"You saved our lives, sir," he said to Clay. "Those savages would have overwhelmed us if you hadn't come to our assistance."

"Just luck we came along when we did," Clay said, taking out his own pipe. "We were headed upriver with a load of pelts, bound for Lisa's fort." Clay was somber as he packed his pipe, then got a blazing twig from the fire and lit it. "Those plews are all on the bottom of the Yellowstone now, along with our supplies."

"I'm dreadfully sorry about that. Is there any hope of recovering your goods?"

"I reckon I can dive down and get some of the pelts, the ones I can find. Water won't hurt them. All of our supplies'll be ruined, though."

"We have plenty of provisions," Franklin declared. "We'll be glad to share them with you, of course. After all, you and your friends saved our lives."

As a matter of fact, several men had delved into the packs they carried with them and were cooking a stew made with dried beef, wild onions, and roots. One man already had pan bread ready to cook over the fire. The smell of the food reminded Clay it was past time to eat.

He looked at the professor and asked, "What in blazes are you folks doing out here, anyway?

I didn't think there were any white men in these mountains except fur trappers."

"Well, as I told you, I'm an instructor in botany at Harvard. I'm also something of an amateur naturalist, like my friend Tom Jefferson." Franklin's words came faster as he warmed to his subject. "I'm on a botanical expedition, financed by President Jefferson and the American Philosophical Society of Philadelphia. Our purpose is to retrace the route of Lewis and Clark, collecting plant specimens, taking measurements, and the like. I don't know if you're aware of the scientific significance of the discoveries made by Captain Lewis and Captain Clark—"

"I was with them," Clay said. "I stuck more than one weed in a sack for Cap'n Lewis."

"Really?" Franklin's eyes widened. "You were a member of the Corps of Discovery, Mr. Holt?"

"Yes. All the way to the Pacific and back."

"Well, this is a most fortuitous meeting indeed!"

Clay was not sure he liked the sound of that, so he said nothing.

After a moment, Franklin went on, "You're aware, then, of all the information Lewis and Clark brought back with them, as well as the many specimens of their discoveries. However, you may not know that their findings were greeted with skepticism by some members of the scientific and philosophical community. Why, a few of my fellow naturalists have insisted that Lewis and Clark are madmen and simply imagined all the adventures they claim to have had."

"Kind of hard to do when they brought so much proof back with them, isn't it?" Clay said.

Franklin chuckled. "Never underestimate the stubbornness of the academic mind, my friend. At any rate, since President Jefferson sent the expedition to the Pacific for scientific as much as political purposes, I know that the doubt and resistance his ideas have met have been a great disappointment to him. I've come west to corroborate the discoveries of Lewis and Clark and try to convince the skeptics in the scientific establishment of their veracity."

"I reckon I follow most of what you just said," Clay mused. "But if these scientific rascals don't believe what Cap'n Lewis and Cap'n Clark had to say, what makes you think they'll believe you?"

"Preponderance of evidence, Mr. Holt, preponderance of evidence. Simply put, I'm going to beat them over the head with the proof until they finally open their eyes and look at it. Figuratively speaking, of course."

Clay could not help but like the professor, long-winded though he might be.

"Why'd you bring your daughter with you?" he asked. "The wilderness is no place for a young woman."

Franklin sounded genuinely surprised by the question as he replied, "Lucy goes everywhere with me. She's my assistant. She transcribes all my notes and helps me with my cataloguing and classifying."

"Reckon you've noticed by now this isn't Massachusetts, Professor," Clay said dryly. "There're all kinds of dangers out here you'll never run into back East. Indians, wild animals, bad weather—"

"Of course, of course," Franklin agreed. "I'm well aware of that, Mr. Holt. But I've read the journals of Captain Lewis and Captain Clark, and I'm also aware that they had a woman with them for most of the trip."

"An Indian woman," Clay pointed out. "A Shoshone named Sacajawea. Janey, we called her. She made the trip, all right, Professor, but it's not the same thing."

"You have your wife with you," Franklin said stubbornly, and Clay remembered what he had said about academic minds.

"Shining Moon is a Hunkpapa Sioux, born, bred, and raised in these mountains. This is her home. But I wouldn't drop her down in the middle of Cambridge, Massachusetts. She'd be plumb scared to death, I reckon." *I know I would be,* Clay added silently.

"Well, perhaps you're correct, Mr. Holt, but really, this discussion is pointless. Lucy is here, whether I should have allowed her to accompany me on this expedition or not."

"That's true," Clay agreed grimly. "And I guess that makes her your concern, Professor." Without waiting for Franklin to say anything else, he walked over to the fire and squatted on his haunches next to Shining Moon.

The man Clay had backhanded on the island was standing nearby, and after giving Clay a hard look for a moment, he said, "After we eat, we'll get organized and move on again. That all right with you, Professor?"

"Whatever you say, Mr. Lawton," Franklin replied. "After all, you are in charge."

Clay looked up sharply. "This gent's running the show?"

"Mr. Lawton is our chief guide, Mr. Holt. I hired him back in St. Louis, along with these other gentlemen."

Clay snorted in disgust, and that drew another glare from Lawton.

"No wonder you walked right into a Blackfoot ambush," Clay said.

Lawton stiffened. "Listen, Holt, I'm getting mighty tired of the way you're acting. I've heard talk about you, back in St. Louis and in some of the settlements along the Missouri. You're supposed to be some sort o' big skookum he-wolf. Well, you don't look like so all-fired much to me."

Slowly Clay stood up and faced Lawton across the fire. "I don't tell folks what to say about me or what to think about me," he said. "But I never tried to run out on folks I'd signed on to protect."

Lawton's hand went to the knife sheathed at his hip. Clay tensed and reached for his own blade. He felt an instinctive dislike for Lawton.

Might as well get this trouble over and done with now, Clay thought.

Neither Shining Moon, Proud Wolf, nor Aaron Garwood said a word. They were well aware that Clay would not take it kindly if they intervened. Likewise, the others in the professor's party seemed willing to stand back and wait.

"Stop it!" Lucy Franklin cried. She had gotten to her feet without any of them noticing, and the hood of her cloak was thrown back so that her reddish-blond hair shone in the sunlight. She trembled as she went on, "We just escaped from those awful savages! We shouldn't be fighting among ourselves!"

"Lucy's right," Professor Franklin said, moving over so that he was between Clay and Lawton. "There's no need for this animosity, gentlemen."

A buckskin-clad man spoke up, his voice cool and arrogant. "I say let them settle it, Professor. A duel is the thing. That's what we would do back in Heidelberg."

Clay glanced at the man who had spoken. He was fairly young, probably in his mid-twenties, and for the first time Clay noticed that although he wore buckskins, he hardly looked natural in them. He had sleek dark hair and good looks that were almost too pretty for the surroundings. His hands were soft and uncallused, and he carried no weapons. A large leather case was propped against a rock next to him. Clay realized that he had been too busy earlier to notice the differences between this man and the others.

"I don't think we need a duel, Rupert," Franklin said sharply. "We're not back in Europe, you know. We don't settle things with sabers or dueling pistols at dawn."

The young man called Rupert shrugged. "Of course, Professor. And I certainly would not wish to see anything occur that might upset Miss Lucy."

"Why don't you all just sit down and be quiet?" Lucy said shakily. "There's been enough fighting today."

His gaze still fixed on Lawton, Clay said, "Reckon the young lady's right. I'll stay out of your way, Lawton, and you stay out of mine."

"Sure," Lawton replied, his lip curling into a sneer. Clay knew by looking at him that the man considered this a victory; Lawton believed that Clay was backing down.

Let him think whatever the hell he wants to, Clay told himself. Anyway, this was none of his business. The professor was the one who had hired Lawton, so it was up to Franklin to deal with him.

The young man who looked out of place in buckskins approached Clay and gave a half-bow. "Rupert von Metz, at your service, Herr Holt. Professor Franklin neglected to introduce us earlier. I am honored to make the acquaintance of such a famous wilderness man as yourself."

So this Metz fellow has heard of me, too, just like Lawton, Clay thought. He'd had no idea folks

50

were talking about him back in St. Louis. The trappers who had gone down the Missouri with him the previous autumn must have carried tales about his clash with Duquesne and the fight at the fort with Zach Garwood.

Even though von Metz had claimed to be glad to meet him, the young man's eyes were cold and calculating, Clay decided. He wondered what von Metz was doing on this expedition.

The explanation was not long in coming. Even though Clay had only grunted in acknowledgment of von Metz's self-introduction, the man went on as if Clay had asked for his life story.

"I'm an artist, you see," von Metz said. "I have painted portraits of most of the noble lords and ladies in Europe, but my real ambition is to capture on canvas all the spectacle and majesty of the American West. To this end, one of my patrons, Comte Defresne, has generously sponsored my trip here and allowed me to join Professor Franklin's expedition." He smiled. "This land is much different from my native Prussia. There we have no red savages to menace us."

Aaron Garwood had sauntered over to listen to von Metz's discourse, and when the Prussian paused, Aaron spat on the ground and said, "Some of those red savages, as you call them, are the finest folks I've ever met." Aaron's eyes were narrowed with dislike as he spoke. "Proud Wolf over there is about the best friend I've got in the world."

"Of course," von Metz said, his handsome fea-

51

tures stiff with resentment at Aaron's tone. "I meant no offense."

Clay did not believe that. Von Metz was like a bluejay; he did not care who his squawking disturbed.

"We'd better eat," Clay said curtly. "It's been a rough day."

He sat next to Shining Moon, who gave him a sympathetic glance. She understood his impatience with these pilgrims, he was sure. To Clay's way of thinking, a man had no business venturing into the mountains unless he could take care of himself, or at least pull his own weight in a group.

They ate in silence. Whenever Clay glanced at Lawton, the man was giving him a surly stare. With Lawton in charge, the professor and his companions were damned lucky to be alive, Clay thought. He had seen Lawton's kind before—a bully when the odds were on his side, a coward when he had to stand up alone. There was a good chance Lawton had run into trouble with the law back East somewhere, and heading west had seemed to him a good way to escape his problems.

Well, Clay mused, that description also fit himself in a few ways. He had come west in the first place to get away from Josie Garwood and her ridiculous claim that he had gotten her pregnant; he had returned to the mountains along with Jeff to put an end to the Holt-Garwood feud and all the blood-spilling that went along with it.

And back in Marietta there was a constable who might still want to throw him in jail.

The feud had not ended when Clay and Jeff left Ohio. It had just traveled west with them, culminating in a final showdown between Clay and Zach Garwood, who had been accompanied by his brother Aaron. But now all that was over, the bad blood put to rest with Zach's death. Aaron had befriended the Holts, and Clay had left his past behind to make a life for himself in the mountains, a good life with Shining Moon and her people.

He wanted to get back to that as quickly as possible.

Professor Franklin was talking to Proud Wolf. The young Hunkpapa man was full of questions about Franklin's expedition, and the professor explained how the specimens he was collecting and the information he was gathering would be taken back East to further the knowledge available to the scientific community.

Frowning in confusion, Proud Wolf asked, "You mean there are people who spend all their time studying plants and animals and rocks?"

"Indeed there are, young man," Franklin replied. "They are called naturalists, and I'm proud to number myself among them. In fact, this journey has the support not only of former President Jefferson, but also of the American Philosophical Society of Philadelphia, the country's—perhaps the world's—leading organization of scientists. When I return, my fellow naturalists will pore over my findings until they've extracted every bit of pertinent information to be found."

"I understand your words—most of them— but not why you and the men like you do these things. A plant is here to eat, or to hide a warrior from his enemies, or to make his skin itch. An animal is here to eat and to give its skin to man for clothing. A rock is here to kill the animal—or a man's enemy. All of them—the plants, the animals, the rocks—have always been here, and they will always be here. What else is there to know about them?"

Franklin gave a booming laugh. "You do know how to reduce things to their most common element, don't you, Proud Wolf? That's the mark of a great mind, my boy. You should nurture it. But in the meantime, perhaps I can open your eyes to some things you haven't considered before now."

Clay had been only half listening to the conversation, but now he said, "There won't be time for that. We'll be moving on as soon as we can, and I reckon you will be, too, Professor."

"As a matter of fact, I've been wanting to talk to you about that, Mr. Holt."

Clay tensed. Ever since they had left the island and established this camp, he had had the feeling that something was on Franklin's mind, something that Clay did not particularly want to hear.

Franklin plunged on. "It seems to me that after

the events of today, it would be perfectly logical for you to take over the leadership of our little expedition, Mr. Holt."

"Wait a minute!" Lawton protested, just as Clay had expected. "I'm the chief guide. That's what you hired me for back in St. Louis, Professor."

"And I'm a fur trapper." Clay hated to agree with Lawton but saw no alternative. "I've got business of my own to tend to, Professor."

"But you're a more seasoned frontiersman than Mr. Lawton or any of his, ah, cronies," Franklin pointed out.

Lawton took offense again. "I've been in these mountains before!" he declared angrily.

"Yes, but for how long?" Franklin asked.

"Well . . . a few months."

The professor swung back to Clay. "And what about you, Mr. Holt? How much time have you spent in this wilderness?"

Clay shrugged. "Off and on—about three, four years, I reckon."

"So you see, it makes perfect sense for you to join us."

"Perfect sense to you, maybe," Clay said. "Not to me."

"Clay." Shining Moon spoke up, taking Clay by surprise. "These people may need our help. Besides, our supplies are gone. They sank into the river with the canoes."

Clay glared at Lawton. "It's because of him and his friends that we lost all our possibles."

Lawton returned the hostile stare but said nothing.

"Listen to your wife, Mr. Holt," Franklin advised. "We have more than enough supplies for everyone, you and your companions included. Besides, as I mentioned, I have the financial backing of both Thomas Jefferson and the American Philosophical Society. If you accept my offer, I can promise you enough compensation to recoup all of your losses and to outfit yourself for another trapping journey after our expedition has come to a conclusion."

Clay rubbed his stubbled jaw and grimaced in thought. This encounter had turned out exactly as he had been afraid it would. He did not want the responsibility of shepherding this bunch of inexperienced misfits through the Rockies. Chances were, they would all wind up dead, himself and Shining Moon included.

He looked over at Proud Wolf and Aaron. "What do you two think?" he asked. "You've got a stake in this, same as the rest of us."

"I think we should help these folks," Aaron said without hesitation. Clay saw his eyes dart toward Lucy Franklin, and he knew why Aaron had answered that way. The young man was attracted to her, and Clay could not blame him.

"I too think we should join this expedition," Proud Wolf said. "I would like to learn more of this . . . science and philosophy of which Professor Franklin speaks."

Franklin sensed that Clay was being won over.

He concluded by saying, "Besides, Mr. Holt, if you refuse, we shall have no choice but to continue on with Mr. Lawton in charge."

Clay looked down at the ground for a long moment, and when he finally raised his eyes and looked at Franklin, he said, "You're a slick one, Professor. You reckon you've got it all figured so that I can't turn you down. And I don't suppose I will."

"Then you will take over?" Franklin sounded slightly surprised in spite of himself. "That's excellent, Mr. Holt, excellent!"

Clay stood up and looked over at Lawton. "But if I'm in charge, that means everybody's got to do as I say. That's the only way we've got a chance of getting you folks back to civilization alive."

"Of course, of course," Franklin agreed. "You'll be in complete command."

"Just want to make sure everybody understands that."

Lawton said, "We all know what you're getting at, Holt. I don't appreciate the way you been riding me, but I'll do what you say. Hell, I'm no fool. I reckon you do know this part of the country better'n I do."

"Damn right," Clay said. He turned to Franklin and extended his hand. "We'll do what we can for you and your people."

He just hoped he was not making the worst mistake of his life.

During his time in the Shining Mountains, Jefferson Holt had climbed ridges where no white man had stood before. He had looked out over valleys and mountains and known that he and his brother Clay were perhaps the only human beings, white or red, for fifty or a hundred miles around. Yet he had never felt as isolated as he did now, in the place where he had grown to manhood surrounded by family and friends.

His family was gone, scattered to the east and west. Those who had been his friends had either forgotten him or were uneasy in his presence. More than once in the first few days after his return to Marietta, he had noticed people looking at him as if they were watching a wild animal, fearful that it might spring at them without warning. Maybe Steakley had said something about the way Jeff had jumped him in the office of the trading post.

The worst thing, however, was that Melissa was not here.

There had been two cabins on the Holt family farm. One, the place where Bartholomew and Norah had died, was now a burned-out shell. Jeff could barely bring himself to ride past it. The other cabin, a smaller structure he had built with the help of his father and brothers, was the home to which he had taken Melissa on their wedding night. It held its own memories, most of them pleasant, but the good times were overshadowed by the tragedies that had separated the young couple. It was difficult for Jeff to go there, but he had no place else to stay.

The cabin had not suffered any more damage in his absence than had the Merrivales' place. Jeff chinked some places in the wall, working mud into the openings between logs, glad he had a chore to do that did not require much thinking. His brain was still numbed by the knowledge that Melissa was gone, and he wanted to keep it that way for a while. Maybe it would not hurt so much after time had passed.

It was a futile hope, Jeff knew, but it was all he had to cling to.

After a sleepless night, he rode into Marietta and paid a visit to the county offices, which were located in a building between a blacksmith shop and—of all things—a newspaper office. The newspaper had not existed when Jeff left Marietta two years earlier.

Taxes were due on the farm, as Jeff had known there would be. After he had paid the clerk, he said, "I don't like to see the farm sitting empty like that. The land's good; it needs to be worked."

"You thinking about letting somebody work it for shares, Mr. Holt?" the clerk asked.

"Yes, I believe I am," Jeff replied. "If you run into anybody who'd be interested, tell him to come see me. I reckon I'll be around for a week or so, anyway."

To tell the truth, Jeff had no idea what his future plans were, but he did not feel like explaining that to the county clerk.

The man pursed his lips and said, "That's not much time. But if I come up with anybody who wants to work like that, I'll send him right out to you, sir."

"Thanks." Jeff left the office, glanced up the street toward Steakley's, and considered paying another visit to the trading post. But there was no point in it, he realized. Steakley had already told him all there was to tell. Instead, he got on his horse and swung the animal's head toward the Congregational Church and the burial ground on the little hill behind it.

Jeff left his mount outside the wrought-iron fence around the cemetery and walked among the graves until he found the two he was looking for. His parents, Bartholomew and Norah, were laid to rest there, overlooking the broad sweep of the mighty Ohio River. It was an overcast day, with gray clouds thick in the sky and the air heavy with the threat of rain. Jeff thought that was just fine; the weather suited his mood.

He took off his hat and stood in front of the two gravestones.

"Hello, Ma. Hello, Pa. Reckon you probably thought I'd never be back this way." Jeff swallowed. He had figured he would feel foolish talking to dead folks, even if they were his parents, but somehow this seemed right, as if Bartholomew and Norah were with him somehow, listening to him. "Clay's doing fine. He's married now, to an Indian woman named Shining Moon. I think you'd like her. She's a mighty fine lady. I haven't heard from Edward and Susan and Jonathan, but I'm sure they're all right.

I know Uncle Henry and Aunt Dorothy are taking good care of them. I suppose the only one who's really made a mess of things is me.

"Melissa's gone. Her father took her and went east somewhere with her and her mother. New York, maybe, but I don't even know that much for sure. It'll be pure luck if I ever find her again, and I don't even know if I ought to try. If she loved me—if she *really* loved me—she wouldn't have let Merrivale drag her off like that!"

Jeff trembled as he spoke the angry words. He had not known he felt that way, but now he saw it was true. He was furious with Melissa. *She should have been here when I got back, dammit!*

Suddenly he felt ashamed. He had no right to judge her like that. After all, he was the one who had left to go thousands of miles into the wilderness. True, he'd had a good reason for going, but still, Melissa had been left behind, a vital young woman suddenly without the man she loved. It had been hard for him, sure, hard as hell, but it must have been difficult for her, too.

Jeff took a deep breath, then said, "I wish you were here, Ma and Pa, to tell me what to do. I want to go after her, but what if I never find her?"

He left an even worse question unspoken, although it echoed in his mind: *What if I find her—and she doesn't want me anymore?*

His fingers clenched the hat in his hands, bending it out of shape.

"Jeff?" a voice asked behind him. "Jefferson Holt?"

He spun around quickly, his hand automatically going to the butt of the pistol in his belt. The black-suited man who stood inside the entrance of the cemetery took a rapid step backward, his round face paling in fear.

"Reverend Crosley!" Jeff exclaimed. He took his hand away from the gun as if the butt had turned white-hot. "I'm sorry, Reverend. You startled me. Old habits are hard to break, I guess. But I should have heard you coming."

Jeff knew he was talking too fast and too much, but he was embarrassed not only by his reaction but because Josiah Crosley had caught him talking to himself. At least, that was what it must have looked like. With the line of work Crosley was in, however, he ought to understand about such things, Jeff thought.

"I thought I saw someone come up here," the minister said, some of the color seeping back into his face. "I didn't know it was you, though, Jeff. I'd heard you were back in town. Have you returned to Marietta for good?"

Jeff shook his head without even thinking about the question. When he'd left the mountains, the possibility that he might not return had been an unspoken understanding between Clay and him; that, however, was when he thought he would find Melissa here. With her gone, Jeff was not sure where he was going, but he knew he was not going to stay in Marietta.

He glanced over his shoulder at the tombstones and neatly kept plots.

"You're taking good care of the place, Reverend. I thank you for that. I knew Ma and Pa would rest easy here—if they could anywhere."

Crosley moved closer to him. "You're more than welcome, Jeff. Your parents were fine folks. I guess nearly everybody in town liked them and were sorry when they, ah, passed away."

When they were murdered by the Garwoods was what the preacher meant, Jeff thought. And not everybody in Marietta had liked the Holts. Many had been convinced that Clay was indeed little Matthew Garwood's father and had blamed the Holts for the trouble with the Garwoods.

Jeff pushed those thoughts away. *No point in digging up the past now,* he reminded himself. What he had to worry about was the future.

"Reverend," he said, "did my wife say anything to you about where she was going when she left town with her parents?"

"No, Jeff. I'm sorry. None of the Merrivale family said anything to me. They left rather suddenly, you know."

"That's what Ive been hearing."

"Melissa never wrote to you?" Crosley seemed to find that difficult to believe.

"Not once. I sure never thought things would turn out this way." Jeff squared his shoulders. He did not particularly like Reverend Crosley, and he did not want to pour out his troubles to the man. Anyway, since Crosley did not know where the Merrivales had gone, there was nothing he could do to help Jeff—except pray for him.

A fat drop of cold rain struck Jeff's cheek, followed by another and another. He clapped his hat on his head and brushed past Crosley, bumping the minister with his shoulder as he went by.

"I'll be going now," he said.

"Jeff, is there anything I can do?"

Jeff paused and looked back as the rain fell harder. "Say a prayer for me," he finally said. "I reckon it can't hurt."

IV

Charles Merrivale struggled with the cravat he was trying to tie around his neck. He cursed as he fumbled with the fine silk. His fingers, while not as blunt as a working man's, had not been made for such delicate work.

"Here, darling, let me do that for you."

Merrivale's wife, Hermione, came up from behind and reached around him. Standing on her toes and leaning to one side so that she could see their reflection in the mirror, she quickly arranged the cravat in a stylish knot.

Merrivale turned around, bent over, and brushed his lips across his wife's forehead.

"Thank you, Hermione," he said. "I was having a devil of a time with that thing."

"You were just nervous, dear. You always are when you have important business looming on the evening's horizon."

Merrivale frowned. Sometimes Hermione understood him all too well. It was a sign of weakness in a man, he thought, when his wife knew too much of what he was thinking.

Charles Merrivale was not a man who easily tolerated weakness, in himself or in others. He was tall and broad-shouldered and carried himself with an air of vitality that would have been more common in a much younger man. His thick hair was white, and his stern features gave him the look of an Old Testament prophet, which he resembled in more ways than one. Like those prophets of ancient times, he frequently laid down the law with unshakable conviction, especially where his family and his business were concerned.

So it had been when he resolved to leave Ohio and return to Wilmington, North Carolina, where he had run a profitable mercantile store for years before making one of the few incorrect decisions in his life—to move to Marietta, Ohio, and become a farmer. He had left no room for argument about his decision to return to North Carolina—although Melissa had given him one anyway—and while he had taken a loss on his property in Ohio when the man whom he thought was going to buy the place backed out at the last moment, forcing Merrivale to sell to someone else, he had not regretted his decision for an instant. Unable to repurchase the store he had left behind, he had simply established another one. Business was booming, and his enterprise was so successful that he had already expanded and built several warehouses near the docks. The growing shipping industry was just waiting for his entry into it, he had judged. Trading vessels regularly plied the coast up and down the Atlantic Seaboard, and Merrivale intended to carve out his own niche in this trade.

That was why the dinner that night was so important. He had invited a new business associate, a young man named Dermot Hawley, to join them. Hawley owned a successful freight company, and he would be a natural ally for a merchant like Merrivale.

"What was that?" Merrivale asked suddenly, aware that his wife was speaking to him again. "I'm afraid I let my mind wander, dear."

"I just said I should go see how Melissa is doing," Hermione replied. "I'd so like for her to enjoy herself this evening. She spends altogether too much time brooding."

"Moping over that damned Holt." As usual, Merrivale could not even think about Jefferson Holt without his stomach clenching in anger and hatred. He thumped his chest lightly with his fist as the uncomfortable burning sensation grew stronger.

"Whatever," Hermione said. "I'd just like to see her happy again."

"She'll be happy when she meets Hawley. He's a very handsome young man."

Hermione gave her husband a look of concern, but Merrivale ignored it. He was counting on Hawley's being attracted to Melissa; that would go a long way toward sealing the arrangement Merrivale wanted to make with the young man. Besides, it would not hurt Melissa to think about a man to replace Jeff Holt as her husband. It would be easy enough, Merrivale knew, to have Melissa divorced from Holt; his lawyers had assured him that they could charge Holt with desertion and make the accusation stick. A divorce would cause a scandal, of course, but scandals had a way of blowing over, especially when the person involved came from a wealthy, influential family.

Merrivale glowered into the mirror. His grandson needed a father, blast it, and even if Jeff Holt was still alive somewhere out there in the wilderness, he would never be a suitable parent to a lad like young Michael Holt.

Shrugging into his dinner jacket, Merrivale turned around. He was alone in the room. Hermione had left, and he had not even noticed.

Melissa Holt ran a bone-handled brush through her long, dark brown hair. In the glow of the lamp, her hair shone with brilliant auburn highlights, and she knew it was lovely. She kept it that way only out of habit these days, however. Since Jeff was not there to run his fingers through those silky strands, it really made little difference to Melissa how her hair looked.

In his bed in the corner of the room, nineteen-month-old Michael Holt gurgled in his sleep and rolled over. Melissa stood up from the bench in front of her dressing table and went over to check on the baby.

Of course, Michael was not really much of a baby anymore, Melissa thought, smiling as she looked down at his peacefully sleeping form. He had walked and talked at an early age, demonstrating a precociousness and daring that bordered on recklessness. Most of the time, in fact, Michael was a little terror, forever wandering away, drawn by his curiosity.

He had gray eyes and a thatch of sandy-blond hair, and every time Melissa looked at him, she saw Jeff in him with painful clarity. Michael was both blessing and curse, she thought, a part of Jeff she could cling to but at the same time a constant reminder of what she had lost.

But someday, *someday,* Jeff would come back, and then the three of them would be together.

"My goodness, Melissa, you're not even dressed yet!" Hermione exclaimed as she opened the door to her daughter's bedroom. "Mr. Hawley will be here soon, and we'll be going down to dinner."

At the mention of Dermot Hawley's name, Melissa drew the robe she wore tighter around her throat. She had never met the man, had never even seen him. For all she knew, he could be a perfect gentleman, the nicest man in all of North Carolina. Even so, she practically cringed at her mother's reminder. She knew what her father had in mind; Charles Merrivale's intentions were crystal clear.

"I'm not sure I'll be going down to dinner, Mother," Melissa began. "I'm not feeling very well—"

"No, Melissa," Hermione said sharply. "I'm afraid your father won't stand for that. He won't accept any excuses this time."

"He doesn't know how I feel!" Anger flared inside Melissa. "Surely he wouldn't be so cruel as to force an ill woman to sit through some dreadfully boring dinner—"

"Melissa." Hermione's voice was softer now as she stepped over to her daughter and laid a hand on her arm. "You're not really ill, and we both know it. You just don't want to meet this young man your father has invited."

Melissa pulled away from her mother. She loved her mother, she truly did, but at moments like this she felt almost as much rage toward her as she did toward her father. If her mother really cared about her, why had she never stood up to her husband and defended her daughter from his harsh, arbitrary decisions?

Hermione patted her carefully arranged red hair and straightened her gown. "Now finish dressing and come along downstairs, dear," she said absently. The brief argument was already over as far as she was concerned. "I'll send Sadie up to sit with Michael."

"All right," Melissa said, her voice so soft it was almost a whisper. She knew there was no point in being stubborn about this matter. When it came to stubbornness, Charles Merrivale could not be bested.

Hermione left the room, and Melissa turned to gaze into the cradle again.

"Why did you have to pick tonight to be so good?" she asked the sleeping youngster. "Why aren't you crying and pitching a hissy fit the way you usually do? Then Father wouldn't make me do this."

Michael shifted slightly under his blankets but did not wake up.

Quickly Melissa put on a dark blue gown with white lace bordering the neckline, the wrists, and the hem. She passed the brush through her hair a few more times, then slid her feet into soft leather slippers. She wore no jewelry, no cosmetics. She was not going to fancy herself up for this man her father wanted to show her off to.

There was a quiet, diffident knock on the door, and Sadie, one of the housemaids, opened the door.

"Miz Hermione told me to come up here and sit with the baby," she said.

"That's right, Sadie," Melissa replied, summoning up a smile. It was not Sadie's fault that she was so unhappy, and Melissa did not intend to take out her anger on her. "Come in. And thank you."

Sadie slipped into the room. She was a slender girl of perhaps fourteen; it was difficult to put an accurate age on most slaves if they had been sold more than once, and Charles Merrivale was Sadie's fourth owner. Merrivale was not a strong proponent of slavery, but he felt a man in his position had to have servants. One of the first things he had done after returning to North Carolina and buying their house had been to purchase two maids, a cook, and a man to handle the gardening and the carriage. After a while, when Merrivale was confident they would continue working for him, he would free all four of them, or at least that was what he had promised Hermione and Melissa.

The constant evidence of slavery was one of the things that had shocked Melissa most when she returned to North Carolina. It had not been unheard of for a man to have slaves in Ohio, but it was rare. Out there on what had not too long ago been the frontier, a man might be poor—but he was still free.

"Michael seems to be sleeping soundly," Melissa said to Sadie. "But if he wakes up and gives you any trouble, you come downstairs and fetch me immediately, do you understand?"

"Yes'm," Sadie said. "But I don't figure Mr. Merrivale, he'll want his dinner disturbed. Don't you worry, ma'am. I'll take good care of this little one."

"Yes, I'm sure you will." Melissa understood all too well. An absolute emergency would have to occur before Sadie would be allowed to interrupt dinner. And Melissa could not wish such a thing on her own son, no matter how much she wanted to avoid the evening's ordeal.

"You best hurry, Miz Melissa," Sadie added. "Your daddy's guest is already here. Drove up in a fancy carriage, he did, just 'fore I was fixin' to come up here."

Melissa took a deep breath. So Dermot Hawley had already arrived. She could not postpone this meeting any longer. Grimacing, she left the bedroom and walked to the broad, curving staircase that led to the main floor of the house.

"And here's my elusive daughter now," Merrivale said in his booming voice when Melissa was halfway down the stairs.

She wanted to cringe. Her father's tone held a note of pride, but it was the sound of a man speaking of an inanimate object, a valued possession.

A pleasant expression pasted on her face, she continued to the bottom of the staircase. Her father, mother, and the young man who had to be Dermot Hawley stood in the doorway of the parlor where they could watch her. Merrivale and Hawley each held a glass of brandy.

Melissa could have used a drink herself about now, something to fortify her for this evening. Of course, it would hardly be ladylike or proper for her to take the glass from Hawley's hand and toss back the liquor it contained. Such a move would no doubt shock him beyond words.

She thought about it for all of five seconds, then regretfully discarded the idea.

"Mr. Hawley, may I present my daughter, Melissa," Merrivale said pompously. "My dear, this gentleman is Mr. Dermot Hawley."

Hawley took her hand, bent over it, and kissed it. "The pleasure is all mine," he murmured. "It's a great honor to meet you at last, Miss Merrivale. Your father has told me all about you."

"Then he should have told you that my name is Mrs. Holt, not Miss Merrivale," she said sharply, sliding her fingers out from Hawley's grasp.

"Melissa!" Hermione gasped. "Please, dear, don't be rude to our guest."

"That's right," Merrivale said ominously. "I've raised you to be more polite than that, young lady."

Before Melissa could say anything else, Dermot Hawley grinned and said, "That's quite all right. Actually, you're right, Mrs. Holt. I was aware that you're married. For a moment the fact just slipped my mind."

Melissa met his level gaze and nodded curtly. "Of course. I'm sure you meant no offense, Mr. Hawley."

"None at all, I can assure you." He kept smiling at her.

She had to admit, he was a strikingly handsome man, just as her father had said. In his early thirties, he had curly brown hair, a mustache of the same shade, and blue eyes that sparkled with intelligence and wit. He had a charming air about him. Melissa supposed he had most of the unmarried young women in town—and their mothers—swooning in the hope they might interest him in matrimony.

"Well, why don't we go in to dinner?" Merrivale asked gruffly. He ushered the others ahead of him into the dining room.

Hawley wore a brown suit, a ruffled white shirt, and a cravat of dark gold silk with an impressive-looking stickpin glittering atop it. The clothes were expensive, more testimony to the success of his business even though he was a relatively young man. His hand when he had grasped Melissa's was soft and smooth but strong, an indication that he had done physical labor in the past but not in recent years.

The long mahogany table in the dining room was lit by an array of candles in gilt holders at each end. The polished surface of the table shone brilliantly in the warm yellow light. It was set with fine china and crystal. Hawley commented on the beauty of the room, and when Melissa glanced at her father, she saw the same pride of possession on his face that he had worn when she came down the stairs.

Charles Merrivale was in his element; Melissa had to admit that. She wondered what had ever moved him to give up all this and move to Ohio to farm the land. Whatever it was, she was glad he had made that decision; otherwise, she never would have met Jefferson Holt.

Merrivale was seated at the head of the table, with Hermione at the opposite end, Melissa to his right, and Hawley to his left. The table was so long that Melissa thought her parents would have to raise their voices to be heard if they wanted to talk to each other. On the other hand, Dermot Hawley was relatively close to her, since he was sitting directly across from her.

The meal was every bit the ordeal that Melissa had expected it to be. Her father and Hawley talked business most of the time, and although she paid little attention, she gathered that the young man owned a freighting concern that was doing quite well. She understood why her father was trying to garner Hawley's favor. A partnership between the two men would profit both. Merrivale had the goods to sell—or he would as soon as he filled those warehouses he had built —and Hawley had the means to deliver those goods to people who would buy them. It made perfect sense for them to work together.

But she was damned if she was going to be an inducement for Hawley to strike a deal with her father!

Hermione was content to eat and be pleasantly silent, but from time to time, Hawley tried to draw Melissa into the conversation. For the most part, she responded to his questions in monosyllables, eliciting glares from her father.

At last, though, as he finished his dessert and reached for his brandy, Hawley said to her, "I understand that you have a child, Mrs. Holt."

"Yes, I do. A beautiful boy named Michael." Melissa could not help but smile fondly as she thought about her son. "I'm very proud of him. And I'm sure his father will be, too, when he arrives."

Hawley blinked in surprise. "I wasn't aware you were expecting your husband in the near future."

A dark glare had appeared on Merrivale's face. "She's not," he stated, "in the near future or anytime else. The boy's father went to the mountains and won't ever be back."

"That's not true!" Melissa cried, stunned by her father's blunt declaration. "I'm sure Jeff will come back, and when he does, he'll be just as proud of Michael and love him every bit as much as I do!"

Hawley leaned forward and asked, "You mean your husband doesn't even know he has a son?"

"That's hardly a proper question, Mr. Hawley," Hermione said coolly, "even if you are a guest."

Melissa could have hugged her mother for that show of support, but her father said harshly, "No, Holt doesn't know anything about the child. He ran off before Melissa could tell him."

"That's not the way it was," Melissa protested. "You're making it all sound so awful—"

"It *was* awful," Merrivale cut in. "It was a dreadful mistake for you to ever marry that man. I knew from the start he'd come to a bad end. Why, he's been gone for over two years! I'm sure he's been killed and scalped by some of those wild red savages in the mountains."

76

"Charles!" Hermione cried.

Melissa paled. For the first time in her life, she was so angry with her father that she could have struck him. At the same time, a ball of sick fear had formed in the pit of her stomach. Her father had just put into words the horrible prospect that had haunted her for most of the past two years. All kinds of things could have happened to Jeff out there in the Rocky Mountains. Logically speaking, it was entirely possible he was dead.

But Melissa refused to believe it. She was sure she would know if Jeff were dead. She would know it in her heart.

"I'm not even going to dignify that absurd statement with a denial, Father," she said, forcing herself to sound much more calm than she felt. "You've always been wrong about Jeff, and you're wrong now."

Merrivale's face flushed brick-red with anger. "How dare you speak to your father that way?" he demanded. "Why, if you were still a child, I'd send you to your room—"

"But I'm not a child, am I?" Melissa interrupted. "I'm a grown woman with a child of my own and a husband who will be coming back for us. Mark my words, Father. You'll see."

"I'll see no such thing," Merrivale said coldly. "In fact, I've been considering instructing my attorneys to begin divorce proceedings so that this ridiculous union of yours will be dissolved!"

Melissa stared at him, as stunned as if he had just slapped her across the face.

At the other end of the table, Hermione said tentatively, "Charles, you can't mean—"

"I mean every word of it. I didn't intend to say anything about it just yet, but all this talk of Jeff Holt has convinced me that something has to be done. Otherwise, this foolish little girl is going to waste the rest of her life pining away for a phantom, a man she'll never see again."

Melissa was out of her chair before her father had finished speaking. Shaking with a rage she could barely control, she stalked across the dining room to the big french doors that led into the garden behind the house. She threw them open and stepped into the warm spring night. It was either get out of the house or start throwing things at her arrogant, pigheaded father, and she knew it.

Behind her, she faintly heard her mother saying in embarrassment, "Oh, Mr. Hawley, I'm so sorry about all this! I wanted you to have a nice dinner with us, not be subjected to such a—a scene!"

Melissa could not hear Hawley's reply, but she did not really care. It was none of his business. She had not wanted to meet him in the first place.

She was glad her father had not come after her and tried to force her back into the house. If he had, she was not sure what she would have done, but one thing was certain: It would not have been pleasant. The Merrivale family had already suffered enough embarrassment for one evening. The best thing that could happen now would be for Hawley to leave.

The sound of footsteps behind her made her turn around sharply to see who had followed her into the garden. A bright moon floated overhead, casting more than enough silvery illumination for her to recognize Hawley as he walked toward her. He was shorter than Merrivale, and he moved with a grace the older man had never possessed.

For a second Melissa thought about running deeper into the garden, where Hawley could not find her. But she stayed where she was. Her upbringing prevented her from being overly rude to anyone, even someone whose company had been forced on her. It was hardly this young man's fault that Charles Merrivale was such an awful, unfeeling parent.

Dermot Hawley came to a stop about five feet from her. She stood there, arms crossed over her chest, waiting.

After a moment he said, "I'm sorry, Mrs. Holt. I didn't mean to cause unhappiness between you and your father."

"It's not your fault, Mr. Hawley," Melissa said.

"Well, it was my question about your son that started things, even if it was indirectly. It wasn't my intention to bring up any unpleasant subjects. I didn't know what the—situation with your husband was."

Melissa relaxed slightly. Hawley sounded genuinely concerned and contrite, and she reminded herself that he was not the one who deserved her anger.

"That's all right, Mr. Hawley. I know you meant no harm. It's just that my father and I will never see eye to eye on the subject of my marriage, I fear."

Hawley chuckled. "I'll admit I haven't known your father for very long, but I have a feeling Charles Merrivale doesn't see eye to eye with people on a great many subjects, unless they agree with him, that is."

"You're right. He can be a maddeningly stubborn man."

"And what about his daughter?"

Melissa had to smile. "I suppose I can be a bit stubborn at times, too. But I come by it honestly, as you've seen."

"Indeed. Well, I just wanted to apologize for my part in this—"

"And as I've told you, it's not your fault. My father and my husband never got along well. But I'll never let my father bully me into a divorce! I won't hear of it!"

"Good for you," Hawley said firmly, which rather surprised Melissa. "You have to do whatever you think is best for you and your child." After a few seconds' hesitation, he added, "However, if your husband has been gone for over two years in the wilderness, perhaps—"

"No. I won't stand for any suggestion that Jeff may be dead. He's a good man, a strong man, a smart man. And he is with his brother, and

Clay Holt knows those mountains as well or better than any other white man in this country. He was with Lewis and Clark, you know."

"No, I didn't." Hawley sounded impressed. "I'm sure Clay Holt must be quite a frontiersman. Were he and your husband going to trap beaver?"

"How did you know that?" Melissa asked.

Hawley shrugged his shoulders. "Most of the men who have gone into the Rockies are fur trappers. I hear there's a great deal of money to be made in that business, if one can endure all the hardships that come with it. Your husband may return from the mountains a rich man."

"I don't care about that. I just want him to come back."

"Of course. And I'm sure he will, if it's humanly possible. After all, what man wouldn't come back to a lovely woman like you?"

Melissa cast her eyes toward the ground, wishing that Hawley would not make such comments. He had somehow moved closer without her noticing it, so that now he stood only a couple of feet from her. She could smell his clean masculine scent, and it made her feel strangely disconcerted.

"Mr. Hawley—"

"Dermot."

"Mr. Hawley," Melissa insisted. "I'm not sure we should be out here like this. After all, I am a married woman."

"Which doesn't mean that you and I can't be

friends. It's highly likely that your father and I will be doing a great deal of business together, Melissa, which means that you and I will be seeing more of each other."

"There—there shouldn't be any need for that. Father has an office in which to conduct business."

"Of course. But I've always believed in mixing business with pleasure whenever possible, and there's nothing more pleasurable than spending time in the company of a beautiful young woman."

"You dare too much, Mr. Hawley," she told him coldly.

He shook his head, and she could see him smirking in the moonlight. "Not at all. If I were going to dare too much, I'd be kissing you right now—Mrs. Holt." He drawled her name mockingly.

She wanted to slap him, but she sensed that would not bother him. In fact, he might regard it as the mark of a small victory. So she said, "I'm going in now. The night is getting rather chilly."

"Of course. I'll walk you."

"That's not necessary."

However, she could not stop him from striding along beside her as she retraced her path to the house. When they entered the dining room, they found Charles Merrivale still seated at the table, a goblet of brandy in his hand and the curved stem of his pipe clenched between his teeth. From the expression on his face, it was taking all his self-control to keep from biting right through that pipe stem.

"I see you found her, Dermot," he said to Hawley. "My thanks. My daughter is a rather delicate young woman and should not be out in the night air like that."

Hawley smiled. "We had quite an interesting conversation, didn't we, Mrs. Holt?"

"Yes," Melissa said. "Interesting." She looked at her father. "Where's Mother?"

"Your mother has retired for the evening. She was quite upset by your behavior, Melissa. You should apologize to her in the morning."

"I should apologize?" Melissa caught hold of her temper as it started to get away from her again. It would do no good to prolong this argument. Icily, she said, "I'm rather tired, too. Good night, Father." She turned to walk out of the room.

Merrivale stopped her with a sharp word. "Melissa!" When she paused and turned around, he went on, "Aren't you going to say good night to our guest?"

She looked at Hawley, whose expression was still enigmatic. "Good night, Mr. Hawley."

"Good night, Mrs. Holt," he replied. "I'm sure we'll be seeing each other again."

"I'm sure." With that, she got out of the dining room before anyone could stop her again.

Trembling with anger, she went up to her room, opening the door so sharply when she got there that she startled Sadie, who was dozing in a rocking chair near Michael's cradle.

The maid jumped up and blinked at Melissa. "The baby's been sleepin' just fine, Miz Melissa," Sadie said quickly. "Don't you worry, I been keepin' an eye on him—"

Sadie must have seen the fury on her face, Melissa realized, and mistakenly thought it was directed at her. "That's fine, Sadie," she said, softening her expression. "Thank you for watching him. You can go now."

"Good night, ma'am." Sadie scurried out of the room.

Melissa went over to the bed and looked down at the still-sleeping Michael. The sight of him drained the anger from her, and it was replaced with feelings of love and longing.

"Your father will come," she whispered to him. "Someday he'll come for us and take us away from here, and then we'll all be happy for the rest of our lives."

V

Marietta is principally inhabited by New Englanders, which accounts for the neat and handsome style of building displayed in it.

—Fortescue Cuming
"Sketches of a Tour to the Western Country"

Of all the people in Marietta whom Jefferson Holt did not want to run into during his return visit, he wanted to see Josie Garwood the least. And yet as he stepped out onto the porch of the trading post, there she was, just starting up the steps. She held the hand of a little boy, four or five years old, who Jeff knew had to be her son, Matthew.

Jeff stopped in his tracks and for an instant thought about retreating into the store. He would have preferred to face a party of hostile Blackfoot than Josie Garwood.

But it was too late. She had seen him, and after a split-second's hesitation, she continued up the steps, bringing Matthew with her.

"Hello, Jeff," she said, pleasantly enough. "I heard you were back in town."

He nodded and lowered the bag of supplies in his hand to the porch. "Hello, Josie. How are you?"

"Keeping well enough, I suppose. You know how it is."

He did indeed. He knew about Josie Garwood, just as everyone else in the area did.

Josie was still a very attractive woman in an earthy way. Raven-black hair framed a face that was not beautiful but possessed a sensuousness that immediately drew the eye to it. Her figure had always been lush, and if her waist was a bit thicker now than when he had last seen her, her breasts were also fuller and more prominent. Her nipples prodded against the fabric of her dress. Jeff chided himself mentally for even noticing that fact, but it was hard not to notice Josie, and that was a fact, too.

The little boy at her side had the same coarsely handsome features and black hair as his mother. That was not surprising, and it was even less so considering that Matthew's father was none other than Zach Garwood, Josie's older brother. Josie had blamed Clay Holt for making her pregnant, an accusation that had caused the bad blood between the Garwoods and the Holts, but Jeff knew the truth. Zach himself had admitted it before Clay killed him in the savage knife fight at Manuel Lisa's fort the previous autumn.

But Josie was probably not aware that her secret had been revealed, and as far as Jeff was concerned, things could stay that way. Josie was already known far and wide as a trollop, and he had no wish to add to her shame.

Not that it was any shame to be viciously molested, as Josie had been by Zach. It was hardly her fault that her brother had forced her to give in to his perverted lust. But at the same time, Josie had lied about Clay, and that lie set in motion the chain of events that had ended with the deaths of Bartholomew and Norah Holt and Luther and Pete Garwood. If none of that had happened, Clay and Jeff would not have been forced to leave Ohio in hopes of avoiding any further bloodshed.

That was all over now, Jeff reminded himself. He smiled politely at the woman. "I'm glad to see you, Josie," he lied. "It's been a long time."

"It certainly has." She hesitated, then said, "Is Clay with you?"

"No, I'm afraid not. I don't know where he is." That was true; Clay had been planning to spend the spring trapping with Shining Moon, Proud Wolf, and Josie's youngest brother, Aaron, and they could be anywhere along the Big Horn or Yellowstone rivers by now.

"Oh," Josie said, her face and voice mirroring her disappointment. "I knew I hadn't heard anything about him coming back with you, but I was hoping. . . ." She let the words trail off and shrugged.

Josie had always been half in love with Clay, even when they were children, Jeff remembered. That was most likely why she had claimed he was the father when she learned she was pregnant. She had to have hoped that Clay would marry her. But Clay had not returned her feelings, and things had not worked out the way Josie had planned. Instead, Clay had headed west, joining up with the expedition led by Lewis and Clark. Josie had been left behind to denounce him bitterly.

"Have you seen him since you left?" she asked. "Everybody said the two of you had probably gone west together."

"I've seen Clay," Jeff admitted. He did not see any harm in easing her mind a little. "He was just

87

fine the last time we got together." For a moment, he considered telling Josie that Clay was married now, but he stopped short of that. It would be better in the long run, he decided, to keep things as vague as possible.

Josie lifted her chin. "I'm glad to hear it. Clay and I, we had our differences, but I never wanted any harm to come to him. I never wanted any of that trouble—"

"I know, Josie." Jeff did not want her to hash over the past. "What's done is done. Let's leave it that way." A thought occurred to him, and he asked, "You knew Melissa, didn't you?"

"Melissa Merrivale?" Josie frowned. "Why are you asking *me* about her? You're the one who married her."

"That's right. But when I got back here, she was gone. Her father went back East and took Melissa and her mother with him. I was wondering. . . . Maybe you talked to Melissa before they left?" Jeff recalled that Melissa and Josie had not been what anyone would call friends, but he was unwilling to pass up any possible chance for information.

Josie sadly shook her head. "I'm sorry, Jeff. She didn't say anything to me. Do you mean to say you don't know where they are?"

Jeff sighed heavily, then said, "Mr. Steakley thinks they might have gone to New York, but he's not sure. Melissa didn't leave a letter for me or anything."

"That's awful!" Josie looked down at Matthew,

who was impatiently tugging on her hand. "Just hold on," she said to the boy. "We'll go inside in a minute, as soon as I'm through talking to Mr. Holt."

"I want to go now," Matthew said, giving Jeff a surly look.

Jeff was sure the boy had been raised to hate the Holts.

"All right, all right!" Josie gave in, letting Matthew pull her toward the door of the trading post. Then she stopped abruptly and turned to Jeff, provoking a groan of frustration from Matthew.

"Zach and Aaron left here, too, Jeff. I guess you didn't know that."

Jeff had been hoping that she would not ask about her brothers. She would probably be happy to hear that Aaron was all right and had made peace with the Holts, to the point of joining them in their fur-trapping endeavor. But Jeff did not want to tell her that Zach was dead—and at Clay's hand.

"I had heard that they were gone," he said, still hoping to evade any direct questions about her brothers.

Thankfully, Josie did not ask any. Instead, she said, "Before they left, Zach talked about what a great place the West is going to be. There are all kinds of opportunities out there for somebody who's smart and willing to work, he said."

That sounded a little too perceptive and forward-looking to be a direct quote from Zach

Garwood, Jeff thought, but he decided not to contest it. "That's right. I reckon it's going to be a fine place one of these days."

"I—I was thinking about going west myself. Making a new start. There's not much left for me here. Pa's dead, and I'm the only one left. I can't work the farm. All I can do is . . . well, you know what I mean."

Jeff could well understand why she would want to leave Marietta. Yet he worried that she might be intending to find Clay. The last thing Clay needed now, just as he was making a new life for himself with Shining Moon, was for Josie Garwood to show up, bringing Matthew along with her.

"What do you think?" she pressed him. "Do you think I should do it?"

"That's up to you, Josie. You're the only one who can make that decision. You should know, though, that the frontier is a hard place. St. Louis is the last real settlement. There's not much other than Indian villages and a few fur-trader's forts beyond it. It's not much of a place for a woman, especially one with a small child."

Josie's gaze darted back and forth along the street, and Jeff knew she was seeing the disapproving stares of the women, the knowing and lecherous glances of the men.

"Any place would be better than here," she declared fervently. She took a deep breath. "I'm glad I ran into you, Jeff. I think I've made up my mind."

Jeff bit back a groan. "It's up to you, Josie."

She patted his shoulder, then turned and continued into the trading post with Matthew. Jeff watched her go and wished he had not picked that afternoon to stop by Steakley's for a few more supplies.

He was going to be leaving soon. He still did not know where he was going, but the urge to be gone from Marietta was growing. As soon as he found someone to take care of the farm . . .

As if providence had just read his mind, the county clerk was walking along the street at that moment, and when he spotted Jeff on the porch, he called out, "Mr. Holt! I've been looking for you."

Another man was with the clerk. They were a mismatched pair, for the second man towered over the short, slender county official. Not only was this man taller, but he was wide enough to have made about three of the clerk, Jeff figured. He wore a thick, bushy black beard, and a battered felt hat was crammed down on his black hair. A coat that looked as though it had been made out of bear hide was stretched over his massive shoulders. Deep-set dark eyes squarely met Jeff's gaze.

"Mr. Holt, this gentleman is interested in talking to you about your farm," the clerk said.

The bearded man stomped up onto the porch of the trading post and extended a hamlike hand.

"Howdy, Holt," he said in a rumbling voice. "Glad to meet you. Name's Castor Gilworth."

Jeff shook hands with Gilworth, fully expecting the giant to crush his hand, but although there was immense power in the man's grip, he tempered it with restraint.

"Pleased to meet you, Mr. Gilworth," Jeff said. "Interested in some good farming land, are you?"

"Yup. Not to buy it, though. This feller—" Gilworth jerked a blunt thumb at the county clerk—"he says you got a place you need somebody to work for you. That sounds just like what me and my brother Pollux are lookin for."

"You'd be willing to work the land on shares? I can tell you right now, I'm willing to be more than generous in the split. What I'm really after is somebody to take care of the place so that we can keep it in the Holt family."

"Sounds good to me," Castor Gilworth said. "You see, me and Pollux lost our place in Pennsylvania, and we got it in our heads that we want to head west one of these days. Ain't quite ready to do that just yet, though, so we need some work and a place to live. This farm of your'n sounds just right."

"Well, it sounds good to me, too."

Despite Gilworth's rough appearance, Jeff felt an instinctive liking for the big man. He had always been a pretty good judge of character, he thought, and his time on the frontier had honed that quality. Out there, a man had to know whom he could trust, and such decisions sometimes had to be made quickly.

"Draw up the papers any way you want," Castor Gilworth said. "Reckon I trust you, so that's good enough for Pollux and me. We'll sign 'em." He grinned. "We can read and write, you know. Most folks figger we can't, but our ma taught us real good."

"I'm sure she did." For some reason Jeff's meeting with this massive man had lifted his spirits after that distressing conversation with Josie. "Where is this brother of yours, Mr. Gilworth?"

"He's still down to the county office. Ol' Pollux, he's a mite shy when he gets in a big town like this, so I figgered I'd come talk to you by myself first."

"Well, let's go get him," Jeff suggested. "We can work out all the details later, but right now I think you and me and old Pollux ought to have a drink."

Castor licked his lips. "I reckon we're going to get along just fine, all right, Holt. Come on."

He slung a huge arm around Jeff's shoulders as they started down the street.

"You'll like Pollux. Him and me are twins. Damn near as identical as two peas in a pod, 'cept he don't have no hair on top of his head. Bald as a stone. But he's a good feller, and we don't hold that agin him."

"Of course not," Jeff agreed.

"I hear tell you been to the Rockies. You got to tell us all about it. We're goin' to be out there one of these days, me and Pollux."

"I'm sure you will," Jeff said, realizing now that becoming friends with Castor and Pollux Gilworth would probably be somewhat akin to being swept up by a force of nature such as a flood or a cyclone. The chances of surviving would be pretty slim—but if you did, it would be one hell of a ride while it lasted.

The bend of the Yellowstone River where the Blackfoot attack had taken place was as good a place to camp as any, so Clay proposed that the expedition stay there for a few days, for a variety of reasons. He wanted to recover as many of the sunken pelts from the river as he could; that would mean diving to the bottom of the icy stream and taking considerable time to warm up between each dive. Also, he wanted to teach Professor Franklin, Lucy, and Rupert von Metz as much as he could about surviving in the wilderness. Finally, spending a little time there before continuing with the expedition would give Clay a chance to evaluate the skills—and the trustworthiness—of Harry Lawton and the men he had brought with him from St. Louis. From what Clay had seen of them so far, he was not impressed. However, he could deal with them being green as grass—as long as he could trust them.

Lawton raised more doubts in Clay's mind. As the party sat around the campfire that night after burying their dead, Clay announced his plan. Immediately, Lawton frowned and then spat expressively into the flames.

"Sounds to me like a damned foolish notion," he said.

Keeping a tight rein on his temper, Clay asked, "Why's that?"

"We already had to fight them Injuns once. Staying here's just begging 'em to come back."

Clay did not agree. "The Blackfoot's normal stomping grounds are a good ways north and east of here, though every now and then they come raiding down in these parts. That's what you ran into, a war party a long way from home. They've already been beaten once, so chances are that's where they're headed right now."

"You can't know that," Lawton said.

"No, I can't. But I know one thing: An Indian can be stubborn as a rock, but he's not stupid. Those Blackfoot may be nursing their wounded pride, but they won't regroup and come back this way until we've had time to be long gone."

"I think your idea is an excellent one, Mr. Holt," Professor Franklin said. "We need some time to lick our own wounds, so to speak, and you do have those furs to recover. I agree with you that we should camp here for a few days."

Lawton grunted. "Do what you want to do. I ain't in charge no more, am I?"

Clay wished the man was not so hostile, but under the circumstances, he would not have expected any other reaction. After all, Lawton's position as leader of the expedition had been yanked out from under him and handed over to somebody else, and a newcomer at that. No wonder he was angry.

But Clay had not asked for the job, either. Now that he had accepted Professor Franklin's offer, he intended to do the very best he could.

The Blackfoot raiding party that had clashed with the travelers earlier in the day was no longer a threat, in Clay's estimation, but that did not mean no other dangers lurked in these mountains. Consequently, Clay, Shining Moon, Proud Wolf, and Aaron Garwood took turns standing watch during the night. Clay would have let Shining Moon sleep, but he knew from experience that she would be angry if she was not included in any task that needed to be done.

For breakfast the next morning, Clay cooked hotcakes over the fire, and Proud Wolf picked berries from nearby bushes. Professor Franklin exclaimed over the tastiness of the berries and asked Proud Wolf how he had known they were safe to eat and not poisonous.

The young man just shrugged. "Any child of the Teton Sioux knows what to eat and what not to eat."

"You must give me a list," Franklin said enthusiastically, pulling out a sheaf of paper, a pen, and an inkwell from one of the supply bags. Breakfast was forgotten now that his scientific curiosity had been aroused.

When the meal was finished, Clay told Aaron to keep an eye out for trouble, then walked over to the riverbank. Shining Moon went with him.

"You will look underwater now for the pelts?" she asked.

Clay nodded. He handed her his pistols and one of his knives, then tossed his coonskin cap on the ground and removed his shirt and moccasins. His skin prickled at the touch of the cool morning air. It might have been better to wait until later in the day when the sun was warmer, but he was anxious to recover as many furs as he could.

"Keep an eye on Lawton," he said in a low voice to Shining Moon. "I don't think he'll cause any trouble, but you never can tell."

"I will watch him," she promised solemnly.

Clay took a deep breath and waded into the chilly water, heading for the deeper part of the river. Some folks said it was better to go slow and get adjusted to icy temperatures, while others advocated plunging right in. As far as Clay was concerned, neither method had much to recommend it. There was just no good way to get into water this cold.

The frigidness hit him like a blow as he dove in, the stream closing over him as he stroked toward the bottom. At this point, the Yellowstone was not overly deep, perhaps ten or twelve feet, and it was clear enough for Clay to see the sunken canoes and their cargo. He swam quickly to them, trying to ignore the cold.

The pelts had been tied into bundles with rawhide thongs, which were then tied to the canoe. Quickly Clay cut the leather strips that lashed the furs to the sunken craft. He took hold of one bundle and tried to lift it, but a few of the water-soaked furs had caught on the canoe. Grimacing, he dislodged the bundle, then kicked off the rocky bottom of the river and knifed back to the surface of the stream.

He exploded from the surface, and droplets of water sparkled brilliantly in the morning sunlight. His teeth chattering already, Clay swam to the bank and pulled himself out. Shining Moon was waiting for him with a blanket she had borrowed from the expedition's supplies. Clay shivered violently as she wrapped it around him.

"Come to the fire," she urged. "I asked Proud Wolf to build it up while you were in the river."

The campfire was indeed leaping higher now, and soon after he was seated beside it, the warmth from the flames seeped into his chilled body and put an end to his shivering.

"I can reach the pelts without any trouble," he said to Shining Moon, "but I'm going to have to take a rope down and tie it to the bundles. It'll probably take a couple of us to lift them out of the water. They're heavy from being soaked."

"Rest now," Shining Moon replied, "and let the cold leave you before you go in again."

Clay was not going to argue with that advice. He huddled beside the fire for a good half hour before he felt up to entering the river again.

The task went more quickly than he had expected. Using one of the expedition's ropes, he swam down to the sunken cargo, tied the rope to the rawhide thongs binding a bundle, and gave it a tug. That was the signal to Proud Wolf and two of Lawton's men who had been drafted to help. The three of them hauled the pelts out of the river while Clay swam to the surface.

Diving in and out of the icy water took its toll on Clay, and during the afternoon he needed more time to warm up between trips down to the canoes. By late in the day, with the help of the others, he had salvaged all the pelts he could. The binding around two bundles had come loose, and the furs had been washed away by the river's current.

Proud Wolf and Aaron Garwood had opened the bundles and spread the furs out to dry. The sunshine would do a good job of that, but it would take several days before the plews were ready to bind up again. Clay did not mind the delay, since it would give him the time he needed to familiarize his charges with the wilderness.

Harry Lawton had spent most of the day sitting with some of his men, talking and laughing. Clay had paid little attention to them, since he was so busy with his own tasks. At one point Rupert von Metz joined Lawton and the others, took a small easel and canvas from his packs, and painted the lounging frontiersmen, who did not seem to mind the Prussian's attention.

A small hunting party had gone out during the afternoon and returned with a good-sized deer, so the group had venison stew that evening. By that time Clay, who was chilled to the bone and seemed unable to warm up no matter how much time he spent by the fire, was more than ready for hot food.

Lucy Franklin carried a steaming bowl of stew to Clay, who took it and said, "Thanks, Miss Franklin. You don't know what this means to a man as cold as I've been all day."

"I hope it helps, Mr. Holt. I made it myself, you know."

"No, I didn't know," Clay said. Lucy's demeanor led him to believe that she had recovered from the frightening experience of the day before. He spooned the stew into his mouth, then winced a little because it was so hot. But it tasted wonderful. He could almost feel the strength and warmth flowing back into him as he ate.

"It's good," he told Lucy. "Mighty good."

Her smile widened. "I'm glad you like it."

Clay glanced to the side. Shining Moon, Proud Wolf, and Aaron were waiting for their food, but Lucy was not in any hurry to take it to them. She seemed content just to stand there and watch him eat, Clay thought.

Feeling a little uncomfortable, he suggested, "How about some for my friends?"

"Of course. I'm sorry. I wasn't thinking." Lucy hurried back to the stew pot to dish up more of the savory concoction.

"Reckon I can fetch my own." Aaron stood, hitched up his buckskin trousers, and strode over to the fire. A few seconds later, Proud Wolf followed. They joined Lucy and took the bowls she handed them.

"Aaron and my brother have noticed that Miss Franklin is an attractive young woman," Shining Moon said quietly.

"Shoot, they probably figured that out right away," Clay said.

Shining Moon looked at him. "But Miss Franklin would prefer that *you* notice."

"What do you mean? You can't figure that gal is—is—" Clay frowned.

"Interested in you? That is exactly what I mean."

"But she just met me yesterday."

"When you helped save her from a band of bloodthirsty savages," Shining Moon said wryly. "You cannot blame her for feeling grateful. And when a young woman feels grateful to a handsome man, it can easily become something else."

"But, hell, I'm a married man!"

"That may not matter to her."

Clay suppressed a groan. "Lord, I hope you're wrong about this. I've got enough troubles right now without having to worry about some young girl making cow eyes at me."

Shining Moon lowered her own gaze and murmured, "Just so you do not return those looks."

"Not much chance of that!" Clay assured her.

He paid more attention now as Aaron and Proud Wolf continued talking to Lucy Franklin. Maybe the two young men could distract Lucy from her budding interest in him. He fervently hoped so.

Warmed by the stew, Clay went over to speak with Professor Franklin for a few minutes, explaining that the expedition would stay for several days while the pelts dried on the riverbank.

"That's fine," Franklin said. "I've been picking the brain of that Sioux lad all day whenever he wasn't helping you, and I tell you, Mr. Holt, he's a veritable font of information. I've learned as much in one day about this land and its flora and fauna as I learned in all the weeks since we left St. Louis."

Clay could believe it. "Yep, Proud Wolf likes to talk, all right. Before we push on, though, I want to see how each of you handles a rifle. We need to go over your charts and maps, too, just to make sure they're accurate."

"Of course. And if anyone would know, it's you, Mr. Holt. After all, you've been over this ground before."

"Not all of it. This is a big country, Professor. There's plenty of it I haven't seen yet."

"Well, I'm sure you'll remedy that before you're through. You strike me as a man who needs to see all there is to be seen."

Clay shrugged. "Never really thought about it that way, Professor, but it could be you're right."

Exhausted by the day's grueling work, Clay went back to the other side of the fire, ready to lie down for the night. Using borrowed blankets, Shining Moon had made their bed just on the edge of the circle of light cast by the fire. She was nowhere in sight when Clay slid into the blankets, and he knew she must be off in the darkness tending to her personal needs before turning in. He planned to wait for her to join him before going to sleep, but weariness claimed him. His eyes closed as he drifted off.

He was not sure how much time had passed when he was roused from slumber by a soft, warm presence moving against him. Instinctively his arms went around the slender woman beside him. He recognized the scent of Shining Moon's hair as she pressed her face against his shoulder.

"You are awake, Clay Holt?" she whispered.

"I am now."

"And are you still cold?"

"A mite chilled," he admitted.

"You must be given warmth so that you will not become ill. And I know the best way to do that," she murmured. "It is an old Hunkpapa method."

"I'll bet." Clay chuckled. Then his mouth found hers, and his hand stroked her side, finding smooth, bare, silky skin that seemed to burn with its own special fire.

"She was right," Clay thought. He was warmer already.

On the other side of the campfire, which had burned down to little more than coals, Lucy Franklin shifted uneasily in her blankets. She had seen Shining Moon slide in next to Clay Holt, and although they were being very quiet about it, she knew what they had to be doing.

Lucy's face flushed. There was nothing wrong with what they were doing, she told herself. After all, Clay and Shining Moon were married. Or at least they had been joined in some sort of Sioux ceremony, which was the same thing, as far as the two of them were concerned.

Lucy was not quite convinced of that, however. How could anyone be truly married without standing up in front of a preacher? When Lucy was quite young, her mother had died, and her father had never been comfortable with any sort of moral or religious instruction—despite the fact that Lucy probably knew more about botany than any other female on the continent—but even so she knew a real marriage had to be blessed in a church, not in the middle of some godforsaken wilderness.

At first, shaken and emotionally drained after the battle with the Blackfoot, she had not even realized that Clay and Shining Moon were a couple. It had seemed so much more likely that the Hunkpapa Sioux woman was paired with the other Indian, the young warrior called Proud Wolf. But Lucy understood now that Shining Moon and Proud Wolf were brother and sister. As for Aaron Garwood, he was just a friend and partner to the others.

Lucy was not blind. She knew from the way Proud Wolf and Aaron had hovered around her at supper that they were both quite taken with her. Aaron seemed to be a nice enough young man, but he was not nearly as impressive as Clay Holt. And Proud Wolf was an Indian, so Lucy knew there could be no relationship between them. But as for Clay . . . ah, Clay Holt was a different matter.

She had never seen a man who struck such a chord deep within her. He looked so stern, yet he was surprisingly gentle. And he knew everything there was to know about life on the frontier. He was the most compelling man Lucy had ever met.

Maybe she felt this way because she realized Clay was her best chance of surviving this horrible expedition. She wished she had never come along, but her father had never doubted that she would accompany him and assist him, as she had for the past several years, and Lucy had not wanted to disappoint him. So here she was, deep in the most hostile landscape she had ever encountered, probably surrounded by more savages, hundreds of miles from the nearest outpost of civilization. It was enough to make her weep with fear and desperation.

Except when she looked at Clay Holt.

Right now, that squaw might be enough for him, Lucy thought. But sooner or later, she vowed, Clay would realize that what he really needed was a white woman to love and care for. And that woman might as well be her.

She drifted into sleep with that thought in her mind and a faint smile on her lips.

VI

Holding his pounding head, Jefferson Holt staggered to the doorway of the cabin and threw open the door. A horrible noise filled the air; to Jeff's ears it sounded like a dozen waterfalls roaring at once. However, he saw it was just the Gilworth brothers, asleep in the back of their wagon and snoring so loudly the earth seemed to shake under Jeff's feet.

He was sick from drinking too much rum at Monsall's tavern the evening before, Jeff realized. He had bought a tankard for Castor and Pollux, and then each of them had insisted on buying one for him in return, and by that time Jeff had been fuzzy enough to start the whole thing around again. Where it had ended was impossible to say, since he remembered almost nothing after the sixth tankard.

Leaning on the doorjamb, he closed his eyes to shut out the brilliant morning sunlight and massaged his aching temples while wishing that the Gilworths would stop snoring. He must have managed to get on his horse and lead Castor and Pollux here in their wagon the night before. He had felt the same instinctive liking for Pollux Gilworth that he had for Castor, and settling the deal with them had been simple. They would work the farm and live in the cabin, taking care of the place and keeping all but ten percent of the profits. That ten percent would go into an account Jeff would open in Marietta's recently established bank, which was owned by old Rufus Putnam, the retired soldier who had led the first settlers down the Ohio River. In turn, Castor and Pollux had agreed to remain on the farm for at least two years, or until they heard otherwise from Jeff. They had shaken hands on the arrangement, and that was enough for Jeff.

Now all he had to do was decide what to do with his own life.

As Castor had said, Pollux was rather quiet, preferring to let his brother do most of the talking. But Pollux had said one thing the night before that came back now to Jeff. Talking about the reverses that had led the Gilworths to lose their farm in Pennsylvania, Pollux had said, "A man can't sit still when things're falling apart all around him. He's got to jump one way or tother."

That was the choice facing Jeff now, he realized. Going west would take him to the frontier, back to the Rocky Mountains and his brother Clay. But Melissa had gone east. . . .

New York was a big place, sure, and he had no guarantee that was where the Merrivales had gone. But Jeff knew suddenly with crystal clarity that he was not ready to give up on being reunited with Melissa. She was his wife, and he loved her. They were meant to be together.

He straightened, his growing resolve helping him to forget about his headache and the uneasy feeling in his stomach. Now that he had made his decision, another idea occurred to him. The natural path to New York led up the Ohio River to Pittsburgh, where his two younger brothers and his sister were living with their aunt and uncle, Dorothy and Henry Holt. He could stop there and visit with Edward, Susan, and Jonathan on his way to New York. It would go a long way toward easing his mind to know that the youngsters were all right.

Jeff grinned. Despite the hangover, he felt better than he had at any time since returning to Marietta and discovering that Melissa was gone. He strode out to the Gilworth wagon, reached into the back of it, and shook Castor by the shoulder.

"Wake up!" he shouted cheerfully. "Rise and shine, Castor! Time to take a look around your new farm."

Castor stopped snoring. He rolled over and propped one eye open to regard Jeff balefully. He moaned. Beside him, Pollux stirred reluctantly as well.

"What the hell . . ." Castor muttered. He lifted a hand to his shaggy head. "Lord! Is that me yellin' like that?" He winced as he spoke.

"Come on," Jeff said, his enthusiasm clearing his head more with each passing moment. "We've got a lot to do before I leave."

"Leave?" Pollux echoed as he sat up and ran a hand over his bald head, which as Castor had said was as smooth as a polished stone. If anything, though, his beard was longer and bushier than Castor's. "So you made up your mind what you're going to do?"

Jeff nodded. "That's right. I'm going after my wife. And I'm going to find her no matter how long it takes."

Castor clambered down from the wagon and slapped Jeff on the back, the force of the blow staggering the smaller man.

"That's the spirit!" he bellowed at Jeff, forgetting about his hangover. "I don't reckon you Holts ever give up, do you?"

"No, I guess not," Jeff said slowly.

He was beginning to realize that about himself and the rest of his family. They were Holts, and when they wanted something, or when there was a wrong to be righted, they went after it with every bit of their strength and determination.

And Lord help the man who got in their way.

Lucy Franklin was going to be a problem. Clay sensed that quite plainly over the next few days. It seemed as though every time he looked up, she was there in front of him, wanting to know if he needed anything or if she could do something to help him.

Maybe it was ungracious of him, he thought, but he wished to hell that the professor had left her back in Massachusetts.

Clay had a feeling Harry Lawton was going to give him trouble, too. So far the former chief guide had done nothing but mutter behind Clay's back, but whenever Clay caught the man looking at him, he saw hatred in Lawton's gaze.

The first thing Clay had done to prepare for the rest of the expedition was to make sure the supplies were in as good shape as Franklin claimed. He was glad to see they did indeed have plenty of everything—powder, shot, sugar, salt, flour, salt pork, jerky, and beans. That was enough for the trip to the Pacific, provided they were able to hunt game along the way. Franklin and his group were not planning to return overland. A ship chartered by the American Philosophical Society was scheduled to sail around the Cape of Good Hope and meet them at the mouth of the Columbia River. The ocean voyage itself was something of a scientific expedition, the professor had explained.

After checking the supplies, Clay and Franklin, with the help of Shining Moon and Proud Wolf, spent a day poring over the maps the group had brought along. Clay recognized some of them as copies of the charts made by Lewis and Clark during their journey. He recalled sitting by the campfire many a night while the two captains made laborious notes in their journals and struggled to get each detail correct on the maps they were making. Evidently much of the information gathered by the Corps of Discovery had been made available to scientific

110

societies, such as the one in Philadelphia, although it had not yet been released to the general public. That time was coming, Franklin insisted, and perhaps not too far in the future.

"There's a great clamor among the population for more knowledge about the West," Franklin said to Clay as they looked over the maps. "They've heard a great deal about the expedition of Lewis and Clark, but much of what is being bandied about is just rumor and innuendo. Did you know, for example, that some people insist these mountains are inhabited by great woolly mammoths such as those that existed thousands and thousands of years ago?"

"Don't know about mammoths, whatever they are," Clay said, "but there's just about every other kind of critter out here."

"Some foolish individuals claim, however, that Lewis and Clark never reached the Pacific Ocean, that the entire journey was just a figment of the imagination of some scrivener hired by the government to dupe the public into accepting President Jefferson's purchase of the Louisiana Territory."

Clay shook his head. "Well, I know that's not true. I was there, from St. Louis all the way to Fort Clatsop at the mouth of the Columbia and back. If you ask me, nobody could make up something as farfetched as what we did, no matter how much imagination they had."

"I agree wholeheartedly." Franklin traced a line on the map with the tip of a blunt finger. "Now, about this stream here and its location on the map . . ."

For the most part Clay found the professor's charts to be accurate, although he, as well as Shining Moon and Proud Wolf, did find a few mistakes to correct. By the time he and the others were finished studying the maps, Clay felt confident about using them.

The next morning—after Lucy had hovered over him so much during breakfast that he wanted to shoo her away like a troublesome insect—Clay announced, "Since we've got plenty of powder and shot, I want to see how everybody handles a rifle. You may all need to do some shooting before this trip is over."

"I handle a gun just fine," Lawton protested, "and so do the boys I hired."

"You won't mind showing me, then," Clay said.

"You're the boss, ain't you?" Lawton said bitterly.

Rupert von Metz folded his arms across his chest and stared at Clay. "Well, I for one refuse to be subjected to such a test."

"Why's that?" Clay forced himself to keep his tone civil and not show the impatience he felt.

"I am a Prussian," von Metz replied, as if the answer should have been obvious. "And despite the fact that I also have artistic abilities, I possess all of the natural Prussian aptitudes."

Clay waited a moment for a better explanation. When it became apparent he was not going to get one, he asked, "And just what does that mean?"

Von Metz regarded Clay with disdain. "It means that as a Prussian, I am naturally better with a firearm than some unwashed backwoodsman."

"Really, Rupert—" Professor Franklin began.

But Clay held up a hand to stop the botanist. "That's all right, Professor. Reckon I know how Mr. von Metz feels. It's all right to be proud of the place you come from." Clay's mind was working rapidly as he spoke. Von Metz's arrogance was going to cause more and more trouble unless he was taken down a notch or two—now.

Clay continued, "Just because a fellow is from a certain place, though, doesn't mean he can do everything that other folks around there can."

Von Metz glowered at him. "You doubt my word?"

"Let's just say I need convincing." Clay's flintlock was cradled in the crook of his left arm, as it usually was when he was not busy doing something else. He shifted the Harper's Ferry rifle around so that it was held ready to use, then hefted the weapon and suggested, "Why don't we have a shooting match?"

"A competition? Between you and me?" Von Metz sounded surprised at first, but then his eyes began to shine with interest. The proposal seemed to appeal to his competitive nature. "Of course, Herr Holt. But why not expand the scope of this contest, say, to include cold steel as well?"

"What do you mean by that?" Clay felt a tickle of unease at the back of his neck. Von Metz was up to something.

"After our shooting match, as you call it, I propose that we also match our skill with sabers. I happen to have a pair of fencing sabers with me."

Somehow it did not surprise Clay that somebody like von Metz would haul a pair of fencing sabers hundreds of miles into the wilderness. You never knew when you might have to fight a duel, he thought, chuckling to himself.

He glanced at Shining Moon, Proud Wolf, and Aaron and saw the concern on their faces.

"Sure. Sounds like a good idea to me." Without warning, Clay tossed the rifle to von Metz, who reacted quickly and snatched it midair. "First let's see what you can do with this, though."

Von Metz lifted the rifle, checking its balance. He raised it to his shoulder and rested his cheek against the polished wooden stock, then squinted and sighted over the long barrel. Finally, he nodded.

"This weapon is crude, but it will do."

"It's loaded and primed," Clay told him. "All you have to do is cock it and fire."

"And what is my target?"

Clay looked around and spotted a small mark on a tree trunk about a hundred yards away. He pointed.

"See the blaze on that tree? A bear did that, rubbing up against the trunk until he knocked the bark off. See if you can put a ball into it."

Von Metz sniffed as if the challenge was too easy, but Clay thought he saw a glimmer of uncertainty in the young Prussian's eyes. Everyone in the group had gathered around by now and was watching with great interest as von Metz lifted the rifle to his shoulder again. He pointed it at the tree and settled his cheek against the stock.

"Better be careful," Clay warned him in a quiet voice. "You hold the gun like that when you fire and the kick's liable to bust your jaw."

"I know that," von Metz snapped. "I was simply trying to estimate the accuracy of these primitive sights."

Clay noticed that von Metz readjusted his grip on the rifle, however.

After a moment von Metz pulled the cock all the way back, sighted again, and took a deep breath. Clay saw his finger whiten on the trigger as he squeezed off the shot. With a burst of smoke, noise, and flame, the rifle fired. Just as Clay had expected, the recoil of the heavy weapon knocked von Metz back a step.

A bit pale faced, he caught his balance and asked quickly, "What happened? Did I hit it?"

The distance was too far to be sure, so Aaron Garwood said, "I'll go check." One of Lawton's men hurried along with him as he trotted toward the tree.

When they reached it, both men examined the trunk intently. Then Lawton's man turned and held his hands about six inches apart. "That far under the blaze!" he called.

"Good shooting, Rupert!" Lawton exclaimed,

and some of his companions echoed his congratulations.

Clay thought von Metz looked displeased, however, as he handed the rifle over.

"I should have done better," von Metz said. "If I had been more familiar with this weapon, I would have."

"I reckon so." Clay reloaded the rifle. "But that is good shooting, von Metz. That's no easy target I picked out. We'll see how I do."

He poured powder from his horn into the barrel, then dropped a ball on top of it and used the ramrod and wadding to seat the charge. After priming the lock and waving Aaron and the other man away from the tree, Clay lifted the rifle to his shoulder and cocked it. He sighted for only a couple of seconds before pressing the trigger.

The gun boomed again. As the smoke cleared, Aaron ran to the tree and let out a whoop of excitement. He placed his finger in the middle of the blaze and shouted, "Dead center!"

Clay's face was carefully expressionless as he asked von Metz, "Want to go again?"

The Prussian looked about ready to chew his way right through that tree trunk, Clay thought. Through clenched teeth he said, "You have already bested me. But there is still the test of steel."

"That's right. Let's get on with it." Clay handed the empty rifle to Proud Wolf.

Shining Moon put a hand on Clay's arm and asked, "Are you sure you want to do this?"

"Why not?" Clay grinned at von Metz. "This is just a little sport, isn't it, Rupert?"

"Of course," von Metz replied tightly.

Clay read another answer in the Prussian's eyes, however. Von Metz was serious about this, and Clay knew that if the man got a chance, he would run that saber right through Clay's vitals. He could always claim that the killing had been an accident. With Clay dead, Lawton would probably resume command, and Lawton and von Metz seemed to be friends. Besides, Clay had humiliated von Metz, at least in the eyes of the young artist; he would be eager to have his revenge.

Von Metz stalked to his tent and disappeared through the canvas flap to get the sabers. Meanwhile, Aaron dug both rifle balls out of the tree and rejoined the group, tossing the misshapen lumps of lead up and down in the palm of his hand.

"Good shooting, Clay," he said quietly to his friend. Echoing Shining Moon, he added, "Are you sure about this saber business?"

Clay smiled a little and looked at Proud Wolf. "Aren't *you* going to ask me the same question?"

Proud Wolf shook his head. "You will show that European fool how a true man of the mountains fights."

"Glad somebody's got some confidence in me," Clay said.

"I have confidence in you, my husband," Shining Moon said. "But I do not want you spitted on a long knife like a rabbit ready for roasting."

Before Clay could reply, von Metz emerged from the tent carrying two long, slender, slightly curved sabers in brass scabbards. As von Metz brought the weapons over, Professor Franklin frowned.

"I'm not certain this is a good idea, Mr. Holt," he said.

Beside him, Lucy looked concerned as well.

"It'll be all right," Clay said quietly, hoping to reassure them. He was not as confident as he sounded, however. Von Metz moved with athletic grace, like a cat, and Clay knew that a single misstep could be fatal. Still, he had gotten himself into this, and now there was nothing he could do except go through with it. If he backed down, none of the group would follow him.

Von Metz held both sabers toward Clay and said, "You shall have the choice of weapons, even though by all rights it should be mine as the offended party."

"I thought we said this was sport, not a duel," Clay replied.

Von Metz's response was, "Pick your weapon, Herr Holt, and let us get on with this."

"Sure, if that's the way you want it." Clay wrapped his fingers around the bone handle of the hunting knife at his waist and slid the heavy blade from its sheath. "Don't need either one of those pigstickers. I'll use this."

There were exclamations of surprise from

those gathered around, including Clay's companions and the professor and his daughter.

Von Metz coolly asked, "Are you certain of this decision?"

"Yep."

Von Metz inclined his head. "Very well, then." He handed one of the sabers to a bystander, then slid the other from its scabbard, the blade emerging with a slight rattle of steel against brass. He tossed the scabbard aside.

Clay knew what the other man had to be thinking. The weapon Clay held had a long blade for a knife, but it was still only about a foot in length. The saber in von Metz's hand was close to two and a half feet long. In a fight like this, that extra eighteen inches represented a tremendous advantage in reach.

But Clay was certain that he would be lost if he used that flimsy little sword. A man was better off staying with what he knew. The bone handle of the hunting knife fit his palm as though it were part of him.

Von Metz put his feet together, lifted the saber in a salute, and said, "En garde!"

The onlookers moved back, forming a large circle with Clay and von Metz in its center. Nobody wanted to get in the way of a wildly swinging blade.

Clay said to von Metz, "Whenever you're ready."

The Prussian came at him then, sunlight flickering on the blade of the saber as it described

119

a complicated arc through the air and flashed toward Clay's face. Clay took a quick step back, and the thrust missed. He brought his knife up, and steel rang against steel as it clashed against the saber, ruining any fancy move von Metz might have had planned for his backswing. The heavier hunting knife, with Clay's strength behind it, had no trouble turning aside the saber.

Von Metz stepped back and regarded Clay. "Very good," he said. "Very smooth, Herr Holt. You have fought with blades before."

"Once or twice," Clay said dryly.

Von Metz launched another attack, this time to the accompaniment of cheers from some of Lawton's men. Lawton had probably put them up to it, Clay thought fleetingly. Then he turned his full attention to von Metz. The Prussian's saber was leaping around like something alive, darting and jumping and slashing forward. But each time the blade approached Clay, the frontiersman's hunting knife parried the blow.

A light sweat broke out on von Metz's forehead as Clay used his knife to turn thrust after thrust aside. Clay seemed content to fight a defensive battle. That was sound strategy, given the longer blade his opponent possessed. He was going to have to bide his time, he thought, and wait for the right moment to strike.

That moment was not long in coming. Becoming angrier and more frustrated by the second, von Metz's movements grew wilder, more reckless. The saber swung wider as he slashed at Clay, who either ducked, dodged, or blocked each attack. Gradually, von Metz abandoned any pretense of fencing and merely hacked at his opponent. Clay retreated a little, drawing von Metz on. The Prussian cursed in his native language and lunged forward, swinging the saber wildly.

Clay knew the time had arrived. He darted aside, and as von Metz stumbled past him, Clay's knife slashed down and rang loudly against the saber. The lighter weapon snapped as Clay twisted his wrist in a time-honored maneuver to break an enemy's blade. Von Metz let out a howl of rage and tried to catch his balance.

He was too late. Clay's foot shot out and went between von Metz's calves. He hooked his toe behind the Prussian's left leg and jerked. Von Metz went over, landing hard on his back.

Before he could move, Clay dropped one knee lightly on von Metz's chest, then put the blade of the hunting knife against his throat. Von Metz froze motionless as the keen edge touched his skin. A surprised and horrified silence fell over the onlookers as they realized how close Clay was to cutting von Metz's throat.

But it was not really that close, Clay thought. If he had wanted von Metz dead, the Prussian would have a bloody gash from one side of his neck to the other right now. Shining Moon, Proud Wolf, and Aaron understood that and knew von Metz was in no real danger as long as he stayed still, but the others had no way of knowing the true situation.

Lucy gasped in horror, and Professor Franklin cried out, "For God's sake, Mr. Holt, don't kill him!"

In one lithe motion Clay got to his feet, taking the blade with him. He stood over von Metz. As he slid the knife back into its sheath, Clay said, "Never meant to kill him. If I did, he'd be dead already." He held out his hand to the prone von Metz. "You handle a blade pretty good, mister, and in case I didn't mention it before, that was fair shooting, too. I reckon you'll do to go over the mountains with."

At least that was true as far as von Metz's skill with weapons was concerned. His attitude, however, left one hell of a lot to be desired, Clay thought.

Von Metz sat up and pushed himself to his feet, ignoring Clay's outstretched hand. It seemed he was in no mood to be mollified by Clay's words of praise.

"You—you backwoodsman!" he said, his handsome face purple with rage. He turned on his heel and stalked off.

Clay shrugged. He had knocked some of the arrogance out of von Metz, but the young Prussian evidently still had a plentiful supply.

Turning to Harry Lawton and the other men, Clay said quietly, "You boys were going to show me how well you shoot."

"Yeah, we'll do that," Lawton said, giving Clay

an ugly grin. "But you'd better watch out for that youngster, Holt. Next time, he's liable to shoot at you."

Clay doubted that. Rupert von Metz might be thoroughly unpleasant—and Clay knew the Prussian would not hesitate to kill him in fair combat—but he did not believe von Metz was the kind of man to shoot from ambush.

Lawton, now, was an entirely different story. As long as Lawton was around, Clay was going to do his damnedest to have eyes in the back of his head.

That night, as the campfire became embers and one by one the members of the expedition turned in, Rupert von Metz found himself sitting alone in front of his tent. No one had had much to say to him since the debacle that afternoon. He had already lost Lucy Franklin, of course, to Clay Holt. During the first weeks of the journey, Lucy had been taken with von Metz, who thoroughly enjoyed being charming whenever young women were involved. He had been hoping she would prove an entertaining diversion during this trip through the wilderness. Only the relatively close quarters and the fact that Lucy's father demanded a great deal of her time had prevented von Metz from instigating a dalliance already.

All that had changed with Holt's arrival on the scene, von Metz reflected. Now, not only did Lucy ignore him, but so did the other men in the group. Von Metz had no desire to become lifelong friends with any of these frontier ruffians, but their company was better than nothing.

In disgust, he stood up, brushed off the seat of his trousers, and turned to enter the tent.

"Wait up a minute, Rupert," someone said to him before he could push past the canvas flap.

Von Metz turned and saw a shape looming between him and the glow of the fire. He recognized his visitor as Harry Lawton, who had probably been the most cordial member of the expedition so far.

"What do you want, Harry?" the young Prussian asked.

"A bit of talk." Lawton chuckled. "Holt showed you up pretty good today, didn't he?"

Von Metz stiffened with anger. Lawton had no right to speak to him that way. "As I recall, you have had your own less than sterling moments against Herr Holt." Following Lawton's lead, von Metz kept his voice pitched low so that it could not be heard around the campfire or in any of the other tents.

"I reckon you could say that. I'm planning to do something about it, though."

"What?" von Metz asked scornfully. "So far you have done nothing but complain and utter vague threats."

"That's because I'm waiting for the right time," Lawton snapped. "You can take my word for it. Mr. High-and-Mighty Clay Holt is going to regret coming in here and bullying me out of a job."

"You will still be paid."

"That ain't the point!" Lawton insisted. "It's a matter of honor, too."

Von Metz tried not to laugh. It was ludicrous to hear a man like Lawton, little better than a filthy savage, talking about honor. Von Metz seriously doubted there was anyone on this misbegotten continent who fully understood the word.

"What is it you want with me, Harry? I'm rather tired."

"Sure, sure, I'll make it fast. I just wanted to know if you'd be interested in helping out when it comes time to settle the score with Holt."

Von Metz raised his eyebrows in surprise at the question. He had honestly thought Lawton lacked the courage to do anything about Holt except whine and complain.

"You have a plan?" he asked, curious.

Lawton shook his head. "Not yet. But I'm thinking on it. Can I count on you when the showdown comes?"

"Against Holt? You certainly can." There was a part of von Metz that believed Lawton would never get around to doing anything, but just in case he did, it would not hurt to form an alliance of sorts with the man. And if Lawton did not exact vengeance on Clay Holt, then von Metz would deal with the problem himself.

Lawton slapped him lightly on the arm, and Rupert tried not to show how distasteful he found the contact.

"Glad to hear it," Lawton said. "We'll show that—"

"You men better get some sleep," someone called from the other side of the camp. "We'll be pulling out in the morning."

Both Rupert and Lawton recognized the voice as Clay Holt's.

Lawton turned and gave Clay a wave of acknowledgment, then swung back to face von Metz and growled, "Ain't that just like the son of a bitch? He don't ever get through giving orders, not even when a man's fixing to turn in."

"So, we resume the journey tomorrow, eh?" von Metz mused. "Sometime during our trek, that opportunity of which you spoke will arise, Herr Lawton, and we must be ready to take advantage of it."

"Yep. And when we do, Clay Holt is a dead man."

Von Metz nodded slowly. He liked the sound of that; he most certainly did.

Castor and Pollux Gilworth went down to the landing to see Jeff off. It was a fine spring morning with a fresh breeze from the southwest. That breeze would fill the sail on the riverboat waiting at the slip and help carry the vessel upstream to Pittsburgh. Also aboard was a full crew to pole the boat along; against the current of the mighty Ohio, they needed all the help they could get.

Jeff had bought a new coat of brown wool, as well as some new shirts, from Steakley's Trading

Post. He wore the same floppy-brimmed felt hat and carried the same weapons as when he had ridden back into Marietta. The Ohio could be a rough place to travel. Sometimes the boats were attacked by river pirates, and thieves and cutthroats might be traveling as passengers as well. But Jeff was not thinking about any of the hazards of riverboat travel that morning. He was filled with excitement and anticipation.

"Well, good luck to you," Castor said as he shook hands with Jeff. "Hope you find what you're lookin' for."

"Same here," Pollux echoed, also shaking hands with Jeff.

"I'm sure glad I ran into you boys," Jeff said. "You've taken a load off my mind, agreeing to work the farm. Once I've stopped off at Pittsburgh and made sure my brothers and sister are all right, I'll be able to turn all my attention to finding Melissa."

It would be good, too, just to see Edward, Susan, and Jonathan, not to mention his uncle and aunt. Jeff had not seen Henry and Dorothy Holt for more than ten years, when Bartholomew had taken the family to visit his brother Henry and Henry's family. That was the last contact Jeff had had with any of the Pittsburgh relatives.

His step was light as he crossed the gangplank to the deck of the riverboat, his powder horn, shot pouch, and possibles bag bouncing against his hip. He was traveling light, just the way he liked. He could move faster that way. In the mountains a man learned not to carry any more than he really needed.

Jeff turned at the low railing and lifted a hand in farewell to Castor and Pollux. The burly, bearded Gilworth brothers returned the wave.

Jeff had been the last passenger to board. Not many people traveled upriver; most of the traffic still headed west. One of the crew members pulled in the gangplank, and within minutes other men had poled the boat away from the dock and turned it to catch the southwest wind.

Once again, Jefferson Holt was leaving his old home behind. And just as before, he had no idea what he would find when he got where he was going.

Part II

The Ohio into which we had now entered, takes its name from its signifying bloody in the Indian tongue, which is only a modern appellation bestowed on it about the beginning of the last century by the five nations, after a successful war, in which they succeeded in subjugating some other tribes on its banks. It was called by the French La belle Riviére, which was a very appropriate epithet, as perhaps throughout its long course it is not exceeded in beauty by any other river. It was always known before as a continuation of the Allegheny, though it more resembles the Monongahela, both in the muddiness of its waters, and its size: the latter being about five hundred yards wide, whereas the former is only about four hundred yards in breadth opposite Pittsburgh.

—Fortescue Cuming
"Sketches of a Tour to the Western Country"

VII

"Could I interest you in a game of cards, Mr. Holt?"

Jeff was sitting on a stool atop the keelboat's cabin watching the steep, wooded hills slide by on either side of the Ohio River. The fellow passenger who had spoken to him was a man with red hair and a ginger beard. He was sporting a fancy waistcoat, a ruffled shirt, tight buff-colored breeches, and a beaver hat, canted on his head at a jaunty angle.

"No, thanks, Mr. Burke," Jeff said. "I think you'd find I'm not much of a card player."

The man called Burke smiled. "To a man in my line of work, Mr. Holt, that's not always a disadvantage. However, I won't press you." He ducked back into the cabin from which he had emerged a moment earlier.

Burke was one of only half a dozen other passengers on the boat. Jeff had met him the day the boat set out from Marietta, and Burke had not hesitated to declare right away that he was a gambler. He hailed from Pittsburgh, where he was returning after a trip downriver to pick up a recent purchase—one of the most impressive horses Jeff had ever seen.

"His name is Beau," Burke had explained to Jeff as he brushed the big, magnificent black animal. "He's been running races all over Ohio and Illinois for the past year, and he's never been beaten. I had to pay a pretty price for him, but he's going to win back that much and more once I get him to Pittsburgh."

Jeff recalled seeing horse races around Marietta in the past, but he had never heard of this Beau. From what Burke had said, however, the horse had not started winning races until well after Jeff had gone west with Clay.

The keelboat was a large one, nearly eighty feet long and eighteen feet wide. The walkway where the crew members poled the vessel took up only eighteen inches on each side, so there was plenty of room amidships for passenger cabins as well as a sizable cargo hold. The hold was only about half full, mostly with barrels of salt, so Beau was staying there, supported by a broad sling that passed under his belly and hung suspended from the ceiling.

The horse's new owner, Eugene Burke, divided his time between the cargo hold and the crude saloon that had been set up in one of the empty cabins. The bar consisted of several planks laid atop whiskey barrels. Barrels of salt had been rolled in from the hold to serve as tables, and the passengers and off-duty crewmen who frequented the place used kegs for seats.

A game of cards was usually going on, presided over by either Burke or one of the other passengers, a surly character named Wiggins, who also dressed well and had the look of a professional gambler. From what Jeff had seen, he concluded that Burke and Wiggins knew each other, but there was no friendship between them. In fact, they seemed to go out of their way to avoid each other.

Traveling against the current, the keelboat did not make particularly good time, and Jeff was keenly aware of each passing moment. He was eager to get to Pittsburgh, and even more eager to reach New York and begin his search for Melissa. Aided by the sail and a half dozen oarsmen in the boat's bow, the crew used their long poles to push the craft along, only a few yards offshore, where the water was shallower and the poles could reach the bottom. The captain—or patroon, as Jeff had heard the crew call him— stood aft on top of the cabin, controlling the long steering sweep and watching the river ahead so that he could call out instructions to his men.

Each night the riverboat was tied up to the shore, since traveling in the dark was too hazardous, but from dawn to dusk, the tall, gaunt, muscular crewmen in buckskin trousers and red flannel shirts followed a grueling routine. Standing at the bow, they planted their poles on the bottom of the river and walked toward the rear of the vessel, pushing it forward. Then they gripped the poles tightly and walked toward the bow and repeated the entire process. Their efforts moved the boat along at a slow but steady pace. In return, the boatmen received wages of approximately twenty-five dollars a month and meals consisting of hardtack, corn, and potatoes.

It made Jeff shudder just to think about it. He missed the mountains more than ever, the freedom, the clean air of the high country, the taste of water from an ice-cold mountain stream. These rivermen drank cups of muddy water dipped straight from the Ohio, usually followed by a cup of raw whiskey from the ever-present keg on deck.

Another day and the boat would reach Wheeling, the major settlement between Marietta and Pittsburgh. It also marked the approximate halfway point to Pittsburgh. Jeff was thinking about how surprised his relatives would be to see him when he heard a shout from the cabin beneath him.

"Don't be a fool, man! Put that gun down!"

Jeff tensed as he recognized Eugene Burke's voice. The saloon cabin was right under him, and it sounded as though Burke was in trouble. Jeff stepped to the edge of the roof, dropped lightly to the walkway, and ducked his head as he went down the three steps into the cabin.

The room was lit not only by the light coming through the open door but also by an oil lantern hanging from a hook on the ceiling over the makeshift bar. The boat's cook had been pressed into service as the bartender. Looking worried, he stood behind the bar. Five more men were gathered around one of the salt barrel tables, cards and money scattered on its lid. Burke stood on one side of the barrel, his hands held up in front of him, palms turned toward the three men opposite. The fifth man, whom Jeff recognized as the gambler called Wiggins, stood off to one side.

One of the three men who stood facing Burke had leveled a pistol at him. The flintlock was cocked and ready to fire.

"What the hell's going on here?" Jeff asked sharply, hoping he would not startle the man with the gun into pressing the trigger.

"Thank God you're here, Mr. Holt!" Eugene Burke exclaimed. "Perhaps you can talk some sense into these gentlemen. I seem to have offended them in some way—"

"Cheated us, you mean, you fancy-pants bastard," the man with the pistol growled. "We know all about you. Should've figured out before now why you always win more than you lose at these friendly little games." The man spat on the cabin floor in disgust.

To judge from their clothes, he and his two companions were tradesmen. They were better dressed than riverboat men but not as dandified as Burke and Wiggins. Jeff had exchanged few words with any of them during the voyage.

"What you're implying is just not true." Carefully Burke waved a hand toward Wiggins.

"You've had your minds poisoned against me by the smooth words of my esteemed colleague here. I assure you, if I've won more than I've lost, its only because of my greater experience at these games of chance."

"Experience at bottom-dealing, you mean," one of the other men said. "Go ahead and shoot him, Carl. It's what he deserves."

Burke looked wildly at Jeff again.

"Nobody's going to shoot anybody," Jeff said.

"Stay out of this, mister. It ain't none of your business. You ain't been playing cards with this fella, but we have. And we've all lost money."

"Then that's your own fault," Jeff said bluntly.

Wiggins spoke up for the first time since Jeff had entered the cabin. "Not entirely. Not when a man like Burke is sitting at the table."

Burke shot him a venomous glance. "You're just angry because I beat you to Beau!" he accused. "You wanted to buy him, too."

"I would have given that stupid farmer a better price for him than you did," Wiggins said coolly. "But if you think I'm holding a grudge against you, Burke, you're wrong. I simply told these men the truth about you because I thought they deserved to hear it."

Wiggins was lying, and Jeff knew it. He could see hatred glittering in Wiggins's eyes whenever the man looked at Burke. It was almost beyond comprehension to Jeff how a man could be so jealous over a racehorse that he would try to get another man killed. From what he had seen so far during the trip, Burke and Wiggins had a history of animosity toward each other; he supposed the horse was the last straw.

Jeff looked over at the bartender. "Better go tell the captain what's going on down here. I don't reckon he'll want anybody getting shot on his boat. Be hard to get bloodstains out of those planks."

Burke paled a little at that comment, and the bartender took a step toward the door.

"Hold it!" the man with the pistol barked. "We don't need the captain to settle this for us. We handle our own problems." He extended his arm a little farther. The muzzle of the pistol was only a foot from the forehead of the terrified Burke.

Jeff thought rapidly. His own pistol was tucked under his belt, and it was unlikely he could draw it and cock it in time to do Burke any good. The same was true of his knife. By the time he could slide the blade from its sheath, pull his arm back, and launch the knife in a throw, the man could easily put a pistol ball through Burke's brain. Jeff's rifle was in his cabin with his other gear; he had not expected to need it on what had started out as a peaceful day.

And that was my mistake, he realized, *thinking that a day would stay peaceful just because it started out that way.*

Jeff's gaze fell on a whip hanging on a peg beside the door. It was there, he knew, because sometimes when keelboats got stuck in shallow water or on sandbars, mules had to be used to pull the boat free. They would be brought to the riverbank, and ropes would be tied between them and the boat. In cases like that, the captain would use the whip to keep balky mules pulling on their ropes.

Right now, Jeff Holt put the whip to another use.

With his right hand he snatched the coil of braided leather from the peg. He had used a whip on mules and oxen back in his days of working the Holt family farm, but it had been awhile since then. Still, after one learned the necessary snap of the wrist, it was hard to forget. Letting instincts and old habits guide him, Jeff lashed out with blinding speed.

The whip uncoiled and then wrapped itself around the gunman's wrist with a sharp popping sound. Jeff jerked it back. The pistol boomed, but the ball thudded harmlessly into the cabin wall, missing Burke by several feet. There was another thud as the pistol fell to the floor, followed by a howl of pain as its owner clutched his wrist, which was circled by a bloody welt.

Everyone in the cabin was startled into a momentary state of inaction. Jeff took that opportunity to pull and cock his pistol. He aimed it in the general direction of the three men, but the muzzle menaced Wiggins a bit as well. With a slight shift of Jeff's aim, he would hit the gambler.

"Stand still, all of you," Jeff said. "Are you all right, Burke?"

Sweat beaded on Burke's forehead and trickled down his cheeks into his beard. He pulled a handkerchief from his pocket and mopped away some of the wetness.

"I'm fine," he said shakily. "Thanks to you, Mr. Holt."

The captain appeared in the doorway, drawn by the shot. Angrily he shouted, "What in blue blazes is going on down here? Who's shooting on my boat?"

"Just a misunderstanding, Captain," Jeff said without taking his eyes off the men he was covering with his pistol. To the redheaded gambler, he added, "It *was* a misunderstanding, wasn't it, Burke? I'd hate to think I risked my life for a fellow who cheats at cards."

Jeff's voice was cold and hard, and Burke seemed to realize he had better tell the truth. He swallowed and said, "You have my word, Mr. Holt. I didn't cheat these men. There was no need to."

"Are you willing to accept that?" Jeff asked the three men.

The one called Carl was still nursing his injured wrist. He glared at Jeff for a second, then jerked his head in an angry nod. "Don't reckon we've got much choice, do we?"

Jeff looked at Burke. "It'd be a gesture of goodwill if you were to offer them their money back, Burke."

"Give back money that was fairly won?" The gambler looked astounded.

"I know you have a hard time understanding that, but it might make the rest of the trip a bit easier."

Burke sighed heavily. "Very well. I suppose I should follow your suggestion, Mr. Holt. After all, you did save my life with that whip. Whatever gave you the idea of grabbing it like that?"

"Just luck, I reckon. Being in the right place at the right time, maybe."

Burke reached forward and picked up some of the money from the barrel, leaving most of it lying there. "That's my share of the pot. You gentlemen are . . . welcome to the rest. " He winced as if the words pained him.

Carl and his companions scooped up the remaining money, and one of the other men said to Jeff, "You can put up that pistol now, mister. This is all over."

"How about you, Carl?" Jeff asked. "You're the one who got hurt. You holding any grudges?"

The man shook his head. "I guess not. I can be a little hotheaded sometimes, and I figure this was one of those times. I shouldn't have pulled a gun."

"I reckon you had some encouragement." Jeff looked over at Wiggins, who had watched the entire exchange stoically.

"I've heard enough of this to know what was going on," the riverboat captain said, "and it had better not happen again. I'm used to rough behavior from my crew, but they generally stop short of shooting at one another. I expect the same from my passengers. If there's any more trouble, I'll close this bar down, understand?"

The men all nodded, and Jeff finally lowered his pistol. As he tucked it away, Wiggins gave him a cold-eyed look, and Jeff sensed that the gambler's circle of enemies had expanded to include him. If Wiggins had succeeded in goading one of the other men into killing Burke, he might have been able to claim the racehorse for himself. Jeff Holt had ruined that scheme.

Burke stepped over to Jeff and said, "I can't thank you enough, Mr. Holt." With his handkerchief, he patted away the last of the perspiration from his forehead. "I shall never be able to repay you—"

"There's one thing you can do," Jeff cut in.

"Whatever you say."

"Stay out of trouble. I like you, Burke, but I've got other things on my mind right now besides pulling your bacon out of the fire."

With that, Jeff left the cabin to watch the landscape pass by and wait impatiently for the boat to get to Pittsburgh.

The crew and the other passengers on the keelboat were anxious to reach Wheeling for a variety of reasons. Instead of representing the halfway point to Pittsburgh, as it did to Jeff, Wheeling meant to the others a chance to go ashore to a settlement, to have a hot meal, to buy a drink in a real tavern, to sample the charms of the young women who worked in the waterfront dives.

Under other circumstances, a drink and a hot meal would have appealed to Jeff, although he could have withstood the temptation to hire a wench. He was not interested in the temporary pleasures of the flesh, not when his wife was out there somewhere waiting for him. He stayed on board the keelboat while the other passengers, the captain, and the crew went ashore.

During the night something disturbed Jeff's sleep, and he reached for his rifle as he rolled out of his narrow bunk. The boat was quiet now, but something had roused him, and Jeff trusted his instincts. Each of the cabins opened directly onto the walkway that ran all the way around the boat. Jeff swung the door back slowly to keep its hinges from squealing, then stepped out into the cool night air.

His thumb was looped on the cock of the flint-lock, ready to press it back instantly into firing position. He stood stock-still, letting his eyes and ears do the work. From one of the other cabins, he heard the sound of snoring. Some of the other passengers or the crewmen must have returned to the boat after a night of carousing. Maybe that was what he had heard, Jeff thought—someone stumbling aboard, blind drunk.

Maybe . . . but maybe not. His instincts were warning him that something was wrong.

He turned quickly but quietly as the sound of a small splash reached his ears. It came from aft, and he stepped lightly toward the rear of the boat, listening for the noise to be repeated.

142

Moonlight washed over the scene. Nothing moved on the river. Other keelboats were tied up at the Wheeling docks, but they were silent and dark. Jeff reached the aft end of the vessel and stood next to the long sweep. Still nothing.

Several yards away a fish broke the water in a shallow leap, then splashed back under the surface. During the brief moment when it was out of the water, moonlight glittered on its scales.

Jeff grinned ruefully. The sound of the fish jumping was the same as the splash he had heard a few minutes earlier; he should have recognized it the first time. Nothing was happening on the keelboat. Everything was as quiet and peaceful as it should have been.

He tucked the rifle under his left arm and headed back to his cabin. His nerves were on edge from being anxious to get to Pittsburgh, he told himself. Nearly every waking moment he thought about Melissa, and at night his dreams were haunted by visions of her. No wonder he was jumpy.

He returned to his cabin, placed the rifle beside the bunk, and crawled under the blankets. Within moments he was sleeping.

The next day, as the boat resumed its voyage, Jeff noticed more traffic on the river. Keelboats and flatboats, barges and crude log rafts, the Ohio carried them all. Some, such as the boat on which he rode, were going upstream, but most were headed downstream.

Folks going west, Jeff thought as he watched

the boats slide past. *Going after their dreams and hopes.* So was he, although his dream lay in a different direction.

Around midmorning the wooded, gently rolling hills they had been passing gave way to rugged, rocky bluffs, which rose over twenty feet on either bank. This formation ran as far as Jeff could see as he peered upstream, at least for two miles. As it happened, no other boats were traveling along this stretch of the Ohio at the moment. The breeze was fresh and strong, filling the sail, and with the efforts of the crewmen and their poles, the keelboat reached the fastest speed yet of the journey.

That did not last long, however. Jeff was sitting on the roof of the cabins near the bow, his usual spot, when he heard a commotion from the cargo hold aft. Eugene Burke emerged from his cabin, a frown on his bearded face as he listened to the same bumping and thumping Jeff heard.

"That's Beau!" Burke exclaimed. "If that son of a bitch Wiggins is trying to hurt him—"

The gambler left the rest unsaid and hurried to the door at the rear of the boat that led into the cargo hold. Jeff swung down and followed him.

The captain was already at the door of the hold, his attention drawn by the noises coming from inside.

He turned to Burke and said, "That's that horse of yours, Mr. Burke, acting like the very devil himself is after him. I knew I shouldn't have

144

agreed to carry that animal. If he kicks a hole in our hull—"

As he spoke, the captain swung the door open, and what he saw inside shocked him into a momentary silence. Jeff and Burke crowded next to him, peered past him, and saw Beau jerking around frantically as swirling water rose around the horse's hocks.

Throwing his head back, the captain bellowed, "We're taking on water! Head for shore!"

Looking around, Jeff realized that there was no shoreline suitable for bringing the boat aground, only those steep bluffs. Warning bells went off in his head. This was more than a simple leak in the cargo hold, he sensed.

As the boat veered toward the shoreline, the captain splashed into the rising water in the hold, searching for the source of the leak. Burke went after him, reached for Beau's harness, and tried to calm the horse. Jeff stayed on deck, watching the shoreline.

Suddenly he spotted a narrow opening in the bluff about fifty yards ahead. At that point a small creek ran into the Ohio from the northwest, and as he watched, rowboats carrying men wearing buckskins and rough work clothes emerged from the opening and turned toward the foundering keelboat.

Following his instincts, Jeff lifted the flintlock rifle in his hands and reached for the cock.

"Pirates!" he shouted. "Pirates up ahead!"

He had heard plenty of stories about river pirates and how they operated; now he knew that the splash he had heard the night before had been caused by someone sabotaging the keelboat. The pirate had bored a hole in the hull, plugged it loosely, and waited for it to work itself out. The scheme had worked perfectly, putting the boat in jeopardy here in this section of river between the bluffs, where the creek provided a good hiding place until the pirates were ready to make their move.

Of course, Jeff thought quickly, this was just speculation on his part. Maybe the approaching rowboats were not carrying pirates after all.

They answered that question by opening fire on the keelboat a second later. Rifle balls whined in the air above the boat and thudded into its sides. Jeff snapped his own rifle to his shoulder, settled the sight on the chest of a man in the lead rowboat, and pressed the trigger. The rifle boomed and bucked against his shoulder, smoke billowing from its muzzle. After the smoke had cleared, Jeff was able to see his target sag to the side, then topple into the water.

Lowering the rifle, Jeff drew and cocked his pistol. The range was still rather far, but he aimed and fired anyway and saw another pirate clutch a shattered upper arm.

The pirate rowboats were all to the port side of the keelboat, so Jeff decided to take the shortest route to the relative safety of the starboard side. He leapt onto the roof of the cabins and ran across it, then dropped to the walkway on the opposite side, where he crouched down to reload. The crew was gathering on that side of the boat as well, and the vessel began to list.

Jeff stood up, took aim with his rifle, and fired. This time he missed, the ball splashing into the water beside a rowboat. Grimacing, he snapped off a shot with the pistol. He could not tell if he hit anything.

The captain came bounding out of the hold and pulled an old-fashioned blunderbuss pistol from under his long coat. Snarling an oath, he pointed it at the pirates and pulled the trigger. The weapon went off with a roar like a small cannon, and the heavy lead ball smashed into one of the rowboats with an explosion of splinters.

Burke emerged from the hold and joined in the battle, snapping off a shot with a small pocket pistol. The pirates were close enough now for the gambler's shot to have an impact. One of the men went over backward, clasping both hands to his face. Blood welled between his fingers.

More shots were fired by the keelboat's crew, most of whom carried pistols tucked under their belts, and as they fired a ragged volley, several raiders were hit. But the pirates had the rivermen outnumbered by more than two to one, and the rowboats were almost close enough now for the men in them to leap over to the keelboat. A moment later, while the crew members were still reloading, that was exactly what happened.

The pirates swarmed over the boat, and the fighting, now hand-to-hand, grew fierce. Jeff was in the thick of it. He reloaded his pistol and looked up in time to see a pirate leap across the cabin roof at him, an oar upraised to smash his skull. Jeff jerked the pistol up and fired without aiming, letting instinct guide his shot. The ball smashed into the pirate's midsection and knocked him backward, as if he had been punched by a giant fist.

Another raider took his place, however, hurling himself at Jeff, knife in hand. Jeff dropped his pistol and caught the man's wrist in time to turn the blade aside, but in the next instant the pirate crashed into him, and Jeff felt himself driven back toward the edge of the walkway. Suddenly nothing was under his feet but air, then a split-second later, the surface of the river itself. He and the pirate went under with a huge splash.

Twisting desperately, Jeff pulled himself out of the pirate's grip and searched with his fingers until he found the hilt of his hunting knife. He slid it out of its sheath. As the man grappled with him again, forcing his head underwater, Jeff struck out with the knife and sank the blade into his opponent's body.

The man gave a strangled yell of pain that was cut off by river water gurgling into his open mouth. His hands locked around Jeff's throat, holding him under the water. Jeff ripped the knife free and struck again and then again, plunging the blade well into the pirate's belly each time. The fingers fell away from Jeff's throat.

He kicked with his feet and stroked with his

free hand, launching himself up and out of the water onto the shore. Inhaling a deep breath of air into his burning lungs, he shook his head to clear his eyes and looked up at the nearby keelboat. The fighting was still going on, but the crew was slowly getting the upper hand over the raiders. Men were battling all along the walkway, as well as in the water around the boat.

Eugene Burke was standing near the bow, and as Jeff watched, the gambler knocked one of the pirates into the river with a sharp right cross. Movement behind Burke caught Jeff's eye. It was the other gambler from Pittsburgh, Wiggins, creeping out of a cabin, gun in hand. Wiggins was finally getting into the fight, it appeared.

A second later Jeff realized he was wrong. Wiggins lifted the pistol and aimed it not at one of the pirates but instead at Burke's back. Instantly Jeff understood: Wiggins was going to use the confusion of the battle to get rid of his rival once and for all. Everyone would think Burke had either been killed by a pirate or hit by a stray shot.

From the shore, Jeff drew back his knife hand and shouted, "Wiggins!"

The man half turned toward him in surprise. Jeff's arm whipped forward, the knife flickering as it spun across the distance between them. With a solid thump, the blade caught Wiggins in the chest. He staggered back against the cabin wall. The gun in his hand dipped toward the walkway and went off as a death spasm caused his finger to jerk the trigger.

Burke whirled around at the sound of the shot so close behind him, turning in time to see Wiggins paw futilely with his other hand at the knife sticking out of his chest. Wiggins slid down into a sitting position, and his head fell limply onto his left shoulder as he died.

"Give me a hand!" Jeff called to Burke as he swam to the keelboat.

Burke knelt on the walkway next to Wiggins's body, grasped Jeff's upraised wrist, and helped him get out of the river. As water streamed from his clothes, Jeff bent over and pulled his knife from Wiggins's chest, causing the body to slump all the way over.

"It looks as if you've saved my life again, Mr. Holt," Burke said. "I'm quite grateful."

"Never mind that," Jeff said shortly. "Let's worry about the rest of those pirates."

They quickly realized, however, that the pirates were not going to cause any more trouble. The criminals who had survived were jumping back into their rowboats and pulling away from the keelboat as fast as they could. The price required to capture the boat was more than the pirates wanted to pay.

But the danger was not entirely over, for the keelboat was wallowing low in the water. With the pirate threat rapidly diminishing, the captain disappeared into the hold again, followed by several of his men. The leak had to be found and stopped before the boat sank.

"I've got to get Beau out of there!" Burke said

anxiously. "He can swim, but not if he's trapped in that hold!"

Jeff followed Burke down the steps into the big compartment. The horse was still thrashing around as much as it could in its restraints. Burke reached for the sling to unfasten it.

"No need for that, Mr. Burke," the captain called from the other side of the room. "We've got the leak plugged. If you want to help, grab a bucket and give us a hand bailing the water out of here."

For the next hour passengers and crew pitched in together to empty the boat of the water that had nearly sunk it. Soon the keelboat righted itself, and the hole bored by the pirates was temporarily plugged. As soon as the boat reached a spot where it could safely tie up, a more watertight patch would be put in place and covered with pitch.

"We'll be able to reach Pittsburgh; have no doubt of that," the captain assured Jeff and the other passengers. "This is only a minor setback."

A minor setback that could easily have proven fatal, Jeff thought. Luck had been with them, and although several of the crew were wounded, none had been killed or hurt so badly that they would not be able to pole the boat. Other than the pirates who had been killed in the fighting, the only one to die had been Wiggins.

Later in the day, when the keelboat was again heading upriver, Burke sought Jeff out and thanked him once more. "As I told you, you'll

151

find I can be quite grateful, Mr. Holt," the gambler said. "I'd be glad to reward you—"

"No. I didn't do it for a reward," Jeff said curtly. He liked Burke, but he did not particularly care for the idea of having the man feel indebted to him. "I would've done the same thing for anybody about to be gunned down from behind like that. Didn't even really think about it much."

"Well, whatever you say. Just remember that I owe you a great favor. Perhaps when we reach Pittsburgh I can do something to repay you."

"We'll see," Jeff said.

He was not interested in being paid back, but the idea of reaching Pittsburgh greatly appealed to him. He was eager to see his relatives and then get on with his search for his wife. And if there was no more trouble along the way, that would suit him just fine. He had been apart from Melissa for much too long already.

VIII

North of the border, on the edge of the Canadian Rockies, the finishing touches were being put on a sprawling fort surrounded by a high stockade fence made of unpeeled logs. Within the fort were several barracks, two storage buildings, a quartermasters depot and store, a powder magazine, a smokehouse, a blacksmith's shop, and what would have been officers' quarters and the regimental offices—if this had been a military installation.

This was not an outpost of Her Majesty's Royal Army, however. It was privately owned and had been built by the fur-trading company known as the London and Northwestern Enterprise. The agent in charge of the company's Canadian operations had ordered the fort built, and he was the one who had named it Fort Dunadeen.

Fletcher McKendrick looked around at his handiwork and was well pleased.

He was a tall, rawboned, middle-aged Scotsman with curly, graying red hair and large, rough hands that still showed the marks of manual labor, even though McKendrick had spent most of the past few years behind a desk. Even in the wilderness he was well dressed, wearing tight brown breeches, a waistcoat, a silk shirt, and cravat. One of the D'Orsay beaver hats made with furs provided by the London and Northwestern Enterprise perched on his head.

Until recently, McKendrick's base of operations had been the military post at Fort Rouge, to the northeast. However, he had decided it would be easier to accomplish the task given to him by his employers in London if he was closer to the border, and the company had backed his judgment by building Fort Dunadeen for him. Now, he had to deliver on his end of the bargain.

McKendrick's job was simple: He was to expand the company's fur-trapping operation south into American territory by any means that he deemed necessary.

The London and Northwestern Enterprise was a latecomer to the fur industry in North America. The Hudson's Bay Company and the North West Company dominated the fur trade in the Canadian wilderness. Therefore, the owners of the London and Northwestern were more willing to cut a few corners in order to expand their business as quickly as possible. That suited McKendrick just fine; he was not a very patient man.

There were political considerations to his job, too, McKendrick knew. Borders in this part of the world were an uncertain thing, and the exact demarcation of the line between Canada and the United States had yet to be determined. When that time came, it would certainly strengthen England's claim to the territory it desired if the British leaders could point to a successful ongoing fur-trapping operation in the lower Rockies. Added to the greed of the London and Northwestern's owners had probably been some not-so-subtle urgings to expand, from ministers high up in the government.

Fort Dunadeen was only the first step. McKendrick had plans, indeed.

Several men were still working on the roof of one of the barracks buildings, but once that was completed, the fort would be finished. The stockade fence had been the first thing erected, to provide protection from the Indian bands that marauded in the area from time to time. When that had been finished, McKendrick had instructed most of the men to trap, leaving only a small contingent to continue the construction of the fort. The first buildings they had erected were the storehouses, to hold the furs brought in by the trappers. It was late spring, and the weather was more than pleasant enough for sleeping in the open in bedrolls until the barracks were completed.

McKendrick headed for his office. He liked to start the day with a stroll around the fort, but now he was ready to get to work.

His secretary, a man named Lloyd Hodgkins, was waiting for him. Hodgkins had recently been sent over from company headquarters in London, just as McKendrick had been a couple of years earlier. But unlike the burly Scotsman, Hodgkins had never done a day's physical labor in his life, and his slender frame, delicate hands, and pasty complexion were testimony to that. A pair of pince-nez perched on the narrow bridge of his nose as he regarded McKendrick sternly over the lenses. Hodgkins hated it on the frontier, as McKendrick well knew, but he was good at his job. He could keep up with the paperwork and had an eye for details that McKendrick sometimes overlooked.

"We now have enough furs in the storehouse to make up a load that can be taken east," Hodgkins said as McKendrick entered the office.

"Aye, and good morning to ye, too, Lloyd,"

McKendrick said dryly. Hodgkins had no time for small talk.

"And you're going to have to draft a letter to Lord Harbridge sometime soon detailing your plans for the upcoming expansion of the company's trapping territory."

McKendrick hung his hat on a peg near the door and stepped behind his desk.

"You're right, as usual," he said. "The lord and his partners will be getting impatient to hear what's going on out here."

McKendrick took out his pipe and tobacco pouch, then filled the pipe and packed it as he leaned back in his chair and frowned. Lord Harbridge was his superior in the London and Northwestern Enterprise, and he was not a man tolerant of failure. When McKendrick had reported the collapse of his first effort to extend the company's trapping south of Canada, he had received a scathing reply from Harbridge. The lord's attitude had softened a bit in recent letters, and he had provided the funds for McKendrick to have the fort built. But he would not be forgiving of another failure, and McKendrick was well aware of that fact.

As he raised his bushy red eyebrows, McKendrick asked, "What do ye think, Lloyd? You weren't here last year when we made our first try, but you've heard about it. What do ye think went wrong?"

Hodgkins sniffed. "Well, since you've asked me, sir, I believe you placed too much reliance in that man Duquesne. The French are so undependable, you know."

"Aye," McKendrick said slowly. "Mayhap you're right."

He had indeed placed a great deal of faith in the little mercenary who called himself Duquesne. The man had seemed to McKendrick to possess the guile and ruthlessness necessary to establish a foothold in the American Rockies. Duquesne had been well on the way to doing just that by stirring up trouble between the Indians and the American trappers when two men, brothers named Holt, had interfered. Duquesne had ended up dead. The only good thing to come of the whole affair had been that Duquesne's efforts could not be traced back to McKendrick. At least the Scotsman hoped that was the case.

"Duquesne made some mistakes," McKendrick continued, "but the real error was mine. I thought it best to operate behind the scenes and not come out into the open until all the Americans had been driven out. I can see now that's not going to happen so easily."

"What do you intend to do, then?" the secretary persisted.

McKendrick had been toying with an idea that would answer that very question. "We're going into that territory just as if we owned it and have nary a doubt of our right to be there," he declared. "The Americans can try to push us out if they want to, but they'll be risking an international incident if they do. Parliament has not recognized the boundaries of that land the Americans bought from Bonaparte, so they'll be quick to set up a howl if some of Her Majesty's subjects are harassed."

For a moment Hodgkins considered. Then he nodded and said, "A plan that is stunning in its simplicity, sir. But what if those barbarians don't care about causing an international incident?"

"We'll be there with enough force to keep them from running us off." McKendrick brought a knobby fist down on the desktop for emphasis. "I'll tell the men to lie low until they get a fort of their own built, and then the Americans can attack us—if they dare."

"You're going to build another fort?" Hodgkins sounded as if he regarded the suggestion with quite a bit of skepticism.

"Aye." Now that he had made up his mind, McKendrick was not the type to back away from the idea. "Not as fancy as this fort, mind ye. It will not cost much. But it'll be plenty strong to hold off those heathen Americans."

"I hope youre right, sir."

"I know I'm right," McKendrick said. "What I need now is somebody to take charge of the group that'll be going south."

"I'll make a list of the available men so that you can decide from among them."

McKendrick waved a hand in dismissal, and Hodgkins retreated into the smaller office set off to one side of McKendrick's chamber. After taking paper, pen, and inkwell from the desk,

McKendrick began to compose the letter he would have Hodgkins copy to Lord Harbridge.

Never one who handled words easily, the Scotsman had to concentrate heavily on the task before him, and all of his attention was still fixed on the paper in front of him half an hour later. It was covered with blots, smudges, and crossed-out words, but Hodgkins would be able to make sense of it. That was his job.

Suddenly the outer door opened, and McKendrick glanced up in annoyance. He did not like to be disturbed when he was working on something like this. He glared at the two men who stood there, both of them wearing the buckskins and fur caps of trappers. They looked as nervous as cats.

"Well, what is it?" McKendrick demanded. "What in blazes do ye want?"

"Get in there, both of you," a man's voice said harshly.

The two trappers in the doorway stumbled into the office. Another man entered behind them, and McKendrick could see now that the third man had prodded them at gunpoint. He had a brace of flintlock pistols trained on their backs.

"What's the meaning of this?" McKendrick asked, blinking in surprise. "Hodgkins!"

The secretary hurried in from the other office but stopped short as he saw the two men standing in front of McKendrick's desk and the third man covering them with a pair of guns.

"What is this, sir?" he asked tentatively.

"I was hoping ye'd know." McKendrick got to his feet and peered past the two prisoners—because that was what they were, no doubt about that—at the third man. "You're Brown, aren't you?"

"That's right, sir," the man with the pistols said. "Simon Brown, at your service."

Simon Brown was a tall, strapping, handsome man with regular features, intelligent blue eyes, and thick brown hair. He wore a fringed buckskin jacket, whipcord trousers, and high black boots. McKendrick knew almost nothing about him except that he was one of the trappers, but he recalled now that Brown had impressed him before as being somewhat out of place in the wilderness. Looking at him now, McKendrick was struck by the thought that Brown would have looked more at home wearing an expensive suit and striding down a London street.

However, there was no mistaking the casual ease with which Brown held the two pistols. His attitude was that of a man accustomed to the threat of violence.

"What are ye doing here, Brown?" McKendrick asked. "And what have these two men done to warrant such treatment?"

"They've been stealing from the company, that's what they've done. I caught them hoarding pelts that should have gone into the storehouse."

McKendrick glowered at the two men, who

refused to meet his gaze. In a voice that quivered with rage, the Scotsman asked, "Is this true?"

"N-no, sir, I swear it's not," one of the men said. "This is all just a misunderstanding. We'd never cheat the company, sir."

"I can show you the pelts, Mr. McKendrick," Brown said coolly. "Also the cave not far from here where these two have been storing them. I noticed them sneaking around there the last time I left the fort, so I thought I'd best see what they were doing."

Frantic, the other man said, "It's not true! Brown's out of his head—"

"Shut up." Brown prodded him in the back of the neck with a pistol muzzle. "I know what I saw."

"I believe ye, Brown," McKendrick snapped. "I thought it was taking longer than it should have to accumulate enough furs for our first shipment from this fort. Now I understand why." He looked over at Hodgkins. "Have these two locked up in the smokehouse, Lloyd. When the first shipment goes east, they'll go with it. I want them sent back to England to stand trial for their theft."

"Yes, sir," Hodgkins said.

Brown held up a hand. "Wait a moment. You're convinced of their guilt, Mr. McKendrick?"

"Indeed I am."

"Then there's no need to waste time and money putting them on trial, is there?"

With no more warning than that, Brown lifted the pistols in both hands and pulled the triggers.

The blast of the shots was deafening. The hapless thieves jerked forward, eyes bulging grotesquely, as the balls from Brown's pistols entered their heads from behind. Blood ran from their noses and ears as they pitched to the puncheon floor. The stench of death filled the room.

McKendrick stood behind the desk, rooted to the floor, his features frozen in a mask of shock. Hodgkins stared at the twitching corpses and let out a high-pitched wail before crumpling as if his bones had turned to water.

Finally McKendrick regained the use of his tongue. "My God, man!" he shouted. "What have ye done?"

"Simply carried out the will of the man who represents law and order in this part of the world, sir," Brown said as he reloaded the pistols. "I'm referring, of course, to you."

"But I didn't tell you to kill them!"

"You said they were guilty. I thought this was the simplest, most direct way of dealing with the problem. I assure you, sir, once word of this gets around—and you know how the men talk amongst themselves—anyone who's been considering a spot of pilferage will think twice before they kipper off with any of the company's plews."

McKendrick passed a trembling hand over his face. His normally ruddy features were pale.

Slowly he said, "You're undoubtedly right about that, Brown. I trust you'll, ah, dispose of these two?"

"Of course, sir." Brown tucked away the guns.

Hodgkins let out a moan and pushed himself into a sitting position. His eyes were closed, and when he opened them and confronted the grisly sight before him, he swayed as if he might pass out again. But McKendrick's whiplash of a voice drove him to his feet before that could happen.

"Notify the company that these two men were killed in an unfortunate . . . accident, Hodgkins." McKendrick clasped his hands behind his back and rocked on his toes. Now that he had regained his composure, an idea occurred to him. "And, Hodgkins, never mind about that list of possible commanders for the expedition across the border. I think I've already found the right man for the job." He fixed his gaze on Brown. "Interested?"

"I'm not sure exactly what job you're talking about, Mr. McKendrick, but I'm always interested in anything that will help the company— and myself, of course."

McKendrick stepped around the desk, carefully avoiding the bodies and the puddles of blood that surrounded them. He extended a hand to Brown and said, "Get rid of these two, as I told ye, and then come back here. I think we have a great deal to talk about, ye and I."

"Yes, sir," Brown agreed.

And as he shook the young man's hand, McKendrick felt a surge of satisfaction. With Brown in charge of the group going south, the London and Northwestern could not fail to establish a foothold in the American Rockies—because Simon Brown would not hesitate to kill anyone who got in his way.

Clay Holt looked over the group gathered beside the Yellowstone River and tried not to dwell on the misgivings he felt. The majority of them were inexperienced or hostile toward him—or both. It would take more than a little luck for them to make it safely to the Pacific coast. And luck was sometimes in short supply out on the frontier.

"I believe were ready to move out, Mr. Holt," Professor Franklin said with an eager expression.

"All right, Professor. We'll head northwest starting off. You've strayed a mite from your original path. If you'd kept going in the same direction, you'd have wound up down in Colter's Hell. Might've got through the mountains that way, but it would've been rugged."

"Whatever you say, Mr. Holt. You're in charge."

Clay felt the baleful gaze of Harry Lawton on him as Franklin made that statement. Lawton, after all, was the one who had gotten the party off the trail in the first place. It had to be galling to him to listen to this.

Not that Clay cared much about Lawton's feelings. As long as the man did as he was told, that was all that really mattered.

With Shining Moon at his side, Clay strode to the front of the group and angled away from the river. Professor Franklin and his daughter Lucy were behind him, followed by Rupert von Metz, Lawton, and the other men. Proud Wolf and Aaron Garwood brought up the rear. Clay wanted someone he could trust to keep an eye on their back trail.

Clay carried a bundle of beaver pelts on his back, as did Shining Moon and most of the others in the party. Despite the weight of the furs, Shining Moon would keep up with him all day and never lose a step. He knew that she prided herself on things like that.

They would be on foot for several days, perhaps a week or more, and the going would be tough. But once they reached the land of the Shoshone, they could trade furs for horses, and after that the trip would go more quickly. For the most part the Shoshone got along well with other tribes, even the Piegans and Bloods, and they had provided horses for Lewis and Clark's expedition several years earlier. He might even run into some who remembered him from that journey, Clay thought. He wondered how Sacajawea and her baby, little Pomp, were getting along.

The day was beautiful, with bright sky and towering clouds that seemed to mirror the snow-capped peaks below. The snow would remain on most of the peaks all summer long, despite the heat at the lower elevations. Today the spring air was crisp, not too warm, not too cool, and filled with the sweet scent of flowers blooming in the meadows that filled the valleys.

No wonder he loved this country and never wanted to live anywhere else, Clay thought as he walked along through it. It could be stark and hard at times, even brutal, but there was beauty here the likes of which could be found nowhere else on God's green earth.

The expedition pushed on all morning with few complaints, only those uttered in muffled voices by Lawton and his cronies. Clay had expected Professor Franklin and Lucy to tire quickly, but neither of them asked for extra rest stops, even when their pace slowed toward midday. Rupert von Metz also kept up, although his face grew taut with anger every time he glanced at Clay. Clay was aware of how von Metz felt, but he did not care as long as the Prussian caused no trouble.

They left the Yellowstone behind during the morning and stopped for the noon meal in a verdant park at the foot of a mountain. The men sank gratefully to the ground to sit cross-legged and gnaw on biscuits and hardtack.

Proud Wolf and Aaron moved up from the rear to join Clay and Shining Moon, and as they did, Clay asked them, "Any sign of people behind us?"

"I sure didn't see any. How about you, Proud Wolf?"

The young Hunkpapa agreed. "Those Blackfoot will not bother us again."

"Wasn't worried about the Blackfoot in particular," Clay mused. "But it's good to know they're not back there."

Professor Franklin and Lucy joined them, and as Franklin sat down, he gestured with a hand holding a biscuit. "These mountains around us, they're still part of the Rockies range known as the Absarokas, correct?"

"The upper end of the range known as Absarokas," Clay replied. "Another day or two and well be cutting west, through the valley of the three tongues of the Missouri. The going'll really get rough then, because we'll be heading up to the dividing ridge."

"The top of the shining mountains," Franklin said, awe in his voice. "I wasn't sure I'd ever get to see it for myself."

"We're not there yet," Clay pointed out dryly.

Franklin chuckled and said, "No, but you'll get us there, Mr. Holt. I have every confidence in you."

Clay was not sure he liked having somebody put that much trust in him, especially not a pilgrim like Franklin. However, he would do the best he could to keep his charges alive and get them where they were going.

Once they were past the dividing ridge it would still be a hell of a long way to the Pacific, Clay thought, but if they could get their hands on some horses, the route to the Columbia River would not be too hard to traverse. And when they reached the Columbia, they could build canoes to carry them the rest of the way. With luck they would reach the Pacific by early fall. If the boat from the American Philosophical Society was waiting, Clay and his companions could get this bunch off their hands and settle down to wait out the winter there on the Pacific coast. That would mean not returning to this part of the country until the next spring. He would lose a season's trapping, but Franklin had promised to make up for the loss. Besides, he could not leave these folks on their own out here in the wilderness; they would die for sure, and Clay did not want that on his conscience for the rest of his days.

Might as well make the best of it, he told himself. There were worse ways to spend a summer than trekking across this wild and glorious country.

Aaron Garwood pushed himself to his feet when the meal was over and Clay had called out the command to get under way again. The months he had spent with Clay, Shining Moon, and Proud Wolf had toughened him more than he would have thought possible. Even his left arm, weak from being broken by Clay during the bad times in Ohio, had grown stronger. When he had first come to the frontier with his brother Zach, Aaron had figured he would wind up frozen to death, drowned in some river, or stuck full of Indian arrows. He could still die in those ways, of course. But with what he had already learned from Clay and the things he would learn in the future, he figured he at least had a fighting chance for survival.

Nearby, Rupert von Metz was also getting to

his feet, struggling with the cases that contained his canvases and paints.

"Would you like me to give you a hand with some of that?" Aaron said without giving it a thought.

Von Metz looked up at him and frowned. "No, I would not like for you to give me a hand, as you so quaintly phrase it. Do you think for an instant that I would entrust any of my work or materials to a man who is only half a step above the level of an aborigine?"

"Didn't mean to offend you," Aaron said shortly, reining in a surge of anger. "I just wanted to help."

"Well, I don't need your help."

"Fine." Aaron turned away, wondering if von Metz had been born with that burr under his longjohns.

Aaron drifted back to the rear of the column as it formed up again. Proud Wolf walked beside him.

"That man von Metz does not like you," Proud Wolf said quietly.

"I don't reckon he likes much of anybody except himself," Aaron said.

That was not strictly true, however, he saw a moment later. Although loaded down with the goods he was carrying, von Metz went over to Lucy Franklin and extended a hand to help her up. Aaron could not hear what she said to von Metz after he had assisted her to her feet, but she was smiling, and then she laughed at something he said in return. When the group set out, von Metz was walking beside Lucy and conversing with her.

Aaron's eyes narrowed. He did not trust von Metz, did not trust him at all, and he figured Lucy would be wise not to trust him either. Of course, it was not his place to say anything to her—

"Clay told us to keep an eye on the back trail, remember," Proud Wolf reminded Aaron, breaking into his thoughts.

"You're right. I reckon Miss Franklin can look after herself. After all, she is a grown woman."

And that, Aaron reasoned, was part of the trouble.

The afternoon passed without incident, although the party did not cover as much ground as it had during the morning. The professor and Lucy grew more exhausted, and Clay was smart enough to recognize that and adjust the group's pace accordingly. Aaron felt grateful for that; he did not want Lucy to suffer.

Von Metz walked alongside her most of the afternoon, allowing Aaron no opportunity to talk to her. But that evening, as they were making camp in a little bowl in the foothills of the Absarokas, Aaron saw his opportunity. Lucy had sat down on a large rock and slipped her shoes off, and she was rubbing her sore feet. He went over to her.

"Bear grease is good for that," he said.

Lucy looked up at him. "I beg your pardon?"

"Bear grease is good for foot miseries like that."

Flushing in embarrassment, Lucy quickly put her shoes on again. "My feet are fine, thank you, Mr. Garwood."

Aaron sensed that he had offended her, but he did not see how. Hurriedly, he added, "I was just trying to help—"

"Is this buffoon bothering you, Miss Franklin?"

Aaron's head jerked around when he heard Rupert von Metz's voice. The Prussian stood there, an expression of annoying smugness on his face.

Aaron knew he might be making a mistake, but he could not prevent himself from saying, "You just keep out of this, von Metz. It's none of your business."

"Perhaps it is," Lucy snapped. "Rupert is just trying to make sure I'm all right, and I appreciate that."

Von Metz smiled, then glanced coldly at Aaron. "I think what Miss Franklin is trying to say is that you should leave her alone, Garwood."

Aaron ignored the man's mocking tone and looked at Lucy. "Is that what you're saying, Miss Franklin?"

Lucy appeared more confused and upset with every second. She hesitated, then said, "I meant no offense, Mr. Garwood. You just took me by surprise, that's all."

"Then you don't want me to leave?" Aaron shot a triumphant look at von Metz, who glowered back at him.

"I don't know what I want."

Clay Holt stepped up behind her and said, "I think what Miss Franklin really needs is for you two young bucks to leave her alone. I reckon we've all got enough to think about without you two acting like a couple of bull moose."

"Damn it, Clay—" Aaron ended his objection midsentence. Clay was right, of course; he nearly always was. There were more important things to worry about than scuffling with von Metz over a woman. There would be time enough for that once they had reached the safety of the Pacific coast.

Aaron sighed. "I'll gather some firewood."

"Good idea," Clay said dryly. "Why don't you help him, Mr. von Metz?"

Von Metz drew himself up and declared, "I do not turn my talented hands to such common tasks."

"Well, then, you might not turn them to eating, either," Clay said. "Everybody in this bunch pulls his weight from here on out, understand?"

For a long moment the tension in the air was thick as Clay and von Metz stared at each other. Lucy stood between them, turning from one man to the other.

Finally von Metz shrugged his narrow shoulders. "As you wish. I will be magnanimous enough to go along with your request, Holt, ridiculous though it may be."

"Don't care what you think of what I tell you,

just as long as you do it," Clay shot back. He strode away, and Lucy watched him go.

Aaron took a deep breath and wished that he could handle himself as well as Clay did. He was not sure he would ever have that much confidence.

"I will gather firewood, but not with the likes of you," von Metz said icily to Aaron. "I will go that way. I would appreciate it if you would choose another direction."

"Fine by me," Aaron replied curtly. "I'm not that fond of your company, either." He turned on the heels of his buckskin moccasins and walked away.

"Wait, Mr. Garwood!" Lucy called after him.

Aaron stopped and looked over his shoulder. Von Metz had stalked off, too, but he also came to a halt and watched as Lucy walked over to Aaron.

"I'm sorry, Mr. Garwood," she said. "I didn't mean to cause trouble between you and Mr. von Metz.

"I don't reckon you caused the trouble," Aaron said, glancing at von Metz's taut expression.

"Well, I just wanted to say that I appreciate your concern."

And then she smiled at him.

Aaron felt as though his throat had constricted and he couldn't breathe. He could hear his heart pounding, and his face was getting warm. God, he had never known that the smile on a woman's face could be so potent!

Suddenly he was aware of the bustle of the camp going on around him. His friends Clay, Shining Moon, and Proud Wolf were only a few yards away, as was Lucy's father. None of them were paying much attention to the conversation now that Clay had broken up the potential trouble, but to Aaron it seemed as though all of them were staring at him.

He swallowed hard and said, "That's all right, Miss Franklin. Just don't you worry about it."

"Thank you, Mr. Garwood. I'll let you get on with your chores now. And I'll try that bear grease as you suggested."

Still smiling, she walked away.

Aaron forced his muscles to work. He strode out of the bowl where they were camped into the trees of the surrounding hills. He had no trouble finding branches on the ground there for firewood.

When he was about twenty yards from the edge of the bowl, von Metz stepped out from behind a nearby tree and said, "Garwood."

The two syllables were fraught with menace, and Aaron turned quickly toward the Prussian, halfway expecting to see a gun or a knife in the mans hand. He was ready to drop the armload of firewood and grab a weapon of his own if need be.

Von Metz, however, was unarmed, except for an armful of branches.

"Thought you were going the other direction," Aaron said.

"I circled around here so that I could talk to you in private," von Metz replied. "I abhor conducting personal business in full view of everyone else. It's quite undignified."

"What the hell is it you want?" Aaron asked bluntly.

"Just this: Stay away from Miss Franklin. She is a refined young lady who has no need of attention from a man like you."

Aaron's jaw tightened. "That's none of your damned business, is it?"

"You may dispense with the hostile attitude, my unwashed friend."

Somehow, von Metz made the word *friend* sound like a curse.

"I did not come here to fight you," he continued. "My wish is not to battle with you over Miss Franklin like two dogs squabbling over a bone. My sense of honor will not allow me to stoop to that level. However, I do wish to ask you a question. Just what do you believe someone like yourself could offer a woman such as Lucy?"

Aaron blinked. He had not thought about it that way. In fact, he had not really thought about the matter at all, other than to form a liking for Lucy and an intense dislike for this arrogant young Prussian. But he realized with a sinking feeling that von Metz was right. Lucy was accustomed to finer things than Aaron could ever hope to give her. And she was probably a lot smarter than he, too, considering that a professor had raised her. Aaron did not have

175

a thing to offer her, at least nothing that really mattered.

"You made your point," he said quietly to von Metz. "Now get the hell away from me and stay away."

"As you wish." Von Metz gave a mocking smile, then headed back toward camp, still carrying the firewood.

Aaron followed a moment later, his expression bleak. He had been fooling himself thinking that Lucy might be interested in him. That would not happen again.

They would probably be scalped by the Blackfoot anyway, he thought, so what the hell did it matter?

IX

The situation of Pittsburgh is unrivalled with respect to water communication, with a great extent and variety of country; and would also be so in beauty was it not hemmed in too closely by high and steep hills.

—Fortescue Cuming
"Sketches of a Tour to the Western Country"

Pittsburgh had grown since Jeff Holt had last visited the settlement. In fact, it could no longer be considered a settlement, he thought as he stood on the walkway of the keelboat and re-garded it as they drew nearer. The place was now a city.

Situated in the triangle created by the Alle-gheny and Monongahela rivers as they came together to form the Ohio, Pittsburgh had orig-inally been settled by the French from Canada and called Fort Duquesne. Eventually it had been taken over by the British and renamed Fort Pitt. The town of Pittsburgh had grown up around the fort. The British were long gone, of course, having been driven out during the Revolution, and now Pittsburgh was about as American a place as anybody could find.

The rivers and the city were enclosed by high, steep, wooded hills to the north, south, and east. The point of land on which Pittsburgh had been established was fairly level, as was the terrain to the southwest, where the Ohio flowed. As the keelboat passed Robinson's Point and Smoky Island, just south of the city, Jeff spotted several large buildings, which he de-cided must be factories of some sort, although he had no idea what was manufactured there. It appeared that Pittsburgh had become a center not only of trade but of industry.

Eugene Burke stepped up beside Jeff and laid a hand on his shoulder. "Well, what do you think, Mr. Holt?"

Jeff gave a whistle. "I never expected the place would have changed this much."

A faint tingle of unease went through him.

Accustomed as he had become to the wide open spaces of the West, he had felt a little confined by Marietta, which was not much more than a village compared to Pittsburgh. How was he going to cope with all the buildings and the people? And if the thought of visiting Pittsburgh made him so uncomfortable, how the devil would he survive in New York?

Jeff swallowed hard and stared at the houses and stores rising on the point just ahead.

"Yes, Pittsburgh's come a long way from the frontier community it used to be," Burke said. "Why, when I first came out here, there were fewer than half a dozen taverns in the whole town. Now there are at least four times that many."

"Is that so," Jeff replied. He supposed people measured progress in different ways.

The keelboat veered into the Monongahela. Pittsburgh's wharves and shipyard were on the left bank, just past the main part of town. Jeff watched the streets and buildings slide by, then tried to count the vessels anchored ahead. He gave up when he reached two dozen—which, according to Eugene Burke, was approximately the number of taverns in Pittsburgh.

Henry and Dorothy Holt lived on Wood Street, about six blocks from the riverfront—at least that was what Jeff recalled from his previous visit to his uncle and aunt's house. He was certain he could find the place, but if he had any trouble, he knew someone would be able to direct him. Henry Holt was a cabinetmaker, one of the best carpenters west of the Appalachians, and surely well-known in the town.

As the crewmen tied the keelboat at a vacant dock, making fast a rope from the wharf to the cordelle in the center of the vessel's roof, Burke turned to Jeff and extended a hand.

"I hope you'll pay me a visit while you're here, Mr. Holt," Burke said. "You can find me at the Green Archer Tavern just about any evening. The least I can do is buy you a drink after you saved my life twice."

"I told you not to worry about that," Jeff said as he shook hands with the gambler. To take any sting out of the words, he added, "If I get a chance, I'll stop in and say hello."

"I hope so. Now, I'd best see about getting Beau unloaded."

Jeff could hear the racehorse moving restlessly below in the cargo hold. Beau was going to be glad to get his hooves back on dry land, Jeff thought.

One advantage of traveling light was being able to disembark easily. With his possibles bag, powder horn, and shot pouch slung over his shoulder and his Harper's Ferry rifle in his hand, Jeff was able to step across to the dock without waiting for a crewman to run a plank over the gap.

People, horses, wagons, and carts were everywhere, or so it seemed to Jeff. The air was full of shouts, laughs, and curses. Aptly named, Water Street ran the length of the town along the riverfront, and as Jeff took a deep breath to calm his jumping nerves, he plunged into what appeared to him to be utter chaos.

You could spend a year on the frontier and not see this many people, he thought as he wove his way through the crowds. To his left was the river, to his right a long line of warehouses and other businesses. Finally, after what seemed like a mile but was actually four blocks, he reached a broad avenue with a signpost declaring it to be Wood Street. Jeff had been hoping that Wood Street would not be as busy as the promenade along the river, but even more people were there.

He made his way past bakeries, tobacconists, saddlemakers, butcher shops, barbers, millineries, and general mercantile stores. His eyes were wide with amazement as he strode along. He had thought Steakley's Trading Post had carried a little bit of everything, but there were many more goods to be had here, a hundred times more.

And the taverns! Burke had been right about the taverns. Since getting off the boat, Jeff had not been able to walk a block without passing at least two of them. It seemed that people in this town worked a great deal and played just as hard.

But he noticed other signs of civilization, too. Up ahead on a corner were an Episcopal church and a Presbyterian meetinghouse. Beyond them, the street was lined with residences, and the heavy traffic thinned out somewhat.

He hailed a man in a wagon as he passed the sanctuaries and said, "Excuse me, sir, but do you know if Henry Holt still lives near here?"

The man hauled his team to a halt and looked down at Jeff. "Henry Holt," he repeated slowly. "Any relation to Ned Holt?"

Jeff had a cousin named Ned, who had been about ten years old the last time Jeff visited. "That's right."

The wagon driver spat into the dust of the street. "I know where Ned Holt lives. Right up there. Third house on the left." He pointed to the house, and from the way his expression twisted, Jeff could tell that he was not fond of Ned.

That puzzled Jeff. He remembered Ned as an active, friendly boy. But he only said, "Thank you," then started down the street again.

The man in the wagon called after him, "If you've got a score to settle with Ned Holt, watch yourself. I hear he's a tricky one."

Jeff was bewildered. Why would the man assume he held a grudge against Ned? It sounded as if Ned was not thought highly of around here, which was surprising.

On the other hand, some folks in Marietta did not think much of the Holts, either. It was all a matter of how you looked at things.

The young blond man stretched lazily on the soft bed, enjoying the feel of the bed linens. The warm, silky smooth skin of the woman nestled against him felt even better.

It was the middle of the day, and sunlight was streaming in through the lace-curtained window of the bedroom. Somehow that made what had happened here earlier seem even more deliciously sinful. Affairs such as this were customarily carried out under the cover of darkness, when it was easier to slip in and out of a married woman's bedroom.

The young man propped himself up on an elbow and threw the sheet back. Preening under his gaze, the woman rolled onto her back and stretched her arms over her head, giving him a good look at her full, pillowy breasts, her generously rounded belly, and the lush curves of her hips and thighs. Her dark hair spread out on the pillow around her head.

"Do you like what you see, Ned?" she asked with a giggle that was only slightly unbecoming in a woman of thirty-some years. It was clear that the young man's attention made her feel like a girl again.

"You know I do, Phyllis," Ned Holt replied, leaning over to brush his lips against hers. He traced the kiss along the line of her jaw, then down to the soft hollow of her throat. Phyllis closed her eyes, tilted her head back, and shivered as his lips drew closer to the coral tip of one breast.

A door slammed downstairs.

Ned sat bolt upright, the passion that had gripped him an instant before fleeing as if it had wings. Phyllis gasped, brought her hands to her mouth, and uttered a mewling sound that was almost a moan of terror.

"Not your husband," Ned said hoarsely. "That couldn't be your husband."

"There's no one else it could be," she whispered. "But he wasn't supposed to be back until tomorrow!"

Heavy footsteps were coming up the stairs. The steps sounded purposeful, and Ned had no doubt where they were heading.

He saw no point in arguing about why Phyllis's husband had returned to Pittsburgh a day early; he had to get out of there—fast.

He was out of bed in a flash, no longer interested in Phyllis's brazenly displayed charms. Snatching up the breeches that he had hastily thrown aside earlier, he jammed his legs into them and pulled them up around his hips. He grabbed his shirt, which lay crumpled in a corner, tossed it over his shoulder, and picked up his boots as he hurried toward the window.

Next to it was a sturdy latticework trellis. Ned had checked on that out of habit the first time he had paid a visit to Phyllis Hastings. They had met in a Liberty Street tavern. She was quite beautiful—although he sensed her attractiveness would desert her before too many years passed—and so he had forgotten all about the pledge he had made to himself not to become involved with married women again.

That had been several weeks earlier, several

quite enjoyable weeks. But now Ned listened to the footsteps coming down the hall and knew he had been a fool—again.

He slid the window open, threw a leg over the sill, and tossed his boots down into the alley behind the house. Then he tugged his shirt on over his head. Leaning to the side, he reached for the trellis.

Inside the bedroom, the door was thrown open, and a red-faced man stormed in to glare at Phyllis, who was still cowering nude and terrified on the bed.

"I knew it!" the man shouted. "I knew you were nothing but a no-good trollop—"

Ned did not wait to hear any more. Finding a handhold and foothold, he swung over onto the trellis. Phyllis's husband continued to rave at her, and Ned hoped that by reaching the ground in time, he might get away without having a shot taken at him.

It was awfully tiresome being shot at by angry husbands. That was one reason Ned had vowed to leave married women alone in the future.

"Fred! He's out here, Fred!"

The shout came from below Ned and startled him so badly that he almost lost his grip on the trellis. Grabbing the latticework more tightly, he pulled himself against the house and craned his head around to see who was down there yelling. He saw another pudgy, middle-aged man, probably one of Fred Hastings's friends or business associates.

Hastings's head emerged from the bedroom window. "Come back here!" he shouted at Ned. "Come back here, damn you, and face it like a man!"

Ned had no intention of doing that. He was only eight feet off the ground now. He jerked his head back and forth, looking from Hastings in the window to the man waiting in the alley, who called, "I'll get him, Fred! The bastard won't get past me!"

We'll see about that, Ned thought.

Suddenly Hastings stuck his hand out the window—and in it was a pistol. "Stop or I'll shoot!" he cried.

The whole situation was so ludicrous it would have been laughable, Ned realized, if he weren't the one with a pistol aimed at him. Stuck halfway up a wall outside a married woman's bedroom window . . . It was the kind of story that would have given him quite a chuckle had he heard someone else tell it.

But from the livid look on Hastings's face, the man was ready to shoot him.

With a yell, Ned pushed himself away from the wall and plummeted toward the man on the ground.

They crashed together with bone-jarring impact and fell to the dirt of the alley. Luckily, Ned landed on top, so that while he was shaken by the collision, the other man was stunned and had the wind knocked out of him. He lay there thrashing around and gasping like a fish out of water as Ned rolled quickly to one side and leapt to his feet.

His eyes searched wildly for his boots until he spotted them in the dust a few feet away. He lunged toward them and grabbed them up as Hastings shouted from the window, "Stop, damn you!"

Ned heard Phyllis cry, "Leave him alone, Fred!" He glanced up and saw her face over Hastings's shoulder as she struggled with him. Her arms were around his chest, trying to tug him back from the window. He shoved her away roughly.

While Hastings was distracted, Ned seized the opportunity to run. He dashed down the alley, away from the house. Behind him, a pistol cracked.

Grimacing, he hunched his shoulders as he ran, anticipating the horrible impact of a pistol ball striking his back. Nothing happened, though, and he kept running toward the narrow lane at the end of the alley. Hastings's shot had missed, and by the time the man could reload his pistol, Ned knew he would be out of range.

He had always been a fast runner, even as a boy. He put that skill to good use now.

Never again, he told himself as he sprinted toward safety. Never again would he dally with a married woman, no matter how lush or willing she was. Forbidden charms were often the sweetest, but they were not worth the danger involved.

Maybe this time he would keep that promise.

Behind him Fred Hastings leaned out the

window and bellowed, "I know you! And you'd better stay away from my wife, by God, or next time I'll kill you, Ned Holt!"

Henry Holt's house was a whitewashed frame structure with two stories. He had built it himself with the help of his four sons, the youngest of whom was Ned. As a youngster Jeff had thought it large and roomy, and looking at it now, he was still impressed. His uncle had done well for himself.

Flagstones formed a walk leading across the neat front yard to a small porch. Jeff stepped up to the door and used the brass lion's-head knocker to rap sharply. After a moment he heard quick footsteps on the other side of the panel, and then it swung back to reveal a pretty young blond girl about ten years old. Her eyes widened as she looked up at the visitor, and after a second she squealed, "Jeff? It *is* you!"

He had to look twice to be sure of the girl's identity, so much had she changed since the last time he had seen her. But then he grinned and said to his sister, "It's me, Susie."

Susan Holt threw herself into Jeff's arms and hugged him tightly around his waist.

"Edward! Jonathan!" she cried. "Come quick! Jeff's here!"

Rapid footsteps sounded in the hall just inside the door, and two young boys bounded out of the house. Both of them grabbed Jeff, staggering him. His little brothers had grown, too.

Dark-haired Edward, who would be thirteen years old now, was only about a foot shorter than Jeff. Jonathan, sandy-haired and stockier than any of his brothers, was eight. He hung on Jeff's left arm and whooped exuberantly.

His expression having lit up, Edward now tried to look more solemn as he stood back and held out a hand to Jeff.

"It's good to see you again," Edward said, holding back his joy in favor of the maturity he had always sought. But when Jeff grasped his hand, Edward gave up and pumped it for all he was worth before throwing an arm around Jeff's shoulders again.

"What's all this uproar?" a deep male voice asked. A slender man with iron gray hair appeared in the doorway and looked out at the happy group gathered on the step.

"Hello, Uncle Henry," Jeff said.

Henry could be a dour man at times, but a smile creased his leathery face as he recognized his nephew. He shook hands with Jeff, his grip as strong as ever from his carpentry work.

"Jefferson Holt! What in blazes are you doing here in Pittsburgh? We all thought you were out west somewhere, trapping beaver and fighting Indians."

"I was until a while back," Jeff replied. "But now I'm heading east, and I couldn't come this way without stopping to see the youngsters, and you and Aunt Dorothy."

"Well, I should say not!" Dorothy Holt stepped

out of the house to stand beside her husband. A diminutive woman, still attractive despite the silver streaks in her dark hair, she stepped forward and hugged Jeff tightly. "We're so glad to see you, Jeff! I couldn't believe my ears at first when I heard Susan saying that you were here."

"I'm here, all right, big as life and twice as ugly."

"You're not ugly!" Susan protested. "You're just . . . rugged-looking."

Jeff laughed. He supposed that was the polite way to describe him. He had a week's worth of beard on his face, and it had been longer than that since he'd had a bath—not counting the dunking in the Ohio during the battle with the river pirates. But the members of his family were certainly a sight for sore eyes, and he supposed they were looking at him the same way.

"Well, there's no need for all of us to stand around outside like this," Henry said. "Come in, Jeff, come in. Welcome to our home."

Henry took Jeff's hat and rifle, then led the group into a spacious parlor furnished comfortably without being ostentatious.

"I'll fix us some tea," Dorothy said. "Jeff, you just sit right down and make yourself at home."

Jeff settled himself on a sofa as Dorothy bustled off to the kitchen. Susan and Jonathan sat with him, while Edward took a wing chair at the end of the sofa. Taking out a pipe and tobacco pouch, Henry sat down in an armchair nearby.

"How long are you going to be with us, Jeff?" Henry asked as he filled his pipe with tobacco.

"Not very long, I'm afraid." Jeff hesitated, unsure of how much to say about the quest that had brought him there. Then he decided to plunge ahead and tell them the whole story. They were family, after all.

"I'm just passing through, heading for New York."

"New York?" Henry repeated in surprise, and the youngsters reacted the same way.

"You mean you haven't come to take us back to Ohio?" Susan asked.

"Why in the world are you going to New York, Jeff?" Edward said.

Jonathan just looked disappointed.

"I'm looking for Melissa," Jeff said heavily. "She's not living in Marietta anymore."

Henry put the pipe in his mouth, struck a match, and puffed. Then he said, "In that letter she sent upriver with the children, she didn't say anything about not staying in Marietta. In fact, I got the feeling that was what she was planning."

"That's what I thought, too." Jeff paused, then said, "Maybe I'd better back up a mite. I don't reckon I've ever thanked you for taking in these youngsters, Uncle Henry. I don't know what I would have done if it hadn't been for you and Aunt Dorothy."

With a wave of his hand, Henry said, "Don't you worry about that. We couldn't have been happier when they showed up and said they needed a place to stay. All of our own young'uns have married and moved away, you know. Except for Ned."

In his uncle's voice was a peculiar heaviness when he mentioned Ned, Jeff thought, and again he wondered why people acted strange when the subject of his cousin came up. But now was not the time to pry into that.

"Well, you really eased my worry," Jeff said, "and Clay's, too. Melissa was supposed to come with the children, but she must have changed her mind at the last minute."

"You mean her father talked her out of it," Edward said. From the expression on his face, anyone could see that he did not care much for Charles Merrivale. "We were looking forward to her coming with us."

"I wish she had, Edward, I wish she had. Then I would have known where to find her. She and her folks were gone when I got back to Marietta, and the most I could find out about where they went was from Mr. Steakley. He seemed to remember something about them heading for New York."

Henry grunted. "Doesn't sound very certain to me."

"No, sir, it's not. But it's the only lead I've got."

"Well, I can understand why you're going there," Henry said. "It must've been quite a blow when you got to Marietta and found your wife gone."

191

"I felt as though I'd been punched in the stomach," Jeff said.

Henry puffed on his pipe one last time, set it in the ashtray on the table next to his chair, then clapped his hands on his knees. "Well, no point in dwelling on that now. Tell us what you've been doing with yourself these past couple of years."

"Yes," Jonathan echoed excitedly. "Tell us about fighting the Indians!"

"Actually, I haven't fought that many Indians, Jonathan. Most of the ones I've met have become good friends. In fact, you've got a sister-in-law who's a Hunkpapa Sioux woman named Shining Moon."

"No!" Susan exclaimed. "Clay married an Indian woman?"

"And she's as fine a lady as you'll find anywhere," Jeff said. "She's got a younger brother named Proud Wolf, and I reckon he's just about the best friend I've got out there in the West. Proud Wolf and Shining Moon saved our skins a time or two. And I mean *our* skins, not the beaver pelts."

Before Jeff could say anything else, the front door of the house opened again, and a man entered the foyer, slamming the door behind him and stopping short when he reached the parlor entrance and saw Jeff sitting there. He was tall, broad-shouldered, and brawny, with blond hair. He stared at Jeff in surprise.

"Hello, Ned," Henry said in a flat tone. "Come

in. Your cousin Jeff was just telling us about his life in the West."

"Jeff?" Ned Holt acted as if he could not believe his eyes or his ears. "Is that really you, Jeff?"

Jeff stood up and held out a hand to his cousin. Just like Pittsburgh, Ned had grown considerably since Jeff had seen him last. Ned was four or five inches taller and about forty pounds heavier than his older cousin.

"It's me, all right," Jeff said. "How are you, Ned?"

A couple of long strides brought Ned face to face with Jeff. He ignored the outstretched hand and with an exuberant whoop swept Jeff into a bone-crushing bear hug. "Son of a bitch! How the hell are you, cousin?"

"Ned!" Henry said sharply. "Put the lad down, son. And watch your language! There are still children in this house, you know."

Ned set the startled visitor back on the floor and said sheepishly, "Sorry, Jeff. Hope I didn't squeeze the daylights out of you."

Jeff was trying to draw some air back into his lungs. "No, that's . . . that's all right, Ned. I reckon you're just glad to see me."

"Damn right!" Ned winced and went on, "Sorry again. Guess I'm just a little carried away."

Jeff could smell whiskey on Ned's breath, and he realized that his cousin was a little drunk, even though it was the middle of the day. That came as a surprise. Henry and Dorothy were Congregationalists, like most of the Holts, and they had never approved much of drinking.

"Sit down and go on," Ned said eagerly. "I want to hear all about the West." He pulled up a straight-backed chair, reversed it, and straddled it as Jeff took his place on the sofa again.

A moment later Dorothy entered, cast a stern glance at Ned, and said tightly, "I thought I heard you come in, son. Have some tea with us. It'll do you good."

"No, thanks, Ma," Ned said. "I just want to hear all about Cousin Jeff's adventures out West."

"I'm not sure I'd call them adventures," Jeff said wryly. "Misadventures, maybe."

For the next half hour, he talked about some of what he and Clay had seen and done in the West, leaving out most of the violence and bloodshed and glossing over the rest. He explained about Shining Moon and Clay, and that he and Clay had been accepted into the Hunkpapa tribe almost as brothers. To his surprise Ned was even more full of questions than the children, and as Jeff looked at his cousin, he saw something shining there that did not come from liquor.

What he saw, Jeff realized, was wanderlust, the same thing that had gotten hold of Clay at an early age and sent him west at the first good opportunity. Jeff himself had experienced that feeling at times, although his odyssey to the mountains had come about by necessity rather than any

194

great desire to roam. But he could understand how Clay had felt, and he saw the same thing now in Ned.

"I'm going out there one of these days," Ned said when Jeff paused in his storytelling. "I've got to see that country before it gets all civilized."

"I reckon it'll be awhile before that happens. It's a big land, and it's going to take a lot of people to fill it up. I don't know if that's even possible."

"Are you going back?" Ned asked.

Jeff answered without hesitation. "Someday. But I don't know when."

"Well, when you do, maybe I can go with you."

"If I were you, son," Henry said, "I'd worry more about exploring some unknown territory right here in Pittsburgh. Say, the inside of that factory where you're supposed to be working."

Ned shrugged off his father's sarcasm. "That's just a job, Pa. It doesn't mean anything. It's not like what Jeff and Clay have experienced out on the frontier. That's a whole different way of life."

"Not really," Jeff said, not wanting Ned to romanticize things too much. "A man has a job to do out there, too, and most of the time it's pretty hard work. But he does what he has to if he wants to survive."

"Yes, but he's free. There's no freedom in working for wages."

Henry scowled. "I don't believe I'll ever understand you, Ned. Why, if I felt like you do, this family wouldn't have any—"

"Jeff, you'll be staying a few days with us, won't you?" Dorothy asked, her question cutting across her husband's rapidly rising voice. It was clear she did not want the discussion to escalate into an argument. She gave Henry a stern look, and he settled back in his chair.

"I can stay for a few days. I'm anxious to get on to New York and start looking for Melissa, though."

"Why, I can imagine! It must have been horrible to go home expecting to find your wife and then her not be there."

"It's about as bad a feeling as I've ever run across."

Dorothy stood up. "We still have a spare room, even with the children here. Edward, why don't you show your brother where it is?"

"Sure," Edward said, bounding up from his chair. "Come on, Jeff."

As Jeff got to his feet, Ned popped up, too, and slapped Jeff's back.

"It's going to be great having you here, cousin," he said. "I know the best places in town to have a good time, and I'll show them all to you!"

"Well, I don't—"

"You'll do no such thing," Henry cut in. "It's bad enough you seem to have dedicated your life to carousing, boy. You're not going to drag your cousin into it as well!"

Ned shrugged. "We'll see. Come on, Jeff."

As Jeff followed Ned and Edward through the house, Susan and Jonathan trailed along behind, unwilling to let their big brother out of sight just yet. Despite the circumstances, Jeff had to admit that he was happy to see the three of them again. Knowing they were all healthy and in good spirits would make it easier to continue his search for Melissa.

Ned and Edward escorted him to a cheerful, airy room on the second floor of the house. A four-poster bed with an embroidered spread stood in the center of the room. Jeff rested a hand on the bed and pushed up and down.

"A bed to sleep on," he murmured. "The past couple of years I've gotten used to a rope bunk or a blanket roll on the ground."

"Sounds like a hard life," Edward said.

"It can be," Jeff admitted. "But it's got its advantages. When a man gets accustomed to the open sky over his head, it's hard to leave it behind."

"Damn, but that sounds good! You've got to tell me more about it, Jeff." Ned lowered his voice a little. "I, ah, might have to leave town before too much longer, and I've been thinking about heading west myself. Edward, not a word of this to my ma and pa."

Edward nodded. "Sure, Ned. I understand."

His brother might understand, but Jeff did not. "What's wrong, Ned? Are you in some sort of trouble?"

"Nothing you need to worry about, cousin." Ned grinned broadly and slapped Jeff on the back again. "You've come a long ways. You'd better get some rest. Before you move on, you're liable to need all the strength you've got!"

Jeff did not like the sound of that at all. But Ned was probably exaggerating, he reasoned.

From what Jeff had seen so far, Pittsburgh looked like a busy, industrious, but peaceful town. But appearances, as he knew all too well, could be deceiving.

Jeff talked more in the days that followed than he had in the past year. At least that was how it seemed to him. A man got used to silence on the frontier, to speaking only when necessary and keeping his words and thoughts to himself. But under the nearly constant questioning of his siblings, not to mention his cousin Ned, Jeff spun yarn after yarn. He answered their queries tolerantly and cheerfully, glad to be with them and remembering how he himself had reacted when Clay first returned to Ohio after his journey with Lewis and Clark. Jeff had been the one full of questions then.

He got some respite while the children were at school and Ned was at work. He spent that time helping his uncle in the cabinet shop behind the house. Unlike the others, Henry was as taciturn as a frontiersman himself, and he kept his attention focused on the work at hand.

Jeff enjoyed the sawing and hammering, the smell of cut wood, the faint hot tang of a saw blade warm from use. He had never minded hard work, and he found it kept his mind off his reason for being in Pittsburgh.

Always lurking at the edge of his thoughts, however, was Melissa. He had been willing to postpone his search for a few days to visit his family, but his patience was not as great as he had hoped it would be. By the time he had been in Pittsburgh a day and a half, he was itching to get started on his quest again, but he swallowed that impatience and forced himself to concentrate instead on his brothers and sister, his aunt and uncle, and his cousin. He enjoyed the time he spent with them, almost in spite of himself, although he resisted Ned's invitations to accompany him for a night on the town.

By his third night in Pittsburgh, though, he knew he would have to be moving on soon. He had enough money left to buy a good horse, so he decided that at supper that evening he would ask Henry to recommend a stable where he might find such a mount.

Shortly before the evening meal, Dorothy entered the parlor, looked around, and said, "Ned's not here yet. Where do you think he could be?"

Henry was sitting in his favorite armchair, puffing on his pipe and reading the current issue of Mr. John Scull's *Pittsburgh Gazette,* which boasted on its masthead that it had been established in 1784 as the first newspaper west of the Allegheny Mountains.

He rattled the newspaper and snorted. "Knowing that boy, he could be in any of a dozen or more taprooms."

"He always comes home for supper," Dorothy said. "You know that, Henry. I'm worried about him."

Jeff looked up and said, "Ned seems to be the type who can take care of himself, Aunt Dorothy." He was seated on the sofa, examining some of the schoolwork Susan and Jonathan had been proudly showing him.

"Oh, I know that, but I still worry. It's a mother's job, I suppose."

Jeff put down the paper Susan had given him. "I'd be glad to go look for him and make sure he's all right."

"Would you, Jeff? Supper won't be ready for a while. I'll tell you where to find the nail factory. You'll probably meet him on the way there."

Henry lowered his newspaper and sat forward in the chair. "You don't have to put yourself out, Jeff. I'm sure Ned's all right."

"I don't mind," Jeff said as he stood up. "I've been wanting to see a bit more of the city before I move on, and this will give me a chance."

"Can we come with you?" Susan asked.

Jeff glanced out the window and saw the shadows of evening. "No. It's getting dark, so I think it would be better if you two stayed here, Susan."

Both youngsters looked disappointed. Jeff

was glad Edward was up in his room working on his studies; otherwise, he would have been asking to come along, too.

As Dorothy told him how to find the nail factory, located on Grant Street several blocks away, Jeff went into the foyer and put on his jacket and hat. His rifle was leaning in a corner, and his pistol was lying on a small table, but as he reached for them, he hesitated. He was going on a simple errand, and he should have no need for the firearms. If he did run into trouble, he always had his hunting knife. But it was unlikely he would encounter any problems in as civilized a place as Pittsburgh.

He strode out into the evening, enjoying the warmth that lingered in the air. Fewer people were on the streets now, since most were sitting down to their evening meal.

Jeff walked briskly toward Grant Street, which ran along the eastern edge of town. The closer he got to that district, the more taverns he saw. Given Ned's fondness for liquor, Jeff agreed with Henry that Ned had most likely stopped at one of them for a drink before going home. He decided to look into the ones he passed.

He had checked two taverns and seen no sign of Ned when a shout from up the street caught his attention. In the thickening dusk, he saw a figure dart out of another drinking establishment and run in his direction. The man was moving so quickly that his feet went out from under him, and he went sprawling on the cobblestones, rolled over, and sprang back to his feet. As he did, other men boiled out of the tavern.

"There he is!" one of them cried. "Get the bastard!"

Jeff froze as the fleeing man ran toward him. There was something all too familiar about him. . . .

"Come back here, Holt!" shouted one of the pursuers. "Stop, damn you!"

It was Ned, all right. His aunt had been correct, Jeff thought. Her youngest son was definitely in some sort of trouble.

"Ned!" Jeff called. "Over here, Ned!"

Ned was already racing in Jeff's general direction, but he veered directly toward him in response to the shout. As his cousin pounded up to him breathlessly, Jeff caught his arm and jerked him to a halt.

"What is this, Ned?" Jeff demanded.

Panting, Ned threw a frantic glance at the four men chasing him. They were not far away, but they were slowing down slightly since they had caught sight of Ned being confronted by someone else.

"Come on, Jeff!" Ned said desperately. "We've got to get out of here!"

"I'm not going anywhere until I find out what this is all about." Jeff owed a great deal to his aunt and uncle for taking in the children, and he was not about to turn his back on his cousin while Ned was in trouble—but he was not going to step into a fight without learning what it was about, either.

Ned hesitated, his wide-eyed gaze leaping wildly from Jeff to the other men and back again.

"They say I owe them money," he finally admitted, "but it's all a big mistake!"

The four men were close enough to hear what Ned was saying. They slowed to a halt ten feet away, and one of them laughed harshly.

"A mistake?" he growled. "You made it, Holt. Now pay up, or we'll take the debt out of your hide!"

"You've been gambling, haven't you, Ned?" Jeff asked.

Again Ned hesitated, but then he jerked his head in a nod.

Jeff asked the other men, "How much does he owe you?"

"It ain't us he owes," the spokesman replied. "It's our boss. But the debt's a hundred dollars."

Jeff gave a low whistle of amazement. One hundred dollars was a hell of a lot of money. He looked at Ned, who gave him a sheepish grin and shrugged.

"All right," Jeff sighed. "I'll pay you. But I'll have to go back to the place I'm staying."

"That won't do," the spokesman for the group said. "We got to have the money now. Either that, or Holt gets a beatin'. And he'll still owe the money after that." The man squinted at Jeff in the gloom. "Why're you trying to help this bastard, anyway?"

"He's my cousin."

"So you're a Holt, too, eh?"

"That's right," Jeff said sharply. He did not like the scornful tone in the man's voice.

"Well, get the hell out of here. You ain't got no part in this, even if you are related. Go ahead, turn tail and run like your cousin here."

Jeff looked at Ned, who was nervous and agitated and was clearly restraining himself from fleeing. The block they were standing on was practically deserted, and the other pedestrians in sight seemed to be avoiding the confrontation. In this part of town, it was doubtful that anyone would even summon a constable in the event of trouble.

Jeff took a deep breath. "I don't like the way you talk, mister. I said I'd pay you if you'll let me go get the money. You'll have to be satisfied with that."

The four men exchanged glances.

"Nope." The spokesman shook his head. "You're outnumbered two to one, mister. You got no right dictating terms."

"Then you'll have to settle for nothing," Jeff said coldly.

"Jeff . . ." Ned's voice was tight with anxiety. "I don't think this is such a good idea."

A faint smirk played over Jeff's mouth. None of the men were carrying guns as far as he could tell.

"You can run from this pack of dogs if you'd like, Ned. I'd rather not."

The leader of the toughs said, "You're a stupid bastard just like your cousin, mister. But don't say we didn't warn you."

With a shouted curse he leapt forward and swung a fist at Jeff's head. The other three hired ruffians were right behind him.

Jeff ducked the wild, roundhouse punch and stepped closer to the man, hooking a hard blow to his belly. A quick shove sent him staggering back into one of his companions.

In the meantime, one of the other two had slammed a punch into Ned's jaw, staggering the younger Holt. Ned caught his balance, blocked the next punch, and crashed his own fist into his opponent's face. The man's nose flattened under the impact, and he let out a howl of pain.

Jeff went on the offensive, tackling the fourth man and bearing him backward. The man's heel caught on a loose cobblestone, and he fell heavily, taking Jeff with him. Jeff landed on top of him and heard a satisfying *crack* as the man's head hit the street.

In the next instant a booted foot smashed into Jeff's side. The kick lifted him off his fallen adversary and sent him rolling along the grimy street. The man who had kicked him pounced after him and drew back his foot for another blow, but as his foot lashed out, Jeff twisted his head out of the way and grabbed the man's leg. A quick yank sent him tumbling.

Ned traded punches with the man Jeff had tangled with to start the fight. Now that the fracas was under way, he was holding nothing back. He slugged his opponent, took a punch, and slugged again, then reached out suddenly to grab the man's shoulders and jerk him forward. Taken by surprise, the man had no chance to resist. Ned lowered his head and butted the man in the face as hard as he could.

A few feet away Jeff threw himself on the man he had just spilled and hit him twice, a left and a right that drove the man's head first one way, then the other. The man went limp, stunned by the combination of blows.

Jeff rose to his feet and turned to face the next opponent, but he saw that he and Ned were the only ones left standing. Three of the men were either out cold or too stunned to keep fighting, while the fourth huddled on his knees and held both hands over his shattered nose. Blood made dark trails on the backs of his hands in the twilight.

Breathless, Ned said, "Well, I reckon we taught them a lesson. Come on, cousin. Let's go home."

"Hold on, Ned," Jeff said sharply. "Do you have any money?"

Ned blinked in surprise. "Some."

"A hundred dollars?"

"Not hardly."

"Give me what you've got." Jeff held out his hand.

"Wait a minute! What's the idea, Jeff?"

"A man ought to at least try to pay his debts," Jeff said stubbornly. "Give me the money."

Grumbling, Ned reached into his pocket and pulled out a handful of coins and a couple of folded bills. He handed them to Jeff, who walked over to the leader of the ruffians. The man was half conscious now, moaning and moving around a little. Jeff dropped the money on his chest.

"That's a start," he said, not knowing or really caring if the man heard what he was saying. "I'll see that your boss gets the rest of what he's owed." Jeff prodded the man in the side with the toe of his boot. "But stay away from my cousin. Holts don't take kindly to being pushed."

He turned and walked away, then looked over his shoulder and snapped, "Come on, Ned."

Ned hurried after him. "That was one hell of a fight, Jeff. You can really handle yourself. You must've been in a lot of brawls out there on the frontier."

"Not many," Jeff replied tightly.

He did not mention the urge he had felt during the fight to pull his knife and sink it into his opponent's belly. To Ned this had been nothing more than a rough game, but to Jeff, after spending two years in the wilderness, a fight was usually a matter of life and death. You killed your enemy before he could kill you.

He took a deep breath and pushed those thoughts away. He was back in civilization now, and things were different. But he was still the same man, and he knew now what he had suspected all along: No matter where he went, he would always carry some of the frontier with him.

X

As the expedition headed west through the valley where the three branches of the Missouri River ran, Clay was glad to see that Aaron Garwood and Rupert von Metz were keeping their distance from each other. Von Metz was a natural-born troublemaker, Clay had decided after their clash of a few days before, and the last thing he wanted was to have the two young men at each other's throats over Lucy Franklin.

Lucy seemed to be fond of both of them, although Clay had caught her casting longing glances in his direction several times. He ignored the looks—and hoped that Shining Moon would continue to do so, too.

The land of the valley was a flat, grassy plain, with the Absarokas falling away in the distance behind the travelers and the main body of the Rockies rising far ahead of them. Called the Shining Mountains by the Indians, the Rockies looked almost close enough to touch, but Clay knew he and his companions would have to travel for days before they reached the foothills.

As they hiked across the valley, Professor Franklin moved up alongside Clay and Shining Moon and asked, "Did you come through here with Captain Lewis and Captain Clark, Mr. Holt?"

Clay gestured to the north. "We were up that

way about eighty miles or so on the westbound leg of the trip. On the way back, Captain Clark traveled through this area, but I wasn't with him. He and Lewis had split up into separate groups so they could cover more ground. I went with Lewis. And I've done most of my trapping south and east of here, around the Yellowstone and Big Horn rivers, so this is all virgin territory to me. I've heard plenty about it, though, from John Colter."

"John Colter," the professor repeated. "Oh, yes, I've heard of him. Supposed to be quite an adventurer. People have begun calling him a mountain man."

"Good name for him. He's seen more of these mountains than any other man alive, white or red, I reckon."

"I remember you made some mention several days ago of something called Colter's Hell. What's that?"

Clay chuckled as he replied, "John was out on one of his tramps through the mountains a couple of winters ago when he came upon a valley where hot mud bubbled up from the ground, boiling-hot water shot a hundred feet in the air, and demons rumbled around in the earth right under his feet—or so he said. The smell of brimstone was so strong it liked to have overpowered him. At least that's the way he tells it. Folks got to saying that he'd found the back door to hell, so it wasn't long before they started calling that area Colter's Hell."

"Incredible! Was there any truth to the story?"

"Most people didn't think so at first," Clay said. "But I've talked to enough Indians who have seen the same things that I sort of believe it now, even though I've never been there myself."

"This fellow Colter must be an amazing man."

"Tell the professor about the race," Shining Moon suggested.

"What race?" Franklin asked.

"Between Colter and about five hundred Blackfoot warriors," Clay said. "The stakes were his life. I know this one's true because I was at Fort Lisa when he came stumbling in after it was all over, naked and skinny as a rail with his feet cut almost to ribbons."

Franklin listened with rapt attention.

"Seems Colter was over on the other side of the Jefferson Fork." Clay pointed ahead of them. "That's on the far side of the valley. The Jefferson's the farthest west of the three tongues of the Missouri. Anyway, last fall he and another trapper name of Potts were up there on the canyon rim, about where it starts sloping down to the river. They got jumped by the biggest bunch of Blackfoot either one of them had ever seen. Potts tried to get away, but the braves filled him full of arrows. John had the sense to stay put. He figured he was dead either way, but he didn't see any point in rushing things.

"So the Blackfoot took his clothes and tortured him a mite—nothing too serious, you understand—then decided to have some real fun with

210

him. They gave him a little start and told him to run for his life. Of course, they figured they'd catch up to him right away and kill him."

"How horrible!" Franklin muttered.

"Colter didn't care much for the idea, either," Clay said. "He'd told them he wasn't much of a runner, but that was an out and out lie. John Colter's about as fast on his feet as anybody you'll ever see. So he took off, running barefoot over those rocks, and when the Blackfoot came after him, they found they couldn't catch him after all. One by one, they fell back, their tongues dragging like a dog that's been running all day.

"All but one of them. He was the only one who could keep up with Colter. Now, John was heading for the Jefferson as fast he could, but he couldn't shake that one warrior. So when he got close to the river, he did the last thing that Blackfoot ever expected him to do: He turned right around and came straight at him.

"The Blackfoot was so startled that he tripped as he tried to throw his lance. He fell, and the lance went into the ground in front of John. That was all the chance John needed. He grabbed up that lance and stuck it right through the Blackfoot."

Clay glanced around and saw that Lucy Franklin and Rupert von Metz had moved up within earshot, too. He felt a little uncomfortable about relating the ghastly details while Lucy was listening, but he also knew from the expressions that she and the professor and von Metz wore that they would not be satisfied without hearing the ending.

"That Blackfoot was dead, but John knew the others would be coming along before too much longer. So he jumped into the river and found himself a place to hide, under a pile of driftwood that had floated along until it got snagged. Even in the fall, the Jefferson was mighty cold from snow melt, but Colter stayed there in that hiding place while the rest of the Blackfoot came looking for him. There was enough room under the driftwood for him to get air. Luck was with him; none of the Indians looked under that mess of wood. They went off searching for him, and he waited until it got dark. Then he slipped out from under the driftwood and swam downstream.

"Colter stayed in the river for about five miles, then got out and rested some. There didn't seem to be any Blackfoot around, so his luck was still with him. He knew where he was well enough and figured the best thing to do was to strike out across country toward Fort Lisa. It was only about two hundred miles, and he walked it before."

"Two hundred miles! But he had no weapons, no food!" Professor Franklin observed.

"And he was buck naked, to boot," Clay agreed. "But he figured being hungry and footsore would be better than what the Blackfoot would do to him if they caught him. There were plenty of creeks along the way where he could get water, and for food, berries and bark were better than nothing. He started out that same night."

Clay concluded by saying, "Took him eleven days to cover that two hundred miles, but he made it. Like I said, I was there when he came in. I never saw anybody so worn out. But less than a week later, he'd outfitted himself and taken off again for the high country."

Into the awed silence that followed, Rupert von Metz said scornfully, "What a preposterous story! No one could possibly do such a thing."

"My husband does not lie," Shining Moon said coldly. "I, too, was there at the fort when John Colter arrived from his ordeal."

Von Metz scowled but was silent, as though unwilling to cast doubt on the word of a woman, even an Indian woman.

Quietly Clay said, "You'll find that lots of things happen out here on the frontier that might seem unbelievable to folks who have never been west. A man can do damn near anything, even outrun five hundred Indians or walk two hundred miles in his bare feet, if he wants to live bad enough."

"I'd like to meet this man Colter and talk to him," Franklin said. "I'm especially interested in that area you say he discovered called Colter's Hell. It sounds like something a scientist should investigate."

"Well, if we happen to run into him, I'd be glad to introduce the two of you, Professor," Clay said. "Or maybe sometime in the future, you and I could go take a look at the place ourselves."

"I'd like that, Mr. Holt." Franklin smiled. "I'd like that very much."

213

So would he, Clay realized. There were plenty of sights out here he had not yet seen, mountains he had not yet climbed, high grassy meadows he had not yet trod. The frontier was a beautiful place, and the best thing about it was that there were always new things to see and experience. This rugged wilderness was full of surprises.

Before he was through, Clay Holt vowed to himself, he would see all of it, from one end to the other.

They made camp that night beside the first fork of the Missouri. They had been able to trace its course for several hours before actually reaching it because the trees along its banks were visible as a low green line for many miles across the plain. The cottonwoods and willows grew to a respectable size here, and they would provide shelter and firewood so that the travelers would not have to burn dried buffalo chips.

Proud Wolf was given the job of gathering wood, and while a part of him wanted to protest that such a chore was woman's work, he did not argue with Clay. The time Proud Wolf had spent with his brother-in-law had taught him that everyone had to share in such tasks.

He picked up his rifle and ranged along the riverbank, heading upstream as he collected branches and twigs suitable for kindling. He had been in this broad valley once before, several years earlier, when the elders brought him and other young men there to teach them the buffalo hunt. The elders had demonstrated how to stalk the great shaggy beasts, using hides for conceal-ment until they were close enough to bring down the massive creatures with lances and arrows. It had been a thrilling time for Proud Wolf, al-though he had never killed any of the buffalo himself. In fact, he had tripped and fallen on the hide he had been using as a disguise, and his feet had become so tangled in it that he could not get up. The debacle had almost caused a stampede, but Proud Wolf nevertheless remem-bered the experience with fondness, as it was the first time he had hunted with the warriors of his tribe.

Someday they will fully accept me as one of them, he thought as he filled his arms with firewood. *I will perform great deeds, and the women will sing songs of my bravery. . . .*

"Help! Dear Lord, someone help me!"

Proud Wolf's head snapped up. The cry was coming from somewhere behind him. He had traveled farther than he had intended, he realized, so caught up had he been in his recollections. The camp was probably a mile downstream.

The shouts continued, perhaps only a couple of hundred yards away, much closer to him than the camp was. Then he realized that he was hearing Professor Franklin's voice—and the man sounded terrified.

Proud Wolf dropped the firewood, grasped his rifle, spun around, and ran back the way he had come. As he ran he checked the weapon, making sure it was ready to fire as soon as he full cocked it.

He raced around a bend in the river, ducked past some cottonwoods, and came to a stumbling halt. The professor was fifteen feet up a willow, clinging to the trunk. Proud Wolf was a little shocked at the professor's climbing ability, given his bulky shape, but terror could give a man wings, and few things were more terrifying than a grizzly bear . . . like the one reared up on its hind feet at the base of the willow, swiping at Professor Franklin with a big paw.

The bear was a good-sized one, about seven feet tall and weighing at least six hundred pounds, Proud Wolf judged. He had seen larger bears before, but this one was undoubtedly big enough to pose considerable danger. Those paws with their long, curved, razor-sharp claws could open up a man from groin to gizzard. The beasts lost their temper easily, and Proud Wolf wondered what Professor Franklin had done to anger this one.

"Hang on, Professor!" he shouted. "Climb higher if you can, but do not slip!"

Proud Wolf was not sure if Franklin heard him over his own shouts and the bear's growling and snuffling. The grizzly's head swung around, and Proud Wolf knew it had noticed his presence. Silvertips like this one did not have good eyesight, but their hearing and sense of smell were keen.

The young Sioux lifted his rifle and cocked it, then hesitated. Killing a grown bear with one shot was a difficult feat, and once he fired, he would need at least half a minute to reload. In that amount of time the grizzly could easily reach him. Already riled, the beast would be angered that much more by being shot.

Proud Wolf had heard of men killing grizzlies with their knives, but he knew that was out of the question. He would be no match for the massive bear; the creature would tear him apart in seconds. But he had to do something. . . .

Then he heard a sudden rattling in the brush along the bank not far from him. Acting on a hunch, he darted toward the noise and pushed back the undergrowth. There he saw a single bear cub. The grizzly that had Professor Franklin treed let out a bellow of rage and lumbered toward Proud Wolf.

"Watch out, lad!" Franklin cried.

His pulse pounding in his head, Proud Wolf leaned over and scooped up the cub. It was still small enough for him to lift, but he had trouble hanging on to it as it struggled in his grip. He ran to the edge of the river, hesitated, and looked over his shoulder. The bear had covered more than half the distance between them and was closing rapidly.

Proud Wolf tossed the cub into the water.

The cub was crying as it landed with a splash, and the pitiful sound almost made Proud Wolf regret what he was doing. *Almost.* But he had to distract the mother bear some way, and the quickest method was to put the cub in danger.

Not that the cub was threatened too badly. The river's current was not swift, and Proud Wolf knew that bears could swim, even young ones such as this. But the cub's mother would probably dive into the water after it, anyway, so that she could grip the scruff of its neck with her teeth and haul it out of the river.

Proud Wolf was betting his life on that. He darted to the side, dropped the flintlock, and leapt toward a low-hanging branch as the bear thundered past him. Swinging his feet up, he hooked his knees over the branch and pulled himself up frantically, just in case the bear paused to swipe at him. However, the grizzly paid no attention to him, plunging into the river instead with a huge splash, sending a spray of water high into the air. It swam toward the cub.

Proud Wolf dropped from the tree and called, "Get down, Professor! Get down and run!"

Awkwardly, Franklin clambered down the willow, losing his grip near the bottom and falling the last few feet. He landed heavily and toppled onto the ground, and by the time Proud Wolf had picked up the rifle and raced over to him, he was sitting up and holding his left leg.

"I think I've twisted my ankle." Franklin looked up at Proud Wolf, his normally ruddy features pale and drawn with fright and pain. "You run back to camp while that beast is occupied."

"No," Proud Wolf said curtly. "I will help you."

He tucked the rifle under his left arm, then bent and slid his right arm around Franklin.

"But I can't run!" the professor objected. "That bear—"

"The bear is worried about her cub. If we can get out of here, she will forget about us." With a grunt of effort, Proud Wolf tried to lift Franklin.

The professor helped, levering himself to his feet with his other arm and his good leg while Proud Wolf supported the injured one. Proud Wolf looked over his shoulder again and saw that luck was with them. The grizzly was emerging from the stream with her cub—but on the opposite bank.

"Come on," Proud Wolf said, his voice showing the strain of hoisting even part of Franklin's considerable bulk. "We must hurry."

He thought about firing his rifle in the air in hopes of summoning help from the camp, then decided against it. Clay and the others might think he was just taking a shot at a deer to cook for their supper. Besides, he did not want to waste the time that would be needed to reload. It was more important to put distance between them and the grizzly.

Limping heavily, Professor Franklin made his way along the river with Proud Wolf's help. Every couple of minutes, the young Hunkpapa looked over his shoulder to make sure the bear was not in pursuit, but the brute seemed to have forgotten about them, just as he had hoped.

The last glimpse he caught of the grizzly was of it disappearing into the brush on the far side of the river.

"We can slow down now," Proud Wolf told Franklin. "The bear will not bother us. They are quick to anger but equally quick to forget."

"Thank God for that! I certainly never intended to upset the beast. In fact, I didn't know she was anywhere near until I stumbled over that cub while I was studying the vegetation along the stream." Wincing in pain, Franklin went on, "All I could think to do was run and climb a tree. It wasn't until I was already halfway up that willow that I remembered bears can climb, too."

"The bear would have, when she got tired of swiping at you with her paw." Dryly he added, "You should not leave the camp alone, Professor."

"I know. But everyone else was busy, and I thought this would be a good opportunity to take a look at the foliage while there was still some light."

An idea occurred to Proud Wolf. "Next time you want to study something, will you take me with you?"

"So that you can protect me?"

"So that I can learn from you," Proud Wolf said sincerely. "This—this *science* of yours interests me. I wish to know more of it."

Professor Franklin smiled down at him. "You want to be my student, eh? That sounds like a fine idea, Proud Wolf. And at the same time you can keep me from getting into such trouble as I did today. It's a deal, my boy."

Proud Wolf beamed. He had already learned that the world contained many things about which he knew nothing. The arrival of the white men in the mountains had told him that; now, with the help of Professor Franklin, he would learn more about what lay beyond the territory roamed by the Hunkpapa.

He had already decided that one day he would travel to far lands and see the wonders they held. Great warriors were also great explorers, and he would be the greatest warrior of all.

"Oh, my God!" Lucy Franklin cried.

At the young woman's exclamation, Clay looked up sharply from his task. He had been forming a circle of rocks in which to build a campfire once Proud Wolf got back with the firewood, but that could wait. From the sound of Lucy's voice, there was trouble.

Proud Wolf and Professor Franklin were entering the camp. Franklin was limping heavily as though injured and was leaning on the young Hunkpapa man. Lucy ran forward to meet them. Clay followed at a slower pace.

"Father, what happened?" Lucy asked as she clutched the professor's arm. "Are you hurt?"

"Just a twisted ankle, that's all," Franklin told her. "But it would have been much worse had it not been for this lad. He saved my life."

Clay joined them and asked Proud Wolf, "Saved the professor's life from what?"

"Just a grizzly bear," Proud Wolf said in mock nonchalance.

"Old Ephraim?" Clay used the trapper's favorite term for the bears. "Don't see too many of them out on the plains like this."

"She was staying close to the river," Proud Wolf explained, "and she had a cub with her—as the professor found out."

"Oh, so that's what got her dander up. How'd you get her away from the professor?"

"I threw the cub in the river, then got out of the way."

Lucy stared at Proud Wolf. "You threw an innocent little bear cub in the river?" She sounded outraged by the admission.

"I had to get the bear's attention away from your father, Miss Franklin. She had him trapped in a willow tree."

"And soon she would have had me for dinner," Franklin put in. "Don't berate the boy, Lucy. His quick thinking saved my life."

"I'm sorry," Lucy said to Proud Wolf. "I didn't mean to snap at you. This—this wild country out here is sometimes beyond my comprehension."

Shining Moon, Aaron Garwood, Rupert von Metz, and Harry Lawton had gathered in time to hear what Proud Wolf and Franklin were saying, and following Lucy's comment, von Metz snorted and said, "It would take a lunatic to understand this land, my dear, since it seems to be wholly populated with them already."

Clay ignored von Metz and said to Franklin, "What were you doing when you got into trouble, Professor?"

"I'm afraid I wandered off quite carelessly while I was studying the trees along the river. I assure you, it won't happen again, Mr. Holt."

Lawton spoke up. "Next time you want to go off adventuring, Professor, let me know and I'll go with you."

The offer was one way for Lawton to get back in Franklin's good graces, Clay thought.

The professor winced with pain. "Thank you for your consideration, Mr. Lawton, but that won't be necessary. Young Proud Wolf here has agreed to accompany me each time I leave the camp."

"Sure, if that's what you want," Lawton said in a surly voice, then walked away.

Clay watched him for a second, then turned back to Franklin. "We've stood around here talking long enough. You'd better get off that bad leg, Professor. How'd you hurt it, anyway?"

"Falling out of the tree where that bear had chased me." Franklin limped to the center of the camp with Proud Wolf supporting him on one side and Lucy on the other. He sank down on the ground and stretched the injured leg in front of him. "I'm afraid I twisted my ankle rather badly."

"Well, this isn't a bad place to camp," Clay said

as he hunkered on his heels next to the professor. "We've got more than enough supplies, so we'll stay here for a day or two or even longer, until you feel up to walking again. No point in pushing things and hurting that leg worse than it already is."

"Thank you, Mr. Holt," Franklin said fervently. "I'm sorry to be causing so much trouble—"

"Don't worry about it," Clay said. "This is your expedition, Professor, not mine."

"Perhaps, but we've put ourselves in your hands. I appreciate your understanding."

Clay clapped Franklin on the shoulder and then stood up. "We still need some firewood," he said, looking at Proud Wolf.

"I will return for it," Proud Wolf said.

Clay picked up his long rifle and cradled it in the crook of his left arm. "I'll go with you, just in case you run into Old Ephraim again."

Franklin lifted his head to look up at Clay. "Excuse me, Mr. Holt, but this is the second time I've heard you refer to the grizzly bear by that name. Can you tell me why?"

Clay had never really considered the question before. After he had thought about it for a moment, he said, "You saw that bear, with all the silver fur among the brown, like a grizzled old man. Didn't it look like somebody who'd be called Old Ephraim?"

"You know, now that I think about it in that light, you're correct. The name does seem suitable."

Clay strode off upriver, Proud Wolf beside him.

While the two of them gathered firewood, Shining Moon carefully removed Professor Franklin's boot and bound the injured ankle with wide strips of rawhide, tying them tightly so that the swelling would go down. Lucy watched as Shining Moon worked over her father's leg, as if suspicious that the Hunkpapa woman might try some heathen healing ritual. What Shining Moon was doing, though, was nothing more than good common sense. When she was finished binding the ankle, she propped Franklin's foot up on a round stone.

"Keep it higher than the rest of your leg, and that will help prevent more swelling," Shining Moon told the professor. "Tomorrow, I will make a poultice of roots and herbs and river mud to take some of the pain from your leg."

"Thank you, my dear," Franklin said gratefully.

"Are you sure that's such a good idea, Father?" Lucy said. "I mean, you won't know what's in this concoction Shining Moon prepares."

"I will be glad to tell you the things I will use, Professor."

"And I'd be very interested to know, Shining Moon," he said, "although I certainly trust you. But the medicinal and healing arts of your people are another area I'd like to investigate during this trip. I'm sure we'll have a profitable discussion."

Shining Moon traded smiles with the professor, and Lucy looked vaguely frustrated before she went back to unpacking the provisions.

That evening, as the entire group sat around the campfire, Professor Franklin related the story of his misadventure with the grizzly bear one more time. Proud Wolf looked rather embarrassed by the praise that Franklin heaped on him, but Clay thought the young man was enjoying being the center of attention.

After everyone had turned in for the night, except for the lookouts, Clay rolled up in his blankets with Shining Moon. There was nothing better than lying here, he thought, looking up at the brilliant stars in the huge vault of night sky, his woman's head resting on his shoulder.

She whispered, "Proud Wolf did a brave thing today."

"He did a smart thing today. Using that cub to distract the mama was quick thinking. But you're right about his being brave. It could've got him killed."

"I do not think Lucy Franklin realizes that. She does not like Proud Wolf or me."

"Oh, I reckon she just doesn't know what to make of you. Likely she never saw any Indians close up until she came out here. But I figure she wishes she were back in Massachusetts about now, right enough."

"Perhaps—if she could take you with her," Shining Moon said.

Clay looked at her in the starlight and saw that

she was grinning. She was teasing him, but he did not mind. He leaned closer, intending to kiss her soundly.

A wink of light, seen for an instant from the corner of his eye . . .

He lifted himself on an elbow, peering toward the dark bulk of the distant mountains. Beside him, Shining Moon caught her breath in surprise at his reaction. She had been expecting a kiss, not this sudden tension on his part.

"What is it?" she whispered.

"Thought I saw something." His gaze was still fixed on the peaks. "A light, over yonder in the mountains."

Shining Moon twisted around to peer behind her at the Rockies. "They are too far away. You could not have seen anything."

"The light of a fire can carry a long way on a clear night." Clay lay down again. "But it's gone now, whatever it was."

"Perhaps it *was* a fire. It could belong to other trappers or to some of my people."

"Or to a band of Blackfoot or Arikaras."

She lifted a hand and rested her fingertips on his cheek. "Whatever you saw, it is far, far away and cannot touch us tonight. But you and I are together, as we should be."

"Can't argue with that. His head dipped toward hers, and his mouth found her warm, waiting lips.

But even as he kissed her, his mind was in the distant mountains, and he knew that what-

227

ever it was that had stirred his warning instincts was still there.

Waiting.

XI

From the number of religious houses and sects, it may be presumed that the sabbath is decently observed in Pittsburgh, and that really appears to be the case in a remarkable degree, considering it is so much of a manufacturing town, so recently become such, and inhabited by such a variety of people.

Amusements are also a good deal attended to, particularly concerts and balls in the winters, and there are annual horse races at a course about three miles from town, near the Allegheny beyond Hill's tavern.

On the whole let a person be of what disposition he will, Pittsburgh will afford him scope for the exercise of it.

—Fortescue Cuming
"Sketches of a Tour to the Western Country"

Jeff knew he could not stay in Pittsburgh any longer; his impatience to resume his search for Melissa was too great. The day after he had intervened in the trouble between Ned and the four toughs, he paid a visit to a nearby stable and bought a sturdy-looking bay mare.

"She'll make a good saddler for you, young fella," the liveryman said as he patted the mare's flank. "She's got a good gait, a pleasant nature, and plenty of sand."

"I'm sure I'll be well-satisfied," Jeff replied. "I'll need a saddle, blanket, and harness, too."

"Got quite a ride in front of you, eh?"

"All the way to New York City," Jeff said.

The livery owner, a short, slender, middle-aged man, squinted up at Jeff. "New York, did you say? You look to me more like the type to head west. What's in New York that'd take you back there?"

"A dream," Jeff heard himself saying.

That was true, he thought as the stableman went to get a saddle and the other gear he would need for the journey. As a young man—only a few short years ago, though the time seemed longer—he had dreamed of having a home and family: a good farm, a beautiful wife, a cabin full of rambunctious Holt kids. Melissa had been the centerpiece of that dream.

When Melissa and he were married, he had taken the first step toward fulfilling that dream. But their wedding had been marred by violence and death, and their happiness together had been short-lived. Fate, it seemed, had cruelly conspired to steal his dream away from him.

Jeff's jaw tightened. He was being maudlin, and he knew it. He and Melissa had had more than their share of bad luck, but there was no use in crying over it. The best thing to do was to forge ahead and try to put the situation right.

"Here you go," the liveryman said as he brought out a saddle, harness, and colorful blanket. "That'll take care of you. Whole thing'll run you, say—forty dollars?"

"Done," Jeff agreed. He took a pair of double eagles from his pocket and handed them over, then saddled the mare.

"Jeff!" a voice called from the street outside the livery barn. "There you are!"

Jeff saw Ned lunge through the entrance where the barn's double doors were swung back.

"Pa told me where he thought you'd headed. I need to talk to you, Jeff."

"I'm a little busy."

"This won't take long."

Jeff sighed. "All right. Wait until I get this horse saddled."

The liveryman looked Ned up and down and said to Jeff, "Friend of yours?"

"My cousin, Ned Holt."

"Oh." The man's voice was flat, hard. "I've heard the name."

Jeff looked at Ned. "Does everybody in this town know you?"

Ned just shrugged. "Word gets around."

"That it does," the liveryman said coldly. He walked off into his office.

Ned ignored the man's reaction and said to Jeff, "Let's go get a drink."

"Sort of early in the afternoon, isn't it?"

"Never too early for good whiskey. And I know a place that has the best in town."

Somehow that claim came as no surprise to Jeff. He cinched the saddle in place, then rigged the harness and bridle over the mare's nose. He took up the reins and led the horse out of the barn. Ned walked alongside him.

"The tavern's not far away. Come on."

Jeff let his cousin lead the way. Although he did not want a drink, playing along with Ned would be the quickest way to find out what he wanted to talk about. Jeff had a feeling he was not going to like what he heard.

Ned's destination was on Liberty Street, one of the two thoroughfares that paralleled the Allegheny River on the northwest side of town. As he and Jeff approached a sturdy-looking building, Ned indicated a signboard hanging from a pole outside the door. The sign showed the silhouette of a bowman with arrow nocked and bowstring pulled taut. The figure was painted a bright emerald green, and under it, in the same shade, were the words Green Archer Tavern.

Something about the name struck Jeff as familiar, but it took him a moment to recall that Eugene Burke, the gambler from the riverboat, had told Jeff that he could be found there. Surely there was only one Green Archer Tavern in Pittsburgh.

"I've heard of this place," Jeff said as he looked up at the sign.

"I haven't been here for a while, but the last time I paid it a visit, it had the finest liquor and the friendliest serving girls in the whole city,"

Ned said. "And that's all a man really needs to be happy, I always say."

Jeff could believe that, as well. Ned lived for the moment and had no concept of happiness that had to be worked for.

At the edge of the cobblestone street in front of the tavern was a hitch rail, and Jeff looped the mare's reins over it and fastened them with a jerk. "This won't take long," he murmured to the animal as he patted her.

"Here we are," Ned said, opening the door and ushering Jeff into the building. When Ned closed the door, the rectangle of afternoon sunlight that had fallen through the opening was cut off, and the interior of the tavern returned to its usual shadowy state.

Even in the early afternoon the shutters over the windows were closed. Lanterns burned at either end of the bar. The floor was sprinkled with sawdust. Thick beams stained a dark brown from clouds of pipe smoke supported the ceiling. Scattered around the room were heavy tables flanked by benches, and on the far side was a huge fireplace topped by a stone mantel. The fireplace was filled with cold ashes now.

A large circular table surrounded by chairs was tucked into a corner near the fireplace, and several men sat around it playing cards. Jeff glanced at the men, thinking that Burke might be one of them, but he did not see any familiar faces.

Women in low-cut dresses carried buckets of

beer and glasses of whiskey on trays to the various tables, about half of which were occupied. A pair of bartenders in waistcoats toiled behind the long bar. The Green Archer was no common dive, Jeff decided as he looked around, but neither was it a high-class establishment. From the looks of things, it catered to men who took their drinking and gambling seriously.

The buzz of conversation in the room diminished slightly when Jeff and Ned entered, but it resumed so quickly that Jeff was unsure he had even heard correctly. Chances were, some of the men in the place had recognized Ned, who seemed to be known all over Pittsburgh, especially in places like this.

Ned steered Jeff toward an empty table and signaled to one of the bartenders by holding up two fingers.

"I don't want whiskey," Jeff said quickly. "Beer will be fine."

"Make it beer instead," Ned called out to the bartender, who nodded.

Jeff and Ned sat opposite each other, and a few moments later a serving girl brought them a bucket of beer and two mugs. Ned flipped her a coin and slapped her on the rump, drawing an outraged gasp and then a giggle from her.

"What did I tell you, cousin?" As she walked away, Ned watched her swaying hips. "Lovely, isn't she?"

Jeff had not paid much attention to the young woman, and if he had, he knew he would not find her nearly as attractive as Melissa. He grunted noncommittally.

"Why did you bring me here, Ned?"

Before answering, Ned dipped both mugs into the bucket, set one in front of Jeff, then took a deep swallow from the other. He wiped foam from his upper lip with the back of his free hand and leaned forward.

"I want to ask you a question, Jeff. It's about your trip to New York."

Jeff waited, and when Ned did not go on, he said, "Well? What about it?"

"Can I go with you?"

The words came from Ned in a rush, as if he'd had to summon up courage to voice it and did not want to wait until his determination bled away. For a change, the cocksure grin that bordered on arrogance was not on his face. Instead, he looked nervous and unsure of himself.

Jeff did not answer right away. He had been halfway expecting the question, but he was not sure what to say. To give himself time, he leaned back on the bench and drank from his mug. The beer was cool and, as Ned had promised, good.

"Why do you want to go to New York?" he finally asked.

"You saw the reason last night—or at least part of it."

"Those men who were after you?"

Ned lowered his eyes. "They're not the only

ones," he said quietly. "There are others I owe money to, and—well, there are some men who seem to be holding grudges against me."

"Now, why would they do that?" Jeff asked coolly. "It wouldn't have anything to do with their wives, would it?"

Ned managed to look proud and a bit ashamed at the same time, no easy task.

"Some women do seem to find my charms very appealing. I keep telling myself I should confine my attentions to the unmarried ones, but—"

"But it's hard for you to keep that vow, isn't it?"

Ned said nothing.

Jeff did not know whether to laugh at his cousin or chide him for his behavior. Ned was a wastrel, no doubt about that; his life was consumed by gambling, women, and liquor. *But he's so damned sincere about it,* Jeff thought.

"I take it you're really in danger," he said.

"As long as I stay in Pittsburgh, I am. But I could make a fresh start in New York—"

"A fresh start on more trouble, you mean."

"No. All that's behind me now, Cousin. No more women and no more gambling. I swear to that."

Jeff did not believe him for a second. Ned might think he meant that pledge, but Jeff knew it would prove impossible to keep. Still, Ned might be good company on the journey.

"What about Uncle Henry and Aunt Dorothy?"

he asked. "How would they feel about your leaving?"

"They might be upset at first, but I'm sure they'd rather I go than stay here and get beaten up in some alley—or shot."

Ned had a point. For his own good he needed to get out of Pittsburgh. Jeff would be doing him a favor by helping him accomplish that, and surely his aunt and uncle would see it the same way, once they thought the situation over. It was a shame Ned had gotten himself into such trouble, but leaving town was probably the best solution.

He and Clay had left Marietta to prevent further bloodshed, Jeff recalled. Ned's problem really was not much different, except that it was of his own making, instead of being caused by some twist of fate.

Jeff was about to tell Ned he could come along to New York when the door of the Green Archer opened and a man entered, paused just inside the door, and peered around as if letting his eyes adjust to the dimness. Then he riveted his attention on the table at which Jeff and Ned were sitting. Quickly he yanked a pistol from his belt, cocked it, and leveled it at them, shouting, "I told you I'd find you, Holt!"

"Damn!" Ned grated. "Hastings!"

"That's right," the man said as he advanced toward the table, covering Jeff and Ned with the pistol. Behind him the other patrons of the tavern scurried for cover. "Fred Hastings. You've good cause to remember me, Holt, but I'll wager you remember my wife Phyllis even better. I thought you'd have the sense to stay away from her after I chased you out of her bed once! Instead, I find out you've still been sneaking around to see her!"

"Blast it, Ned!" Jeff exclaimed. "Have you completely lost your mind?"

"You don't know Phyllis, Jeff. That's really all I can say." He lifted his hands, palms outward, toward the man with the gun. "But I can promise you, Hastings, I won't bother her again. In fact, I'm leaving town. I'll be far away from Pittsburgh."

"You're not leaving," Hastings said grimly.

"Yes, I really am. I'm going to—"

"You're not going anywhere! You're going to be buried here in Pittsburgh, where I can visit your grave and have a good laugh every day, you goddamned—"

Hastings had moved up alongside Ned and Jeff's table. Jeff saw the man's finger tighten on the trigger of the pistol, so he did the only thing he could: He upset the table, shoving it right into Ned and Hastings.

Hastings's flintlock pistol went off with a roar as he fell. Jeff could not tell if the shot hit Ned or not, and he did not take the time to find out. Instead, he jumped up from the bench and vaulted over the table. Hastings was struggling to get out from under it as Jeff landed on him. The man threw up an arm to block Jeff's blow, but he was too late. Jeff's fist caught him in the jaw, driving the back of his head against the sawdust-covered floor. Hastings went limp, his eyes open but glazed.

Jeff whipped around and knelt beside Ned, who was sprawled loosely on the floor. "Ned!" he said urgently. "Are you all right?"

Ned pushed himself into a sitting position and shook his head. "Banged my skull on something when I fell. But I'm not hurt. Hastings's shot missed, thanks to you."

Grasping Ned's upper arm, Jeff said, "Don't thank me. Let's just get the hell out of here."

As they stood up and turned toward the door, it was slammed open, and more men pushed into the tavern.

"There he is!" one of them exclaimed, pointing at Ned. "Where's Hastings?"

"Look there!" another cried, pointing to Hastings, still lying on the floor. "They've killed him!"

"Wait a minute—" Jeff began.

With clenched fists, the men moved forward.

"Fred wanted to do this by himself," one of them said grimly, "but now that you've killed him, Holt, we'll take care of you and your friend."

The odds were bad, but at least the men had not drawn more guns, Jeff thought. It looked as if once again, for the second time in less than twenty-four hours, he and Ned were going to have to fight their way out of trouble.

"Hold it!"

The voice crackled through the air from behind the bar. Jeff glanced in that direction and saw the familiar dapper figure of Eugene Burke. The gambler held a pistol, as did each of the two bartenders, and all three weapons were trained on the group advancing toward Jeff and Ned. The men stopped in their tracks.

Jeff noticed an open door behind the bar and figured that Burke had come through it, probably from a back room. The pistol shot must have drawn his attention.

"There's not going to be any more fighting in my place," the gambler said firmly. "Wrecked furniture costs money to replace, not to mention broken bottles of whiskey. Now, you men turn around and get out of here, and take your sleepy friend with you."

"But they've murdered Fred Hastings!" one of the men protested.

"No, they haven't, you damned fool," Burke said scornfully. "Look at him. He's coming around."

Indeed, Hastings was shaking his head and moaning. Jeff and Ned stepped away from him, and a couple of his friends hurried forward to help him to his feet. Hastings did not seem to know where he was or what was going on, but he was coherent enough to glare at Ned and start cursing.

"Get him out—now!" Burke said.

Hastings did not resist as his friends led him out of the tavern, but several of them cast baleful glances over their shoulders at Ned. Judging from their expressions, Jeff concluded that the matter was not yet settled.

After Hastings and the other men had left, Burke replaced his pistol under his coat, and the bartenders put their weapons under the bar. Burke went around the bar and walked toward Ned and Jeff, and for the first time he acted as if he recognized Jeff.

"I suppose that takes care of half my debt to you, Mr. Holt."

"As far as I'm concerned, the score is even." Jeff extended his hand toward Burke. "I have to admit, I was damned glad to see you. I remembered the name of this place and looked for you when we came in, but I didn't know you owned it."

"Yes, the Green Archer is one of my pride and joys, Beau being the other. He's running for the first time this Saturday. Why don't you come with me to the racecourse?"

"I'd like to," Jeff said, "but we won't be here by then. I'm heading on to New York, and Ned here is going with me. This is my cousin, by the way. Ned Holt. Ned, Mr. Eugene Burke."

"Oh, I know the notorious Ned Holt," Burke said dryly as they shook hands. "When we were coming up the Ohio on that keelboat, I didn't connect his name and yours, I'm afraid."

"I don't owe you any money, do I, Mr. Burke?" Ned asked nervously.

"No, my boy, you don't. You've always taken

care of your losses to my satisfaction. Were those gentlemen after you because of a debt—or a woman?"

Ned looked sheepish. "A woman, I'm afraid."

"A man should never have more than two vices," Burke said. "That's all anyone can manage. You're just trying to do too much, Ned. That's your problem."

Jeff said, "We appreciate the help, Mr. Burke, but we'd better be going now. Ned probably has some getting ready to do if were going to leave Pittsburgh tomorrow."

"I think that's a good idea," Burke agreed. "Sure I can't interest you in another drink to replace that spilled beer? On the house, of course."

"No, thanks," Jeff answered quickly, before Ned could accept the offer. "We've got to get going. Thanks again for the help."

"You're more than welcome. I'm glad you got to see my place—although it wasn't under the best of circumstances."

Jeff took hold of Ned's arm and steered him firmly out of the tavern. They paused just outside to look around in case Hastings and his friends were waiting for them, but they saw no sign of the men. Jeff untied his horse and led it down the street. Ned strode alongside.

"Do things like this happen to you every day, Ned?" Jeff asked.

"Well, not every day. But often enough that I think it's a good idea I'm leaving town."

"I hope your parents understand. But I'm glad you asked me if you could come along."

"Are you sure? I was afraid you'd say no."

"I thought about it," Jeff admitted. "But I don't think I could leave you behind now. I don't want you on my conscience, Ned Holt."

Henry and Dorothy Holt were understandably upset when their youngest son announced his intention of leaving town.

"Was this your idea?" Henry asked Jeff when he learned of Ned's plan.

"Don't blame Jeff, Pa. I was the one who asked him if I could go along. I just think it would be a good idea if I got out of Pittsburgh for a while. You know, until things cool off a bit."

"You mean until people forget about your gambling debts and your philandering?" Henry snapped.

"There's no need for talk like that, Henry," Dorothy said quietly. "We both know Ned has done some things he shouldn't have, but there's no point in dwelling on that now."

"I'm glad you understand, Ma. I'm only doing what I think is best for the whole family."

"And there are the other young men to consider, too," Dorothy went on. "It pains me to say it, Ned, but you haven't been setting a very good example for Edward and Jonathan."

"I know. And I'm sorry about that, too."

Henry looked at Jeff again and said, "Are you sure you want this rascal going along with you?"

242

"I don't mind. I think he'll be safer traveling to New York than he would be if he stayed here, at least for a while."

"How long will the two of you be gone?" Dorothy asked.

"I can't say. It depends on how long it takes me to find Melissa." *And I'll look until I do find her,* Jeff added silently.

"Good luck to you," Henry said as he shook hands with Jeff. "When will you be leaving?"

"First thing in the morning. I've tarried here long enough, not that I haven't enjoyed my stay. But it's time to be moving on."

"I understand." Henry paused, then added, "The young ones, though, they're going to be disappointed."

Jeff had already thought of that. He was not looking forward to their reaction, but the time had come to tell Edward, Susan, and Jonathan of his decision.

The first thing Edward said when Jeff had explained that he was leaving the next morning was, "Take me with you, Jeff. I'm old enough."

"No," Jeff said firmly. "You're still in school, Edward. All of you are. And you're helping Uncle Henry in his business. You're needed here."

"You mean you don't need me?" Edward asked in a voice tinged with bitterness.

"I never said that. But I'm going to be traveling quickly. That's why I decided to go cross-country on horseback, rather than continuing on up the

Allegheny by keelboat. It's going to be a hard trip."

"I'm up to it," Edward said.

"You probably are. But that wouldn't stop me from worrying about you, and that would slow us down. My mind will rest a lot easier knowing that the three of you are in good hands here in Pittsburgh."

"I still don't think it's fair."

"It wasn't fair for my wife to disappear, either," Jeff told him, the words a little sharper than he intended. "Life takes all sorts of turns that aren't fair. All we can do is deal with them the best we can."

Edward nodded gloomily. "I guess you're right. But I don't have to like it."

"I don't like it, either," Susan said. She hugged Jeff tightly. "I was just getting used to you being here, Jeff, and now you're going off for who knows how long. Will we ever see you again?"

"Of course you will," Jeff promised. He returned Susan's hug, then slid an arm around the shoulders of Jonathan, who was struggling manfully not to sniffle. "I'll be back. One of these days, all the Holts will be together again. You have my word on that."

That promise mollified the youngsters a bit, and the family was able to enjoy a last quiet evening together. Ned stayed in, rather than going out one last time. It made no sense, he said, to risk getting killed on the very eve of putting all his troubles behind him.

Jeff made no comment, but he knew all too well that some of Ned's troubles might well follow him to New York. As long as Ned had such a healthy appetite for cards and women and whiskey, there was always going to be trouble in the vicinity.

Before dawn the next morning, Jeff was up, dressed, and going down the hall to Ned's room to shake him awake. Ned groaned and tried to bury his head beneath the pillow, but Jeff grasped his ankle and pulled him out of the bed, dumping him unceremoniously on the floor.

"Time to get stirring," Jeff told him. "I want to put a lot of miles behind us today."

"You're a cruel man, Jefferson Holt. It must be the middle of the night!"

"It'll be daylight by the time we leave. There'll be plenty of light to see the road. Come on."

Still grumbling and muttering, Ned got dressed, then followed Jeff downstairs. Dorothy was already in the kitchen cooking cornbread and ham and eggs for their breakfast.

"I'll send what's left of the cornbread and ham with you to eat on the road," she told them. "That way you'll have a little home cooking to start the journey."

"Thanks, Aunt Dorothy." Jeff sat down at the kitchen table in front of a steaming mug of tea.

"Henry's tending to your horses," Dorothy went on. "He knew you'd want to get a good early start."

She did not look at her son as she served breakfast to the two young men. When all the food was on the table, she said, "I'll go pack your things, Ned," and hurried out of the room before he could respond.

"Your mother's going to miss you," Jeff said into the silence that followed Dorothy's departure.

"I reckon so," Ned said gloomily. "I guess I've been quite a disappointment to her. All my brothers turned out so good, and me . . . Well, you've seen how I turned out."

"You're young yet," Jeff told him. "Things can change."

"Not easily. I figure some people were just born to trouble, and I'm one of them. But I'm going to try hard to make a fresh start in New York."

Jeff admired his cousin's determination while privately doubting Ned's ability to avoid the same sort of problems that had plagued him in Pittsburgh. Maybe Ned would surprise him, he thought.

Henry Holt came in from the small barn behind the house and said, "Your horses are saddled and ready to go, boys. Got your gear together?"

"Ma's tending to mine," Ned replied.

"Won't take me long to pick mine up," Jeff said. "I travel light."

"Comes from living in the mountains, I reckon," Henry mused as he slumped into a chair at the table. "I'd like to see those mountains one of these days."

"You, Pa? I figured you were the kind who'd

be happy staying right here in town the rest of your life."

"There are things you don't know about your old man, son," Henry told him. "Bartholomew and I had a few rip-roaring times of our own, back in the days when everything west of the Alleghenies was dangerous ground. There comes a point in a man's life when he has to put all that behind him—but that doesn't mean he forgets what it feels like to be young and wild and anxious to see what's on the other side of the next hill."

Ned stared at his father as if he was amazed to hear such sentiments coming from Henry Holt's mouth. "You should have told me about all this sooner, Pa. I'd have liked to hear about it."

"You had enough of the wanderlust in you already," Henry said. "You didn't need me filling your head with stories and stoking that fire. Besides, your mother would've taken a broom to me if she'd heard me telling you about those days."

"What days?" Dorothy wanted to know as she came back into the kitchen carrying a pack for Ned.

"Never mind, dear," Henry said smoothly as he rose to his feet. He brushed a kiss across his wife's cheek. "The lads are ready to go. You'd best wake the young ones so they can say good-bye."

This was the part Jeff was dreading. He steeled himself for the tearful farewells, and that was exactly what he got from Susan and Jonathan as the youngsters entered the kitchen still in their nightshirts and hugged him tightly. Edward's eyes were damp, but he managed to keep the tears from spilling as he shook hands with his brother.

"Next time you set off on some adventure, I'm going with you," he declared.

"I'd like that," Jeff said. Then he threw his arms around Edward for a last hug, not caring if he embarrassed his brother.

Meanwhile, Ned was saying his farewells to his parents. Dorothy was the only one crying, and she sobbed unashamedly as she hugged Ned and then Jeff, too. Jeff shook hands with his uncle while Ned said good-bye to his young cousins.

Then it was time to go.

They strode out into the gray dawn, two tall, brawny young men, carrying rifles and pistols and looking almost as grim as if they had been going off to war.

He was going to miss Pittsburgh, Jeff thought as he swung up into the saddle on the bay mare's back. He was going to miss his brothers and sister and his aunt and uncle. The visit had been a good one.

But it had only been a stopover on a much larger journey, and Jeff had known that from the first. It was time now to turn his eyes back to the goal that had led him away from Ohio in the first place.

It was time to go find Melissa.

"Well, that wasn't quite as bad as I expected," Ned said half an hour later as they rode their horses at a fast walk down the eastbound road from Pittsburgh.

Neither of them had spoken since the emotional parting at the Holt house. Now, Ned's flippant tone did little to disguise the fact that he had been shaken by the farewell, too, Jeff thought.

"To change the subject," Jeff said, "Looks like it's going to be a warm day. The sun's only been up a little while, but it's already heating up."

"That's all right with me. I've had enough of the cold, gray winter. Give me some warm sunshine any day—and a pretty girl to share it with me."

Jeff heard the sudden thunder of hooves behind them and jerked his head around. Several riders came racing out of a lane Jeff and Ned had passed a moment earlier. They spurred their horses toward the two Holt cousins, the early morning sun glinting on pistol barrels.

"Hastings and his friends!" Ned said. "Damn it, I didn't think they'd come after us like this!"

"Ride!" Jeff called to him. "If we've got luck on our side, we'll outdistance them!"

As Jeff heeled the bay into a gallop, he slid his pistol out from behind his belt. He had no desire to kill any of their pursuers, but a well-placed shot might discourage them.

Twisting in the saddle as he and Ned pounded along the road, Jeff cocked the pistol and lifted

249

it, then squeezed off a shot. He saw dust spout up in the road in front of the men chasing them. Several of the riders in the lead faltered as they flinched involuntarily from the shot, and that slowed down the others as well.

"Come on!" Jeff shouted to Ned, hunching forward over the neck of the mare and urging it on to greater speed. "We can make it!"

Ned's mount, a big buckskin gelding, ran neck and neck with the mare. Slowly the two of them pulled away from the pursuers.

Shots boomed behind them, and Jeff heard the faint whine of pistol balls passing near his head. He leaned forward even more, to make himself a smaller target. Beside him, Ned turned enough to throw a shot of his own over his shoulder, and then as Ned swiveled back to the front, Jeff saw that he was grinning.

This was all just an adventure to Ned, Jeff realized. And then to his shock he found that he was smiling, too.

He took off his hat, slapped it down on the rump of the mare, and cried out, "Faster, girl, faster!"

The mare surged ahead. Then Ned's mount drew even with the bay mare again, and side by side they plunged down the road, gradually drawing farther and farther away from their pursuers.

The chase was exciting, all right, Jeff admitted to himself. But he hoped fervently that the entire journey to New York was not going to be like this.

Part III

It may not be improper to mention, that the back-woodsmen, as the first emigrants from the east-ward of the Allegheny mountains are called, are very similar in their habits and manners to the aborigines, only perhaps more prodigal and more careless of life. They depend more on hunting than on agriculture, and of course are exposed to all the varieties of climate in the open air. Their cabins are not better than Indian wigwams. They have frequent meetings for the purposes of gambling, fighting and drinking. They make bets to the amount of all they possess. They fight for the most trifling provocations, or even sometimes without any, but merely to try each others prowess, which they are fond of vaunting of. Their hands, teeth, knees, head and feet are their weapons, not only boxing with their fists, (at which they are not to be compared for dexterity, to the lower classes in the seaports of either the United States, or the British islands in Europe) but also tearing, kicking, scratching, biting, gouging each others eyes out by a dexterous use of a thumb and finger, and doing their utmost to kill each other, even when rolling over one another on the ground; which they are permitted to do by the bye-standers, without any interference whatever, until one of the parties gives out, on which they are immediately separated, and if the conqueror seems inclined to follow up his victory without granting quarter, he is generally attacked by a fresh man, and a pitched battle between a single pair often ends in a battle royal, where all present are engaged.

—Fortescue Cuming
"Sketches of a Tour to the Western Country"

XII

Although Clay Holt kept his eyes open as the party he led crossed the valley of the three forks of the Missouri, he did not see any more unusual lights in the foothills of the Rockies main range. As they drew nearer, what some members of the group had taken to be gray, overcast skies above the foothills were revealed to be the mountains themselves, towering seemingly to heaven.

As they paused one noon for a meal of jerky and hardtack, Professor Franklin peered in awe at the peaks that seemed to loom over them, although they were still miles away.

"My God," Franklin said. "They're so . . . majestic. But how in heaven's name will we ever get over them?"

Clay, squatting on his heels nearby, was smoking his pipe.

"It won't be easy, Professor," he said, "but there are ways. Trails and passes known to the Indians—"

"And to men such as yourself," the professor put in.

Clay shrugged. "I know some of them. But I'm mighty glad Shining Moon and Proud Wolf are with us. Any of the trails they haven't been over themselves, they've heard about from other members of their tribe."

Kneeling beside Clay, Shining Moon said to Franklin, "Teton Sioux do not like the high mountains, even though it is told by the old ones how our people came from them a long time ago. The hills and the plains are better. In my lifetime our people have moved slowly eastward and southward, coming down from the mountains in the land called Canada. We were driven to this land by the Blackfoot, the Crow, the Gros Ventre, and the Assinniboin. There is no shame in this, because always we have found better land awaiting us. And one day the Hunkpapa and the other bands of Teton Sioux will turn, and our enemies will regret ever rousing us from our sleep."

Soon the group packed up and resumed the journey, crossing the final and most westerly fork of the Missouri that afternoon. The land gradually sloped upward now, and they entered an area of sparse vegetation. This was the rugged, rocky terrain, dotted with cactus, over which John Colter had run his already legendary race with the Blackfoot. It was hard to imagine any man running naked and barefoot over such ground, let alone being able to outdistance attackers. But as Clay had said, people were able to accomplish amazing things when their lives were at stake.

Late in the afternoon, as they were looking for a place to make camp for the night, Clay's gaze swept across the foothills before them, and he stiffened.

"Professor," he said, turning to Franklin, "you've got a spyglass in that gear of yours, don't you?"

"A telescope? Yes, indeed I do, Mr. Holt. Do you have need of it?"

"Break it out. I want to take a closer look at something."

"What is it?" Shining Moon asked.

"Not sure yet," Clay replied, his attention focused on the hills. "Thought I saw something moving around up there."

What he had seen could have been a family of bears, Clay thought, but the movement that had caught his eye had seemed human. He took the telescope that Franklin handed to him, then opened the instrument to its greatest length and lifted it to his eye. As he peered through the lens, the foothills seemed to leap closer to him. He moved the instrument slowly, scanning from side to side. After a moment he froze and held it steady.

"I thought so," he breathed as he watched a party of half a dozen or so white men outfitted in buckskins move along a ridge. He handed the telescope to Shining Moon and said, "Take a look. Right there above that white outcrop of rock." He pointed at the landmark.

"What is it, Mr. Holt?" Lucy Franklin asked.

"Looks like some other trappers."

Shining Moon handled the spyglass rather awkwardly, but finally she was able to hold it steady and locate the ridge where Clay had spotted the men.

"I see them," she said. "They are white men, that is certain. They have no pelts with them, though."

"Probably out on a scout," Clay said. "They must have a camp somewhere up there. Better let them know we're here." He turned to look at the group and ordered, "Three of you men fire your rifles into the air, one at a time."

Harry Lawton scowled. "Why would we want to do that? Waste of good powder and lead, if you ask me."

Clay suppressed the urge to tell Lawton that no one had asked him.

"Those fellows are right in the direction we're going. Chances are we'll be spending a night or two in the vicinity of their camp. I want them to know we're out here and heading toward them so that they'll be on the lookout for us. Life out here in the mountains is a pretty harsh, lonely existence most of the time, Lawton. Folks like to get together whenever they have the chance, swap some tobacco and a few yarns. You'd know that if you'd spent much time out here."

Lawton flushed angrily at Clay's last comment, but he said nothing. He nodded curtly to his men, and three of them raised their flint-lock rifles. One by one they fired into the arch of sky, and the echoes of the blasts rolled across the hills.

Clay took the spyglass back from Shining Moon and again turned it toward the party of white men. He had located them and steadied the glass when the sounds of the shots must have reached them, for he saw them stop suddenly and lift their heads to listen, then look around. Even through the spyglass, he could discern little about their immediate reaction. But he did see that they turned abruptly and hurried in the direction they had come from, soon disappearing from view over the ridge.

"That's funny," Clay muttered as he lowered the telescope. "They took off like a grizzly was after them."

Lawton spat on a nearby clump of cactus. "Reckon they wasn't as anxious to make friends as you thought, Holt."

"Reckon not," Clay agreed, still puzzled by the men's reaction. But it was really none of his business, he supposed. Out here people did not force their company on others.

He waved his hand forward. "Let's move on. We've still got ground to cover before nightfall."

Simon Brown brought the ax above his head, then sent it slashing down against the log in front of him. The sharp edge of the axhead bit into the wood with a solid thunk. Brown grunted as he levered the ax free and lifted it for another strike.

He was shaping the log to join the others he had cut for the gate in the half-finished stock-

257

ade fence that would soon enclose this outpost in the wilderness. The fort would be the London and Northwestern's first permanent foray into what was widely regarded as American territory.

But not much longer, Brown thought. Before he and his men were done, this entire area would be under British control—specifically, the control of the company and Fletcher McKendrick.

And McKendrick would be very grateful to one Simon Brown for all his help, grateful enough to pay Brown whatever he wanted. When he returned to England, it would be as a wealthy man, and he would spit in the faces of his father and older brother.

Damn the whole system of primogeniture anyway, Brown thought as he sunk the ax into the log once again.

The idea that Gerald was entitled to inherit his father's title and wealth simply because of an accident of birth was ridiculous as far as Simon Brown was concerned. If anyone deserved to become Lord Tarrant, it was he, not that simpering fool Gerald.

It was a shame that the doctor attending his mother at the birth had not been a bit more incompetent. Then he might have mixed up the order in which the twin boys had been born, might have said that Simon had come into this world first at five minutes before midnight on December thirty-first in the Year of Our Lord 1781, instead of five minutes after midnight on the first day of 1782. Twin boys, born in different years. How absurd . . . how unfair.

But Gerald was the eldest, and the law was unequivocal. Someday, everything would go to him, and Simon would be left with nothing. Gerald had made that perfectly clear before Simon left England. Of course, the way Simon had tormented his older but smaller, more fragile brother since they were children might have had something to do with Gerald's lack of generosity, Brown thought now with a cold, wry smile.

The ax bit once more into the log. Gerald had deserved it, Brown told himself. He was weak, so he had deserved the practical jokes, the beatings, the public humiliations, the nights when he had mewled in pain as Simon grunted above him and taught him all the ways a weak boy was meant to be used.

Brown warmed a bit as the memories came back to him. Those had been good days, and their parents—their damned, stupid parents—had never had any idea of what was really going on.

In the end, the system, and Gerald, had won, of course. But only for the time being. One day Simon Brown would return to England to reclaim his true identity. Gerald could have the birthright. Simon would be richer by far, and anyone who said money could not purchase contentment and prestige was a fool indeed.

Brown sleeved away the sweat from his forehead as he worked at shaping the log. The sun was sinking toward the mountain peaks, and night would be falling soon. He rested the ax over his shoulder.

"That's enough, lads," he called to the men working on the fence and the buildings of the fort. "Pack it in for the night."

No one argued with the order to quit for the day. Of course, no one argued with Brown anyway, no matter what his orders were. Word had gotten around quickly about his killing the two thieves in McKendrick's office, and no one wanted to cross him. The men probably regarded him as either a lunatic or the cruelest bloke on the face of the earth—or both. That was fine with Brown.

To keep them off balance, he had set a fairly easy pace so far, both on their trip down from Canada and in the construction of the fort. Keep them guessing, that was his plan; make them wonder when he might explode into violence again. They stayed on their toes that way and did good work.

The fort was located in a small valley in the foothills. This was good beaver country, with many small streams running southeast from the mountains to join the Jefferson River. Brown had men out scouting those creeks at the moment, and as soon as the work on the fort itself was completed, they would begin trapping in earnest. Later, if anyone challenged their right to be there, they would have the fort itself to show as evidence that they had been trapping in the area for quite some time and therefore should have the right to continue.

Brown strode toward the long, low barracks building, the first structure the men had completed. It allowed them to sleep inside while they continued to work on the rest of the outpost, and it provided protection in case of Indian attack. The walls were made of thick logs, well-chinked with mud. In a number of places, loopholes had been cut so that rifles could be fired from inside in case of trouble. There were no windows and only one door. With enough food and water, a small force inside could hold off an army.

Brown had not yet reached the building when he heard someone hailing him. He stopped, turned around, and was surprised and not a little annoyed to see a half-dozen men—the men he had sent out earlier to scout—hurrying toward him. As he walked forward to meet them, Brown saw that several of them looked worried.

"I didn't expect you boys back this soon," he said. "I expected you to camp out tonight and look for more beaver tomorrow."

"Sorry, Mr. Brown," the leader of the scouting party said. He was a slender, sallow man named Dobbs. "We saw something and figured we'd best get on back here and tell you about it. Might be important."

"Well, don't keep it to yourself," Brown said with impatience.

"Yes, sir. There're folks coming this way. White men."

"What?" Brown blinked in surprise. "How many? Two? Three?"

"More like a dozen and a half," Dobbs said.

A puzzled frown appeared on Brown's face. "Where?"

Dobbs waved toward the valley where the three tongues of the Missouri ran.

"Down on the plain," he said, "just this side of that nearest branch of the big river, the one called the Jefferson by the Americans. They spotted us first and fired their rifles."

"They shot at you?" Brown asked in amazement.

Quickly Dobbs said, "Oh, no. They were too far off to be shooting at us. I'd say they were signaling, sir. Trying to get our attention."

"What did you do?"

"We got out of sight as quickly as we could, just like you told us to if we ran into anyone, white or Indian. I'd say that if you want to keep our presence in these mountains a secret, sir, it's too late now."

Brown took a deep breath and tried to calm his raging pulse. Fury welled inside him, a blinding red haze of anger that threatened to overwhelm him. He wanted to lash out at Dobbs, to raise the ax and drive it deep into the man's neck. He could almost feel the satisfying crunch of steel against the man's spine, could almost see Dobbs's head topple off his shoulders to roll away, still in its coonskin cap. That would be an amusing sight indeed, Brown thought.

Gradually he brought his rage under control and said quietly, "How good a look did they get at you?"

"Fairly good, I'd say. I thought I saw the sunlight reflecting off the lens of a spyglass."

"But there was still quite a distance between your party and them, correct?"

"Yes. A couple of miles or more."

"So what they really saw was just a small group of white men moving through the foothills. They don't know whether you were American or English, so they'll assume you were just a party of American trappers."

"I suppose that's the most likely conclusion they could draw," Dobbs said.

"No harm done then." Brown looked around and saw that most of the men from the fort had gathered to listen to the discussion. He lifted his voice and went on, "But all of you men know our orders. We're not to reveal our presence here until the fort is complete and our trapping operation is established. You understand how important this is."

Some of the men muttered their agreement.

"We won't let this incident worry us," Brown continued. "But in the future, should any of you accidentally encounter Americans—and if they're close enough to see that there's something unusual going on—you're to deal with the situation immediately. Don't hesitate. Just kill them."

"Kill them?" one of the men exclaimed. "I say, is that really necessary?"

Brown fixed the man with a cold stare. "It is. And if you don't have the stomach for it, just take them prisoner and bring them here to the fort. I'll take care of the matter personally."

Judging from the uneasy looks on their faces, none of them doubted that for an instant.

Brown shouldered the ax again. Dobbs was a lucky sod, he thought. The man had no idea how close he had come to having his head lopped off. Brown was going to have to give that method of killing some consideration. If there were prisoners to be disposed of, it would be quite effective to use one of the broad-bladed axes and cut their heads off in front of the whole group. That would show his men that he meant business—and it would be quite entertaining at the same time.

Brown turned back toward the barracks. The day's work had given him an appetite that even Dobbs's bad news could not dispel, and he was looking forward to supper.

The botanical expedition camped that evening at the base of the foothills, and Professor Franklin took advantage of the opportunity to gather samples of the prickly pear, which grew in profusion in the area. Proud Wolf accompanied him, holding the box in which the professor placed his specimens. Franklin kept up a running lecture on what he was doing, explaining how scientific analysis would differ from casual observation.

In their quest the two had moved a short way up the gentle slope. Franklin bent over a plant with a large, pale blossom and studied it at length.

"What might this be, what might this be?" he muttered to himself.

"Bitterroot," Proud Wolf said. He bent beside Franklin and reached out to grasp the plant at its base. As he pulled it out of the ground, a small, immature root shaped something like a carrot was revealed.

"Too early to eat this one," Proud Wolf went on, "but later in the year, when they are grown, these roots are peeled and eaten by my people. They are very good."

"I'm, ah, certain they are," Franklin said, regarding the scrawny root somewhat dubiously. "We'll take it with us. Lucy, come over here and make a note of this."

Lucy took her father's journal from one of the packs and carried it to the professor and Proud Wolf, along with pen and ink. She sat on a large rock and, as Franklin described the plant, wrote rapidly in the journal, making a sketch of the bitterroot as well.

Nearby, Rupert von Metz was doing some sketching of his own, using a large pad and a piece of lead from his gear. He roughed in the shape of the mountains that towered above them, then added pockets of light and darkness.

Seeing that the work of setting up camp was proceeding smoothly, Clay strolled over to the young Prussian and looked over his shoulder at the sketch.

"That's mighty good," Clay said after a moment. "Looks just like those mountains."

"It's supposed to," von Metz replied curtly. "Why else would I be doing it?"

"Just trying to give you a compliment, son."

"Oh. My work, which has won the praise of nobility and scholars across Europe, is now facing the critical judgment of an American backwoodsman whose only other exposure to art is the pitiful daubings of savages on rocks and tipis."

Clay's jaw tightened as he struggled to get a grip on his temper. "You're a mighty hard fellow to like, von Metz."

"I have never asked you to like me, Herr Holt. Attaining your friendship is not one of my goals in life."

"I reckon surviving this trip is, though. You'd best think about that." Clay turned and walked away.

The exchange had been loud enough for most of the others to hear, and it contributed to a subtle air of tension that settled over the camp along with dusks shadows. Clay chided himself for almost getting angry with von Metz. By this time he knew perfectly well that the Prussian artist was not going to accept his leadership with anything but ill will. Von Metz's arrogance, and his memory of being humbled by Clay in the competition with gun and blade, would not allow anything else.

But blast it, Clay thought as he sat by the camp-

266

fire with Shining Moon, Proud Wolf, and Aaron, *the boy has talent.* He could draw pictures that did more than just look like their subjects. It was as though von Metz saw not only the outside of things but the inside, too, and a sense of that came through in his work.

Too bad he was such an unpleasant bastard.

That night, as Clay lay rolled in his blankets with Shining Moon, he heard the distant rumble of thunder and noticed a faint flicker of lightning near the mountains. Sometimes there were thunderstorms in the high country, brief but violent, full of pounding rain and crackling lightning. With any luck this one would blow over quickly and miss them. He knew the coming days would be difficult enough as they climbed toward the highest peaks of the Rockies; they did not need extra problems.

Contrary to his hopes, the rain came before morning. At first the drops, although large, were few and far between. Then they increased, and the wind picked up, bringing with it a raw chill as the group got ready to break camp after a cold breakfast. With the rain it was impossible to keep a fire going. As soon as they found a sheltered place, Clay thought, he would call a halt and have a fire built so that they could wait out the storm in relative comfort.

"Let's get moving," Clay called when the group was ready to go. "The sooner we find a good place, the sooner we can get out of this weather."

Everyone in the party looked miserable. Water

trickled from the wide brim of Professor Franklins hat down his back. Lucy had donned an oilcloth slicker, but it kept her only somewhat drier than the others. Rupert von Metz kept up a constant muttering in his native tongue, and Clay suspected he was cursing not only the weather but also everyone involved in this ill-fated expedition, especially him. As for Lawton and the other men, they had gone about the morning's tasks without complaint, but Clay caught more than one of them glaring at him through the drizzle. Even the normally exuberant Proud Wolf was more subdued than usual as he took his place at the rear of the party with Aaron Garwood.

Shining Moon, a blanket thrown over her head and shoulders, moved alongside Clay and said, "This rain is not good. It began in the mountains last night."

"I know," Clay said. "I heard it. But we'll stay out of any gullies that might flood. We'll be all right. You know of any caves around here?"

"Never have I heard any of my people speak of caves in these hills, but that does not mean there are none to be found."

"We're bound to find someplace to get out of the wind and rain. Keep your eyes open."

Clay knew Shining Moon's eyes were even keener than his, and he was glad she possessed such sight. It was hard to see anything through the rain and fog forming in the valleys between the hills. The sun was completely hidden by thick banks of gray and black clouds. The warm spring they had been enjoying seemed to have deserted them.

Throughout the morning the rain continued, sometimes hard in a brief downpour, but mostly in a steady drizzle. The muddy ground made footing difficult and slowed their pace considerably, but Clay did not push the group to hurry. They were cold, wet, and uncomfortable, and he knew he might be faced with a full-fledged mutiny if he rode them too hard.

The beaver pelts got soaked again, and as they did, their weight increased until Clay considered abandoning them. But he hated the idea of giving them up; he and his companions had worked hard for the plews, and there was a chance the expedition might run into other trappers who would be willing to take the furs and split the profits. It would have to be someone Clay knew and trusted, however, before he would be willing to let him hold the money until he and the others got back from the Pacific coast, a year or more in the future.

Still he found no suitable shelter. The group had passed a few overhangs that looked promising, but the wind was swirling, and the formations would not have provided enough cover for a campfire. They had to have a fire, Clay had decided, not only for warmth and comfort but also to ease their minds. The professor, Lucy, and von Metz had to be frightened as well as uncomfortable, and a crackling fire to huddle next

to always made one feel more secure and less inclined to panic. The Indians who had made their
home in these mountains since time immemorial
knew the truth of that: Give a person a nice snug
cave and a circle of flame, and the world did not
look nearly as bad as it might otherwise.

Suddenly the wind and rain lashed at them even
harder than before. Clay bent forward against its
force and heard a whimpering cry behind him.
He looked over his shoulder to see Professor
Franklin comforting Lucy, who was stumbling
along beside him. Franklin had one arm around
his daughter's waist and with his other hand
held his hat on his head. In the dim, gray light
their faces looked pale and haggard. Von Metz
was behind them, equally unsteady on his feet.

Clay felt his wife's hand on his arm. "Clay,
we must find some shelter soon. These people
cannot go on."

"I know. Let's move over by that stand of pine
and let them rest for a few minutes. I want to
talk to Proud Wolf, too. Nobody's going to be
coming up on our back trail in this kind of
weather, so I think I'll send him ahead to scout."

Shining Moon agreed with his idea. As she
walked along, her moccasins slipped in the
mud, and Clay put his hand under her elbow
to steady her.

They veered toward the trees, a sparse clump
of pine that would offer some shelter from the
rain but not much. The narrow trunks would
not cut the wind at all. Normally, Clay would

270

have avoided trees during a storm to lessen the chance of being struck by lightning, but other than the faint flickering in the sky and the distant rumbling the night before, no lightning had accompanied this storm. It was just wind and rain—but that was enough.

As the group huddled under the trees, Clay motioned Proud Wolf over to him and asked, "You feel up to going on ahead and taking a look around, maybe finding us a spot where we can get out of this mess?"

"I will go," Proud Wolf said. He loped away with a seemingly tireless gait and within moments had disappeared into the thick curtain of rain.

Clay lowered his bundle of pelts to the ground and told the other men carrying furs to do the same. Those with the lighter packs of supplies kept them on their backs. Clay leaned against the trunk of a pine and closed his eyes. His body had been hardened by the rugged existence he had led for the past five years, but he was no more immune to weariness than anyone else. He was tired, tired of slogging through the mud, tired of stumbling into trouble every time he turned around, tired of people depending on him. . . .

Shining Moon snuggled against him and rested her head on his shoulder. Her presence instantly drove away the gloomy thoughts. Life had its problems, but it also had its rewards, and the feel of his woman in his arms was one of the best rewards of all. Clay put an arm around her shoulders and drew her more tightly to him.

An ominous rumbling sound came from somewhere above them.

Rupert von Metz lifted his head sharply and asked, "What is that?"

"It sounds like—like . . ." Frowning, Professor Franklin groped for an explanation.

Clay knew what it was. "An avalanche," he said grimly, stepping away from Shining Moon and into the rain to peer up at the foothills and mountains. The rain pelted his face and made him feel almost as if he were underwater, in danger of drowning. He controlled his faint sense of panic and searched for the source of the steadily increasing roar.

Shining Moon gripped his arm tightly and said, "The mountains are falling."

Clay shook his head. "Just a few tons of rock and mud. The mud gave way under all this rain."

"We must get out of here," von Metz said wildly. "There is an avalanche coming, and you stand here calmly discussing it! We must run!" His voice trembled; he was on the verge of losing control.

"Can you see where it's going, von Metz?" Clay asked sharply. When the Prussian made no reply, Clay raised his voice to be heard above the thunderous rumble. "I can't, either. We might run right into its path if we leave here. At least these trees offer us some protection."

"Proud Wolf!" Shining Moon suddenly exclaimed. "He is out there somewhere!"

Clay caught her arm to prevent her from running out of the clump of trees. "There's nothing we can do to help Proud Wolf now. He's mighty fast on his feet, Shining Moon. If anybody can dodge an avalanche, it's him."

The noise was incredibly loud by now, and Clay had to shout to make himself heard. He had seen giant waterfalls, had heard thunder so deafening that it shook the very earth—but this sound was worse.

"Get behind the trees!" he bellowed, motioning for the others to move. If the pines were directly in the path of the avalanche, they would be swept away like everything else. However, if the main body of the slide passed on one side or the other, so that the trees were on the fringes of the disaster, they might provide enough protection for the explorers to survive. It was their only chance.

Suddenly, just when it would have seemed impossible, the noise grew even louder, like giant fists slamming against the ears of the terrified group huddled among the trees. Clay wrapped his arms around Shining Moon and leaned his shoulder hard against the trunk of a pine, bracing himself as best he could.

Then, looming up from the rain and fog like a monstrous beast, a gray wall of mud and rock appeared, dotted with trees it had uprooted higher in the foothills. The avalanche surged toward them like a wave. Several of the men screamed in sheer terror, broke away from the trees, and ran down the slope.

"Come back, you damned fools!" Clay called after them, but even though he was shouting at the top of his lungs, his words were lost, swallowed up by the roar of the slide.

Eyes wide, heart pounding, Clay watched as the bulging forefront of the avalanche swelled closer and closer—and then passed to the right. Rocks and clumps of mud pounded the grove of trees. Everyone was screaming now, Clay supposed—he knew he was—but nothing could be heard except the tumult of the avalanche. He pressed Shining Moon harder against the tree, shielding her with his body. He shuddered as rocks thudded against him, most of them small but packing significant impact. The tree shivered as it took the brunt of the blows. Mud swept around Clay's feet and tried to tug him away from Shining Moon, but he held on for all he was worth. The others were doing the same, using the trees for protection from the rocks and as anchors to keep from being swept away.

Clay twisted his head and saw the men who had made the fatal mistake of trying to outrun the avalanche. The leading edge of the slide was just now catching up to them, and as he watched, they disappeared into the boiling gray madness. He thought he heard their death shrieks, but he knew that had to be his imagination.

The mud was up to his knees now, pulling

at him like giant hands. This time he really did hear a scream and jerked around to see Lucy Franklin being torn from her father's grip by the swirling mud. She started to fall, her face frozen in terror.

But before she could disappear under the surface of the mud, Aaron Garwood was there beside her, grabbing one of her flailing arms to hold her up. At the same time, Professor Franklin caught the back of Aaron's coat. The tough buckskin held without tearing, and together Franklin and Aaron were able to pull Lucy back to safety.

Then the air seemed clearer, the rumble of the avalanche having subsided slightly. Clay let himself hope that the worst of it was over. He leaned to the side to peer past the tree trunk, hoping he could see the end of the slide.

What he saw was a huge boulder weighing at least several tons bounding down the hillside toward them like a pebble kicked by a little boy.

And it was coming straight at the tree where he and Shining Moon were crouched.

For a split second the thought flashed through Clays mind that it would be ludicrous for him to be killed by something as unpredictable as an avalanche after all the other dangers he had survived. Then he was reacting instead of thinking. He flung Shining Moon to the side, the corded muscles of his arms and shoulders bunching under the buckskin shirt as he threw her to relative safety. He saw the flow of mud pull at her, spin her around; then her hands caught the rough bark of another tree trunk, and she held fast to it. Clay launched himself after her as the boulder slammed into the tree where he had been huddled an instant earlier. The pine was uprooted, plucked from the ground like the bitterroot plant the professor had found earlier. It spun crazily through the air.

Clay felt something hit the back of his shoulders just below his neck. He stumbled, the impact throwing him forward. Stunned by the blow, his balance deserting him, he fell. Cold gray mud slapped him in the face—

Then it closed in around him, drawing him deeper and deeper. He let himself go, surrendering to the inexorable pull as the grayness around him turned to black.

XIII

He is truly a philosopher, contrasting his former with his present situation, with much good humour and pleasantry.

—Fortescue Cuming
"Sketches of a Tour to the Western Country"

Cantering his horse along the New Jersey palisades, Jeff Holt drew rein and looked across the

Hudson River at New York City. He had thought Pittsburgh was impressive, but the Pennsylvania city paled when compared to the sprawling settlement spread out before him. The entire lower end of the island of Manhattan was crowded with buildings and people, and houses were scattered over the rest of it. A ferry loaded with travelers, horses, mules, wagons, and carriages traveled on the Hudson River, heading for the distant city.

Beside Jeff, Ned Holt let out a low whistle of amazement. "Did you ever see anything like it, Cousin?"

"No," Jeff admitted. "I never have."

During the past two months the young men had followed the Allegheny River out of Pennsylvania into New York, then headed east through the Finger Lakes region. It was beautiful country, full of wooded hills and valleys and deep, sparkling lakes. The roads were generally good, and there were quite a few farms in the area. An air of tranquillity hung over the entire region, and it was difficult to believe that less than fifty years before, smoke from the burning cabins of settlers had filled the sky as the Mohawk Indians fought a bloody, futile war to stem the tide of white expansion.

Jeff and Ned had taken their time on their journey. In each settlement they had come to, Jeff had questioned everyone he could find, hoping that someone had heard of the Merrivale family or knew of Melissa's whereabouts. He placed advertisements in newspapers, offering rewards to anyone who could furnish the information he needed. He had also checked the records of property transactions at each county courthouse, hoping to find some mention of Charles Merrivales having bought land.

They angled northeast through Syracuse and Utica, continuing their search as they worked their way farther north into the Adirondacks. Everywhere it was the same story: people were hospitable and wanted to help, but no one Jeff encountered knew anything about Melissa or had even heard of the Merrivales. Finally he and Ned had turned south again and headed down the Hudson River Valley, where again Jeff was struck by the beauty of the land.

Ned had enjoyed the journey, taking in the sights with wide, eager eyes. Once they had left Pittsburgh—and escaped from Ned's vengeful enemies—the young man had relaxed. He helped Jeff in his quest as much as possible; whenever they entered a community, they split up to cover more ground, and if Ned had any doubts about the potential for the success of their mission, he kept them to himself.

Jeff was grateful for that; he was plagued with enough doubts of his own. The task he had set for himself was impossible, he realized more with each passing day. The only way he would ever find Melissa was by sheer luck. He had to accept the possibility that he might never see her again.

But he was not yet ready to give up. Across the river was the most populous city not only in the state but also in the nation. More than sixty thousand people made their home in New York —and Jeff would talk to each and every one of them if he had to.

"We have relatives over there, you know," Ned said as they looked across the river at the city.

"No, I didn't," Jeff replied, surprised.

"We used to get letters from a cousin Irene. She was Pa's cousin, I think, which would make her your father's cousin, too."

"We were out of touch with everyone in the family except your folks in Pittsburgh," Jeff said. "I never heard anything about a cousin Irene."

"Ma and Pa haven't received a letter from her in several years, as well as I can remember. But she ought to be alive still. We could look her up."

"I suppose. New York's a big place, and it wouldn't hurt to have someone we know help us find our way around. Do you have any idea how we could locate her?"

Ned's forehead furrowed in concentration as he tried to cull details from his memory.

"Let me see. . . . She was married to a man named Marshall or Marsh or something like that—March, that was it! Her name was Irene March. Seems to me her husband was a ship-wright."

"If we ask around at the docks, we can probably find him. If the family is still here." Jeff heeled his horse into motion. "Come on. Let's see about getting a ride on that ferry."

They rode along the heights until they found

a path that led down to the shore. The ferry was already making the return trip, and by the time they reached the landing, it had tied up at the small loading pier. More passengers were boarding.

Jeff paid for both of them, handing a silver dollar to the man collecting the fares. He and Ned led their horses on board the big bargelike ferry and found a place to stand near the railing around the edge.

Jeff felt a tingle of nervousness. It was partially because so many people surrounded him, and he was not used to being crowded. But his anxiety was even greater because New York City represented perhaps his last chance to find Melissa, and he knew it.

When the boat was full, it left the landing and made its way across the river, its steam engine thumping and roaring. The crossing took less time than Jeff had expected.

The boat docked at another pier on the western shore of the island. The main waterfront area was to the south, along the lower tip of the city. Jeff and Ned could see the tall masts of the many ships anchored there, showing plainly over the roofs of the buildings along Water Street and Wall Street. That was probably where they would find this man March whom Ned had mentioned.

Before they began checking into that, however, Jeff wanted to do something else. As they led their horses off the ferry, he spotted a sign that read *New York Weekly Journal* on a nearby building. He pointed it out to Ned.

"Let's stop there first. I want to place an advertisement."

"Might as well," Ned replied. "Can't hurt, can it?"

Jeff did not answer. They both knew all too well what a long shot it would be if someone saw the notice about Melissa and her family and could actually provide information about them. But Jeff was not ready to give up—not yet.

They entered the building and found a small reception area separated from the main part of the room by a waist-high railing. On the other side of the railing, the chamber was filled with bulky machinery, rolls of paper, and jars of ink. Jeff knew that the machine, which looked vaguely intimidating to him, had to be a printing press, but he had no idea how it worked.

Also beyond the railing was a man sitting on a chair tipped back so that his feet could rest on the scarred surface of an old desk. He had a magazine propped open on his legs and was scowling as he stared at its pages. Jeff read the name on the magazine, *Salmagundi,* and that made as little sense to him as the intricate arrangement of gears, levers, and plates that formed the printing press.

The man looked up, saw Jeff and Ned standing on the other side of the railing, and closed the magazine, then tossed it onto the desk.

"Scandalous." He grunted. "I don't know why people read such drivel." He lowered his feet to the floor, then put his hands on his knees, pushed himself upright, and said, "Can I help you gentlemen?"

"I want to put a notice in your paper," Jeff said. "When will the next edition come out?"

"Three days from now. We're a weekly, you know. Is that soon enough for you?"

"I suppose it'll have to be. I want the notice to request that anyone having knowledge of a young lady named Mrs. Melissa Holt or her parents, Mr. and Mrs. Charles Merrivale, should please contact me as soon as possible, in care of this newspaper. My name is Jefferson Holt."

The newspaper man raised his eyebrows. "You're the husband of the lady in question, I take it?"

"That's right."

"Ran away from you, did she?" The question was accompanied by a cynical expression.

Jeff wanted to lunge across the railing and knock the expression off the man's face, but he controlled the impulse.

"That's not important to you. What matters is that I intend to pay you whatever your going rate is for the space required to print that announcement."

"Of course." The mention of payment sobered the man. "I'll write up the notice and have it in the next edition. Let me figure out how much it will cost."

Ned patted the stock of the long rifle cradled in his arms. "Make sure you figure correctly, friend."

The newspaper man swallowed, blinked, and named a price that sounded fair to Jeff considering that the *New York Weekly Journal* was probably the largest paper in which he had yet placed a notice. He held a pair of coins over the railing, and the man stepped forward quickly to take them.

Now that the arrangement was completed, the man relaxed a bit and said, "If you want to reach a different group of readers, you might consider placing a notice in that magazine I was looking at. It doesn't have nearly as large a circulation as the newspaper, of course, but I suppose it's read by quite a few people."

"I thought you said it was scandalous," Jeff said.

"Oh, it is. But I know the man who puts it out. In fact, I do his printing for him." The newspaper man waved toward the building's grimy front window. "I see him coming right now. That's what led me to suggest you might want to place a notice in it."

Intrigued, Jeff turned and looked out the window to see a well-dressed man walking down the sidewalk toward the newspaper office. He wore a beaver hat, a silk shirt with an elegant cravat, a tailcoat, and high black boots over tight, fawn-colored breeches. His handsome features and air of elegance gave him the look of a fop, but there was genuine warmth on his face as he entered the office.

"Good morning, Collins," he said to the publisher, then turned to look at Jeff and Ned. "What have we here? Some gentlemen newly arrived from the wild frontier, by the looks of them."

Jeff was not sure whether to bristle at the man's tone or not. He nodded curtly to the newcomer.

"Washington Irving." The man smiled at Jeff and Ned as he held out his hand. "I'm glad to meet you."

Jeff shook hands with him and said, "I'm Jeff Holt, and this is my cousin Ned Holt."

"Glad to meet you, Mr. Holt, and you, too, Mr. Holt," Washington Irving said. "What brings you to the land of Knickerbocker?"

Warming to the man, Jeff said, "I'm looking for my wife, Mr. Irving. I just arranged to have a notice placed in Mr. Collins's newspaper asking for information about her. He suggested that I might advertise in your magazine, as well."

"We'd be glad to have your business, of course," Irving replied in a concerned tone. "And I'm sorry to hear that youve been separated from your wife, Mr. Holt. Was the separation . . . involuntary?"

"If you mean did she run away from me, the answer is no," Jeff said emphatically. "Melissa's father is the kind of man who likes to get his own way. When he and Melissa's mother left Ohio, he talked Melissa into going east with them, even though she and I were already married."

"Where were you at the time, Mr. Holt? I realize this is not really any of my business, but—"

"That's all right. I don't mind telling you. I was trapping furs in the Rockies with my brother."

"Really!" Irving exclaimed. "How fascinating. I must speak to you at length about this, Mr. Holt. For now, however, if you'll tell me how you want your notice to read, I'll see about getting it in the next issue of *Salmagundi.*"

Jeff repeated the same information he had given Collins, then said, "If you could word the notice so that anyone responding to it can get in touch with the *Salmagundi,* I'll check with you from time to time to see if anyone has answered."

"That'll be fine with me," Washington Irving agreed.

"Now, we've got to get down to the docks and look up another cousin of ours. He's supposed to be a shipwright, or at least he has something to do with boats."

"What's his name?" Irving asked. "Perhaps Collins or I know him."

Jeff looked at Ned, who said, "I'm pretty sure his last name is March."

"Not Lemuel March?" Washington Irving's eyebrows lifted in surprise.

"That's it, all right!" Ned said. "I remember now, Lemuel was his first name."

Collins and Washington Irving exchanged a look, and it was obvious to Jeff that both recognized the name.

Collins said, "You go down to the Tontine Coffee House, at the corner of Wall Street and Water Street. You'll either find March or someone who can tell you where he is."

"Thanks." Jeff shifted his rifle. "Let's go, Ned."

When they were on the street again, Ned said, "Did you see that look they gave us when we mentioned March?"

"Yes, I did. Reckon they've heard of him, all right. I wonder what it's about."

"We'll find out in that coffeehouse they mentioned, I suppose." Ned looked at the hustle and bustle all around them as they walked along the street toward the waterfront, and his gaze was eager and excited. Jeff wished he could share his cousin's anticipation.

The Tontine Coffee House was located at the angle where Wall and Water streets came together a block from the harbor. It was an impressive three-story building of brick and stone and mortar, with a flag flying from a pole on its roof and a railed wooden porch along the front of the building. The first floor was decorated with brick columns and arched windows, while the upper stories were less fancy. A dozen or more well-dressed men stood on the porch, sipping coffee from cups and talking animatedly. From the look of them, they were men of commerce—merchants, brokers, bankers, and traders—and successful ones at that.

The hum of conversation lessened as Jeff and Ned approached the steps leading to the porch and climbed them. Jeff in his buckskin and homespun and Ned in his rough store-bought clothing were out of place here, and naturally they attracted some attention. The weapons they carried made them stand out even more. None of the coffeehouse's patrons seemed to be armed. They were the kind to settle disputes with words and lawyers and money, not fists or knives or guns.

Jeff kept his face and voice civil as he said into the lull, "I'm looking for a man named Lemuel March."

That made them stare even more, and Jeff felt his jaw tighten in anger. Just because he was not from their city, they were regarding him as though he were some sort of lunatic.

He forced himself to go on politely, "I believe this man March has something to do with boats."

That drew a laugh, and a tall, slender man strode forward from the rear of the group. He had gray hair and a weathered face, and although he carried himself with the grace of a younger man, he had to be in his middle to late forties. He stepped in front of Jeff and Ned.

"So this fellow has something to do with boats, eh?" the man said. "Why are you looking for Lemuel March?"

Jeff returned the level stare. Although the man was dressed as expensively and elegantly as the others, something about him was different, a sense of personal strength that the rest of them did not possess.

"Not that it's any of your business," Jeff said coolly, "but Lemuel March is married to my father's cousin."

"My God, you're a Holt!" the man exclaimed. He looked at Ned and added, "And so are you. I should have known."

Jeff's eyes narrowed in surprise. "That's right. I'm Jefferson Holt from Ohio and more recently the Rocky Mountains. This is Ned Holt from Pittsburgh. And if you don't mind my asking, sir—who the hell are you?"

A grin spread across the man's face as he stuck out his right hand.

"I'm Lemuel March, of course. And I do have something to do with boats, as you put it." He jerked the thumb of his left hand over his shoulder, toward the waterfront. "I own about six of them back yonder."

Now it was Jeff and Ned who looked surprised. Jeff recovered first and shook hands with Lemuel March.

"It's good to meet you, sir. We meant no offense—"

March waved off the apology. "None taken, I promise you. It's been awhile since my wife has been in touch with either of your families. Come along and let me get you some coffee. You'll have to tell me all about your reasons for coming to New York."

Now that Jeff and Ned had been welcomed by March, the other men on the porch of the coffeehouse went back to their conversations.

Grateful that he and Ned were no longer being gawked at, Jeff accepted a cup of the strong black coffee from a waiter summoned by March. Then Jeff explained the errand that had brought them to New York City. March listened intently as Jeff told him about the disappearance of Melissa and her parents from Ohio.

"You don't know for certain that they came here to New York, do you?" March asked when Jeff had concluded the tale.

"No, sir, I don't. And I've found no sign of them so far. But I can't give up."

"No, no, of course not," March agreed. "I have business connections not only here in the city but throughout the state. I'll be glad to pass the word that you're looking for your wife and try to help you locate her. If this man Merrivale has gone into business anywhere in the Northeast, we should be able to find him."

A surge of gratitude went through Jeff. For too long, Ned had been his only ally in his search. Now, with an influential man like Lemuel March on his side, perhaps he really did have a chance of locating Melissa.

"I'm sorry I had the mistaken impression that you were a shipwright," Jeff told the older man.

"I'm to blame for that," Ned said. "All I remembered for sure from Cousin Irene's letters was that you had something to do with boats, Mr. March. I never figured you owned them."

"That's all right, Ned," March said. "And both of you call me Lemuel. I don't stand on ceremony where family is concerned. Irene's going to be very happy to see the both of you. She loves to have visitors."

"Wait a minute," Jeff said. "We don't want to inconvenience you—"

"Nonsense. We have plenty of room, so both of you will stay with us while you're here in New York. Agreed?"

Jeff and Ned looked at each other, and Jeff said, "We'd be happy to. We've seen enough rented rooms in taverns and roadhouses over the past couple of months, haven't we, Ned?"

"Amen to that," Ned said fervently. "And slept out under the stars enough, too, although that never seemed to bother you much, Jeff."

"I got used to it in the mountains."

Lemuel said, "I want to hear all about that. You must have had quite an amazing experience out there. But I can wait until we're home so that you won't have to repeat everything for Irene and the girls. I'm sure they'll be interested, too."

"The girls?" Ned said.

"Our daughters," Lemuel explained. "Irene and I have three of them, you know." He clapped one hand on Jeff's shoulder and the other on Ned's. "I hope you lads enjoy being surrounded by beautiful females, because the March household is full of them!"

The March house was a two-story frame structure, its walls whitewashed and set off by trim painted a pleasant shade of green. It was about half a mile north of the Tontine Coffee House, facing a dirt street called Broadway that ran almost the length of Manhattan Island. Along the street were flagstone sidewalks, and the houses that lined it were set behind narrow yards that barely had room for a tree or two. The March house had a small brick entrance porch, little more than a pair of steps, built onto the front of it. The windows were narrow, and the shutters were thrown open on this warm day. Lemuel had insisted on driving Jeff and Ned in his carriage, which he handled himself. Their mounts were tied behind the vehicle.

Lemuel brought the team of matched black horses to a stop in front of the house and lithely stepped down. He had a hint of a rolling gait in his walk as he led Jeff and Ned up to the house, and that was enough to tell Jeff that at one time Lemuel had been a sailor. Lemuel ushered them inside, then removed the beaver hat he had reclaimed from inside the coffeehouse before leaving. He tossed it on a small table in the foyer.

"Irene! Girls!" he called out. "Come down here. We have company!"

A moment later an attractive blond woman appeared at the top of the stairs.

"Is that you, Lemuel?" she asked. "What are you shouting about?" Then, catching sight of the two visitors, she smoothed her dress and petticoats and started down the stairs. As she drew nearer, Jeff could see a few strands of silver among the blond hair, but her lovely features were unlined, and she looked youthful.

When she reached the bottom of the stairs, she smiled at Jeff and Ned and said, "Good afternoon, gentlemen." If she was surprised by her husband's bringing home two strangers, she did not show it.

"Do you know who these two lads are, Irene?"

As she glanced at Lemuel, Jeff detected a faint flicker of annoyance in her eyes, but the smile on her face did not budge.

"You know I don't, dear," she said. "Why don't you introduce them to me?"

"Of course. This is one of your cousins, Jefferson Holt, and another cousin, Ned Holt."

Irene March's green eyes opened wider when she heard the names.

"Ned?" she repeated. "You're Henry and Dorothy's youngest boy?"

"That's right, ma'am," Ned said.

Without hesitation Irene threw her arms around Ned and hugged him.

"Heavens, I haven't seen you in years!" she exclaimed. "And you've grown so much! Why, the last time I saw you . . . well, you don't even remember it, you were so small."

"I'm afraid I don't," Ned admitted.

Irene turned to Jeff. "And you're Jefferson? I'm afraid I don't remember you. You're not one of Ned's older brothers, are you?"

"No, ma'am. My parents were Bartholomew and Norah Holt."

Irene's mouth opened slightly as she stared at Jeff.

"Bartholomew and Norah," she said, her voice little more than a whisper. "I haven't seen Bartholomew since I was a little girl, but I knew he had married and had children. How is your father?"

"He's been dead for a couple of years," Jeff told her. "My mother, too."

"Oh, I'm so sorry! I had no idea—"

"It's all right," Jeff assured her. "I know you didn't. Our families have been out of touch for a long time."

"It's hard to keep track of everyone," Lemuel put in. "The country's so large, and the mail service isn't what it should be. But the two of you are here now, and that's what matters."

From the top of the stairs, a clear young voice asked, "What's going on down there? What's all the commotion?"

Jeff looked up as three young women started down the stairs with a clatter of heels. They came in descending order, from oldest to youngest, excited and eager to see who the visitors were.

The first one was a brunette, eighteen or nineteen years old, with a slender figure and brown eyes that studied Jeff and Ned with frank curiosity. Behind her was a blond like Irene, perhaps seventeen, whose already lush beauty foretold that she was going to be spectacularly lovely in a few years. Bringing up the rear, but not particularly liking it, to judge from the expression on her lightly freckled face, was a girl of fifteen or sixteen with green eyes and strawberry blond hair, which she pushed back out of her elfin face as she reached the bottom of the stairs. She gaped up at Jeff and Ned, unconcerned that she was staring.

"Girls," Lemuel March said, "these are your cousins, Jeff and Ned Holt."

Irene said, "Allow me to present my daughters. This is Rachel." She touched the brunette's shoulder. "And Jeanne." That was the lovely young blond. "And Barbara." Irene slid her arm around the shoulders of the coltish fifteen-year-old.

Rachel March stepped forward, held out her hand to Jeff, and in a husky voice said, "Hello."

"It's an honor to meet you, Miss March." Jeff took her hand awkwardly, unaccustomed to shaking with women.

"No need to be so formal, Cousin Jeff," Jeanne said brightly, bumping her older sister aside. "We're related, after all." She threw her arms around him and hugged him.

Jeff blinked in surprise as he found his arms full of soft, warm young woman. He managed to slip out of the embrace and hoped he did not offend Jeanne by doing so. She did not seem to mind because she immediately turned to Ned and repeated the greeting. Ned did not release her so quickly, Jeff noticed. Cousin or no cousin, Ned was in no hurry to let go of a pretty girl.

Barbara offered a shy nod and a timid greeting, to which he said, "Hello, Barbara. It's very nice to meet you."

"I told you I had a houseful of pretty women," Lemuel said proudly. "Well, come on in and sit down, you two. I'll have one of the servants take the carriage and your horses to the stable out back."

Lemuel disappeared toward the rear of the house while Irene led Jeff and Ned into a luxuriously appointed parlor. The two young men settled down on a long sofa with elaborately carved legs.

"That's a Duncan Phyfe, you know," Jeanne said.

"Uh, no," Jeff said. "Don't reckon I know this Phyfe fella."

"No, I mean he made the sofa," Jeanne said with a laugh. "He's becoming quite famous."

"Oh." Jeff shifted uncomfortably on the sofa. It might be pretty, but it wasn't much for sitting on. He would have preferred a log bench.

Irene sat in an armchair and gestured for her daughters to take seats on the floor at her feet. The girls lowered themselves gracefully to the large hooked rug on which the armchair sat.

"What brings the two of you to New York? Have you come for a visit?" Irene asked.

"No, ma'am. We're looking for someone. My wife."

Jeff thought Jeanne looked a little disappointed at the revelation that he was married.

Rachel leaned forward a bit and asked, "What about you, Ned?"

"Oh, I don't have a wife," he replied, grinning. "What I mean to say is that I'm helping Jeff. We hooked up in Pittsburgh."

Lemuel entered the room then and went to stand behind his wife's chair, his hands resting on her shoulders.

"Tell them the story, Jeff. I'm sure Irene and the girls will agree that we should help you all we can."

For the next fifteen minutes, Jeff gave Irene March and her daughters one version of the story involving himself and Melissa, Melissa's parents, and his brother Clay and the feud with the Garwoods, omitting the more lurid details so that he would not shock the young women. They all appeared to sympathize, especially when Jeff reached the part of the story concerning his return to Marietta only to find that Melissa was gone.

"That's dreadful, Jeff," Irene murmured when he was finished. "Lemuel is right. If there's anything we can do to help you in your search, we'll be glad to do it."

"They're going to be staying here with us while they're in New York," Lemuel said. "We've already agreed on that, haven't we, lads?"

"If that's all right with Mrs. March, sir," Jeff said.

"Of course it is," Irene said without hesitation. "We have more than enough room. If you want to bring in your things, I'll have the girls show you where to put them."

Jeff looked down at the possibles bag slung over his shoulder and then at the pack Ned had placed at his feet.

"I reckon we're carrying all our gear," he said. "We've been moving around pretty often, so we don't have much with us."

"That's fine," Lemuel said. "Rachel, take the boys upstairs and show them to the guest room."

"Yes, Father," Rachel replied as she got to her feet.

Jeanne and Barbara stood up, too, and Jeanne said quickly, "I could show them."

"No, dear, I think Rachel should take care of that," Irene said firmly, ignoring the look of disappointment on her middle daughter's face. "You and Barbara can go out to the kitchen and get started on dinner."

"But, Mother—" Jeanne began, stopping when she saw her father's face.

Jeff and Ned both looked down at the floor to hide their amused expressions as they stood and followed Rachel from the parlor. She took them up the stairs and led them along a corridor to a large bedchamber at the back of the house. A window overlooked the rear yard and the small stable where the carriage and its team were kept. A four-poster, a wardrobe, a dressing table, and two chairs completed the room's furnishings, which Jeff thought looked quite comfortable. He and Ned had been lucky to find such a place to stay.

If only that same luck would rub off on his search for Melissa. . . .

"If you need anything, let one of us know," Rachel said. She pushed back her long brown hair and looked at them solemnly, which seemed to be her normal expression. "I hope you find your wife, Jeff."

"So do I," he said. "Thank you, Rachel. We appreciate everything."

"Dinner will be in about an hour." With that, Rachel left the room and shut the door behind her.

Ned let out a long, low whistle. "Lord, did you ever see such a lovely crop of young ladies!"

"They're your cousins, Ned," Jeff pointed out.

"Distant cousins," Ned countered. "I think I'm going to like it here."

Jeff closed his eyes for a moment and shuddered, remembering Pittsburgh. Ned's liking it here was exactly what he was afraid of.

XIV

"Clay!" Shining Moon screamed as she saw her husband struck down from behind by a branch as the tree was uprooted and smashed aside by the plummeting boulder. Clay went down hard, landing face first in the torrent of mud and debris sweeping down the hillside.

Shining Moon did not hesitate. She abandoned her position of relative safety and lunged after Clay, reaching for the buckskin shirt he wore. Stumbling and staggering as the mud pulled at her, she managed to grab him and hang on tightly.

"Help me!" she cried as she tried to lift him. "Someone help me!"

She looked around frantically. Professor Franklin and Lucy were huddled behind another tree, one of the professor's arms wrapped around the trunk and the other around his daughter, both of them too terrified to move.

Not too far from her, Rupert von Metz and Harry Lawton were using trees for shelter and support, as were the rest of the men in the party. But neither the Prussian nor Lawton made a move to help Shining Moon. That did not surprise her. They were probably hoping the blow from the tree branch had killed Clay, Shining Moon thought bitterly, and anger surged up in her at the idea. The anger gave her strength, and she tugged harder at Clay's muddy shirt.

She was relieved when Aaron Garwood managed to reach her side. He bent over to get hold of Clay's left arm, and then he lifted while Shining Moon pulled up on his right side. Finally they pulled Clay out of the mud, which grudgingly released him with a great sucking sound.

Shining Moon bit back a sob as she saw how mud coated Clay's face and clogged his mouth and nose. Even if being hit by the branch had not killed him, he might have suffocated while his head was in the mud. Desperately she wiped away the thick, sticky gray mass. The rain, still pounding down, helped loosen the mud and wash some of it away.

The rumble of the avalanche was fading, and the flow of mud had receded a bit. The worst of the danger was over, at least for the moment. Under the circumstances another mudslide was all too possible. The travelers still needed to find shelter. In the back of her mind, Shining Moon knew that, but she could not give it much thought, not with her husband lying limp and motionless in her arms as she knelt there on the muddy slope.

She forced Clay's mouth open wider and dug out another great clot of mud with her fingers. Suddenly a spasm racked his body, a deep gasping cough that shook him and Shining Moon both. Relief welled up inside her. He was alive!

"Help me lift him," she said to Aaron. "We must leave this place."

"Wait just a damned minute," Harry Lawton protested as Shining Moon and Aaron struggled to get Clay on his feet. "As long as Holt's out of his head, I'm in charge again."

Shining Moon paid no attention to the man until he slogged across the dozen or so feet between them and grasped her arm. That made her grip on Clay slip, and he sagged to the ground again. The weakness in Aaron's arm made it impossible for him to support Clay by himself.

"Let go of me!" Shining Moon cried, jerking her arm away from Lawton. "How dare you—"

"Shut up, squaw," Lawton said harshly. "You ain't running this show, and neither's Holt anymore. He's unconscious and may never wake up, so I'm taking over again."

"You're crazy!" Aaron exclaimed. "Clay just got knocked out. He'll come to any minute."

"Look at his head," Lawton snarled. "I've seen men die from clouts like that."

It was true. A large lump on the back of Clay's head was visible now that the rain had washed away most of the mud and plastered his wet hair to his skull. There was a gash on the lump that had bled quite a bit.

Shining Moon felt a coldness in her belly that had nothing to do with the chill wind and rain. Lawton was right; sometimes when a man was hit hard enough in the head, he never woke up. The thought that Clay might be dying caused panic to well up in her, but with a determined effort she controlled that hopeless feeling. She was a Teton Sioux woman, a daughter of the Hunkpapa, and she was strong. Her people had known much hardship, but always they had persevered. She could do no less now.

Tossing her sodden hair back from her face, she met Lawton's hostile gaze squarely. "My husband will not die, and until he is awake again, I will lead us."

"You?" Lawton laughed scornfully. "A squaw giving orders to white men? I don't think so." He turned to Professor Franklin. "What about it, Professor? Who's running things now?"

Franklin blinked, opened his mouth, and closed it again, as though too shaken by what had happened to offer an opinion. The same could not be said of Rupert von Metz, however.

"I think Mr. Lawton should be in charge again," the young artist said. "He knows more about what he is doing than anyone else."

"That is not true," Shining Moon objected. "I have lived in these mountains all my life."

"But you are a woman," von Metz replied with an infuriatingly smug expression. "I would not think it was necessary to point out something so obvious."

"You're wrong about Shining Moon," Aaron said as he knelt beside Clay, holding the unconcious man's head out of the mud. "She knows what she's doing."

"My boys ain't taking orders from a woman. Ain't that right?"

A rumble of tentative agreement came from the other men, most of whom had moved away from the trees now that the avalanche seemed to be over. The flow of mud had almost stopped. The rain had not let up, however, and it was sluicing down as hard as ever.

"This is a foolish argument," Shining Moon said. "We must have shelter. My brother will return soon and lead us to a place where we can get out of the rain and build a fire."

Lawton laughed, a harsh and unpleasant sound. "That brother of yours ain't coming back. The slide got him."

Shining Moon had feared that, but she did not let it show as she said, "Proud Wolf will be back."

"You can think what you want. I'm tired of arguing with you, lady. We're getting the hell out of here." Lawton jerked his head in a curt gesture, ordering his men to follow him.

"No!" Shining Moon cried, knowing that they would stand a better chance of survival if they stayed together. "You must not leave us!"

"Don't try to stop us," Lawton warned. He looked over at Franklin and Lucy. "What's it going to be, folks? You going with us or staying here with this squaw?"

Even though Lawton had not asked him, Rupert von Metz said without hesitation, "I will go with you, Herr Lawton."

The professor still appeared confused and frightened. Lucy huddled against him, not even looking around at the others. Franklin stammered, "I-I just don't know what we should do."

"Then to hell with you," Lawton said savagely. "I'm tired of waiting around here for you to make up your mind. Mr. von Metz, boys, let's go." He hefted his rifle and started along the hillside.

Rupert von Metz followed him, carrying the cases of art supplies he had somehow managed to hang on to during the mudslide. Although the other men muttered among themselves and shifted their feet nervously, none of them followed Lawton and von Metz.

A few moments passed before Lawton glanced over his shoulder and saw that von Metz was the only one behind him. Stopping short, he swung around.

"What the hell's wrong?" he demanded.

After a pause one of the men replied, "We ain't so sure about this, Harry. I mean, the squaw does know these mountains better'n we do."

"But she's a woman!" Lawton protested in disbelief. "Holt's woman!"

"Yeah, but what about that Injun gal who went along with Lewis and Clark?" another man asked. "She showed 'em where to go, and the way I heard it, they might not've made it back if it hadn't been for her."

"My husband knew the woman called Sacajawea," Shining Moon said. "She was Shoshone, and she was a true guide for the white explorers. I, too, will do my best to lead you to safety if you follow me." Even as she spoke the brave words, she wished Clay would wake up. She glanced at him, saw the slack, unconscious features, and wondered if she would be able to stay strong if he did not regain consciousness soon.

"Goddamn it!" Lawton exploded. He pointed along the hillside with his rifle. "I'm going this way. You can squat here with this redskinned bitch if you want to."

Shining Moon caught her breath. If Clay ever found out that Lawton had spoken of her that way, he would kill the man. *If Clay ever wakes up* . . . In the meantime, she had something else to worry about.

"I would not go that way," she said.

Lawton paused and sneered at her over his shoulder. "Oh? And why not?"

"There could be another avalanche. We are safer staying here and going straight up into the mountains. The rocks that will fall easily have already come down."

"That makes sense," Aaron said.

Lawton snorted contemptuously. "You saying there can't be another avalanche come through here?"

"One could, from higher up in the mountains," Shining Moon admitted. "But the chances are much smaller. The rain is still heavy. Rocks may fall in other places."

"Yeah, well, I'll take my chances. And so will the rest of you boys if you've got any sense." Lawton turned away again. "Come on, von Metz."

This time it was the Prussian who hesitated. "I am no longer so sure of this, Herr Lawton. What the woman says is logical."

Lawton swore. He had seen Clay Holt's injury as a chance to regain the control he had lost days earlier, but now it was all slipping away again.

Shining Moon watched him closely, knowing that with Clay unconscious Lawton might decide to seize power by force.

The tension in the air grew as Lawton glared at each of them in turn.

"Shining Moon!"

The unexpected cry made everyone jerk around. Proud Wolf came loping along the hillside, his buckskins covered with mud, his long black hair matted with the sticky gray stuff. When he got close enough to see Clay lying motionless on the ground, Proud Wolf's face twisted with concern, and he ran faster. He approached the others and dropped to his knees beside Clay.

"Is he—"

"He lives," Shining Moon told her brother. "He was hit on the head by a falling branch, but he will be all right." If she said that often enough, she thought, perhaps it would be true. "I knew you would return to us, my brother. Your feet are fleeter than any avalanche."

"Just barely," Proud Wolf said. "I found a cave and was able to hide inside it in time. The slide passed over it. For a while I was afraid the entrance would be completely blocked, but when the rocks and mud were past, there was still a way in and out. We should go there now."

One of the men asked, "How far off is this cave, boy?"

"Half a mile, perhaps." Proud Wolf pointed north along the slope of the foothills, in the opposite direction from where Lawton had been going.

"I say we head up there," another man declared. "Sounds like a good place to get out of this weather."

"The cave is dry," Proud Wolf added. "And we may be able to find enough dry branches inside it to make a fire."

"A fire sounds damn good to me," a third man rumbled.

Lawton hawked up phlegm and spat disgustedly on the muddy ground. "You're going to let a squaw and an Injun kid tell you what to do? Hell, I thought I knew you boys better than that. The whole damn lot of you make me sick." He strode over, picked up a pack of supplies, and turned to walk off again.

"Wait," Shining Moon said sharply.

Lawton stopped and looked around with a scowl. "What is it now?"

Shining Moon pointed to the pack in his hand. "You cannot take those supplies. The rest of us may need them. We lost several packs in the avalanche."

For a few seconds Lawton just stared at her in surprise. Then he shifted his body so that the barrel of his rifle was pointed in the general direction of the others.

"I'm not staying with a bunch of crazy people," he declared, "and I'm not going off without provisions. You want these supplies, you can damn well come and take 'em."

That same dangerous tension filled the air again as Lawton faced the rest of the group. Shining Moon's pulse pounded as she tried to figure out what to do. With all the rain coming down, there was a very good chance that Lawton's rifle would not even fire if they jumped him. But she knew he had a pistol under his coat, and the powder in it might be dry enough to ignite. Not to mention the long-bladed knife sheathed at his waist and the 'hawk tucked under his belt. They could overpower him and take the supplies away from him, she had no doubt of that, but how many of them would be hurt in the process? Someone might even be killed.

Clay would have known what to do, Shining Moon thought. So would Bear Tooth, the chief of the village where she had grown to womanhood. And Jeff Holt, who was now far, far away, also could have handled this situation. Perhaps Lawton was right: Perhaps she was just a squaw and had no business trying to lead a group of men.

"Give us the supplies," she heard herself saying, "or I will kill you, Lawton."

The direct challenge was too much for Lawton to bear. He swung the barrel of the rifle toward Shining Moon.

"You red whore!" he rasped. "Nobody talks to me like that!"

In turning toward Shining Moon, however, he took his eyes off Proud Wolf, who sprang forward with the speed of his namesake. The young Sioux's fingers closed around the barrel of Lawton's rifle and forced it up. Lawton grunted in surprise and staggered back a step. Proud Wolf hung on stubbornly to the gun.

Lawton slipped in the mud, caught his balance, and drove a kick at Proud Wolf. Proud Wolf fell, but as he went down he jerked hard on the barrel of the rifle, pulling it away from Lawton for an instant before he drove the butt of it back into the older man's stomach. Keeping his hold on the weapon, Proud Wolf dragged the muzzle down into the mud.

Before Lawton could do anything else, Shining Moon was on him, a fierce expression on her face as she whipped out her own knife and placed the edge of the blade against his throat. The move was too fast for him to counter, and he found himself staring into her eyes from a distance of only a few inches as the keen edge of the knife hovered against his skin.

"Let go of the rifle and the supplies and step back," she hissed.

Lawton's gaze darted over toward his men, and Shining Moon could read the plea for help in them. But she could not take her attention off Lawton to see if that plea was being answered. She stood there next to him, taut as a bowstring, ready to drive the knife into his throat.

"Forget it, Lawton." Aaron Garwood's voice came from behind Shining Moon. "Those fellas have too much sense to help you. They know you're likely to get them killed if they follow you, and they're probably as tired of hearing you run off at the mouth as the rest of us are."

Lawton was trembling with rage, but Shining Moon could see the bitter realization dawning in his eyes. He was on his own. With another shudder, he dropped the pack of supplies and the rifle and stepped back. Proud Wolf pulled the rifle over to him by the barrel. The confrontation was over.

"All right," Lawton grated. "If that's the way you want it, it's fine by me. Go with this stupid squaw and wind up dead for all I care. But you can't send me off into the wilderness with no provisions."

Professor Franklin spoke up. "He's right, Shining Moon. It wouldn't be human to make him leave with no food."

"I would not do that," Shining Moon replied, breathing a little easier now. She sheathed her knife and said, "I did not want him to take the entire pack of supplies, but I am willing to let him have some of them." A faint smile appeared on her face. "Although if he is so much at home in the mountains, he should be able to fend for himself."

Glaring at her, Lawton began, "If you wasn't a woman—"

"If I were not a woman, you would not have tried to impose your will on me," Shining Moon broke in hotly. She controlled her anger by telling herself that a Hunkpapa always remained dignified, then went on, "I will not force you to leave the group. That is your own choice. You can stay with us, or you can go. If you go, you can take rations for four days."

"Four days?" Lawton repeated. "Where the hell can I get to in four days?"

"There is plenty of game in these mountains. Make the supplies last. A man who can make snares and traps can live here for a long time without any supplies bought from a store. My people have done it for hundreds of years."

"I ain't no stinking heathen."

Proud Wolf said coldly, "And the entire Sioux nation is glad of this."

"Are you going or staying?" Shining Moon asked.

"I'm going! I wouldn't stay here with you people if you was to ask me!" Lawton picked up the supply pack, took out some jerky and hardtack, a small pouch of salt and another of sugar, and a spare powder horn. He stored the supplies in his possibles bag, then tossed down the pack and asked, "That suit you, squaw?"

Shining Moon nodded gravely and gestured for Proud Wolf to return Lawton's rifle to him.

"Now go," she said.

Lawton turned and trudged away in the rain. Shining Moon watched his retreating figure for a moment, then turned back to where Aaron knelt on the ground beside Clay.

"Is he coming around?" she asked.

Aaron shook his head gravely. "Not yet."

Shining Moon bent to help Aaron lift Clay

again. "Take us to the cave," she said to Proud Wolf.

Before they could get Clay on his feet, however, two of the other men had stepped forward, and one of them said, "Let us take him, ma'am. We'd be pleased to."

Shining Moon looked up at them and saw the respect in their eyes, respect for the way she had stood up to Lawton. She saw admiration mirrored on the faces of the other men in the group.

"Thank you," she said sincerely, moving aside to let one of the men take her place. The other one got on Clay's other side, freeing Aaron to go over to Lucy Franklin and make sure she was all right. Shining Moon saw the look von Metz gave Aaron and knew the Prussian wished he had thought of that first.

The two men got Clay upright, wrapped their arms around his waist, and slung his arms over their shoulders. They were able to half carry, half drag him that way.

"Your man ain't steered us wrong yet," one of them said to Shining Moon. "Reckon the best thing we can do is let you take his place until he's up to running things again."

"I will do my best," Shining Moon said. She picked up the pack from which Lawton had taken his supplies and slung it on her back. To her brother she said, "Show us this cave you found."

Proud Wolf set off along the slope, quartering steadily up it toward the higher mountains. The others followed him, passing over the huge scar

312

in the earth left by the avalanche. The rocks and mud had swept the hillside clean, leaving a swath of destruction more than a quarter of a mile wide. In a way that made the going easier, since all the obstacles had been wiped away, but the footing was still slippery and treacherous because of the mud and rain.

Eventually they reached a steeper slope, where outcroppings of rock were arranged almost like steps leading up to a narrow, dark opening in the hillside. Shining Moon recognized it as the mouth of a cave, partially blocked by rocks and debris left behind by the avalanche. She and Proud Wolf led the group toward it. As they went up, she glanced over her shoulder and saw that Aaron was still beside Lucy Franklin, helping her father assist her in the climb. Von Metz and the others, including the two who were supporting Clay's limp body, trailed along behind. It was difficult getting Clay up the slope, and several others pitched in to help.

When Shining Moon and Proud Wolf reached the cave entrance, she said to him, "You say you waited in here during the avalanche?"

"I did."

"There were no other occupants?"

"If you mean our friends Bear or Skunk or Badger, I saw and heard nothing of them," Proud Wolf replied, smiling. "I will go in first to make sure they are still not here."

Shining Moon started to object and say that she would go into the cave first, but then she saw the determination on her brother's face and knew from experience that it would do no good to argue with him. When Proud Wolf wanted to do something, only the Great Spirit, the Wakan Tanka, could stop the young man.

Shining Moon contented herself by saying, "Be careful."

Proud Wolf ducked his head and disappeared into the cave. Shining Moon leaned closer to the opening so that she could hear his footsteps as he proceeded slowly and cautiously into the darkness.

After a few moments, he called back to her, "The cave is not large. No one is here but us."

Shining Moon breathed a sigh of relief and stepped through the entrance, motioning for the others to follow. For the first time all day, rain was not pelting against her head, and the absence of it felt rather strange.

She straightened, raised a hand over her head, and her fingers barely brushed the rocky surface of the ceiling. *Good, plenty of head room,* she thought. But they would still need to be careful until they got a fire going and could see. She sank to her knees and felt around her, finding a large open space.

"Bring Clay over here," she said to the men carrying him. "Come slowly, and follow my voice."

She kept talking to guide the men, and a moment later one of them bumped into her with his feet.

"Sorry, ma'am," he said quickly.

"There is no need to apologize. Lay my husband down."

She reached up and helped them guide Clay's body to the floor of the cave. After tucking the depleted supply pack under his head for a pillow, Shining Moon let her fingertips stray over his face and brush his eyes. How she wished those eyes would open, how she longed to hear his lips once again whisper her name. . . .

But details needed to be attended to, and she was in charge now.

"Proud Wolf," she said.

"I am here, my sister."

"Search for dry branches or leaves, anything that we might use to make a fire."

"That is what I have been doing," Proud Wolf replied. "I will soon have enough."

"That is good," she said. "You have flint and tinder?"

"Wrapped up tightly and dry," came the answer.

Confident that Proud Wolf had everything under control, Shining Moon settled back on her heels beside Clay. Gradually, her eyes adjusted to the darkness. Enough grayish light filtered in from the narrow entrance of the cave for her to make out Clay's body, as well as the shapes of the other members of the party as they huddled around the chamber. Everyone was inside now, and Shining Moon could hear the chattering of teeth. They were soaked, and crouching in a hole in the ground did not provide much warmth. The sooner Proud Wolf got that fire going, the better.

He did so a few minutes later. First came only a spark as he struck his flint. Then a tiny flame grew in the tinder he had heaped in the center of a small pile of branches and leaves. The fire grew, caught hold, and spread. More red and yellow flames danced, casting their glow in an ever-growing circle on the floor of the cave.

Soon the fire was burning brightly. As he sat beside Lucy and Professor Franklin, Aaron pointed up at the smoke, which rose toward the ceiling and disappeared.

"Got a natural flue somewhere up yonder," he said. "It's sucking the smoke right out of here."

"That is good luck," Proud Wolf said as he hunkered by the fire, warming himself. "The passage must be small and crooked, for no rain is coming through it."

Shining Moon had noticed the same thing. It was doubtful that Proud Wolf could have found a better place for them to wait out the storm. The cave was big enough for all of them to get inside, yet its confines were close enough for the fire's warmth to spread quickly through the rock-walled room. They were lucky, Shining Moon thought. The avalanche easily could have killed them all, instead of just the few who had panicked and run. As it was, the only serious injury among them was Clay's.

She lowered her head and closed her eyes. Clay

had to be all right. She could think of nothing else. If they had been in the village of her people, she could have brought a holy man to Clay's side to sing over him. Here there were no holy men. She was the one responsible, and she had done what she could for Clay's body: She had led them out of danger, gotten him out of the rain and mud, and had made him comfortable on the floor of the cave by pillowing his head and spreading a blanket over him. Now she had to heal his spirit. Surely the Wakan Tanka would know that she meant no offense by singing the words of the healing song.

Eyes closed, Shining Moon began to sway slowly back and forth. In a clear voice that trembled with love and hope, she sang:

> "Oyate wan waste ca
> Wanna piyawakage-lo!
> Wankanta Tunkasila heya ca
> Wanna piyawakage-lo!"

No ceremony accompanied the song, as would usually have been the case; only the voice of Shining Moon. Then, as she repeated the words, Proud Wolf joined her. Tentatively, Aaron sang as well, struggling with the words. Even though they did not fully understand what was going on, the others must have sensed the gravity of the situation, for they tugged their hats off and sat quietly, solemn expressions on their haggard faces.

Professor Franklin and Lucy watched in awe, their own discomfort forgotten for the moment as they were swept up by the emotions in the cave. Only Rupert von Metz seemed unmoved as he sat with his head and shoulders slumped forward and his knees drawn up.

How long she sang, Shining Moon had no idea. She felt herself being transported away from that place, felt warm sunshine and the gentle kiss of a breeze on her face. The fragrance of flowers and pine trees filled her senses, and when she looked around, she found herself standing in a beautiful meadow, high on the side of a mountain. The sky was a gorgeous blue above her head, and she was looking up at it when she heard her name called. She turned and saw Clay, standing above her on the mountainside, having paused there in his climb. He called her name again, and Shining Moon beckoned to him.

"Come down, Clay! Come down from the mountain."

He hesitated, then started to move, and suddenly he was at the edge of the meadow, running toward her. She stepped forward to meet him, lifting her arms, opening them to draw him into her embrace—

Shining Moon slumped forward, her eyes jolted open by the shock, and she saw that she was not in a beautiful mountain meadow at all but rather inside a damp, cold, smoky cave in the side of a hill. Clay was still stretched out before her, motionless, eyes closed, features pale and drawn.

Shining Moon's lips moved, and the final words of the healing song faded. She knew that she had failed, that her vision had been only that, a dream with no substance. She closed her eyes again and tried to choke back the sob that welled up in her throat.

"Sh-Shining . . . Moon . . ."

Her head jerked up at the sound of the weak, hoarse whisper, and as she looked at her husband's face, she saw something even more beautiful than the vision that had filled her mind moments earlier: She saw Clay Holt open his eyes, look at her, and smile.

XV

Just as Jeff had surmised from his first visit, the Tontine Coffee House was at the center of commerce in New York City. Its proximity to the harbor and the offices of most of the city's shipowners made the establishment a busy place from dawn until after dusk. The day after Jeff arrived with Ned, Lemuel March took both young men to his office and from there to the coffeehouse.

"This is the best place to inquire about Merrivale," Lemuel told Jeff as they entered the impressive building. "If it's all right with you, I won't mention your personal reasons for wishing to locate him. We'll make it sound strictly like a business matter. The men who congregate here understand those motives better than any others."

Jeff agreed. Whatever Lemuel thought was best was fine with him.

Most of the men at the coffeehouse had been there the day before and remembered Jeff and Ned. They were still staring today, some more blatantly than others, but evidently Lemuel March's presence was enough to make them accept the two visitors from the West. Clearly, Lemuel was highly respected in these circles.

He introduced Jeff and Ned to several men, all of whom had ships at the nearby docks.

"My friends here are trying to locate a man named Merrivale," Lemuel explained. "Charles Merrivale. Have any of you heard of him?"

"What line of business is he in?" someone asked.

"I'm not sure," Jeff said. "If I had to guess, I'd say he probably owns a mercantile store. But he could also be involved in shipping."

"Why are you looking for him?" someone else asked.

"It's a business matter," Jeff replied, taking his cue from what Lemuel had said earlier. "I have, ah, a proposition to make to him."

And a simple proposition it is, Jeff added silently. *Tell me where my wife is—or else!*

But all he received from Lemuel's friends were shakes of the head and a few expressions of regret.

"Sorry we can't help you, lad," one of them said. "If we knew this fellow Merrivale, we'd tell you, I can promise you that."

"Could he have set up a business here in New York without you gentlemen knowing about it?"

Lemuel answered, "Not likely. It's our business to know all the store owners in the area. They buy the goods we bring in from England and France, you know. Except for the ones we ship on to other areas."

Ned had been paying little attention to the conversation. He seemed engrossed in the paintings that adorned the walls of the coffeehouse, paintings that featured all sorts of ships, from frigates to brigantines, plying the oceans of the world. His eyes widened as he studied the graceful vessels, their sails billowing with wind. He could almost see them moving across the waves, as if they had come to life before his eyes. Ned had been listening to what was going on with one ear, however, and he heard Lemuel's comment about shipping trade goods to other areas.

"You mean your ships go somewhere else besides New York?" Ned asked, turning to Lemuel.

"Certainly. The main trade routes run between either here or Boston and England, but the March Shipping Company also sends vessels up and down the Atlantic coast, from New Hampshire all the way down to Florida."

Ned glanced at the paintings again. "Lemuel,

do you think we could go down to the harbor and take a closer look at your boats?"

"I don't see why not. Are we through here, Jeff?"

"I suppose so. I knew better than to get my hopes up, but I thought one of your friends might have heard of Merrivale."

"Don't be discouraged, lad," another trader said. "We'll all keep our ears open, and if we hear anything about this Merrivale, we'll get in touch with Lemuel."

"I'd appreciate that," Jeff said sincerely. Then he followed Ned and Lemuel as they left the coffeehouse and turned toward the docks.

Most of the ships in the harbor were the roomy, three-masted cargo vessels known as British East Indiamen, developed for the lucrative trade between England and the East Indies some twenty years earlier. Despite their age, they were sturdy craft with a great deal of life in them, according to Lemuel March.

"We can make the crossing to England in three to four weeks," he said as he pointed out the ships that belonged to him. "Coming back takes about two weeks longer, you understand. Have to sail against the trade winds rather than with them."

"What about the ships that sail up and down the coast?" Ned asked.

"Well, speed is less of a factor there, of course. And the ships make more stops along the way. But the distances involved are shorter, too. One of my ships can make the run from here down to, say, Wilmington, North Carolina, in about two weeks."

"Interesting," Ned muttered as he studied the ships lying at anchor.

"Since when did you become so fascinated with ships?" Jeff asked his cousin.

Ned shrugged his shoulders. "I didn't know I was until I started looking at these. But there's something about them, the way they look and the idea of skimming along over the surface of the sea. It just seems so—so free."

Lemuel clapped Ned on the shoulder and laughed. "You've got it, lad. You've summed it up in that one word. The sea has a powerful lure, just like a beautiful woman. And like a woman, if you're not careful, she'll be the death of you."

"Ned knows all about that," Jeff said dryly.

Lemuel laughed again. "There's nothing like dawn on the ocean with a strong wind at your back. It's a beautiful, powerful feeling, my boy. You should experience it sometime."

"Maybe I will," Ned said, still entranced. "Could I go on board one of them and have a look around?"

"I'll do better than that," Lemuel said. "I'll take you on all of mine that are here."

"Thanks, Lemuel. I really appreciate this." Ned's words were heartfelt.

Lemuel glanced over at Jeff. "What about you, lad? Do you want the grand tour, as well?"

"I don't think so. Since the courthouse isn't far, I believe I'll go there and check the tax and property records. Merrivale could have shown up here without drawing much attention to himself, but if he bought land or set up a business, there's bound to be a record of it."

"Yes, that's a good idea. Well, come along, Ned."

Jeff watched them go up the gangplank that led to one of the ships. Lemuel strolled across with the sure-footed ease of the sailor he had been in years past; Ned, looking a bit uncomfortable, clutched the ropes for support as he made his way on board.

Ned's interest in the ships came as something of a surprise to Jeff. With a shake of his head, he left the docks and walked toward the courthouse a few blocks away.

Back at the docks, on board the *Manchester*, Lemuel pointed out various sails to Ned, then took him into the cargo hold.

"This particular vessel will carry grain to England," Lemuel explained. "We'll start loading any day now. Once she's reached port on the other side of the Atlantic, she'll take on another cargo to bring back."

"What would that be?" Ned asked.

"That's hard to say. Might be manufactured goods, farm implements, or fabric or tea from the Indies. I have agents in London who are always on the lookout for suitable cargos." He cocked a bushy eyebrow. "This shipping is a bit of a hit or miss business. There's money to be made, but you need good luck as well as hard work."

Ned's forehead creased in thought. An idea had occurred to him, and like most of his ideas, it seemed quite appealing at first glance. He was determined to think it through, however, instead of plunging right in.

He pondered for a good ten seconds more before he said, "Sir, do you think I could have a job on one of your ships?"

Lemuel blinked in surprise. "Do you really want to go to sea, Ned?"

"When I stepped onto this vessel, I felt something I had never experienced before. It was the lure of the sea that you mentioned, the freedom to run before the wind and answer to no one but the gods of fate."

Lemuel laughed dryly. "That's quite poetic, lad, but there's not much truth in what you just said. It's true the sea has its appeal, but it can also be a harsh mistress. And as for answering to no one . . . well, you should know that the master of a ship rules his vessel like a king while it's at sea. He can have you striped with a whip or thrown into irons if you cross him. Discipline is stern. It has to be, if everyone is to survive the dangers of a crossing."

Ned looked rather crestfallen. "If you don't think I can handle it, just say so, sir."

A flicker of annoyance passed over Lemuel's weathered features as he said, "I meant no offense, Ned. It's just that you're all caught up in the romance of sailing, and you have no idea what it's really like. If you'd had experience aboard vessels like these, it might be different."

"There's only one way to get experience. Someone has to give you a chance." Ned looked shrewdly at the older man. "How did you become a sailor? Did you run away and ship out as a cabin boy?"

"I did not," Lemuel replied. "I was a cabin boy, yes, but I never ran away. My father was first mate on a ship of the line during the war. When it was over, I sailed with him, a lad of fifteen."

"I'm six years older than that now."

"And every bit as stubborn, I see." Lemuel paused for a moment, then said, "Tell you what, Ned. I'll think about it. If you're sure you want to ship out when Jeff is ready to leave New York, I'll find a place for you. It won't be on one of these big merchantmen on the English route, mind you. I want you to sail on one of my smaller ships on the coastal run. That way you can find out if you really have a taste for it. If you do, there'll be a berth waiting for you on a bigger vessel later." Lemuel held out his hand. "How about it?"

Ned hesitated only an instant before firmly gripping Lemuel's hand. "Fair enough."

"I warn you, though, you'll be sailing as a common seaman. There'll be no special favors for you because you're a relative. You'll follow orders and do your share of the work, or the captain will boot you off at the nearest port."

326

"That's exactly the way I want it," Ned declared.

"Good. Come along, then. I'll show you the other ships in the harbor."

They left the *Manchester* and proceeded along the docks, boarding several other vessels owned by the March Shipping Company. Ned's fascination grew with each visit. He was sure that when the time came, he would still be anxious to go to sea. Of course, that would mean parting company with his cousin Jeff, and Ned would regret that. He had to follow where his heart led, however, and right now it was telling him that his home was destined to be on the briny deep.

Of course, he had also toyed with the idea of going west with Jeff to the Rocky Mountains. He could see now what an immature notion that had been. He had made the right decision; he was sure of it.

As they left the last of the March ships and paused in front of a small office building, Lemuel said, "I've some business with the harbormaster, Ned. Why don't you wait here and watch that ship being loaded? It belongs to one of my competitors, but I imagine you can learn a few things by observing how the cargo's taken aboard. I'll be finished shortly, and then we can go back to the Tontine for lunch."

"All right, sir. That sounds fine to me."

While Lemuel went into the harbormaster's office, Ned turned toward the piers again and tilted his hat back on his head. Several wagons were pulled up on the dock next to the ship Lemuel had indicated, and a dozen or more men had formed a line to unload the crates from the wagons and pass them aboard the ship. From there, more men took the crates and carried them down into the vessel's cargo hold. As Ned watched, more wagons arrived, these loaded with large burlap bags, probably grain, he decided. Most of the workers were stripped to the waist, and a sheen of sweat glistened on their bare torsos.

Ned wandered closer for a better look at the loading operation. He was wondering how the crates were stacked inside the hold when a voice shouted hoarsely, "Watch where ye're goin', ye damned fool!"

Ned looked up and abruptly jumped aside as a crate crashed to the timbers of the dock only a foot or so from where he had been standing. He had inadvertently wandered into the way of a man unloading a wagon, causing him to drop a crate. The red-bearded worker, who was every bit as tall and burly as Ned, glowered at him.

"Sorry," Ned muttered. "Didn't mean to get in the way."

"Oh, ye didn't, did ye?" the man went on angrily. "Ye big landlocked oxen got no business bein' near a ship. Ye're a danger to yerself and to honest sailors who might stumble over ye."

"Wait just a minute," Ned said, feeling his

own anger rise. "You've no call to talk to me that way. I'm going to be a sailor myself."

Redbeard stared at him for a few seconds, then threw back his head and bellowed a contemptuous laugh. "Ye? A sailor? Go back to yer farm, sonny boy. A sailor ye'll never be."

One of the other bare-chested workers tugged at Redbeard's arm and said, "Come on, we got crates to unload."

Redbeard shook off his hand and growled, "In a minute. I got to settle this with yon farmer." He fixed a cold stare on Ned. "And who would ye be shippin' out with, boy?"

"I'm going to have a berth on one of Lemuel March's ships."

"Oh, then that explains it," the man said in a contemptuous tone. " 'Tis well known that March will let anybody sail on his ships—even clumsy brutes such as yourself! That's why his vessels are the laughingstocks of the seven seas!"

Ned had been in enough tavern brawls to know that the bruiser was trying to goad him into a fight. Logically, he knew that if he threw a punch at the man, the man's companions would join in the melee. He would be badly outnumbered and would probably be in for the beating of his life.

That was what his brain told him. But his heart told him that he could not allow the insults to himself—and to his friend and host, Lemuel March—to pass unchallenged.

"You're a damned liar," he said.

Redbeard's eyes lit up. "Oh, 'tis a liar I am, is it? I can't let ye get away with sayin' things like that about me, boy."

"Then do something about it."

"I will," the man said. "I'll do—this!"

With no more warning than that, his ham-like right hand snatched up one of the curved, wooden-handled hooks that some of the men used to help them manipulate the heavy crates. With unexpected speed, he swung the point of the hook right at Ned's head.

Fortunately Ned had the presence of mind to duck, and the hook whistled over him, the point missing him by a matter of inches. He had not wanted this fight, but he was damned if he was going to run from it. Besides, running would not do any good. Redbeard and his companions would quickly overtake him. All he could do was try to end the battle as soon as possible.

While Redbeard was still off balance from the missed swing with the hook, Ned whipped a punch into the man's belly. His fist might as well have pounded into a block of wood, however.

Redbeard backhanded the hook at Ned, and this time Ned dived all the way to the dock to avoid being ripped open. Vaguely, he heard shouts and knew that the other crewmen from the ship were hurrying to witness the fight. If he was lucky, they would stand back awhile to see how Redbeard fared against him instead of pitching in right away.

Ned rolled across the heavy timbers and drove his shoulders into Redbeard's legs. He hung on tightly, heaved upward, and was rewarded by a resounding crash as the man tumbled to the dock. Ned scrambled to his feet and lashed out with a kick, his booted foot catching Redbeard on the wrist, sending the hook spinning. But the move left Ned open for his opponent to return the favor, and while he was balanced on one foot, Redbeard kicked the other out from under him.

Ned fell, but hands caught him before he could hit the dock, strong hands that jerked him upright and thrust him forward. The fight was entertaining and certainly better than working; Redbeard's friends wanted to keep it going as long as possible.

Hoots and catcalls came from the ring that had formed around the two adversaries, but Ned knew better than to be distracted by them. He had to keep his eyes on Redbeard, who was back on his feet and swinging a fist like a mallet at Ned's face.

Parrying the blow at the last moment, Ned tried to sneak one of his own through Redbeard's guard, but the burly sailor knocked it aside easily. Ned was overmatched, and he knew it. In the past he had fought when pride or circumstance drove him to it, but more often he had forestalled battles with his quick wit—or quick feet. Now he was trapped, forced to slug it out with a man who was stronger and more vicious than he.

Stepping back quickly, Ned knew that his opponent would follow, and Redbeard did not disappoint him. As the sailor charged toward him, Ned tried a move that he hoped would take the man by surprise. He ducked his head, dove forward, and rolled completely over. His feet came up together, and as he straightened his legs, using every bit of power at his command, he drove his heels right into Redbeard's groin.

The man's scream must have made the masts tremble on ships at the other end of the harbor. Redbeard folded up over Ned's legs and then slumped to the side, whimpering and writhing. Ned scuttled backward, propelling himself with hands and feet, then stood. The ring of Redbeard's friends was closing in around him, and the other men were muttering in anger and scowling darkly at him. They considered the blow Ned had just struck to be a low one, and they were going to avenge it.

Ned clenched his fists. He would not go down easily, he vowed.

"What the devil is going on here?"

The stern voice roared, and the crowd around Ned fell away almost miraculously. Two men strode through the opening. One was Lemuel March, the other a short, broad-shouldered, bullet-headed individual with graying dark hair clipped almost to his skull. He wore an expensive suit, and the shoulders of it bulged with muscle underneath the fabric. Ned knew that

Lemuel had been intending to see the harbor-master, and he wondered if this man was he.

The man's next words confirmed the guess.

"I'll not have this sort of brawling on my docks! Since your own captains haven't seen fit to order you back to work, I'll take it upon myself to do so. Move!"

The other sailors hurried to follow the order, leaving Ned standing there alone to face Lemuel and the harbormaster. A few feet away, Redbeard was curled up, still mewling in agony.

The harbormaster cast a contemptuous glance in his direction. "Carney always was a trouble-maker, as I've warned his captain more than once. I daresay he started this disturbance, but I want to hear your story anyway, sir." His cold eyes swung back toward Ned.

His pulse still pounding from the exertion of the fight, Ned drew a deep breath to calm him-self and then said, "It was partially my fault. I got in his way while he was unloading a wagon. But then he insulted me and insulted my friend Mr. March, and when I called him a liar, he swung one of those hooks at me."

Lemuel was trying to look stern and disap-proving, but a hint of amusement lurked around his mouth and eyes. "So you were defending my honor, eh?"

"That and trying to keep from getting killed."

"I don't like fighting," the harbormaster snapped. "Never have. But I have to admit I don't mind seeing somebody stand up to Carney for a change. He's accustomed to running rough-shod over whoever strikes his fancy. I'll speak to his captain, but I doubt it'll do much good. Carney may be a bully, but he's also a damned fine sailor. As for you, sir"—he looked at Ned again—"stay the hell off my docks."

Ned blinked in surprise. "But I thought you agreed the fight wasn't my fault."

"I don't care about that. What's important is that Carney will have a grudge against you from now on, and if he doesn't try to settle it, someone else will, in an attempt to curry favor with him. You'll attract trouble down here, mister, and I don't want that."

Grudgingly, Ned said, "I suppose I see your point. And I'll stay away—until it's time for me to ship out."

"You're a sailor?" This time it was the harbor-master's turn to look surprised.

"I'm going to be," Ned declared. "Isn't that right, sir?"

"I, ah, promised the lad a place on one of my ships on the coastal run," Lemuel said.

"Well, that's your business, March," the harbormaster said gruffly. "Just keep your men civilized while they're in port, that's all I ask." With that, he walked toward his office, displaying the same rolling gait as Lemuel.

"Let's get out of here," Lemuel said in a low voice to Ned. He looked at Carney's companions, who had been watching the exchange with surly expressions.

"Get your friend up and take him below," Lemuel told them. He grasped Ned's arm and led him away from the ship.

When they had gone several yards in silence, Ned said, "Honestly, sir, I didn't set out to cause any trouble—"

"I know that, lad. No need to apologize. Sailors have to fight sometimes. It comes as natural to them as breathing."

Ned looked over at him. "Does that mean . . . you think I've got the makings of a sailor?"

Lemuel slapped Ned on the shoulder and said, "We'll see, son. We'll see. Now let's get something to eat. I imagine you've worked up quite an appetite."

The courthouse, which also served as New York's city hall, was an impressive building of three stories, constructed of white marble with a brownstone balustrade running around the top of it. Though not particularly attractive, it was one of the largest buildings in the city. Construction on it had begun in 1803, according to Lemuel, and was still not complete.

Jeff would not have cared if it had been a log hovel, if only it contained the information he was looking for. His search of the county records, however, reached the same dead end it had in all his other stops across the state. If Charles Merrivale and his family were in New York, they had not bought land or paid taxes.

His quest was over, Jeff thought bitterly as he

went back to Lemuel March's house. He would never find Melissa.

Ned was full of talk that night, telling Jeff all about the fight on the docks and Lemuel's offer to let him sail on one of the trading ships that traveled up and down the Atlantic coast.

"I suppose that means we'll be splitting up," Ned said after supper in the room they shared. "That's the only thing I don't like about this, Jeff. I thought for a while I'd go back west with you. I know you never offered to take me, but—"

"You'd have been welcome, Ned. I'm sure Clay would have enjoyed getting to know you. But you've got to do what you think is best."

"What about you? Are you going back?"

Jeff peered out the open window at the night. A breeze was blowing in, carrying with it the salty scent of the ocean. That might hold the promise of magic and adventure for Ned, but to Jeff it just smelled fishy. He preferred the crisp, clean air of the mountains and plains.

"I don't know yet," he said honestly after a moment's thought. "I'm convinced now that I'm not going to find Melissa here in New York, but"—he groped for words—"I hate the idea of going back without her."

Ned rested a hand on Jeff's shoulder in sympathy. "I'm sorry, Jeff, I really am. I was hoping we'd find her, too."

"Well, there's still the advertisement in the newspaper, and the notice in Mr. Irving's magazine. Perhaps someone who knows something about Melissa or her family will see one of them."

"Sure," Ned replied, making his voice sound heartier than he felt. "There's always a chance, isnt there?"

"Yes," Jeff said quietly. "There's always a chance."

Dermot Hawley looked up, his expression automatically brightening as Melissa Merrivale entered the room. Melissa Merrivale Holt, he corrected himself, as she never failed to remind him. She was quite stubborn about that.

Just as she was infuriatingly stubborn about everything else, Hawley thought, his pleasant appearance betraying nothing of his thoughts.

"Mother says to tell you gentlemen that dinner will be served in five minutes," Melissa said to her father. "So you're to conclude your business in that time and not bring it to the table with you."

Merrivale just grunted, but Hawley said, "Of course. We wouldn't want to darken your mother's table with gloomy business talk, now would we?" His charming smile and twinkling eyes took any sting out of the words.

Melissa returned the smile. "Certainly not," she said as she withdrew from the study where the men had been talking.

That smile was a small victory, Hawley thought. But soon she would be smiling at him a great deal. Smiling and gasping in ecstasy and clutching at him and crying out his name as he made love to her, ravishing that beautiful body—

Hawley blinked and forced those enticing thoughts out of his mind. If he allowed his imagination to run wild like that for very long, he ran the risk of losing control and moving too fast.

And that might ruin everything, not only the plans he had for Melissa but for her father as well.

Charles Merrivale puffed on his cigar, then said around it, "That's an intriguing plan of yours, Dermot, taking a wagon train full of supplies overland to those new settlers in Tennessee. When do you intend to do it?"

"Everything is still in the preliminary stage right now, Charles," Hawley replied. He lifted his glass of brandy, sipped from it, and continued, "That's why I'm talking to you now. I wanted to give you the opportunity to be a part of the enterprise right from the start. It will take time to put together a large enough cargo of supplies to make the trip profitable, and I'm visiting several merchants in the area to see if they want to participate."

"Count me in," Merrivale said emphatically and without hesitation. "I can provide, oh, perhaps two wagonloads of goods."

"Excellent! I knew I could count on you, Charles. This arrangement is going to make money for all of us."

"Do you have anyone else lined up to provide supplies?"

"I'm working on that. I've spoken to an agent for a shipping line that brings goods across from England. He's expecting a ship here early next month, and I'm certain I can obtain some of that cargo." Hawley put his hand on Merrivale's shoulder. "You let me worry about these details, Charles. You just think about how you're going to spend all the money you make from this venture."

"I don't intend to spend it," Merrivale said, somewhat stiffly. "I'm going to set it aside for my grandson. Michael will never want for a thing, not if I have anything to say about it."

"That's quite noble, Charles. I'm sure the lad will appreciate it when he's older."

Actually, Michael Holt would never see any of that money, Hawley thought. Once he had married Melissa, it would be only natural for him to assume control of her assets. One way or another, anything Merrivale made out of this enterprise was going to end up in Dermot Hawley's pockets.

Of course, Merrivale was not vital to the success of the plan, but his participation would make things easier. Despite his brusque, sometimes unpleasant personality, Merrivale had a reputation as an honest merchant, and so did the shipping agent Hawley had spoken to. By involving them in the scheme, it would give the whole thing a look of respectability. No one would dream that most of the goods Hawley intended to freight over the mountains into Tennessee were stolen.

Merrivale was talking again, and his words broke into Hawley's musings. "I'm sorry, Charles, what did you say?"

"I was proposing a toast," Merrivale said, lifting his glass of brandy. "Here's to our success, Dermot."

Hawley clinked his glass against Merrivale's. "To success," he said.

And if anyone got in the way? Well, he knew how to deal with such problems.

Merrivale downed the rest of his brandy and, placing the empty glass on a sideboard, said, "We'd better go in to dinner. We don't want to keep the ladies waiting."

"No, indeed," Hawley agreed. "That wouldn't do at all."

He would wait, though. He would wait for Melissa, at least a little while longer. The day was coming, the day that she would be his, totally and completely, to do with as he wished.

Dermot Hawley was still smiling as he and Charles Merrivale left the room.

XVI

So he was alive after all. That had come as a great surprise to Clay Holt. As he leaned back against the rock wall of the cave and warmed his hands on a cup of hot stew from the pot suspended over the small fire, he looked at his wife and felt a grin spread over his face. He could not help it. He had been smiling a great deal, in spite of the ache in his head, ever since he had awakened earlier to find her gazing down at him in wonder.

On the back of his head was a good-sized knot with a gash on it that had bled profusely. The lump was painful to the touch, and other aches and pains spread throughout his body, but all in all he was fine—and grateful to be alive.

Outside, the rain continued to drum down. There had been no more mudslides, and the air in the cave had warmed somewhat, although it was still dank.

Shining Moon saw Clay watching her and asked, "Why do you smile so?"

"Just looking at the prettiest woman I've ever seen," Clay told her.

"That blow on your skull has addled your senses."

"Nope. I'm seeing things clearer than I ever have." After a moment he asked, "What happened to Lawton? Did the slide get him?"

He saw the quick looks the members of the party exchanged. Only Rupert von Metz seemed uninterested. The young Prussian artist was sitting on the opposite side of the cave, his back jammed against the wall, his head slumped forward on his chest, his knees drawn up in front of him. He looked utterly exhausted and more than a little hostile whenever he glanced up at the others.

"Lawton did not wish to stay with us," Shining Moon said. "We gave him supplies and let him leave."

"That's all there was to it?"

"All that matters," she said flatly.

Clay decided not to press the issue. Something had happened—most likely between Lawton and Shining Moon—but he could tell from her expression and tone of voice that she did not want to discuss it. He knew that later he would get all the details from Proud Wolf, complete with colorful embellishments. The boy certainly liked to spin a yarn.

Clay ate more of the stew, then said, "Well, we've got a snug place to wait out the storm, anyway. But there's another problem. Aaron, open those packs of supplies and dig out as many blankets as you can find."

Aaron looked puzzled. "Blankets?"

"That's right. We've got to get out of these wet clothes before all of us catch a chill. It's warmed up in here a mite, but the clothes aren't going to dry very well as long as they're on us."

Professor Franklin was frowning, and Clay knew what prompted his concern. The presence of Lucy, not to mention Shining Moon, was going to cause a problem. But Clay had already thought of that, and he had seen a way to deal with it.

Aaron pulled a blanket from one of the packs, and Clay said, "Take that first one over there and tie a corner of it around that little knob of rock that sticks out. Then give the other corner to Proud Wolf."

Aaron nodded, seeing what Clay had in mind. Proud Wolf was sitting cross-legged beside the fire, but he stood up as his friend followed Clay's orders. When one corner of the blanket was tied around the rock as Clay had indicated, Proud Wolf took the opposite corner and held it up, pulling the blanket taut and forming a makeshift screen.

"You two ladies can shuck your clothes back there," Clay told Shining Moon and Lucy.

Shining Moon stepped behind the blanket, and Lucy followed reluctantly, her face burning with embarrassment. Proud Wolf could be trusted not to dishonor his sister by looking upon her nakedness, and if the young Hunkpapa man was tempted to sneak a look at Lucy, Shining Moon's wrath would discourage him.

"Pass out the rest of the blankets," Clay said to Aaron.

The other men awkwardly stripped off their wet buckskins and homespun. Three of the unloaded long rifles were leaned together in a tipi shape near the fire so that the wet clothes could be hung on them, a few garments at a time.

Aaron tossed two blankets behind the makeshift screen for Shining Moon and Lucy, then handed out the remaining ones for the men to wrap up in. There was no problem until Aaron tried to give one of the blankets to Rupert von Metz.

"Take that vermin-infested thing away from me," von Metz snapped. "If you think I am going to strip myself of my clothes and my last shred of dignity in order to garb myself like some sort of prehistoric aborigine, you are greatly mistaken."

"I think you've forgotten where you are, mister," Clay told him sharply. "If you catch a chill from wearing those wet clothes, it's liable to be the death of you. There's no doctor within a couple of hundred miles, and if you start running a fever, there won't be much any of us can do for you."

"Prussians are a hardy people," von Metz said haughtily. "We are accustomed to the cold and damp."

"All right, but I don't intend to sit around here nursing you if you get sick, von Metz. You may have to fend for yourself."

Von Metz glowered at him. "You would not abandon me!"

Clay thought the man sounded a bit less sure of himself than he had a moment earlier.

"Believe whatever you like. Have you ever seen a man burning up from the inside with the fever? It's not a pretty sight."

The Prussian took a deep breath, then snarled, "Give me that!" and snatched the blanket from

Aaron's hand. His face set in angry lines, von Metz removed his wet clothing and hurriedly wrapped the wool blanket around his pale, slender form. Then he slumped back against the wall to glare around the cave as if daring any of the others to say anything.

Clay was satisfied. He would not have abandoned von Metz if the man had gotten sick, but he saw no point in letting the problem develop in the first place.

He finished the stew and set his cup aside, then pushed himself to his feet and traded his own clothes for one of the scratchy blankets. He was still light-headed from the mishap earlier, so he moved carefully as he went over to Proud Wolf and said, "I'll hold that up now. You get those soaked buckskins off."

Proud Wolf turned over the chore to Clay while he changed, and Clay said, "You ladies about done back there?"

"We are ready whenever you are finished," Shining Moon replied.

Clay looked around, saw that all the men were covered with the blankets, including Professor Franklin, who looked rather ludicrous with his round, pudgy face sticking up above the blanket in which he was swathed. He lowered the screen as Shining Moon and Lucy resumed their places near the fire. Their hair, which had been soaked by the storm, was drying now, and it gave them a soft, fluffy look . . . sort of like a mountain goat after a rain. Clay figured they might not fully appreciate that comparison, though, so he kept it to himself.

Everyone settled back down around the fire, and after a moment Professor Franklin asked, "Well? What do we do now?"

Clay listened to the rain falling outside and gave the only answer he could.

"We wait."

The rain continued all day and well into the night, but sometime before dawn it finally stopped. When Clay stepped out of the cave the next morning, the sun was shining brightly, and a warm breeze moved over the face of the hillside. It felt good.

He had slept surprisingly well with Shining Moon snuggled against him. His slumber had been deep and dreamless, and when he awoke, he felt refreshed and even more clear-headed than the day before. He had been lucky to escape from the avalanche without any worse injuries than he had, lucky indeed, and he knew it.

The long rain followed by the strong southern breeze had cleaned the air, and Clay inhaled deeply as he stared out across the valley of the Missouri's three forks. He could see for thirty or forty miles, all the way to the distant horizon where the Absarokas rose. He lifted his head to scan the mountains looming above him.

A thin plume of smoke twisted into the air, off to the northwest. Clay stiffened as he spotted it. Somebody was up there, a few miles away over the rugged landscape, and he did not think it was Indians. The smoke from an Indian fire was never so easily seen.

Lawton? Clay considered that possibility, but according to Proud Wolf, Lawton had started off in a different direction. Besides, Clay did not think Lawton could have covered that much ground in such a short period of time, considering the storm in which he would have had to travel.

That left the men he had seen through the spyglass, the unsociable group that had left hurriedly when they realized they had been spotted. The thought that they, or some similar bunch, were up there made Clay vaguely uneasy.

Three of the men Lawton had brought out from St. Louis emerged from the cave behind Clay. All of them were carrying their rifles.

"Mornin'," one of them said. "Thought we'd go out and see about pottin' a deer or a bear or an antelope, get us fresh meat."

Clay shook his head and pointed at the rifles. "Not with those. I don't want any shooting for a while unless it's absolutely necessary."

The men frowned at him, and one asked, "Why not? 'Fraid well draw Injuns?"

"If there are any Indians around, they won't need gunshots to know we're here," Clay said. "No, I don't want to start any more avalanches. It's still mighty muddy, and some of those rocks up there could slip and fall without much prodding."

"You're saying the sound of a shot could start another rockslide?" The member of the trio who spoke sounded skeptical, and the other two looked as if they shared that sentiment.

"That's right. There are places in the mountains where you don't dare fire a shot even when it hasn't been raining a lot. I've heard about more than one man who went out to shoot a deer and wound up with half a mountain falling on him."

"Well, what are we going to do for fresh meat, then?"

As if in answer to the question, Proud Wolf emerged from the cave carrying the bow he normally wore strapped to his back. A hide quiver full of arrows was slung over his shoulder.

"I will hunt now," he said to Clay.

"Figured you might be wanting to," Clay said. "I was going to suggest it if you didn't. Be careful, though. Don't try to take down Old Ephraim with an arrow."

Proud Wolf gave Clay a look of amusement. "My people have hunted grizzlies before."

"Well, we can't carry a bunch of bear meat. A deer'll do just fine."

Proud Wolf loped off along the hillside, avoiding the worst patches of mud, and soon disappeared in the heavy timber that covered most of the foothills.

Shining Moon stepped out into the sunshine. She was wearing her buckskin dress and leggings, both of which were decorated with feathers and dyed porcupine quills. Most of the mud that had coated the clothes the day before had dried and flaked off. She ran her fingers through her long raven hair, and as Clay watched her, he thought she had never looked more beautiful.

"Good morning," she said. "You did not wake me."

"Didn't have the heart to disturb you," Clay explained. "You'd been through a lot, and I figured you needed your rest."

"Are you all right this morning?"

Clay reached up to the knot on the back of his head. "It still feels like a mule kicked me, but I'll be fine."

Shining Moon nodded, and as the three men who had been planning to hunt returned to the cave, she went over to Clay and slipped her arms around him.

"It is a beautiful morning," she whispered.

Clay lowered his face to hers and kissed her. It was so good to taste the sweetness of her lips, to feel the warm strength of her body pressed against him. . . .

A tingle of unease went through him.

Shining Moon must have sensed it because she took her mouth away from his and asked, "What is it?"

"Don't know," Clay answered honestly, frowning. He lifted his eyes and scanned the mountaintops again, but no longer could he see smoke. Whoever had been responsible for the fire was gone.

But still he had the uncomfortable feeling of

being watched. And he did not like it, not one damned bit.

Harry Lawton's fingers tightened on the flint-lock rifle in his hands. He wished he could lift it to his shoulder and put a ball through Clay Holt's head. He ached with the desire to kill Holt and that Indian wife of his.

But he was not ready yet. The time would come, but this was not it.

Lawton sank lower behind the boulder that concealed him. He was close enough to see Holt and Shining Moon but far enough away to keep from being spotted, if he was careful. He intended to be mighty careful until he had taken his revenge on the people who had wronged him.

Shivering and miserable in his wet clothes, Lawton closed his eyes and leaned his head against the rock. He wished he could get warm. He was chilled to the bone, and no amount of bright sunshine seemed able to penetrate the frigid cloak that had drawn around him.

He had not gone far the previous day after leaving the group, just far enough to be out of sight. He had firmly believed that some of his men would see the error of their ways and come after him when he stalked off, might even beg him to come back and take over command again—the command that was rightfully his. But that had not happened. The sorry bastards had chosen to cast their lot with Holt and that

Indian wife of his. Well, that was fine, just fine with Harry Lawton. They would *all* be sorry.

When it had become obvious that nobody was coming after him, Lawton stopped and turned around, then trailed the group to the hillside cave. As darkness fell, he had been able to see the warm red glow of the fire within the cave, and it had looked mighty appealing to him. But his pride would not let him go back. Besides, he knew that Shining Moon might have shot him if he had poked his nose in the cave. So he had huddled underneath a tree all night as the rain kept coming down. The tree did not offer much shelter, but it was better than nothing, Lawton supposed. Still, he was soaked to the skin, and with the soaking had come the cold.

Lawton's teeth chattered. Damn, he ought to have warmed up by now, he thought, especially the way the sun was shining. It was a beautiful day.

But it would be an even better day, he thought, when Clay Holt and Shining Moon were both dead. Then those other ungrateful sons of bitches would be glad to have him take over again. He had to handle this just right, though. He had to bide his time and wait until Holt was off away from the others. Better yet, Holt and the woman both.

A lot of fatal mishaps occurred in these mountains, and if an accident claimed their lives, the others would be quick to accept him again as their leader. The professor could not take over; he was an easterner and an inexperienced fool. Aaron Garwood was too green, and nobody was going to take orders from an Indian kid like Proud Wolf.

The thought of Rupert von Metz made Lawton shiver with rage. The Prussian had agreed to help him get even with Holt, but he had remained with him and the others, a traitor of the worst kind. Once he was in control again, Lawton would set the arrogant foreigner straight.

All he had to do was get rid of Holt and his squaw, and everything would be all right, Lawton told himself with great satisfaction. He could wait, too.

He just wished he could warm up.

Proud Wolf returned less than an hour after he had left the cave, the carcass of a young doe draped over his shoulders. He had brought it down with a single arrow, he explained, making the episode sound like an epic battle.

Clay and Aaron went to work skinning and gutting the deer, then carving off several steaks for the group's breakfast. They spent the rest of the morning smoking the remainder of the meat so they could take it with them.

The sun and the breeze dried the ground quickly, and by midday the mud had solidified. Clay and two of the other men scouted in a half-mile circle around the cave and found nothing threatening. The only interesting thing they found, in fact, was Clay's coonskin cap, hung on the branch of a bush that had been in the path of the avalanche. The cap had dried enough to wear it, and Clay settled it gingerly on his head, trying not to put pressure on the lump on his skull.

When he and his companions got back to the cave, Clay announced, "I don't see any reason why we can't move out and head on up into the mountains."

"You are sure you feel like traveling?" Shining Moon asked.

"I'm sure," Clay said. "You know me; I always feel better when I'm on the move."

She said with a trace of humor, "I have noticed this about you, Clay Holt."

Everyone was in good spirits as they gathered their gear in preparation for leaving. Even Rupert von Metz seemed to have recovered from his sour mood of the day before. During the morning he had set up his folding easel and taken a small canvas from his pack of artist's supplies. He had worked for hours depicting the impressive span of landscape around them. From what Clay had seen, von Metz had done a good job of capturing the view across the valley toward the Absarokas.

The remaining men Lawton had hired for the expedition in St. Louis had completely switched their allegiance to Clay, and they complied cheerfully with his orders as the group got moving again, heading higher into the mountains toward the dividing range. Clay suspected some of their newfound cooperation was due to Shining Moon. They had to respect her for the way she had handled herself during the aftermath of the avalanche, including the confrontation with Lawton. Some of that respect was rubbing off on him, as well.

They made good progress that afternoon and for the next three days. The fair weather held as the party climbed higher, leaving the foothills behind and entering the more rugged terrain of the mountains. They worked their way back and forth, following the valleys between the towering peaks and gradually treading higher and higher toward the passes that would take them over to the other side of the Rockies.

Clay had no major aftereffects from the blow on the head. The swollen lump gradually went down, leaving a purplish-yellow bruise that was tender to the touch. His mind remained clear, however.

As they traveled Clay kept a lookout for more smoke, but none was to be seen. If that mysterious group of men was still up there, they were either on the move or had extinguished their campfire, he thought. From time to time he felt that same instinctive crawling of his nerves that told him someone was watching. Whoever they were, they were good at what they were doing, damned good, Clay judged. And that kept him on edge.

If anything, the harrowing experiences the group had been through had brought them closer together. The men joked among themselves and did everything Clay asked them to do. Professor Franklin went back to his collecting and cataloging of specimens, assisted by Lucy and Proud Wolf, who listened intently as the professor gave a running lecture on botany and natural history. Aaron Garwood spent a lot of time with the professor, too, but Clay suspected Aaron's real motive was to be around Lucy rather than to learn more about scientific subjects. Rupert von Metz was the only one who kept to himself, and even he was not as hostile as he had been.

The storm had been the last gasp of winter. The days were mild now, and the new growth of spring was everywhere. The arching dome of sky above the mountains was dotted from time to time with fluffy clouds, but there was no more threat of rain. It was sights like this, Clay thought more than once as he paused to take in the magnificent vista surrounding them, that made the hardships of living in the mountains worthwhile.

On the fourth night after leaving the cave, the group camped in a meadow high on the side of a mountain. The plateau was covered with grass and trees, and a spring bubbled out of the rock base of the steep slope bordering it. The water was cold, clean, and sweet. If he had not promised to take the expedition on to the Pacific so that they could meet the boat waiting there for them in the fall, Clay would not have minded making this place his base camp for a summer of trapping. It was as close to perfect as a man could find. But he was responsible for Professor Franklin and the others, and he was going to get them through or die trying.

That thought crossed his mind while they were setting up camp. He had come close to dying more than once already, but that was the way of the mountains. They gave a man beauty and bounty, but sometimes they demanded a high price. Clay Holt had always been willing to pay that price if need be, and he was not about to change now.

But he wished he could shake that uncomfortable feeling that was gnawing at him. . . .

Harry Lawton shivered as he stared down at the glowing campfire below. Heat as strong as that which came from those flames raged through him, and it was hard to believe that only a few days ago, he had been worried because he could not get warm.

Well, he was warm now. He was a long way past warm.

Deep in the recesses of Lawton's brain, a part of him was still thinking clearly enough to realize that he was burning up with fever, no doubt a result of huddling under that tree in the rain all night after he had been forced to leave the expedition.

That was the way he remembered the confrontation now. They had *forced* him to leave, kicked him out as if he were no better than some mongrel dog. But they would pay for the way they had treated him; all of them would pay. *Especially Holt and his redskinned wife.*

For almost four days now, Lawton had trailed them, guided by instinct and whatever providence controls the fate of madmen. And he was undeniably mad, racked by fever and twisted by hate and resentment until his need for revenge was the only thing that kept him going. At first he had waited patiently for the perfect opportunity to kill Holt and Shining Moon, but he no longer cared about that. All he wanted was a chance, any kind of chance, to kill them all. He sensed that it would come soon.

When they camped in the meadow that evening, Lawton had skirted wide of the spot, staying out of sight as he moved beyond the campsite to the mountain above them. After darkness had fallen, concealing him, he climbed up to his rocky bower, where he would wait for morning. He was confident he could hold off an army up here if he had to. But he would not have to. The bastards would never know what hit them when he started cutting them down. Maybe he would save the two women for last, so he could have a little fun with them before he killed them.

Those insane thoughts were spiraling through his head as he fell asleep, exhausted by effort and illness. How long he slept, he had no idea, but suddenly something roused him, and he sat bolt upright from where he had slumped against the rocks. He saw the rosy glow in the eastern sky and knew that dawn was not far off. Already the predawn light was spreading over the face of the mountain.

Lawton lifted himself up so that he could peer over the rocks in front of him to the right and look down into the camp. But the sight that met his bleary eyes made him stiffen in surprise: Clay Holt was climbing up the steep slope, angling toward him.

Shining Moon awoke suddenly. Her arm went out, her fingers searching for Clay, who should have been lying beside her. Instead, her touch found only emptiness.

During the night she had been restless, unable to sleep. Something about this place bothered her, despite its beauty. Whatever it was had been enough to disturb her so that she did not fall asleep until long after midnight.

Exhaustion gripped her as she tried to pull herself awake now. Her eyes opened, and she saw the pinkish glow of approaching daybreak. She pushed herself into a sitting position, rubbed her eyes, and looked around for Clay but did not see him. No one else was moving around the camp either.

Clay must have gotten up early and relieved whoever was on guard duty, Shining Moon reasoned. She could not remember who that was.

Her gaze went to the outer edge of the plateau, then moved over to the slope that formed the other side. There, movement caught her eye.

Two realizations burst upon her at once. Clay was climbing the slope above the meadow; Shining Moon could see that. The other was the reason this place had looked so familiar to her.

It was the meadow from her vision, the place where she had called Clay back from the mountain of death, summoning him back to life. That was how she had interpreted the vision later, and she knew it to be the truth.

Now, a hundred yards away, Clay was climbing that mountain again.

She threw her blankets aside. As she stood up, she cried as loudly as she could, "Clay! Clay, come back!"

She saw him stop and turn, saw another figure suddenly lurch out from behind a clump of rocks about a dozen feet above Clay. Shining Moon recognized Harry Lawton. He was lifting a rifle, and she heard him howl out a curse as he pointed it at Clay. Then flame and noise belched from the muzzle of the rifle, and Clay fell.

Shining Moon screamed.

Too many things were happening at once. First Shining Moon shouting at him, then the scrape of a booted foot on stone and the insane cry of Harry Lawton from above him. Clay did not waste time trying to figure out how Lawton had come to be there. What the man wanted was all too plain.

He wanted Clay Holt dead.

Clay twisted aside, dropping to the rocky ground as Lawton fired. The rifle ball slammed through the air next to his ear—where his head had been an instant before. As he landed, his rifle slipped from his grip and went clattering down the mountainside.

Lawton tossed his empty rifle aside and reached for the pistol tucked under his belt. His eyes, deep-set in his haggard, bearded face, were shining with madness and, Clay thought, maybe something else. He thought Lawton looked sick, but that did not make him any less of a threat. Rolling over once, Clay jerked out his North and Cheney .56 caliber pistol as the muzzle of Lawton's pistol tracked toward him.

The two men fired nearly at once, and even over the twin blasts of black powder, Clay heard another noise—a deep, growing rumble from somewhere above Lawton. Hard on the heels of that sound came a whine as the ball from Lawton's pistol ricocheted off a rock six inches to Clay's left. A split-second later Clay's shot shattered the grip of Lawton's pistol, blowing it to splinters while neatly taking off the two middle fingers of Lawton's hand. He howled in pain and staggered back a step, shaking his wounded hand and sending a spray of crimson into the air as blood welled from the stumps.

The roaring was louder now, and Clay knew that somewhere up there above them, a rock had fallen, prodded from its precarious perch by the vibration from Lawton's first shot. That rock had kept tumbling and bouncing downhill, taking another with it, and another and another . . .

"Get down, you damned fool!" Clay shouted at Lawton. "Rockslide!"

Lawton ignored the warning. Catching his balance, he used his good hand to jerk his heavy hunting knife from its sheath. He lifted the blade and staggered toward Clay, the knife poised for a killing stroke.

Down in the meadow a rifle cracked. The ball drove into Lawton's chest, pushing him back a step and standing him up straight. At that moment the avalanche caught him. A heavy rock, bounding through the air, slammed into the back of his head. Blood gushed from Lawton's eyes, nose, and mouth as the impact pulped his skull.

Clay barely had time to see that gruesome sight before he was rolling frantically toward a rock ledge overhang to his right. It would offer him some protection from the avalanche, provided the force of the slide did not dislodge it, too. If the overhang fell, Clay would be crushed like an insect. But he was already being pelted by the rocks that swept past Lawton, bearing the dead man with them, and the rock ledge was his only chance.

The roaring filled Clay's ears, and dust clogged

his mouth and nose, choking him. He squeezed his eyes shut against the grit, but he could not keep from breathing it. Huddled there beneath the ledge, his arms crossed over his head for extra protection, Clay waited out the avalanche.

Although it seemed to take hours for the slide to pass him, Clay knew it was only a matter of minutes. Compared to the avalanche and mudslide that had struck the expedition several days earlier, this one was not very large. It was massive enough to have deposited a good-sized heap of rocks and rubble at the base of the slope, however, and protruding from that heap were the feet and legs of Harry Lawton. The avalanche would have killed Lawton even if the shot had not come from the camp.

At the thought of the camp, Clay looked toward the meadow, blinking dust from his watering eyes and wiping them clear. With relief he saw Shining Moon, standing with a rifle in her hands, and he knew she had fired the shot that Lawton had taken in the chest. Clay stood up and waved at her, and she dropped the rifle and ran toward the slope. She scrambled up to meet him as he slowly descended, careful not to start another slide. She passed Lawton's impromptu burial mound without even a glance at it and flew into Clay's arms, holding him tightly around the waist.

"You are not hurt?" Shining Moon asked as she pressed her cheek against his broad chest. "You are all right?"

362

"Reckon I'll be fine. Thanks to you."

"No! It was my fault. I knew this was an evil place. I should have warned you there was danger here—"

"Wait a minute. Slow down, slow down." Clay put his hands on Shining Moon's shoulders and peered into her eyes. "I don't know what you're talking about."

"You do not understand! I saw this place in a vision, when I thought you were going to die. This mountain means death, and I called you back from it." Anger flashed in her dark eyes as she looked up at him. "Why were you not in camp? Why were you coming up here?"

"I just thought it would be a good place to take a look around. I-I don't really know any reason other than that."

"Death was calling you," Shining Moon said ominously. "Death was angry that you cheated it before."

Clay did not know whether to take her claims seriously or not. But Shining Moon believed in what she was saying, so he was not going to scoff at them. *And maybe she's right,* he thought. Maybe Death—in the person of Harry Lawton —*had* been calling him.

He looked down at the camp and saw that everyone was awake now, jolted out of sleep by the gunfire and the rumble of the avalanche. Their anxious faces were turned up toward the mountainside.

Clay slipped an arm around Shining Moon's

shoulders and said, "Come on. They're waiting for us."

And as he led his wife down toward the camp, past the heap of stone where Lawton had been entombed, Clay noticed that the sun had come up, glowing bright and warm above the horizon.

XVII

There were no replies to the advertisements Jeff had placed in the *Journal* and the magazine called *Salmagundi*. Washington Irving was sympathetic when Jeff paid a call to the magazine's offices, which also happened to be Irving's living quarters.

"It's a shame you haven't been able to locate your wife, Mr. Holt," the well-dressed young man said as he leaned back in his chair behind a desk crowded with sheets of paper covered with handwriting. "Your tale is the stuff of great tragedy, worthy of the Bard or the ancient Greeks. Not that I want to trivialize your reality by comparing it to the fancies of literature. I mean no offense."

"None taken," Jeff assured him. He turned one of the sheets of paper on the desk around and looked at it. "What's this, if you don't mind my asking?"

"Oh, it's just one of a series of articles I've been working on for the magazine. The history of New York, you know, as purportedly written by one Diedrich Knickerbocker. The readers seem to enjoy them, even if some of the more old-fashioned among them are a bit shocked from time to time. I've been thinking about collecting the pieces into a book."

"Well, good luck with it," Jeff said. He turned toward the door of the office. "And thanks for trying to help."

"Wait a moment!" Washington Irving said. "What will you do now?"

"I haven't made up my mind," Jeff replied.

It was a question that had been preying on him, however, and he considered it again as he made his way back to the March house. He could not continue to impose on the hospitality of Lemuel and Irene, although they did not seem to mind having Ned and him as guests—and Rachel, Jeanne, and Barbara were certainly enjoying the company of their cousins. But staying in New York would be a waste of time, Jeff sensed. It was time to get on with his life.

The real question was—which way was he going?

Ned gave him the answer to that, at least in the short run. When Jeff went in, Ned was waiting for him.

Ned took hold of his arm and said, "After supper, cousin, the two of us are going out to see what sort of entertainment this town's got to offer."

"I don't think so, Ned—"

"Now, I'm not going to listen to any arguments. I've watched you moping around here for weeks, and I'm tired of it. You need a drink in a place where people are enjoying themselves. And so do I if I'm going to be shipping out in less than a week."

"Lemuel has a berth for you on one of his ships?"

"The *Fair Wind*. Good name, isn't it? She's leaving New York for the Carolinas in three days." Ned smiled. "I'm finally going to be a sailor, after all this time."

Jeff refrained from pointing out that Ned had decided to become a sailor less than a month earlier.

"What about it?" Ned said. "After supper we go find us a good tavern, right?"

Impulsively Jeff agreed. "All right. I suppose a drink or two wouldn't hurt."

Ned rubbed his hands together in anticipation. "I hope we can find an establishment with pretty serving wenches. It's been a long time—" He stopped short as he remembered that he was talking to a married man who had been away from his wife for a much longer time than Ned had gone without the favors of a serving girl.

Jeff read those thoughts on his cousin's face and said, "It's all right, Ned. I wish you good luck, even though I'll not indulge myself in those particular entertainments."

Ned's look of concern vanished, and he slapped

Jeff on the back. "This town won't soon forget that the Holts were here!"

That evening at supper, Lemuel and Ned talked about shipping, but Jeff was unusually silent.

"Well," Lemuel said after the meal had ended and the three men had withdrawn to the parlor, "what do you two lads have planned for this evening?"

Ned shot a startled glance toward Jeff, then looked back at Lemuel and asked, "What makes you think we, ah, have anything planned?"

"Nothing except that reaction of yours," Lemuel said. "It was just an innocuous question. But now I want to know—what *are* you up to, Ned?"

"We thought we'd go out and find a respectable tavern and have a short drink." Ned looked down.

"I see." Lemuel sounded unconvinced. "You didn't intend to pay a visit to some filthy dive, get stinking drunk, and paw the serving wenches all evening?"

"Of course not!" Ned's response was properly outraged.

"Good." Lemuel stood up, went over to the sideboard where his pipe and tobacco pouch were waiting for him, and picked up the pipe. He pointed its long curved stem at Ned. "Because I'm counting on you being a member of the *Fair Winds* crew when she weighs anchor in a few days. If you get yourself killed or hurt in some sort of brawl, or thrown into jail, I'll have to find a replacement for you at the last minute, and I don't like to do that. Do you understand me, Ned?"

"Yes, sir," Ned replied humbly.

"As for you, Jeff, I expect you to have a suitable influence on young Ned here."

"I'm not sure how much influence I can bring to bear," Jeff commented, "but I'll try, Lemuel."

"All right." Lemuel packed tobacco into the wide bowl of the pipe. "Whatever you do, stay away from Red Mike's down on Water Street. A more noisome place you'll never find. There's always some sort of sordid ruckus going on there."

"Red Mike's," Ned repeated. "We'll remember, sir."

"See that you do." Lemuel shooed them out of the room. "Go on, now."

The two young men got their hats and jackets from the rack just inside the front door and stepped outside, leaving their rifles in the house. It was doubtful they would need the long-barreled weapons that night. Both had pistols tucked into their belts, however, and Jeff carried his hunting knife as well.

As they strode down the street, Jeff asked, "Just where did you intend to begin the evening? I'm sure you have someplace in mind."

"Certainly I do." Ned grinned broadly in the twilight. "I thought we'd pay a visit to Red Mike's."

Jeff blinked in surprise. "But you heard what Lemuel said about that place."

"Indeed I did. Can you think of a better reason for going there?"

Jeff had no answer for that. He sighed, shook his head, and followed Ned.

From the outside, Red Mike's was just as squalid as Lemuel had made it out to be. It was located in a small stone building that did not open onto Water Street itself, as Lemuel had indicated, but rather onto a narrow alley running between that waterfront avenue and the next street over. A passerby had told them how to find the place, and the man had also said, "But only a fool'd go there. 'Tis sometimes worth a man's life to venture into such places."

Ned had not been impressed by the warning.

A red lantern hung over the doorway, which was probably what gave the place its name. The stench of human waste and rotting food from the alley made Jeff pause at the entrance to the passage.

"Are you sure you want to go in there?" he asked Ned.

"Of course. Why not?"

The answer seemed obvious to Jeff, but Ned was not in a mood to listen to reason.

"I don't much like the looks of this, Ned."

"It's just a tavern," Ned scoffed. "I've been in dozens worse than this. Come on."

Having been in worse places than Red Mike's seemed to Jeff a dubious reason to boast. He trailed after Ned, who walked boldly down the alley. The passageway was quite dark, the red-painted lantern giving off little light, and Jeff's boots slipped on the paving stones. He hoped he was not stepping in something too disgusting.

When they were halfway down the alley, the door of the tavern swung open, and a slender figure stepped out, silhouetted for a second by the garish light within. The sound of coarse laughter floated out with the figure, and if anything, the smell in the alley grew worse. The man shut the tavern door behind him and walked toward Jeff and Ned.

Jeff could barely make him out against the faint glow of the red lantern. He touched Ned on the arm and said, "Better step aside." The figure was striding toward them with his head down. Jeff and Ned moved over to let him pass.

The stranger stalked by them without a word. The brief glimpse Jeff had was of a man in dark clothes, wearing a floppy-brimmed hat and a cloak with the collar turned up so as to conceal most of his face. Ned turned to watch him pass, then cocked an eyebrow.

"Strange gent, eh?" he commented.

The door of Red Mike's suddenly slammed open again, and this time three men hurried out, carrying themselves with a tense, angry air as they looked up and down the alley.

One pointed toward Jeff and Ned and exclaimed, "There he goes!"

"Get him! Stop that son of a bitch!" another man howled.

Then all three pounded down the narrow alley, straight toward Jeff and Ned.

"Watch out, Cousin!" Ned yelled, grabbing Jeff's arm to jerk him out of the way. The men charged past, brandishing knives and pistols.

Relieved that the trio was not after him and Ned, Jeff turned to watch the pursuit. The man in the cloak had broken into a run, and despite the enveloping folds of the cloak, he moved with a lithe grace and speed. Barely slowing, he whipped around the corner onto Water Street.

"Come on!" Ned urged, tugging on Jeff's arm. "Let's go see what happens!"

Jeff had a pretty good idea of what was going to happen. After the three men caught up to their quarry, there would be a fight, and someone would be hurt, perhaps killed. The cause of the disagreement did not particularly matter: a perceived insult, an accusation of cheating at cards, the wrong look cast at the wrong woman—it could have been any of a hundred reasons.

While Jeff hesitated, Ned broke into a run and chased after the men who had just left Red Mike's. Sighing, Jeff went after him. Ned was just hot-headed enough to get involved with something that did not concern him in the slightest—and get hurt for his trouble.

When Jeff reached the end of the alley and emerged onto Water Street about ten feet behind Ned, he spotted the running figures at the end of the block. No one else was about at the moment, and it was easy to pick them out in

371

the light of a streetlamp. The men were closing in on the figure in the cloak. Jeff drew up alongside Ned, and both of them trotted after the others.

One foot of the fleeing man must have struck a loose paving stone, for he fell, sprawling heavily in the street. With triumphant shouts his three pursuers closed in.

"We got him now!" one of the men yelled, pointing his pistol at the fallen figure.

Almost too quickly for the eye to follow, the man in the cloak rolled over and whipped out a pistol of his own. Coolly facing the muzzle of his adversary's gun, the man fired, his flintlock pistol booming as the orange flash of fire split the darkness. The other man had been too slow. He let out a shriek of pain, doubled over, and was carried past the man in the cloak by his own momentum. He stumbled a second later and went down.

The cloaked man dropped the empty pistol, rolled again, and came up onto his feet in one efficient motion. The other two were practically on top of him when he regained his feet, however, and each of them held a knife. The lamplight glinted off the blades as they were lifted to strike.

Before those blows could fall, the light glittered on yet another length of cold steel, this one long and slender and wielded by the man in the cloak. The sword flashed through the air, its razor-sharp point raking across the wrist of one of the men. He screamed and dropped his knife as blood spurted from the slashed veins, spattering the paving stones at his feet. Dropping to his knees, he grasped his injured wrist, cradling it against him.

The remaining member of the trio lashed out frantically with his knife. There was a tearing sound as the blade tangled for a second in the folds of the black cloak, then ripped free. It had obviously not found flesh, for the cloaked man smashed a fist into his opponent's face with more power than that slender figure should have possessed. The blow rocked the man back a step, and the sword gleamed in the light once more as its edge cut across the man's chest.

He stumbled away from the lethal blade, throwing his own knife down and holding up empty hands.

"Mercy, damn you!" he called. "Mercy!"

Mercy was not in great supply, however. The man in the cloak slashed the sword across the outstretched palms. The other man flinched away from the cutting edge with a cry, then turned and ran, following the example of his wounded companion, who had lurched back to his feet and was stumbling down another alley.

That left only the man who had been shot in the belly. The cloaked figure strode over to him, prodded him in the side with a toe, then nodded in satisfaction. The man was dead.

"You bloody sot!" the victor said in a voice

startling in its clarity. "It's a shame you'll never know you've been bested by a woman."

Ned let out a low whistle of awe. Jeff was too shocked to respond.

The figure in the cloak whipped around and noticed Jeff and Ned for the first time. Her hat had come off in the fall, revealing close-cropped dark hair. She stiffened, then lifted the sword and pointed it at Jeff and Ned.

"Come ahead, if that's your wish," she challenged. "If it's trouble you're after, I can give you all you can handle."

Jeff found his voice first. "We want no trouble," he said. "We saw those men pursuing you and came along to see what was going to happen."

"Odds of three to one don't disturb you, eh?" The words were couched in scorn. The woman's voice had a British accent, and it was low and husky enough to pass for a man's.

Stung by her accusation, Ned said, "We would've pitched in to help you if you had seemed to need it. You handled those three with ease."

"It was a bit dicey for a moment or two," the woman said. She slid the sword into its sheath under the enveloping cloak and bent to pick up her hat and pistol.

Ned stepped forward impulsively and stuck out his hand. "I'm Ned Holt, and this is my cousin Jeff," he declared.

The woman hesitated and glanced over at the body of the dead man.

"This is hardly the time or place for introductions," she said. "Someone probably heard that shot and sent for the constable. I want to be well away from here before he puts in an appearance."

"All right," Ned said. "Come along with us."

"And why in blazes should I?"

"Because I'd like to know a woman who can fight like you can," Ned replied.

"How utterly charming. I'll wager you say that to all the ladies." With a jerk of her head she added, "Come along, if you've a mind to. I could use another drink. You lads might as well buy it."

"But not in Red Mike's," Jeff put in.

"No," the woman agreed dryly, "not in Red Mike's."

As they started along Water Street, heading in the direction of its intersection with Wall Street, Jeff cast a glance at the body lying on the paving stones. He had always been a law-abiding man —well, relatively so, at least—and it bothered him to leave the corpse. Also, even though the killing had been an undeniable case of self-defense, he was not sure he wanted to pass the evening in the company of this mysterious woman. But Ned seemed quite taken with her, and Jeff did not want to abandon his cousin.

"You haven't told us your name," Ned said.

"No, I haven't," the woman replied.

For a moment Jeff thought she was not going to say any more, but then she went on. "It's India. India St. Clair."

"That's an unusual name. A name for an unusual woman, I'd expect."

India St. Clair made no reply.

Jeff waited a moment, then asked, "Why were those men after you?"

"That's none of your business, now, is it?" India asked sharply.

"No, I suppose not. But surely you can understand why Ned and I are curious. It's not every day you see a fight between three men and a woman."

"Not with the woman emerging victorious, at any rate." India mulled it over for a few seconds. "I don't suppose it would do any harm to tell you. Those three didn't know I'm a woman. They saw me only as a potential victim. They were thieves."

"It looked more to me like they considered themselves the injured parties," Jeff commented.

"Well, you're wrong," India snapped. "Not that the attempt would have done them any good, even if they had overpowered me. I've no money. I'm flat broke, as you Americans say, and looking for a job."

"Flat broke?" Ned repeated. "That's absurd. A woman like yourself should always have money."

India paused and then said coolly, "Oh?"

"Of course. There are always means for a beautiful woman to earn a living."

Jeff knew what was coming and did nothing to prevent it. A lesson in manners would not hurt Ned.

India pivoted toward him, hooked her booted left foot behind his right knee, and drove her left elbow into his chest as hard as she could, while yanking his leg out from under him. Ned went down like a sack of grain and landed hard on the pavement. India was on him in a flash, slamming her knees into him and driving him down flat on his back. A small, wicked-looking dagger appeared in her right hand as if by magic, and she held the keen edge of the blade against his throat.

"I'll have none of that kind of talk," she informed him in a low, dangerous voice. "I'm a sailor and a fighter, not some tavern wench willing to let any man paw me for the price of a jug of ale!"

"All—all right!" Ned gasped, his eyes wide. He lay still, not daring to move with the dagger at his throat. His gaze cut over toward Jeff, who stood calmly with his arms crossed, a wry expression on his face. "You could give me a hand here, cousin!"

"It seems to me you're doing fine by yourself, Ned," Jeff said. "I'd rather you didn't cut his throat, though, Miss St. Clair. He *is* a relative of mine, after all."

"There's an old saying about how you can't choose your relatives," India said. Taking the blade away from Ned's neck, she stood up smoothly. "I'll not kill you, but mind your tongue in the future, Ned Holt."

"Oh, you can be sure I'll do that." Ned climbed

to his feet and rubbed his backside, sore from the hard landing on the street. "I'm sorry, Miss St. Clair. I didn't mean to insult you. I spoke without thinking."

"A failing common to most men." She put the dagger away, the small blade disappearing somewhere under the cloak just as the sword and pistol had earlier.

Jeff laughed and gestured toward the Tontine Coffee House, less than a block away.

"Instead of finding another tavern somewhere, why don't we go to the Tontine? I'd rather have a mug of hot coffee than a drink, anyway."

"As long as you're buying, Mr. Holt, I don't care. As I told you, I've no money."

"I'm buying," Jeff said. "Come on, Ned."

Ned was feeling his throat to make sure he was not bleeding. As he fell in step alongside Jeff and India, he complained, "You could have killed me, you know."

"Only if I'd wanted to," she said.

The three of them were soon seated at a table inside the main room of the coffeehouse, which would not close for another hour or so. Few customers were in the place. The barman brought them mugs of coffee, and Ned's was laced with brandy at his insistence.

"I need fortification," he said. "It's been a trying evening. I don't often come that close to having my throat slit by a young woman."

"No, I'd wager you've been in more danger from the husbands of young women," India said, drawing another chuckle from Jeff. She had not known Ned for long, but she already had him pegged.

After she had taken several sips of the bracing coffee, India said, "I'd rather not have it bandied about that I'm a woman, if you don't mind. I've gone to great pains to conceal that fact."

"Your hair, you mean," Ned said.

"And other things." She gave him a cool-eyed stare over the lip of her mug. "It helps being slender."

Ned slowly turned red as the meaning of her words sank in. Jeff would not have thought it was possible for Ned Holt to be embarrassed, but India had managed it.

"I think you must have an interesting story," Jeff said quietly. "If you'd like to talk about it, Ned and I would be glad to listen."

"Why should I talk to you two? I never saw either of you before tonight."

"That's as good a reason as any," Jeff said. "If you've been keeping it a secret that you're a woman, I imagine it's been pretty difficult not having anybody to talk to."

"Aye, that's the truth," India said, then hesitated, as if she realized she might be giving away too much of herself. Abruptly she shook her head, casting away that worry. "I suppose it wouldn't hurt to tell you. You strike me as honest blokes—even if Ned here is a bit too quick to assume he knows everything there is to know about the world."

Ned looked as if he could not decide whether or not to be offended by her comment, but he kept quiet.

"I was born in the slums of London," she began, "and a worse hellhole you're not likely to find. I never knew my father, and you can imagine what sort my mother was, a woman alone like that. She died when I was quite young, six years old, I think. It's difficult to be sure about things like that. Some sort of pox took her; it could have been one of a dozen different illnesses, considering the kind of life she led.

"Don't waste your sympathy on me, lads. I can see it on your faces. I made out just fine for a while. I was small and fleet of foot, the best thief and beggar Whitechapel ever saw. I would have been content to continue in that manner, but when I reached the age of about twelve, some of my mother's old friends showed up and wanted to start the same sort of business with me that they had with her. I was having none of that."

"I should say not!" Ned muttered.

India took another sip from her mug. "So I cropped off my hair, and that let me pass as a boy, at least for a while. I was convinced that wouldn't work forever, though, so I left London. It seemed to be the only thing I could do."

"Where did you go?" Jeff asked.

"To sea, of course," India said.

"That's right, you told us you were a sailor,"

Ned said, "while you were holding that dagger to my throat. I'm going to be a sailor, too."

"Is that so? Well, I began as a cabin boy. The masquerade was easy enough. Thinking I was a lad, the sailors left me alone, except for a few who preferred young boys to women. And they quickly learned to steer clear of me once they saw how well I handled a knife."

Jeff could well believe that.

"And you're still sailing?" Ned asked. "Surely you can't still be working as a cabin boy."

"No, I'm a common seaman. And none of my shipmates have known that I was a girl. Some of the problems I was anticipating never, ah, developed as I thought they would."

Ned blushed again, and to cover his embarrassment, he asked quickly, "So you've been sailing the Atlantic trade routes?"

"For nearly eight years now."

That would put her age at around twenty, Jeff thought.

"I've lived and worked with some of the toughest seamen to stride a deck," she continued. "They taught me how to fight and drink and handle a sword and pistol. And they taught me as well how to do my share of the work. That's all I ask of life—a job and a fair chance to do it."

"What are you doing here in New York?" Jeff asked.

India sat back in her chair. "I grew tired of traveling back and forth between America and

England. I'd rather make a life for myself here. But I can't do that until I can find a job and save some money."

"You're in need of work now?" Ned asked.

"That I am."

Ned leaned forward, his own cup of coffee forgotten in his excitement. "I'm shipping out in three days on a trading vessel called the *Fair Wind*. We're heading down the coast, bound for the Carolinas. If you'd like, I can speak to the owner about getting a berth for you. He's one of our relatives."

"Ned, I told you, I'm of a mind to give up the sea."

"But this is just a trading run up and down the coast. It's nothing like sailing to England and back."

"That's true enough, I suppose," India mused.

"If you were willing to make a few such voyages, your wages might give you enough of a stake to stay in America and do something else," Ned said.

The suggestion was logical enough, Jeff thought, but he had a hunch Ned was more interested in India for her beauty than he was for her abilities as a sailor.

After a few minutes India nodded. "I could give it a try, I suppose. But there's no guarantee this relative of yours would have a job for me."

"Oh, Lemuel will have a job for you," Ned assured her. "Either that, or he'll have to replace me. I won't sail without you, Miss St. Clair."

"I wouldn't back Lemuel into a corner if I were you, Ned," Jeff advised. "If you go giving him ultimatums, you're liable to lose your berth."

"Don't worry. I can handle Lemuel. Besides, I've lived this long without going to sea. If I had to wait a bit longer, I wouldn't be too bothered. But you'll see; it'll all work out."

Jeff wished he could muster up that much confidence about his own problems.

"You'll have to call me Max," India told Ned. "That's the name I've been using since I left London."

"Max St. Clair," Ned said. "I think I can manage that. I must say, though, India suits you better. It's a lovely name."

"Yes, well, I have no idea where my mother got it. She told me once that my father was an army officer who had been stationed there. At other times she told me I was the illegitimate grand-niece of the king or that my father was some sort of duke or earl. Which story she told depended on how much rum she'd had. All flights of fancy on her part, of course." India picked up her mug and drank from it. "You say this trading ship is going to the Carolinas?"

"Yes, but with several stops on the way—"

"Ned," Jeff interrupted, "do you think Lemuel would mind one more traveler on that ship? This one would be a passenger, though, not a sailor." For the first time in weeks, Jeff sounded lighthearted. "I'm afraid I don't know anything about the sea."

"You're going with us, too?" Ned looked genuinely surprised. He reached across the table to slap his cousin on the arm. "That's the best news yet! I really hated to think about us splitting up. We make a good team, you and I."

"I'm just considering it, mind you. But it's obvious I'm doing no good here in New York. And I'm not ready to head west again."

"I think it's a grand idea. We'll both get to see more of the country, and you know how the Holts are about new things."

"Well, I don't," India put in. "In fact, I don't have the foggiest notion what's going on here. But if you'll be sailing on the *Fair Wind*, Mr. Holt, I'll welcome your company. I've a hunch you may be able to help me keep this cousin of yours in line. That is, *if* I get the job, of course."

"I think you will," Jeff said. Now that he had gotten to know India a bit better, he liked her, although he still felt uncomfortable about the ease with which she had killed that man and the callousness that allowed her to leave his body in the street. But he was glad that he had decided to go along on Lemuel's trading vessel. Now that he had made his decision, he realized he had been dreading Ned's departure. If he were left alone in New York, he probably would have given up on his quest and returned to the mountains, never to see Melissa again.

"We need a real drink," Ned declared, signaling to the barman. "I want to celebrate the decisions we've all reached tonight. I think there's even more excitement to come."

"I'm not interested in excitement," India said. "Only in earning enough money to do as I wish for a change."

The barman brought over three jots of rum, and as Ned lifted his glass, he said, "Here's to adventure!"

Jeff and India looked at each other and shrugged. There was no dampening Ned's enthusiasm, and both of them sensed it was pointless to try.

"To adventure," Jeff agreed.

India echoed the sentiment, adding, "And may we have a fair wind indeed to Carolina."

The three glasses clinked together.

Part IV

Volumes might be written to prove the justice of the Indian cause; but in all national concerns, it has never been controverted by the history of mankind from the earliest ages of which we have any record, but that interest and power always went hand in hand to serve the mighty against the weak, and writers are never wanting to aid the cause of injustice, barbarity and oppression, with the sophistry of a distorted and unnatural philosophy; while the few who would be willing to espouse the rights of the feeble, have not enough of the spirit of chivalry, to expose themselves to an irreparable loss of time, and the general obloquy attending an unpopular theme; even in this so much boasted land of liberty and equality, where nothing is to be dreaded from the arbitrary acts of a king and council during a suspension of a habeas corpus law, or the mandate of an arbitrary hero in the full tide of victory.

Is not popular opinion frequently as tyrannical as star chambers, or lettres de cachet?

—Fortescue Cuming
"Sketches of a Tour to the Western Country"

XVIII

There is something tremendously awful in the approach, and raging of a storm at sea, accompanied by dreadful peals of thunder, quickly following each other, and the quick flashes of lightning bursting in streams from the dark and heavy loaded clouds pouring down rain in torrents. This was the case now, and we prepared for it.

—Fortescue Cuming
"Sketches of a Tour to the Western Country"

Dermot Hawley pushed through the crowd in the saloon, paying no attention to the resentful looks he garnered from some of the men he brushed past. This place, not far from the harbor in Wilmington, North Carolina, was called Soapy Joe's, and its inelegant name fit it well. The patrons who drank there were working men: sailors, cargo handlers, freighters, and the like. Mixed in with them were a few individuals in buckskins, hunters back from the Blue Ridge Mountains. Most men in Soapy Joe's earned

389

less money in a year than what Hawley's suit had cost.

Perhaps it had been foolish to come here, Hawley thought. He could have sent for the man he wanted to see and had him come to the office. But Dermot Hawley had never been one to let other men intimidate him, and he was not about to start now. If anyone in this dingy saloon wanted trouble, he would be glad to give it to him.

No one bothered him, however, as he made his way to the long bar and stepped up next to one of the buckskin-clad men leaning on the hardwood.

"Mr. Tharp?" Hawley said. "Amos Tharp?"

The man turned to look at Hawley. He was tall, rawboned, and broad-shouldered, and the buckskin shirt he wore was stretched tight over his muscles. Shaggy, reddish-brown hair hung almost to his shoulders below a wide-brimmed felt hat, and a mustache of the same shade drooped over his wide mouth. Brown eyes under bushy, rust-colored brows regarded Hawley with idle curiosity.

"I'm Amos Tharp," the man said after a moment of studying Hawley. "What do you want with me, mister?"

"A few minutes of conversation."

Tharp lifted his mug of ale from the bar and drained what was left in it. As he lowered it, he looked meaningfully at Hawley.

Hawley signaled the bartender to refill the

mug, and when that had been done, he said to Tharp, "I'd prefer a bit more privacy for our talk."

"We can go over here." Tharp lifted his full mug and gestured toward a table in the rear corner of the room. On either side of the table were a pair of high-backed benches, forming a booth of sorts. Tharp walked over to them and slid into one. Hawley followed and sat opposite him.

"I hope I can count on your discretion," Hawley began after he had introduced himself. "This is a business matter, and it's important that what is said here stays between us."

Tharp grunted. "Nobody ever accused me of flappin' my lips too much, mister. You got something to say, spit it out."

"All right." Hawley leaned forward slightly. "I'm told that you're a tough, dependable man, Mr. Tharp. I have need of just such an individual. I want to offer you a job."

"Figured as much. Doing what?"

"I'm putting together a wagon train of supplies to take over the Blue Ridge into Tennessee. I intend to sell them to the settlers there."

Tharp stared at Hawley for several seconds before saying, "Not a bad idea. I've been over there. Lot of those folks're pretty self-sufficient, but they miss goods from home. I reckon you'll find a market—if you can get your wagons through."

"That's where you come in, Mr. Tharp."

Slowly Tharp lifted the mug to his mouth and drank, then wiped his lips with the back of his other hand.

"You want me to take charge of that wagon train?"

"Exactly. I'm told you've been over the passes and into Tennessee many times. Is that correct?"

"I know the way," Tharp said. "It's pretty rugged in places, but wagons can get through all right. What you really got to worry about are Cherokees and bandits. They're thicker'n flies in those mountains."

"That's what I've heard. And that's why I need a strong man I can rely upon." Hawley lowered his voice a little and went on, "I'm interested in results, Tharp, not in how you achieve them. You'd have a free hand to hire some of the men you want to take with you. I'm not going along with the wagons. You'd be completely in charge."

Again there was a moment of silence as Tharp turned over Hawley's offer in his mind.

"What'd be stoppin' me from takin' the money I get for those supplies and headin' on west, or wherever else I might want to go?"

Without hesitation Hawley replied, "In addition to being told that you're tough and ruthless, I've also heard that you're an honest man. If you give me your word, I believe you'll bring the money back." Hawley leaned back. "Besides, if you don't, I'll hunt you down and kill you like a dog."

For the first time during this conversation, a

hint of a smile played around Tharp's mouth. "I reckon you would, at that," he said. "What's this job pay?"

"Five hundred dollars," Hawley stated flatly.

Tharp cocked an eyebrow, but that was the only sign of surprise on his weatherbeaten face.

"That's a lot of money."

"It's well worth it to me to know that those wagons will get through safely."

Tharp took a deep breath and said, "All right. I'll take the job." He extended a callused hand across the table. Hawley took it and shook hands with him, sealing the arrangement.

Hawley told Tharp where the office of his freighting company was located, then said, "Come by there tomorrow afternoon, and I'll give you all the details. I don't yet know exactly when the wagons will be ready to roll, but it should be within the next couple of weeks."

"You say I can hire the drivers I want?"

"Within reason. I already have several lined up, but we'll need about a dozen more. They'll need to be men who can handle themselves in case of trouble."

Tharp nodded. "I understand. I'll start lookin' around, see who's available. By the time those wagons of yours are ready, I will be, too."

"Excellent."

Lifting his mug of ale, Tharp asked, "Stay and have a drink with me, Mr. Hawley?"

"I'd like to," Hawley lied as he stood up. He did not want to stay in Soapy Joe's any longer than he had to. The smell of stale, spilled beer and unwashed humanity was powerful inside the saloon. "I'm afraid I have to leave, however. I have another business meeting tonight. It's going to be a busy time between now and the wagons' departure. A great many details still remain to be arranged."

"I understand." Hawley raised the mug another few inches. "But in the meantime, I'll drink to the success of our little venture."

"I echo that sentiment," Hawley said. "Good night, Mr. Tharp."

Tharp was too busy swallowing ale to return the farewell, but he lifted a hand and waved to Hawley.

As he moved through the crowd again, Hawley noticed that the patrons did not regard him with as much disdain as when he had entered. His conversation with Tharp and his obvious agreement with the man had changed the opinion of the other customers. A man who met with Tharp's approval was probably not a worthless dandy, no matter how well he dressed. It was an interesting form of status discrimination, Hawley thought as he left the waterfront saloon.

His carriage was waiting for him at the curb, and the driver looked decidedly relieved as Hawley climbed into the vehicle. The man had probably been afraid Hawley would never get out of Soapy Joe's alive.

"We'll go to Mr. Merrivale's house now," Hawley told him.

"Very good, sir," the man said.

As soon as Hawley was settled inside the carriage, the driver picked up his reins and whipped the fine pair of horses into motion. The carriage rolled quickly away from the harbor.

Dermot Hawley leaned back against the rich brocade cover of the padded seat. The freighting business had been good to him. He had started with one wagon—stolen—several years earlier, and no drivers. Hawley himself had handled that chore. In a relatively short period, he had built the business into a thriving enterprise, sometimes honestly, sometimes cutting corners when that was necessary. On a few occasions the wagons of rival freight lines had mysteriously burned or crashed with the loss of their cargo. Hawley did whatever he had to in order to keep the business growing. The scheme he had concocted to dispose of stolen goods in Tennessee was a prime example. If it went off as planned, everyone would be happy—the men who were supplying most of the merchandise; Charles Merrivale, who would make a small, legitimate profit; and Hawley himself, who would make a large, dishonest profit.

He chuckled as he thought about the setup. Merrivale's involvement provided excellent camouflage, and Hawley would appear even more on the up-and-up once he married Melissa and was a part of Charles Merrivale's family. And there were added benefits to be had, too, such as Melissa's smooth white body in his bed.

Just thinking about that made Hawley tap on the roof of the carriage and call to the driver, "A little more speed, dammit! I'm in a hurry."

The ride got a bit rougher as the carriage clattered over the cobblestone streets at a higher speed. Hawley did not care, not as long as his thoughts were occupied with visions of Melissa.

Ten minutes later the carriage came to a stop in front of the whitewashed, two-story frame house that Merrivale had bought on his return to North Carolina. Hawley opened the door and alighted without waiting for the driver's assistance. He was eager to get inside and see Melissa.

"Go on around back," Hawley told the driver, who was only halfway off the seat. "I'm sure one of the servants will give you something to drink."

"Thank you, sir. I'll be ready to depart whenever you are."

Without acknowledging the man's comment, Hawley strode up the flagstone walk to the veranda that ran along the front and both sides of the large house. He went up the stone steps and crossed to the ornately carved front door. A lion's-head knocker was in the center of the panel, and he rapped it sharply.

One of the maids answered. Hawley had heard her referred to by name, but he did not recall it. Not that it mattered, anyway, he thought as he brushed past her and took off his beaver hat and the cloak draped around his shoulders.

"Tell Mr. Merrivale I'm here," he said coldly

as he handed the hat and cloak to the young woman.

"Yes, sir," she said, never lifting her eyes to his. "I'll tell Mr. Merrivale. You can wait in the library if you want."

"Of course." Hawley adjusted the cuffs of his shirt as he walked from the foyer down the central corridor toward the library. He pulled the lace cuffs out just the proper distance from the sleeves of his coat.

By the time Charles Merrivale appeared in the library a few minutes later, Hawley had already poured himself a drink from one of the decanters on a sideboard, which he knew was always kept well-stocked.

"Good evening, Charles. I hope you don't mind my paying a visit this evening and helping myself to some of your fine whiskey." Hawley raised the glass of smoky amber liquid in a salute to his host.

"Of course not," Merrivale replied, although his ruddy face bore an expression of faint annoyance at Hawley's unexpected arrival. "I trust this is important."

"I think so," Hawley said smoothly after he had taken a sip of the whiskey. "I've just hired a man to be in charge of the wagon train. He comes highly recommended as a frontiersman and guide. I'm told he's fought Indians and hunted all over the Blue Ridge Mountains."

Merrivale's expression brightened. Finding the right man to lead the wagon train was one of the most important tasks involved in this undertaking, and Merrivale was as well aware of that as Hawley.

Merrivale crossed the room, took a glass from the sideboard, poured himself a drink, and asked, "What's his name?"

"Amos Tharp. I don't know if you've heard of him or not."

"Tharp, Tharp . . ." Merrivale mused. "No, I don't believe so. You say he was recommended to you?"

"By some other business associates." As a matter of fact, they were the same men who were providing Hawley with the stolen goods that would be transported on the wagons, but Hawley kept that information to himself.

"Well, if you trust him and think he's the man for the job, I'm sure he'll work out fine," Merrivale said. "Is there anything else we need to discuss?"

"Not relating to our business affairs. I was wondering, though—is Melissa here?"

"She has retired for the evening," Merrivale said, the look of vague annoyance returning to his face. "Caring for a young child can be quite tiring, even with servants to help."

"Yes, I imagine so." Hawley hesitated, concealing his disappointment that he would not be able to see Melissa. He had planned on carrying a fresh image of her beauty away with him when he left. But he could still take advantage of this turn of events.

"In that case, I'd like to talk to you about a personal matter, Charles. Have you said anything else to Melissa about that vanished husband of hers?"

Merrivale grimaced. "I've spoken to her until I'm blue in the face. She refuses to listen to reason. I've explained that with the help of my attorneys, she could easily divorce Holt in absentia or even have him declared legally dead, since he's been gone so long." Merrivale tossed off the rest of his drink. "Hell, for all any of us know, he really could be dead."

"One can only hope," Hawley said.

"I'm sorry, Dermot," Merrivale said sincerely. "I honestly thought Melissa would come around before now. I know how you feel about her, and I've considered ordering her to divorce Holt for her own good. She'd be much better off with you. But she's so damned stubborn. It would be just like her to pretend to go along with my wishes, then stand before a judge when the time came and claim that she was being pressured into it against her will. How would that look?"

"Not good," Hawley murmured, frowning. Merrivale was right; it would be much better if Melissa came around to their way of thinking of her own accord. Then she would not be able to back out once it came time for her to marry him. "We'll just have to be more patient, Charles. But I warn you, I'm not going to wait forever."

"I know, I know. I'll do what I can." Merrivale

399

glowered at the floor. "If her mother would just cooperate with me, blast it all. But Hermione's getting more and more intransigent with time. I suppose Melissa gets her pigheadedness from her. But it will all work out, Dermot. You have my word on that."

Hawley hoped Merrivale was right. He would hate to have to postpone his conquest of the fair Melissa for too much longer. Hawley was not a man accustomed to waiting for what he wanted.

He finished his drink and said, "I'll be going, then. I just wanted to stop by and tell you the good news about Tharp. We can proceed with all due speed now."

"My goods are ready. What about the ones coming in by ship?"

"According to what I hear at the harbor, the trading vessel should be here in less than a week. She will have stopped at several other ports on the way down the coast from New York, but I'm sure there will still be plenty of cargo in her hold."

"Do you know the name of this ship?"

"Yes, indeed." Hawley smiled. "And if I were a superstitious man, which I most assuredly am not, I'd think it was a good omen. The ship is called the *Fair Wind.*"

Jeff Holt would not have believed a man could be as sick as he was during the first few days of the voyage and not die. Even though the ship rarely was out of sight of land and the captain spoke glowingly of what good weather they were having, the ever-present up and down motion of the vessel was enough to send Jeff dashing to the railing until it seemed nothing at all was left inside him, that he ought to collapse like an empty sack of skin. But somehow he did not. He survived—although he was no longer sure he wanted to.

Ned proved to be surprisingly adaptable. His features had carried a green hue the first day out from New York, but by the morning of the next day, he had his sea legs, as India put it. Of course, India—or Max, as she was known aboard ship—was not bothered at all with seasickness. She had been riding the plunging decks of ships for years now and was more at home there than anywhere.

It had not proven difficult to secure a berth for India on the *Fair Wind*. Ned had simply explained to Lemuel that he and Jeff had made the acquaintance of a young man named Max St. Clair, an experienced sailor who wanted to return to sea. Each time a ship was in port for any length of time, some turnover in the crew was to be expected, and as luck would have it, there was indeed a need for another crewman on the *Fair Wind*. India, accompanied by Jeff and Ned, had paid a visit to Captain Jebediah Vaughan, and India had told the captain the names of the vessels she had sailed on in the past. Vaughan, a stout, veteran sea dog with snow-white hair and beard, recognized the names of the ships and their captains.

"If you're a good enough seaman to sail with them, lad, you'll do to be a member of the *Fair Wind*'s crew," he had told India. If he had any inkling that there was a young woman's body under India's clothes, he gave no sign of it.

Lemuel had been equally delighted that Jeff intended to sail down to North Carolina as a passenger. "Good luck, my boy," he had said to Jeff when the entire March family congregated on the docks to see the ship off. "I pray that someday your search will finally be rewarded."

"So do I, Lemuel," Jeff said, shaking Lemuel's hand. "So do I."

Irene and the girls had hugged Jeff and Ned good-bye, and as usual Jeanne had been quite ardent in her farewell, especially with Ned. As the young woman hugged Ned, Jeff had glanced up at the deck of the ship and seen India there, watching the farewells, and he thought he detected disapproval on her face.

With Ned beside him at the railing, Jeff had waved to his relatives as the *Fair Wind* cast off and headed out into the harbor. Inside that somewhat protected haven, the waves had not been too bad, and Jeff hadn't minded the motion of the deck under his feet. The farther out to sea the vessel went, however, the worse he had felt, until finally his stomach clenched with nausea.

That had been the beginning. For almost three

days, there had been no end in sight. By that time Jeff was pale and haggard, and he swore a solemn oath that once he reached North Carolina, he would never set foot on a ship again.

Until then, he would simply have to suffer if need be, although the sickness had improved greatly in the past day or so.

Elsewhere on board the *Fair Wind*, Ned Holt was learning what it was like to live the life of a common seaman. It was dirty, boring, exhausting work, he soon discovered. But he did not mind; he got to spend hours each day toiling alongside India, an opportunity that was worth all the effort.

She had not been lying about being an experienced sailor. Even though she had never been on the *Fair Wind* before, she had sailed on enough British East Indiamen that she seemed to know the vessel from stem to stern. Every time Captain Vaughan bawled out an order to trim the sails, India seemed to anticipate the command and hurried to obey it even as the captain's voice boomed out. Ned stayed close to her, and in a low voice she told him what to do.

The only problem with that, as far as Ned was concerned, was that her beauty was distracting. Everyone else on board might see a slender, athletic young man, but Ned knew she was a woman. In the loose white trousers and striped jersey she wore on board the ship, she was lovely, even when her face was coated with beads of sweat from wrestling with some balky rigging.

The ship was off the coast of Maryland when dark, billowing clouds took shape in the sky. Ned and India were sitting cross-legged on the deck, their backs against the wall of the forecastle while they mended one of the spare sails. Ned looked up at the darkening heavens to the northeast.

"What's that?" he asked.

"I'd say we're in for a bit of a blow," India replied. On board the ship, where it was necessary to maintain her masquerade as a young man, she kept her voice pitched low. She did not seem particularly disturbed by the approaching storm, barely glancing at the clouds before resuming her work.

Ned was worried, however. He looked toward the mainland, some two miles to the west.

"Shouldn't we be heading for shore?" he asked.

India shrugged. "That's up to Captain Vaughan. Sometimes it's easier to ride out these squalls if you steer clear of land. I think we should finish what we're doing and let the cap'n worry about it. There'll be plenty of time to finish up on this sail before the wind hits."

She sounded sure of herself, and Ned wanted to believe her. But the clouds were growing blacker now, and they looked to him almost as if they had teeth in them. For the first time since leaving New York, he wished he had not been so impulsive in coming along on this voyage.

Jeff emerged from the hatch where stairs led down to the cabins belowdecks. He spotted Ned and India and strode toward them, adopting the rolling walk that compensated in part for the motion of the ship.

"What's going on?" he asked. "Aren't the waves getting a little rougher?"

"There's a storm coming," Ned told him. "At least that's what Max says, and I believe him."

Looking up at the dark clouds, Jeff muttered, "So do I. Is there anything I can do to help?"

"No. You'd best go back belowdecks," India said. "You're a passenger on this ship, Jeff, not one of the crew. We'll handle things."

With a worried expression that matched Ned's, Jeff asked, "Are you sure?"

"I'm sure," India said.

"Well, all right. But if you have need of me, I'd be glad to lend a hand. I'm no sailor, but I can follow orders."

Captain Vaughan came up behind Jeff in time to hear his last comments. The captain slapped Jeff on the shoulder.

"We appreciate the offer," he said, "but Max is right, Mr. Holt. You go below and leave everything to us. We'll see you and the *Fair Wind* safely through this storm."

"Thank you, Captain," Jeff told him, then went over to the open hatch and ducked through it.

India folded the big square of sailcloth. She had finished patching it while Ned fretted over

405

the approaching squall, and he felt a twinge of guilt as he realized he had left the rest of the work to her. He had not meant to become so distracted.

India rose lithely to her feet and thrust the folded sail into Ned's hands. "Take this below and put it back in the locker where we got it," she said.

"All right. Anything else I can do?"

"Get back above deck and keep your eyes open," Captain Vaughan said. "And do everything that Max tells you to do. He's been through blows like this before. Haven't you, lad?"

"Dozens of times," India agreed. "You're not going to sail for shore, then, Captain?"

"The coastline's too rugged along here. There's nary a good place to get out of a storm. The wind would just drive us ashore and wreck us. Best we try to skirt this squall and outrun the worst of it."

The wind hit then, a cold, swirling force. The sails were already full, but with the sudden change in wind direction, they fluttered.

Vaughan turned and bellowed toward the bridge, "Helmsman!"

The veteran sailor at the wheel was already spinning it, sending the vessel veering to starboard. The sails billowed again as they caught the wind. The ship would have to tack back and forth into the teeth of the gale to keep from being driven out of control. It was a tricky maneuver, but one an experienced captain such as Jebediah

Vaughan would have carried out successfully scores of times.

Ned returned from stowing away the mended sail belowdecks, his face pale and drawn as he hurried to join India. On the way he passed Vaughan, who was striding toward the bridge.

"All hands to your stations! All hands to your stations!" the captain bellowed.

India was waiting for Ned. The wind tousled her short hair and pressed the blue-striped jersey and white trousers to her body. Ned could see the gentle curve of her bound breasts under the jersey.

"Stay close to me," she said to Ned, raising her voice to be heard over the wind, which was steadily increasing to a howl. "We have to watch these lines and make sure they stay taut!"

The two of them clambered atop the forecastle and made their way to the ropes that controlled one of the secondary sails. The *Fair Wind* was a three-master, and Ned and India were assigned to the foresail, along with several other seamen. As long as Captain Vaughan and the helmsman kept the ship on the proper course, there should not be any problems, but with the changeable nature of winds in a squall, that was sometimes impossible to do.

The waves were higher now, and wind drove so much spray over the ship that Ned was soaked in a matter of moments. His stomach lurched each time the vessel plummeted into one of the troughs formed by the storm, and he wondered how Jeff was holding up below in his cabin.

Rain pelted down. Ned's feet, shod in rope-soled sandals he had bought in New York on India's advice, maintained a precarious grip on the deck as he made his way to his station alongside her. Feet spread wide apart to brace himself against the jolting ride, he stayed there for the next fifteen minutes, his hands on one of the ropes that controlled the foresail. He gripped the rope until his hands burned and his muscles felt aflame. He could barely see a foot in front of him, but still the storm raged.

Finally the force of the wind diminished somewhat. Though the squall had been fairly short in duration, to Ned it seemed much longer.

He leaned closer to India and called over the wind, "Was this a bad one?"

She shook her head, her hair plastered to her skull like a tight cap. "I've seen much worse, but this one may not be over yet."

Ned had hoped that within another five or ten minutes, the storm would be behind them, but that was not to be the case. After a lull of a couple of minutes, the wind strengthened again, and the popping of the sails as the wind caught them was like gunshots. Ned hung on tight to the rope in his hands as the ship again plunged wildly.

Suddenly he heard an even louder popping sound, but this one was much closer to India and him. He jerked his head around, and his eyes widened in shock as he saw the big boom of the mainsail whipping toward them, trailing a broken line behind it.

Ned dove to his right, acting immediately when he saw the threat. He wrapped his arms around India's shoulders, and as he crashed into her, the collision sent both of them sprawling to the wet planks of the deck. The heavy boom slashed through the air directly above them. Had it hit them, Ned realized, their backs would have been broken, at the very least.

Men were already leaping to grab the boom and wrest it under control. On the bridge Vaughan bellowed orders again. To Ned it was all chaos, punctuated by slamming gusts of wind and rain. But he did not care. He had saved India's life, and that was all that mattered.

"Get off of me, you great bloody oaf!" she shouted in his ear.

Surprised by her reaction, Ned realized he was lying on top of her, all the weight of his brawny form resting on her slender one. He rolled to the side and sat up, and India did, too, her chest heaving as she dragged air into her body. He had knocked the breath out of her when he landed on her.

"I'm sorry," he said, resting a hand on her shoulder.

"No need to apologize for saving my life. I'm the one who's sorry for shouting at you. I was having trouble breathing, you see."

Ned looked a bit sheepish at the thought going through his mind: If he was going to be lying on top of India, he would much prefer that it be under more pleasant circumstances.

He got to his feet and gave her a hand up. The wildly swinging boom was back under control now. It had torn a hole in the foresail, but that could be repaired. They were all lucky, Ned realized. Someone could have been killed, and the ship could have been crippled.

Minutes later the wind died down again, and this time the storm continued to slacken. Within a quarter of an hour, the clouds were scudding off toward the southwest, and slanting rays of afternoon sunlight were breaking through. The *Fair Wind* rode easily on a sea grown placid once more.

Jeff reappeared on deck, looking pale and drained. He found Ned and India and asked, "Is it over?"

"It's over," India assured him.

"Was it bad up here?"

"Bad enough," Ned answered.

"Your cousin saved my life." India looked over at Ned and went on, "And I don't believe I've thanked him properly yet."

Ned flushed. He wanted more than anything else to take India into his arms and express how glad he was she had not been injured, but of course he could not do that. Not with everyone except Jeff thinking that she was a young man.

"You can tell me some other time," he said gruffly.

"I'll do that," India said, her husky voice unusually soft. "I'll just do that, Ned Holt."

XIX

Three weeks had passed since Harry Lawton's death, and in that time the botanical expedition led by Clay Holt had climbed higher into the mountains. For the past week, however, they had been camped in a small valley just below the last approach to the pass that would take them to the dividing ridge of the Rockies. Professor Franklin had fallen in love with the spot as soon as he saw it and asked Clay if they could establish a temporary base camp there.

"Never have I seen such an amazing variety of vegetation and mineral formations," the professor had declared. "I must have some time in which to study them."

Clay had been happy to go along with Franklin's request. He had suffered no lasting effects from the injury he sustained in the avalanche, and his strength returned quickly. Nevertheless, he and the others had all traveled long and hard and could use the rest.

Spring was in full bloom now, and some days were so warm that they could have been mistaken for those of summer. The members of the expedition were happy to wait in this beautiful valley, surrounded by trees and wildflowers and the towering, majestic beauty of the mountains, while Professor Franklin dug up plants, chipped rocks, and puttered to his heart's content.

Even Rupert von Metz, while still not what anyone could call friendly, seemed satisfied by the decision to camp in the valley. He spent most of each day at his easel, painting the mountains around them. Part of the time, however, he worked on the maps he had been making all during the expedition. He unbent enough to allow Clay to take a look at the charts.

After studying them, Clay commented, "This is a fine job of map-making."

"What did you expect?" von Metz asked brusquely, and Clay did not push the issue any further.

After spending two days in the valley, Clay had come to a decision.

"If we're going to stay here awhile," he told the group, "we might as well fix some better places to sleep, instead of rolling up on the ground in our blankets every night. We'll build tipis, like Shining Moon's people. There're plenty of deer around here to provide buckskin."

So for the next few days, hunting parties went out and returned with deer. Clay, Shining Moon, and Proud Wolf were in charge of the skinning, and after the hides had been cured by the sun, Shining Moon taught Lucy how to sew them together, using thread fashioned from deer gut. The young woman from Massachusetts had been less than enthusiastic about the task, but she went along with what Shining Moon told her to do. In the meantime, the group ate well—venison steaks at some meals, a savory stew made from deer meat with wild onions and roots at others. The venison that was left over was smoked to preserve it so they could take it with them when they finally left the peaceful valley.

And it certainly was peaceful. Clay had been watching for smoke or other signs of habitation around them, but so far there had been none. In a way, that was bothersome.

Shining Moon felt the same way, and one day as they were scraping a hide before pegging it out to dry, she said, "We should have seen Shoshone by now."

"I agree," Clay said. "This is good hunting country for them. Something's got them spooked, I reckon, so they're staying away."

"Those men we saw from the valley of the Missouri? The ones whose smoke you saw?"

"Could be. The Shoshone have always gotten along well with white men, though. I wonder why they're avoiding this bunch."

Shining Moon put down the tool she was using. "I do not know. But dwelling in these mountains is something besides beauty."

Lifting his head to squint up at the peaks, Clay slowly stood up. "You're right. I feel it, too."

But other than keeping their eyes open and making sure guards were posted every night, they could do nothing about whatever was causing their unease—and wait for Professor Franklin to be ready to move on.

Aaron Garwood walked carefully through the woods, his long-barreled flintlock rifle held ready for use, his thumb curled around the cock. The deer droppings that had led him into this thick stand of trees were fresh, and he expected to spot the animal at any moment.

He had been foolish, he supposed, to wander off from the others in his hunting party. But although he had gotten to know the other men and liked most of them, at times he felt the need to be alone, and today was one of those times.

It was hard to believe that Zach had been dead for less than a year. Sometimes it seemed to Aaron that his brother had been gone much, much longer. And in truth, Aaron mused now, the Zach he preferred to remember, the big brother who had protected and loved him, had been dead for a long time—if indeed that Zach had ever existed.

For years Zach Garwood had lived a lie. He had preached hatred for the Holt family, especially Clay, spewing his venom about Clay's having gotten poor Josie pregnant and run out on her—when all along it had been Zach himself who had committed the almost unthinkable sin of raping his own sister. But Luther, Pete, and he himself had listened to the lies and believed them, and they had hated the Holts with the same fanaticism that Zach possessed.

Now Luther and Pete were dead, along with Zach, and Aaron knew the truth behind it all. The way he had once felt about Clay was almost incomprehensible. He'd never had a better friend than Clay Holt, and although not a day went by that he did not feel the weakness in his left arm —the arm Clay had broken in a fight—Aaron never held that against him. Clay Holt might have broken his arm, but he had also repaired the damage done to Aaron's spirit by years of lies and hate.

Clay had not been able to do anything, however, about the melancholy that gripped Aaron from time to time. Aaron tried to keep the memories to himself, memories of watching his brothers die, of seeing his sister turn into a whore and his father grow old and bitter before his death. It was better for him to get out and do something when the recollections started to overwhelm him.

Like joining the hunting party today.

The valley where the base camp was located was two miles away. Aaron and the others had headed northeast along the range of mountains, making their way through other small valleys. They had splashed through several fast-flowing creeks that had looked like prime spots for beaver. Aaron did not have the expert eye that Clay did for such things, but he had learned from Clay and was developing his instincts. This would have been fine trapping country if they still had all their gear, Aaron thought.

He had split off from the rest of the men, telling them he would be back in a few minutes, when he had spotted the droppings. That few minutes had stretched into more than half an hour, and Aaron knew that if he did not spot the deer soon, he ought to return to the hunting party. But it was so quiet and peaceful and beautiful here that he just wanted to enjoy it.

It occurred to him that even if he found the deer, he might not shoot it. Some days were too pretty for killing.

The sound of voices drifted to his ears and made him stiffen. Had the other men circled around somehow and gotten ahead of him? That did not seem likely. Perhaps he was about to run into a band of Indians, Shoshone men out on a hunting party of their own. But as Aaron stopped in his tracks and listened intently, he decided the voices were those of white men, although he could not quite make out what they were saying.

Curiosity warred with his natural caution. Could they be the men Clay had seen a few weeks earlier, the ones who had avoided the expedition? Aaron pondered for a moment, then moved ahead quietly. Walking with the care that he had learned from Clay and Proud Wolf, he moved noiselessly through the woods toward the voices.

After a few minutes he reached the edge of the trees and found himself on a small ridge overlooking another creek. Men in buckskins and fur hats were checking beaver traps that had been submerged in the frigid, snow-fed waters of the stream.

Aaron knelt behind a screen of brush on the edge of the ridge and watched. There were nine men, and several of them carried bundles of pelts on their backs. Now that he was closer to them, he could make out some of what the men were saying. They were talking mostly about the traps. Then there were occasional bawdy comments and accompanying bursts of laughter. Aaron had heard plenty of men talking the same way during his time in the Rockies, especially around the fort built by Manuel Lisa, where he had first been reunited with Clay. But something about the conversation going on below him was different, and then he realized what it was: These men might be speaking English, but they were not Americans. Several had accents so thick he could barely understand what they were saying. A few others spoke in an altogether foreign tongue that Aaron thought might be French.

Canadians, he thought, a conglomeration of Britishers and Frenchmen. But what the devil were they doing down here? Unless he was badly mistaken, it was well over a hundred miles to the Canadian border, even as vaguely defined as that boundary was.

They must be the men Clay had spotted, Aaron thought. But they did not seem to be doing anything except trapping; they'd had no reason to duck out of sight that day Clay had seen them, not as far as Aaron could figure. Maybe he ought to go down there and ask them what the hell was going on.

Before he could make a move, the crackle of a foot stepping on a fallen branch sounded behind him. Aaron turned, instinctively lifting his rifle in case of trouble.

It was trouble, all right, but it came at him so quickly he did not have a chance to respond. He caught a glimpse of two buckskin-clad men lunging at him, both of them carrying rifles. One drove the brass butt plate of his weapon at Aaron's head in a vicious blow.

Aaron threw his left arm up, and the rifle butt thudded against it and sent agonizing pain shooting up his shoulder and neck. He bit back a yelp of agony.

"Hey! Wait—" he cried.

But the two men were not interested in anything he had to say. The second one clubbed him just as the first had. Aaron's left arm was numb. He twisted around to bring his rifle into play, but the second man's rifle butt slammed against his skull, the impact cushioned slightly by his coonskin cap. The blow glanced off to a certain extent because Aaron was trying to jerk his head out of its way. Still, the impact was enough to send him sprawling backward through the brush and over the rim of the wooded ridge.

Tumbling crazily down the slope toward the startled men along the creek below, Aaron tried but failed to hang on to his rifle. Rocks thudded painfully into his body, and gravel chewed at his skin during the fall. He dug in the heels of his moccasins in an effort to stop himself, but that just got him a twisted ankle. Finally, with a bone-jarring thump, he landed on the bank of the creek. Dirt and smaller rocks clattered around him as he lay there, some dislodged as he fell, others kicked loose by the two men who had attacked him as they slid down the slope behind him. The trappers hurried toward them, surprise on their bearded faces.

"Who the bloody hell is that?" one of them called harshly as he came up panting.

The two men who had jumped Aaron covered him with their rifles as they reached the bottom of the ridge.

"Found him up there," one of them replied, jerking his head to indicate the top of the slope. "Spying on you, he was."

The numbness in Aaron's left arm and shoulder was giving way to a burning, throbbing pain. With his good arm he pushed himself into a sitting position. The men who were gathered around him stepped back, and more of them brought rifle muzzles to bear on him. They were treating him like a bigger threat than he was.

"I wasn't spying on anybody," he said thickly, then spat to get some of the grit out of his mouth. After wiping the back of his right hand across his lips, he went on, "I was just out hunting when I heard your voices. I don't know what the hell any of this is about."

"Oh, ye don't know what the hell this is about, eh? Ye don't expect us to believe that, do ye?" The questions came from a slender man with a scraggly black beard.

"It's the truth," Aaron said. "I didn't mean to cause trouble for anybody."

"The only one ye have caused trouble for is yourself, sonny," the man said. To the others, he snapped, "Get him on his feet, and somebody pick up his gun! We'll take him back to the fort."

Another man spoke up, this time with a French accent. "M'sieu Brown said we were to take care of such problems ourselves, *n'est-ce pas?*"

"I know what Brown said, but I'm not a cold-blooded killer. If he wants to dispose of this lad, he can blooming well do it himself!" The Englishman turned away. "Now come on. A couple of you take charge of this lot. The rest of us have beaver to get out of traps!"

Two of the men grasped Aaron's arms, hauling him to his feet. Fresh pain shot through the left one as they lifted him, but he suppressed the urge to scream. A hand plucked the pistol from his belt while another took his knife.

"Ye are a well-armed blighter, I'll give ye that," one of his captors said.

"You can't do this," Aaron began. "You've got no right—"

"The nearest law's a hell of a long way away.

We've got the guns, so we've got the right to do as we please. Now come along and don't give us any trouble. I doubt that our boss'd mind if ye were to get back to our fort a bit more battered up than ye are now."

Aaron swallowed his angry words. He was in trouble, bad trouble, no doubt about that. He had blundered into something not only strange but also dangerous. He was outnumbered and unarmed, and right now he could do nothing to get out of this mess. His only realistic course of action was to stay alive and find out as much as he could about what was going on.

Because sooner or later, he vowed, he was going to get away from these men, and when he did, he wanted to be able to tell Clay Holt what had happened. Knowledge was power, Aaron told himself.

Aaron's hands were not tied, but guards kept their rifles pointed in his general direction, discouraging him from trying anything. The group of trappers made their way along the creek, pulling up traps, removing the drowned beavers from them, and quickly and efficiently skinning the dead animals. These were experienced frontiersmen, Aaron thought. Getting away from them was not going to be easy.

As he listened to their conversation, he was able to pin down their nationalities. Eight of the eleven were English, while the other three were French-Canadians. They were none too careful in their talk, and it was clear to Aaron that they were part of a larger group that had established a fort nearby for the purpose of collecting as many beaver pelts as they could. Aaron wondered if they were Hudson's Bay men or if they worked for the North West Company or one of the smaller British fur-trapping and trading companies. One thing was certain: They had no business in American territory, harvesting the pelts of American beavers.

He was equally sure that they would not have been as free with what they were saying if they expected him to live. When they got back to the fort, wherever it was, this man Brown, whoever *he* was, would kill him. So Aaron knew he had to get away before they reached the fort if he wanted to live. It was as simple as that.

The rest of the hunting party that had accompanied Aaron from the expedition's base camp would know something was wrong when he did not rejoin them. Would they come looking for him? He was fairly certain they would, especially when Clay learned that he was missing. Clay was one of the best trackers west of the Mississippi, but even with his skill, it might take too long for him to find the trail of Aaron's captors. He had to do something himself, Aaron decided.

The trappers ate on the move, gnawing dried venison and hardtack as they continued toward the fort. Aaron was given food, which surprised him until he realized that these men were not much different from the ones he had been living and traveling with for the past year. They were harder and more ruthless, perhaps, than their American counterparts, and he was sure they would kill him if they had to, but they would not allow him to go hungry in the meantime. It was a curious code, but one he was coming to understand the longer he was on the frontier.

At midafternoon the bearded man who seemed to be the leader of the group called a brief rest halt. The creek they had been following had merged with another, creating a larger, fast-flowing river. Spring's warmth had caused the snow on the higher elevations to melt at a faster rate, feeding the mountain tributaries. This one was about fifteen feet wide and five feet deep, and it made pleasant music as it bubbled and raced over the rocks in its bed.

The trappers drank deeply of the cold, clear water. Aaron joined them. He had given them no trouble since his capture, and he sensed that the men who had been told to watch him had relaxed their vigilance.

He looked downstream. About twenty yards away, the water dropped sharply into a falls that was thirty feet high, as best he could estimate. Aaron drank from the river, then stood up and stretched his back as if he was tired and stiff from his tumble down the ridge—which was true enough. At the same time, he took several steps and craned his neck to peer over the edge of the drop where the falls were located.

He could see part of the lower section of the river. It was flowing even faster down there, almost fast enough to be called a rapids.

His plan formed instantly. It was more than daring, he realized. *Foolhardy* would be a better word to describe it. Yet he might not get a better chance to escape, and he knew he could not count on mercy from his captors.

He knelt beside the water again, leaned over as if to get another drink, and kicked out behind him with his feet, propelling himself suddenly into the river in a long, graceful dive.

Shimmering droplets sprayed high in the air as Aaron hit the surface with a splash. The frigid water closed over his head as his momentum took him under, cutting off the yell of alarm from one of the guards. Aaron's left arm still ached badly, but he forced himself to use it anyway, stroking hard with both arms and kicking. He had never been much of a swimmer, but he was swimming for his life now, and that made all the difference.

He stayed under, letting the current help him along, for almost a minute. Faintly, as if from a great distance, he heard the boom of guns going off and knew his captors were shooting at him. They would be able to see him through the water, but their view would be somewhat distorted. He beat back the panic that bloomed in his brain and swam as hard as he could toward the falls. Something tugged at his right sleeve, then again at the left leg of his trousers. *Rifle balls?*

Then, abruptly, he was tumbling half in and half out of the water; the river had dropped out from under him. He rode the falls down, slamming against outcroppings of rock along the way. The drop was not a straight one, but the slope was extremely steep. Aaron barely had time to hope that no jagged rocks awaited him at the bottom before he was plunging into a deep, icy pool.

He had no idea how far down he had sunk, but abruptly he was beating his way to the surface. The current tugged at him, tried to hold him down. Frantically, his desperation growing, he struggled against it, and after seconds that seemed like an eternity, his head broke the surface.

"There's the son of a bitch!"

The cry came from above, and a second later a rifle ball sizzled through the water beside him. Aaron flung water out of his eyes, opened his mouth, and inhaled as much air as he could. Then he dove again, this time into the downstream current, and he let it take him firmly in its grip.

Once the rapids had caught him, there was no getting free—not that he wanted to. With each passing second the racing water carried him farther from the men who wanted to kill him. However, it was also crashing him against the rocks and submerged tree trunks that turned this stretch of the stream into a white, frothing madness. Aaron was aware of the jarring impacts but discovered that he felt no pain, probably because he was numb from the bone-chilling cold of the snow-fed stream. For a few moments he tried to swim, then gave it up as an impossible task. The world had become a dizzying jumble of sky, trees, and water. Sometimes his head popped above the surface, only to be dragged back down a second later. Each time he came up, he gulped another breath and hoped he would not be knocked unconscious on a rock or impaled on a broken tree limb.

Eventually the river widened, and the insane pace of the water slowed. Battered and half-conscious, Aaron drifted along, letting the current carry him for more than a quarter of a mile before he summoned enough strength to kick his way feebly toward the shore. When he finally reached it, he pulled himself onto the grassy bank and collapsed, facedown, gasping for air and quivering.

If the Canadians caught up with him now, they would kill him and be done with it, he thought. He could not move a muscle, not even to save his life.

A few minutes later he was shaking with silent laughter at the audacity of what he had done. Only a madman would have attempted to escape the way he had; sometimes a touch of insanity was the only thing that would work.

Finally he was able to roll over and push himself into a sitting position. He looked back toward the falls, but they were out of sight. The rapids had taken him more than a mile downstream, he realized, and most of that distance was over rugged, rocky terrain that would slow down pursuit. If he could get to his feet and start moving again, he had a good chance of staying ahead of the men who would be after him.

Aaron looked around for a nearby tree with which he could pull himself up, but the closest one was twenty feet away. Slowly he climbed to his hands and knees, then rested for a moment before standing. He staggered, holding his arms out for balance. If he fell, he might not get up again.

He plodded from tree to tree, glancing toward the sky to determine which way was west, the direction he would have to take to find Clay and the others. Every few minutes he stopped and stood absolutely still, listening intently for the sounds of pursuit. Once he thought he heard voices, but they were far, far off to his right. He pushed on, and the next time he stopped, he heard nothing.

His whole body felt bruised from what he'd suffered during the wild ride through the rapids. His twisted ankle throbbed, and his left arm and shoulder ached. But his vision and thoughts were clear, and for that he was thankful.

Aaron walked the rest of the afternoon. The hot sun gave him strength and dried some of the moisture from his soaked buckskins. He was sure he looked like hell after everything he had gone through, but he felt surprisingly good. Escaping death would do that for a man, he supposed. Yet he was aware of a core of weakness deep inside him, and it grew a bit larger with each step he forced himself to take. He hoped he would find the camp soon. Once the sun dipped below the peaks to the west, the air would get chilly, and since his clothing was till damp, he could easily catch a fever, just like Harry Lawton.

As he studied the surrounding landscape in the fading light, Aaron thought some of the mountains looked familiar. He had covered another two or three miles since leaving the creek, and he figured he was somewhere close to the expedition's base camp.

If he'd had one of his guns, he could have fired it into the air and perhaps drawn the attention of his friends, especially if they were already looking for him. But his rifle and pistol were back with the Canadians; anyway, the powder in his horn was useless after that dunking in the creek. All he could do was keep trudging along into the gathering gloom.

He heard voices again, this time ahead of him. Aaron stumbled to a stop. Was it Clay and his friends—or the men who had captured him? Until he was certain, he would be risking his life to go blundering ahead and calling out to them, although that was his first impulse. He noticed a good-sized mound of rocks off to his left, which would afford some concealment and protection, so he started toward them as the voices grew louder.

Aaron clambered into the rocks and hunkered down among them, all the while scanning the line of trees from which the voices originated. He spotted movement, saw several men emerge from the shadows beneath the towering pines. He could tell they wore buckskins and carried rifles, but the light was too dim for him to distinguish any more than that. They might be his friends—or they might be the Canadians.

Then one of the figures that had been partially concealed by the others moved into full view, and Aaron felt a giddy surge of relief when he realized the person was wearing a dress and leggings. It had to be Shining Moon, he thought; there had been no women among his captors and no mention of any back at their mysterious fort. As the group of searchers came closer, Aaron could even make out Shining Moon's long, lustrous raven hair.

He pushed himself to his feet and stumbled out of the clump of rocks, waving his arms over his head and shouting hoarsely, "Clay! Shining Moon! Over here!"

They saw him and broke into a run. Aaron staggered to a halt, and at that moment the core of weakness inside him finally overwhelmed his senses. Everything spun dizzily around him, the earth changing places with the darkening, purple-streaked sky. He felt himself falling but was barely aware of hitting the ground.

Then Clay was beside him, lifting his head

and saying urgently, "Aaron! Are you all right, Aaron? What the devil happened to you, son?"

Shining Moon and the others gathered around him, looking down anxiously at his torn buckskins and the ugly bruises that showed through the gaping holes.

Aaron clutched weakly at his friend's arm and fought off the blackness that was trying to engulf his brain. "Clay," he managed to say. "There's something wrong. . . . I saw them . . . saw the men who . . ."

He slipped away then, carried along on a black tide every bit as inexorable as the rapids in that river.

XX

By the time the *Fair Wind* docked in Wilmington, North Carolina, Jeff had still not gotten completely over his seasickness. Ned was seldom bothered by the pitching of the vessel on the waves, however, and had acquired enough knowledge from India to be considered a capable sailor. As for India, Captain Vaughan was more than pleased with her performance during the voyage.

"You're one of the best sailors these old eyes have ever seen, lad," Vaughan told her as most of the crew prepared to go ashore for the night's stopover in Wilmington. "I hope you won't be running off and joining some other crew once we reach Charleston. I want you with me on the return trip. We'll be heavily loaded with tobacco, and I'll need all the good hands I can find."

"I'll have to think about it, Cap'n," she told him. "But for what it's worth, I've enjoyed sailing on the *Fair Wind* so far. You work a man hard, but you treat him fairly."

"That's what I've always tried to do." Vaughan swung his gaze over to Ned, who stood nearby on the dock trying to catch his breath after unloading cargo. The crates had been put onto wagons and hauled off to nearby warehouses.

Vaughan asked, "What about you, Holt? You coming back with us to New York?"

"Well, I'd like to, Cap'n," Ned replied, sleeving sweat from his forehead. "But that depends to a certain extent on Max here. He taught me all I know about being a sailor, and I guess by now we're partners."

Jeff was listening to the exchange, and he saw the glance of surprise India shot Ned. She had clearly been expecting him to go his own way once the voyage was over. But she did not know Ned Holt as well as Jeff did; his cousin had set his sights on India and was not going to give up easily.

"All right," Vaughan said. "We'll be sailing tomorrow afternoon for Charleston. I don't care what you do tonight, but you'd better be here bright and early in the morning."

"We'll keep that in mind, Cap'n," India assured him.

She picked up her seabag and fell in step between Jeff and Ned as they walked away from the harbor.

When they were out of Vaughan's earshot, she said in a low voice, "You need to make up your own mind about what you do once we reach Charleston, Ned, instead of leaving it to me. I'll be no man's plaything, but neither will I be his keeper."

"Ah, hell, I'm sorry if I put you on the spot, India. I didn't mean to. It's just that I can't imagine signing on for another voyage without you along. We're friends, aren't we?"

"Aye, you've been a good mate," she admitted. "Both of you. And the wages we'll make from this voyage won't be enough to support me for very long. I suppose I'll ship out again, and I'd rather it be on the *Fair Wind* than any other vessel."

Ned clapped a hand on her shoulder and exclaimed, "That's great!"

India stiffened and said, "I put you on your backside and held a knife to your throat once before, Ned. Don't make me do it again."

Quickly Ned lifted his hand from her shoulder. "Sorry. I didn't mean anything by it."

"That's all right. It's just that I don't care for being touched."

Ned got a hangdog look on his face, and Jeff felt a little sorry for him as the three of

432

them walked along. As friendly and helpful as India had been, she was still somewhat reserved, almost as if she had walled off a part of herself. Neither Jeff nor Ned could forget how she had handled herself in that fight back in New York or the way she had so coolly killed a man. India St. Clair's life had been fraught with a great many hardships, Jeff supposed, and the ordeals she had endured had certainly affected her.

Ned was nothing if not determined, however. "Why don't we go find a tavern?" he said. "I could use a drink."

"So could I," India agreed. "What about you, Jeff?"

"Might as well. There's a place up ahead." He gestured to a crudely painted sign over the door of a building that read Soapy Joe's.

India chuckled. "With a name like that, it must be a pub, all right. Come along, boys. First round is on me."

The tavern was a typical waterfront drinking establishment. Several of the sailors from the *Fair Wind* were already there, along with seamen from some of the other ships in the harbor. Quite a few dock workers were also in the place, along with two or three slatternly women serving drinks. Jeff even spotted a man wearing fringed buckskins and a floppy-brimmed frontier hat at a table in the rear.

Ned and India headed for the bar, and Jeff followed.

433

"Three rums," India told the gaunt man working behind the planks of the bar.

"And follow that with a bucket of ale, my good man," Ned added.

The bartender nodded dourly and poured the rum. Jeff wondered idly if he was Soapy Joe himself.

When he slid the smudged glass over to India, she picked it up and tossed off the drink without ceremony. Ned and Jeff followed her example. The rum burned mightily going down Jeff's throat, but the sensation eased as it hit his stomach and ignited a pleasantly warm glow there.

The bartender filled a bucket with ale from a huge keg, then handed it over to Ned along with three mugs. India took the mugs, then rattled a coin on the bar to pay for the rum.

Ned flipped one of his own coins to the man for the ale. "Come on," he said as he turned away from the bar. "Let's find a place to sit down."

They settled on benches beside one of the rough-hewn tables, Ned and India on one side, Jeff on the other. Ned took the mugs from India, dipped them into the ale, then passed them around. As Jeff sipped from his, he studied the surroundings. The walls, ceiling, and floor of the tavern were made of heavy beams, and oil lamps hung from the ceiling, casting a dim yellow light that made a haze of the smoke hanging in the air. The only decorations were several large stuffed fish mounted on one wall. No one came here because the place was elegant; Soapy Joe's patrons came to drink.

The cadaverous bartender was kept busy doling out rum, ale, and whiskey. The room was filled with the low rumble of conversation, punctuated by an occasional burst of laughter, but for the most part the customers took what they were doing seriously.

Ned took a healthy swallow from his mug and licked his lips. Looking across the table at Jeff, he asked, "What are you going to do when we get to Charleston, Cousin? I'm glad you came along with us, but I don't reckon you want to spend the rest of your days as a sailor."

Remembering all his visits to the railing of the ship, Jeff said, "No, I don't think so. In fact, I don't think I'm even going on to Charleston."

"What?" Ned exclaimed. "What are you going to do, then?"

Thoughts on that subject had been on Jeff's mind for several days now, and he said, "I've never been in this part of the country before, so I figured I'd look around for a while and see what it's like. Maybe I'll head on down to Georgia and Florida."

He left unsaid the thought that wherever he went, he would keep looking for Melissa. She was somewhere; she had to be. He would find her sooner or later.

"Are you ever going west again?" India asked. Then she added quickly, "I don't mean to pry."

"That's all right. I'm not sure what I'm going

to do. I came east from the Rockies to find my wife, and I'm not going back without her."

Even as he spoke, Jeff realized that he was finally putting into words what he had felt all along without being fully aware of it. The thought crystallized into rock-hard determination. He missed Clay and Shining Moon and Proud Wolf, and he missed the mountains, but he was not going back without Melissa.

"I wish you luck, Jeff," Ned said sincerely. "I'm sure you'll find her one of these days."

"I am, too," India said. "And if there's anything I can do to help . . ."

"You've done enough by putting this big fella in his place a time or two," Jeff told her, gesturing toward Ned. "When I met him, he could have used being taken down a notch or two, and you've managed to do that."

"Hold on!" Ned said in mock anger. "I don't know where you get such ideas about me, cousin. I've always been the most modest, humble—"

A sudden commotion interrupted Ned's protest, and the three friends turned toward the back of the room to see what had happened. Several sailors had gathered around the table where the man in buckskins Jeff had noticed when they first came into the tavern was sitting. Another sailor was seated across from the frontiersman, and their elbows were on the table, their hands locked in an arm-wrestling stance. Shouts of encouragement went up from the sailors as they urged their friend to defeat the

436

buckskin-clad man. From the sound of it, Jeff figured that several wagers must be riding on the contest.

The frontiersman was red-faced and straining as he pushed against his foe's arm, and the sailor seemed to be putting just as much into the effort, if not more. Their arms swayed back and forth as first one man gained the advantage, then the other.

"I want to watch this," Ned said, standing.

"Don't go mixing in, Ned. Sailors take their games seriously," India warned, still sitting.

"Well, I'm a sailor now, aren't I? Come on."

Jeff and India exchanged a look of concern and followed Ned nearer the table where the contest was going on.

The sailor was huffing and puffing as the back of his hand slowly dipped closer to the table. The buckskin-clad man was still red in the face, but he seemed in control, and it came as no surprise to Jeff when the sailor's strength finally gave out a moment later. The man's hand hit the table with a thud. He let out a groan of disappointment that was echoed by his friends.

The buckskin-clad man released the sailor's hand and pushed back his floppy-brimmed hat.

"That'll do it," he said. "I expect you boys'll be payin' up now."

"Wait just a damned minute," one of the sailors said angrily. "I think you cheated, mister. Nobody can take Peevey here in a fair match."

The frontiersman gave the sailor who had spoken an ice-cold look as he said, "Reckon some-body can, 'cause I just did it. And I don't much like being called a cheater. Now, are you going to pay up or not?"

"Ye got no right to be in here," a sailor said in a loud voice. "This is a tavern for seagoing men!"

"Aye," another said. "We don't want no back-woodsmen in here cheatin' us out of our hard-earned wages."

"Take it easy, boys," the buckskin-clad man advised, his voice clear and firm in the hush that had fallen over Soapy Joe's. "I know you're just on a tear and want a little fun, but you've come to the wrong man for it. You'd best pay up and be done with it."

"Listen to him talk," ranted the first sailor. "He wants our money, but he's too good to fight with the likes of us, he is!"

"Let's show him different," the second man growled. Clenching blocky fists, he tensed, ready to lunge forward and swing a punch at the head of the man in buckskins.

"I wouldn't," Jeff Holt said. As he spoke, he cocked the flintlock rifle cradled in his arms. The unmistakable sound caused a hush to fall over the room. The sailors who had formed a menacing ring around the frontiersman stood stock still.

Ned had a look of anticipation on his face as he asked, "What are you thinking about doing, Cousin?"

"Those odds don't look fair to me," Jeff said. "Thought I'd lend a hand, maybe even things up a little."

Not only were the odds unfair, but Jeff felt an allegiance to the man in buckskins simply because he seemed to be the same type of man Jeff had known in the Rockies. The fellow looked as if he would be right at home in the Yellowstone and Big Horn country. Jeff could not stand by and watch a fellow mountain man being beaten by a bunch of sailors.

"I'm with you, Jeff," Ned said enthusiastically.

"And I as well," India added.

The buckskin-clad man looked at the source of his unexpected assistance, sizing up the three of them. Then he said to the sailors, "Well, boys? What's it goin' to be?"

The man who had been defeated in the arm-wrestling contest spat a curse, then said, "It's not worth getting busted up or shot and missing our ship when it sails. Here's your money, dammit!" He dropped a coin on the table, and his friends reluctantly followed suit. Then they stalked away, trying to salvage some of their dignity by glaring over their shoulders at Jeff and the others.

Jeff was amazed by his own behavior. Clay was the hot-headed brother; Jeff was always the one to use reason instead of resorting to violence. His time in the mountains had hardened him and made him more accustomed to taking fast action when need be, but it was still unusual for him to get involved in a brawl without a sound cause.

"Would've been a pretty good fight, I think," the man in buckskins said to Jeff. "If you gents would like to come with me, we'll find us a place to drink where we won't be bothered."

"All right," Jeff said. "How about you and Max, Ned?"

"Sure," Ned replied. He looked around at the patrons of Soapy Joe's, many of whom were still glowering at them. "The mood's getting uglier now that those gents have had time to think about it. If we stay here, we may have to fight our way out."

"I'll come along, too," India said quietly.

When they reached the street, the buckskin-clad man extended his hand to Jeff and said, "Amos Tharp."

Jeff took his hand. "Name's Jefferson Holt. This is my cousin Ned and our friend Max St. Clair."

"Pleased to meet all of you." Amos Tharp regarded Jeff shrewdly. "You've got the look of a frontiersman about you, friend. Been west?"

"All the way to the Rockies. I trapped beaver out there last year."

Tharp got a misty, faraway look in his eyes. "The Rockies. I've been wanting to see them ever since Lewis and Clark got back. You'll have to tell me all about them. Come along. I owe you gents a drink."

They found another tavern, this one farther from the waterfront and patronized by fewer sailors. Settling into a booth with another bucket of ale, they filled their mugs.

Tharp looked at Ned and India over his drink. "I'm a mite surprised that a couple of sailor boys sided with me like that."

"If my cousin's in the middle of something, then it's my fight, too," Ned said firmly.

"And I stand with my friends," India said.

"Well, here's to the three of you, then," Tharp said, lifting his glass. "You saved me from one hell of a beating, maybe worse. I'd have made those bastards pay for jumping me, but there were too many of them for me to stand up to them for long."

"Why were they ready to go after you like that?" Jeff asked. "Just because they lost some bets?"

Tharp shook his head. "Just looking for a fight, I figure, and they could tell by my clothes I wasn't one of them. If they hadn't come after me, they might've picked you, Holt. You're a frontiersman; anybody can tell that just by looking at you." Tharp downed a long swallow of ale, then studied Jeff. "Say, you wouldn't be looking for work, would you?"

"Work?" Jeff repeated. He had not really thought about what he would do next. He had left St. Louis with a sizable purse, but many months had passed since then, and his funds had shrunk considerably. Before long, he was indeed going to have to find a job, especially if he kept searching for Melissa.

After a moment he said, "I suppose I might be interested. Ned and Max are shipping out again tomorrow, but I've had my fill of the sea."

"Why don't you come with me, then?" Tharp asked. "I'm taking a wagon train full of supplies across the Blue Ridge Mountains into Tennessee. There's a good many settlers over that way now, and more going in all the time. Should be a profitable trip."

Tharp had not struck Jeff as the type to be a businessman. He asked, "Do you own these supplies?"

"Nope. I'm just in charge of the wagons and getting everything there safely. I've got enough drivers, but I've been hiring a few men to go along as guards and outriders. The Cherokees sometimes don't take kindly to folks crossing the mountains, and there're bandits up there, too, who'd as soon slit a man's throat as look at him. Might be a dangerous job, Holt. I got to admit that."

Jeff thought back to his days in the Rockies, to the battles against the Blackfoot and the renegades led by the man called Duquesne. He doubted that Tharp's wagon train would run into more trouble than that.

He knew he was acting on impulse, but the lure of being around men of his own kind and seeing some country besides coastal flatlands persuaded him. He stuck his hand across the table.

"You've got a deal, Amos. I'll be glad to go with you."

"Hope you won't regret it," Tharp said as he shook Jeff's hand. "Well, drink up, you three, and then I'll take Jeff to meet the boss. You'll like him." Tharp lifted his mug and said over the rim, "Fella name of Dermot Hawley."

With papers spread out on the desk in front of him, Hawley was not in the mood for visitors. But when his assistant stuck his head into the office and said that Amos Tharp was there, Hawley wearily agreed to see him.

The preparations for taking the wagon train across the mountains into Tennessee were almost complete. The *Fair Wind* had docked earlier that day, and Hawley had been there to purchase a good portion of the ship's cargo, making sure that plenty of people saw him. The goods had been taken from the ship to one of Charles Merrivale's warehouses for temporary storage until they could be loaded onto the wagons that would form the trade caravan. Hawley expected the wagons to pull out for Tennessee within a day or two, and the only thing Tharp had to do until then was hire a few guards. Hawley wondered if that was why Tharp had come to the office.

Hawley did not stand up as Tharp entered, followed by another man wearing a buckskin jacket and homespun shirt. The second man was younger than Tharp and not as tall, with sandy hair and clean-cut features. A long-barreled flintlock rifle was tucked under his left arm; hanging from his belt was a knife in a fringed sheath. He also carried a pistol. Hawley thought the man looked as if he knew how to use all the weapons.

"Howdy, Mr. Hawley," Tharp said, taking off his hat. "Got somebody I'd like for you to meet. I just hired him as one of the outriders for the wagon train."

Hawley stood up and held out a hand to the stranger. "Hello. Glad you're joining us. I'm Dermot Hawley, and I own this freighting company."

"Nice to meet you, Mr. Hawley," the stranger said, sounding more polite and a bit less rough-hewn than Tharp and most of the other frontiersmen involved in the scheme. "My name's Jefferson Holt."

Only Hawley's experience in hiding his true feelings allowed him to conceal the shock that went through him like a lightning bolt. The smile on his face never wavered as he said, "Holt, eh?"

"That's right."

Could there be more than one frontiersman with the name Jefferson Holt? Hawley wondered. He supposed it was possible, but as he looked into Holt's intelligent eyes, he knew without a doubt that this was the long-vanished Jeff Holt, Melissa's husband.

Swallowing to moisten his suddenly dry throat, Hawley asked, "What brings you to North Carolina, Mr. Holt?"

"Just drifting, I guess. I've been looking for . . . something for a while."

"Oh? And what might that be?"

"My wife," Jeff said bluntly.

Hawley saw Tharp glance at Jeff in surprise. From that reaction Hawley knew Holt had not told Tharp about Melissa. But did Tharp know anything about Merrivale's connection with the wagon train? Hawley tried desperately to remember, his agitation still well hidden behind his bland expression. He didn't remember ever mentioning Merrivale's name to Tharp, and he had certainly never talked to him about Melissa. Perhaps it would be safe to draw Holt out a little more, find out if he had any idea just how close to his goal he really was.

Hawley waved to the chairs in front of the desk, saying "Sit down, both of you. I like to get to know the men who are working for me."

Actually, Hawley had paid very little attention to the men Tharp hired, and he had never invited any of them to sit down and visit with him.

Hawley sank into his own upholstered chair and clasped his hands together on the desk. Looking at Jeff with a sympathetic expression, he asked, "You said you're looking for your wife?"

"That's right."

For the next few minutes, Hawley listened to a sketchy version of the story he had already heard from Charles Merrivale. Every time Holt mentioned the Merrivale name, Hawley waited anxiously to see if Tharp was going to say anything about having heard it mentioned around Wilmington. Tharp kept quiet, however, so evidently he was not familiar with Merrivale's mercantile business.

"I truly sympathize with you, Mr. Holt," Hawley murmured when Jeff had concluded his tale. "I hope you eventually find your wife."

"I'll never give up," Jeff said quietly.

"I'm sure you won't." Hawley straightened in his chair. "However, I'm glad you've decided to join our little venture for the time being." He turned to Tharp. "Amos, take Mr. Holt out to the camp and make him welcome."

"Camp?" Jeff repeated. "What camp?"

"The wagon train is forming just outside of town," Hawley explained. "We'll be leaving tomorrow, so you arrived in Wilmington just in time."

"I was planning to go by the courthouse and check the tax records for Merrivale's name. I know it would be a shot in the dark if I happened to find him that way, but . . ." Jeff shrugged.

His mind racing, Hawley pulled a gold watch from a pocket in his vest and flipped it open. "I'm afraid it's too late for you to find anyone at the courthouse. But I'll tell you what I'll do, Mr. Holt. I'd be glad to go there first thing in the morning to check those records for you. When I see the wagon train off, I can let you know if I found anything."

"Well, I guess that would be all right," Jeff said slowly. "Thanks, Mr. Hawley. It's mighty nice of you to help me like that."

"Glad to do it. I promise you, it's my pleasure." Hawley felt sweat form on his forehead and wished he could wipe it off, but that would draw attention to the tension he was fighting. Instead, he stood up and held out his hand to Jeff again.

"Good to have you with us, Mr. Holt."

"Same here," Jeff said, returning the handshake.

Tharp stood up, too, and said, "We'll be getting on out to the camp now. See you tomorrow, Mr. Hawley."

"Yes. Tomorrow."

Hawley stood there, hoping he did not look as stiff and tense as he felt, until the two frontiersmen had left the office. Then he sank back into his chair with a gusty sigh of relief.

That had been close, too damned close. If Holt had not run into Tharp and agreed to accompany the wagon train, he would no doubt have located the Merrivale family in Wilmington without much trouble. Now Hawley had the son of a bitch distracted and on his way out of town.

But that was not the end of the problem, Hawley knew. Sooner or later, Jeff would be back.

Hawley looked up sharply as the door opened again. Amos Tharp stepped in, pushing past Hawley's protesting assistant as he did so.

"Got to talk to your boss," Tharp grunted. "Now step aside, mister."

"What the hell is this, Tharp?" Hawley demanded as Tharp shut the door behind him. "I thought I told you—"

"I know what you told me," Tharp cut in. "I told Holt how to find the camp and sent him on his way, told him I'd catch up in a few minutes. But I wanted to talk to you first."

"You left Holt on his own?" Hawley's voice rose as he asked the question.

"Yeah, and that bothers the hell out of you, don't it?" Tharp rubbed a thumbnail along his craggy jaw. "What's going on here, Hawley? Why'd you take such an interest in Holt? You never acted that way with none of the other men I hired."

Hawley sat there for a long moment, wondering whether or not to take Tharp into his confidence. Finally he asked, "Just how much does this man Holt mean to you?"

Tharp shrugged his brawny shoulders. "Only met him a little while ago. Seems like a nice enough fella. But it ain't like him and me are brothers, or anything like that."

"Good," Hawley said, reaching a decision. "Since you're here asking these questions, Tharp, I have a proposition for you."

"I'm listening."

"My reasons for being interested in Jefferson Holt are my own. But I want you to keep him out there at the camp until the wagon train leaves. Under no circumstances are you to allow him to come back into town. Do you understand?"

"Sure. There's bound to be more, though."

"There is." Hawley clasped his hands together again. "If he asks you anything else about anyone named Merrivale, you tell him you never heard of anybody by that name."

"Had a feeling you were going to say that."

"One more thing, and this is the most important of all." Hawley took a deep breath and plunged ahead with his idea. "I don't want Holt coming back from Tennessee."

"Don't see how I could stop him."

"Let me make myself absolutely clear. I don't want Holt to survive the trip."

Tharp's eyes narrowed. "You're talking about murder."

"I'm talking about five hundred dollars," Hawley snapped. "Over and above what I've already agreed to pay for your services."

"Five hundred dollars, eh? That's a hell of a lot of money." Abruptly a grin broke out on Tharp's rugged face. "But I reckon I'll try to see you get your money's worth, Mr. Hawley."

Relieved, Hawley returned the smile. "I knew we'd come to an understanding," he said.

"I want half of it now, though. I sort of like Jeff Holt. Might make it easier to keep in mind what I got to do if I've got some money to remind me."

"That can be arranged. Come back here tonight, and I'll have the cash then. You'll get the rest when you return from Tennessee—and Jeff Holt doesn't."

449

Tharp agreed and left the office.

Five hundred dollars, Hawley thought. As Tharp had said, a lot of money, but money well spent if it meant that Jeff Holt would never interfere with Hawley's plans for Melissa. No matter what incredible twist of fate had brought Holt here, so unwittingly close to the goal he had sought for months, it would not do him any good. Jefferson Holt was going to die, just as he should have died in the mountains a long time ago.

XXI

Sitting in a tipi built by the members of the expedition, Clay Holt propped Aaron Garwood up and held a steaming cup of stew to the young man's lips.

"Try to get some of this down," Clay told him. "It'll help you get your strength."

Especially since Shining Moon added herbs to it to make it more potent than usual, Clay thought.

Aaron needed something strong. The boy's body was covered with bruises, including an ugly one on his upper left arm. His torso was wound tightly in makeshift bandages just in case he had any cracked ribs, and a piece of Lucy Franklin's petticoat was bound around his forehead to cover a deep gash there.

After Aaron regained consciousness, he had

gasped out the story of his capture and subsequent escape from the Canadian trappers to Clay, Shining Moon, and Proud Wolf, who were with him in the tipi. The others were waiting anxiously outside to see if he would be all right.

As Aaron sipped at the broth from the stew, Clay looked up at Proud Wolf.

"Go out and tell the others he'll be fine," he said, "once he's rested up and gotten over those bruises."

As Proud Wolf stepped toward the tipi's entrance flap, he paused next to Aaron and rested a hand on his shoulder.

"I am glad you came back to us, my friend," Proud Wolf said. Then he went out.

Clay knelt in front of Aaron and asked, "You feel up to talking some more?"

"Sure. I'm feeling better now."

"These men who captured you," Shining Moon said, kneeling beside Clay, "you are sure they were British?"

"All except for a few Frenchies. I reckon all of them came down from Canada."

Clay agreed. "And they were taking you back to a fort they've built?"

"That's right. Their boss was there, a man they called Brown. He was the one who was going to kill me when we got there."

Shining Moon glanced at Clay. "Why would they want to kill Aaron? How could he be a threat to them?"

"He knew too much," Clay said grimly. "He

could tell they weren't Americans, and they don't have any right to be trapping down here."

"For that they would kill someone?" Shining Moon sounded as if she found it impossible to believe.

Clay took his pipe and tobacco from his pocket and prepared to smoke. "Remember how Duquesne was trying to stir up the Sioux and the other Indians in these parts against the white trappers? We figured then that he might be working for some British outfit up in Canada that wants the furs in these mountains for themselves."

"But there are more beaver than anyone could ever trap," Shining Moon protested.

"To some folks, there's no such things as enough pelts or enough money. I've known men who'd cut your throat for two bits. There's a hell of a lot more than that involved in the fur trade. Not to mention the politics that get all mixed up in it."

"Politics," Aaron repeated as Clay took a burning twig from the fire, held it above the bowl of his pipe, and puffed it to life. "I don't understand."

"One of the reasons President Jefferson sent Lewis and Clark to the Pacific with the Corps of Discovery was to firm up the United States's claim to the Louisiana Territory he bought from that French fellow Bonaparte," Clay explained. "That's why we did so much mapping as we went along. It was sort of like surveying a new piece of property. Now, the agreement we made with Bonaparte sets out the boundaries of the territory, I reckon, but England doesn't have to recognize that agreement. They can sashay down here and claim a lot of the same land, and that claim'll be a lot stronger if they can point to a successful fur-trapping operation in these parts."

"So that's why they want to run everybody else out," Aaron mused.

"That'd be my guess." Clay had been thinking it through even as he explained it, and everything made sense to him.

"These men are dangerous," Shining Moon said. "That is why the Crow and the Shoshone have been avoiding them, as well as us."

"And the Britishers didn't want us getting close enough to see who they are," Clay said. "That's why they ducked away from us."

"What are we going to do now?" Aaron asked.

Clay rubbed his jaw as he thought that question over. As long as he was saddled with the responsibility for the safety of Professor Franklin, Lucy, Rupert von Metz, and the other men, he did not want any part of a clash between British and American fur interests. Every time he thought about how close to dying Aaron had come, anger sprang up in him, but the desire for revenge was overridden by caution.

"We've got our own business here," he said finally. "We'll stay out of their way and hope they stay out of ours. But I'll see if I can talk the professor into moving on right away, so we can put

453

a little distance between us and them. You reckon you can travel in a day or two, Aaron?"

"Nothing wrong with me but some bumps and bruises," the young man replied. "I can travel tomorrow."

"Good." Clay clapped him on the shoulder, taking care to make sure it was the right one and not the left. "You get a good night's sleep. You ought to feel better in the morning."

"I am a mite tired." Aaron had finished the stew and looked stronger already. He set the empty cup aside and rolled up in the blankets that Shining Moon spread for him, and he was asleep almost before they left the tipi. As they stepped outside, Professor Franklin came up to them.

"Proud Wolf tells us the lad is going to be all right," he said.

"I think so," Clay said. "He'll need some rest, though."

"Of course." In the glow of the campfire, the concern in Franklin's face was evident. "The story about the British trappers he told you—is it true?"

"Seems to be. There's no reason for him to lie, and I trust Aaron not to have made any mistakes about what he saw and heard."

Franklin glanced over at his daughter, who was sitting near the fire with von Metz. Quietly he said, "Then we're in danger from them, too, aren't we?"

"We can't be sure of that. They probably don't know for certain that Aaron got back here and told us about them. I think if we stay away from them, we'll be safe enough. But I'd just as soon put this part of the country behind us as soon as we can."

Franklin sighed with disappointment. "I agree. I would have liked to stay here longer—there's so much to see and study—but we must do what's best for everyone. I don't want any more trouble with those men."

"We'll get everything together and move out tomorrow. That is, if Aaron is up to traveling."

"Of course. That gives me a little more time to collect samples."

"Don't wander off, Professor," Clay warned.

"Oh, I've no intention of doing that," Franklin assured him.

Despite what the professor said, Clay instructed Proud Wolf to keep an eye on the naturalist. The last thing they needed was for Franklin to go off and get into trouble.

Clay told the others that they would be leaving the next day, and no one gave him any argument. Aaron's ordeal had cast a somber pall over the expedition, which had recovered from the violence of Lawton's death and had been in good spirits again. Now, yet another threat had reared its ugly head.

Alone in their tipi, Shining Moon asked Clay, "Do you truly think we can avoid trouble with those men?"

"I don't know. But I'm sure going to try."

"You would like to go after them and pay

them back for what happened to Aaron, wouldn't you?"

Clay slipped an arm around her shoulders and drew her close to him. "You know me too well," he said quietly. "But there're more important things now than settling a score. I've got to get this group out of here alive."

"You will," she whispered, lifting her mouth to his.

Now that the London and Northwestern fort was completed, Simon Brown was ready to send out more of his men to set traplines in the streams. The pelts would really start piling up in the storehouses, he reflected as he sipped from a bottle of the brandy he had in his pack. The other men did not know he had such fine liquor in his cabin; they might be envious if they did. But he had a right to enjoy fine things. After all, he was nobility—of a sort.

The man who should have been an earl, stuck in the middle of nowhere in a squalid little fort, he thought. It was enough to make him physically ill. Someday it would all be different.

He was about to drift off into the familiar fantasy of returning to England as a rich man and showing his high and mighty family just how little they really meant to him, when a shout from the sentry at the stockade gate drifted through the open door of the cabin. Brown had been half-reclining on his bunk, but he sat up straight at the call.

Someone was coming in.

He swung his feet off the bunk and went to the door, picking up one of his pistols and a black-hawk ax on the way. The keen-bladed, single-edged ax with its short, straight handle was as dangerous a weapon in his hands as a gun. He could throw it with great accuracy and power over a distance of twenty yards. He had heard that the Indians were good with their 'hawks, but he would match his trusty ax against such primitive weapons any day.

Striding toward the gate, Brown called up to the sentry in the guard tower, "Who's out there?"

"It's Robertson and his group, sir," the man replied.

"You're sure of that?"

"Aye, sir."

"Well, then, let them in," Brown said impatiently. The fort was dark except for a few candles burning in the windows of the barracks, but there was plenty of moonlight for the men at the gate to see his curt gesture as he ordered them to open up.

The rawhide thongs on the gate that served as latches were unfastened, and the small log used as a bar was lifted from its brackets. The heavy gate swung back on its hinges, and a group of almost a dozen men plodded on foot through the opening. They stopped in front of Brown as the gate was being closed behind them.

"I didn't expect you back for a few days yet,

457

Robertson," Brown greeted the leader of the group in deceptively pleasant tones. "You must have had good luck."

"We brought in plenty of plews," Robertson replied. He was a slender man with an irregular patch of black beard on his lean cheeks. "But we ran into a spot of trouble."

"I don't like to hear that," Brown said, his voice still soft. "What happened?"

"An American ran into us. We had to catch him. We were going to bring him to ye—"

"An American?" Brown's voice, no longer soft, lashed at Robertson like a whip.

The bearded man shrugged. "He saw us before we saw him. Weren't nothing we could do but grab him."

"Perhaps not. I assume you killed him immediately."

"Well, some of the fellows brought that up. But I decided to bring him back here to ye."

"Bring him back?" Brown repeated venomously. "I gave orders that if you encountered any Americans close up to kill them!"

Robertson nodded, looking as though he wished he were somewhere else. "Aye, ye did. But I thought you might like to talk to this one, seeing as how he's from that scientific expedition we been dodging."

Brown's grip tightened on the handle of the ax. That group of Americans had been a thorn in his side for weeks now, ever since Dobbs had spotted them over in the valley. His men

458

had remained on the lookout for them and tried to stay out of their sight at all times. No other trappers had been seen in the area, and Brown had congratulated himself on picking such a good site for the London and Northwestern's venture. Now, because of Robertson's carelessness, the Americans probably knew about the British presence in the Rockies.

Keeping a firm rein on his temper, Brown said, "So this man was one of that bunch, eh? We've been keeping an eye on them. They're not doing anything except digging up plants and rocks and measuring trees. I don't believe I need to interrogate the prisoner. Where is he, anyway?"

"That's the problem, Mr. Brown. The bastard's gone and got away, he has."

Rage burst inside Brown's skull. In a voice that trembled with emotion, he asked, "What did you tell this man before he got away?"

"That we were bringing him back here to the fort for ye to deal with."

"So," Brown said slowly, "he knows that you're British and that you have a fort in the area. And he got away and went back to the rest of his party."

Robertson quickly protested. "We don't know that, sir. We took quite a few shots at him, we did, and one of us might've hit him. Besides, he went over a waterfall and down some rapids, so he was pretty well banged up. I don't believe he could've got far through the woods. Probably lying somewhere, either dead or dying."

"But you don't know that," Brown said. "He could have gotten back to the others."

Finally, in a grudging voice, Robertson said, "I guess he could have. But it don't matter, does it? I mean, they were going to find out about us sooner or later anyway."

"Not yet," Brown snapped. "We haven't been here long enough to establish a strong claim. We can't afford to let the American government know what were doing yet."

Robertson took a step closer to Brown and said, "If that bloke did get back to his mates, it's too late to do anything about it now, isn't it?"

"Perhaps not," Brown said softly.

And then he whipped the ax up in a motion too fast to follow in the moonlight and drove the blackhawk's blade into the front of Robertson's skull with a grisly *thunk!*

The blow split the man's head open nearly to the shoulders. A great quiver ran through his body, which stayed upright, and his rifle fell from nerveless fingers. Then, as Brown wrenched the ax free, Robertson's corpse crumpled like a rag doll.

The hideous violence had happened so shockingly fast that the other men present stood transfixed, as immobile as statues. Brown gave them a baleful stare.

"He shouldn't have disobeyed my order," he said calmly. "If he'd killed that American right away, we wouldn't have anything to worry about now." He flicked a hand contemptuously at

460

Robertson's corpse. "Take him out and bury him. I don't want anyone bothering me for a while. I've got some thinking to do."

With that he strode back toward his cabin. He had already forgotten about Robertson; he had dealt with that problem, and it was behind him. His concern now was what to do about the American expedition.

He would feel a great deal better about the situation, he realized, if all of them were dead. And if they were, who would miss them? Who could ever lay the blame for their deaths at his feet? Those were intriguing questions indeed, Brown thought. All he had to figure out now was the best way to dispose of them. He had time to think about it, too. The Americans would not be able to move too fast, not fast enough to escape from him, anyway. After all, he made the rules here. This was his domain.

His lips curved in a smile at that thought. In England, if things had been different, he might have been an earl. Here in the Rocky Mountains he was king.

True to his word, Aaron Garwood was able to travel the next day, although he tired easily and Clay had to call frequent rest halts. But the expedition covered several miles that day, climbing still higher into the mountains. Two days later the party stood at the top of a high pass.

"This is it, Professor. The highest part of the

461

Rockies." Clay held up his hand to bring them to a stop. "Thought you might like to take a look around."

"The top of the world." Franklin's voice was hushed with awe. "It's incredible."

Rupert von Metz sniffed in dismissal. "I see nothing so impressive, just more of these mountains, which have been looming over us forever."

Clay looked at von Metz and shook his head. True, this pass did not look any different from a dozen others they had seen, except that it was higher and the air, colder and thinner. Shining Moon had slipped on her capote, in fact, to ward off the chill. But it was what this place signified that made it important. It was the dividing line of the entire country. Every drop of rain that fell to the east wound up in the Atlantic Ocean, sooner or later, while all the water to the west ended up in the Pacific. That was oversimplifying it, but not by much.

Franklin turned to Clay and asked, "Can we stay here long enough for Herr von Metz to do a sketch?"

"I reckon that won't hurt anything," Clay said.

With a shrug of resignation, von Metz got his sketchbook and charcoal from his pack, and started to work while the others found rocky seats and settled down to rest.

"How are you doing, Aaron?" Clay asked as he sat down beside the young man on a large, flat rock near the wall of the pass.

"I'm all right," Aaron replied. "I feel better today."

Indeed, he looked better, Clay thought. Injuries seemed to heal more quickly in the high country, whether because of the air or the body's recognizing the need for quick recuperation in such harsh surroundings, Clay did not know. But he was glad that Aaron was stronger. It was hard to remember that he and this young man had once been mortal enemies. Aaron had turned into a staunch friend.

After von Metz had finished his sketch, the group moved down from the pass to find a suitable spot to camp for the night. Clay settled for a small, rock-littered bowl two miles downslope, where a tiny spring bubbled out of the stony ground. It would not be a comfortable place to sleep; they were above the tree line, and there were no pine needles or grassy swards to serve as a bed. Soon they would be back in that sort of country.

Two more days passed, and Clay was pleased with their progress. Crossing the dividing ridge had been more than a symbolic advantage; they were going downhill most of the time now, and that made travel easier on everyone. Clay was fairly sure they had left the bloodthirsty Britishers on the other side of the pass, and that eased his mind, too.

The next day they came to a stream that Clay identified as the Flathead River.

"We can follow this to the Columbia," he told

the professor, "and that'll take us to the Pacific. There's still a lot of ground to cover, but if we build canoes, we can use the rivers. I'll get the men started right away."

"Excellent!" Franklin said. He opened his journal. "By my reckoning, the date is June seventeenth, eighteen hundred and nine. A momentous day, indeed."

Clay had no idea whether Franklin was right about the date or not, but June seventeenth sounded likely enough. It had been around the middle of April when he, Shining Moon, Proud Wolf, and Aaron had met up with the expedition, and a good two months had passed since then. *Two eventful months,* Clay thought. With all the trouble they'd experienced and the rugged terrain they had crossed, they had not really traversed much distance in that time. From here on out, once the canoes were finished, they would be able to go considerably faster.

While von Metz did another drawing and the professor, Lucy, and Proud Wolf collected and cataloged more plant specimens, Clay and the other men used their axes to fell birches along the riverbank. The small, supple branches would form the frames of the canoes, while the bark would serve as covering for the small boats. They would need six or seven canoes to carry all the members of the expedition plus the supplies, Clay estimated.

The woods rang with the sound of axes striking tree trunks, and to Clay it was a good sound. It meant they would soon be putting this part of the country, with all its dangers, behind them.

Not soon enough, however, as he discovered less than an hour later. He had stooped over to hack at the base of a tree, and as he straightened to stretch the cramping muscles in his back, something whipped by his ear with a fluttering sound. An arrow was embedded in the tree he had been chopping down, the shaft still quivering.

Then a man a few feet away dropped his ax and staggered forward, screaming. The bloody head of an arrow protruded a few inches from his chest, the feathered shaft sticking out from the middle of his back.

Cries came from the thick stand of trees as the dead man fell forward. More arrows cut through the air around Clay as he snatched up the long rifle lying at his feet. He went down on one knee, brought the primed and loaded weapon to his shoulder, and searched for a target. A flash of bright color caught his eye—streaks of red paint on a face contorted with hate. The Indian's arm was drawn back, ready to throw the 'hawk in his hand. Clay fired first, smoke and flame erupting from the muzzle of his rifle.

The Indian jerked backward, his face disappearing in a crimson smear even brighter than his war paint. Another warrior darted out from the trees and threw himself at Clay, 'hawk raised for a killing strike. Clay dropped the empty rifle and rolled to the side, and the attacker plunged past Clay and landed on the ground. Clay grabbed his knife from its sheath and lunged, driving the blade into the fallen man's back before he could regain his feet.

Clay ripped the knife free and rolled upright. The attackers were Blackfoot, probably from the southern band known as Piegan. It had been a raiding party of Piegan that had attacked the expedition all those months and miles ago, bringing Clay and his companions to their aid. This was a larger group, Clay saw to his dismay. The woods seemed to be full of them.

Guns boomed, arrows hissed through the air, and knives and 'hawks flashed in the sun. The cries of men in mortal agony furnished a grisly punctuation to the chaos.

Shining Moon! Where was she? The thought had barely flashed through Clay's mind before he grabbed his rifle and ran toward the river. But then a Blackfoot raider leapt at him. Clay drove the rifle's brass butt plate into the man's painted face, and the warrior fell away, blood spurting from his smashed nose. Clay sprinted on, hurtling over a body bristling with arrows. He did not pause to try to help the man; one of the arrows had caught the poor bastard in the throat, and he was far beyond what help Clay could give him.

Clay heard gunfire and saw powder smoke coming from a small cut in the riverbank, a gully that led down to the water itself. Part of the expedition must have taken cover there, he figured. He headed toward the smoke as fast as his long legs would carry him, the muscles of his back tensed in expectation of an arrow striking him. He jumped over the edge of the gully, landed hard, and tumbled down the short slope to roll to a stop at the feet of Shining Moon, who was aiming her rifle at the onrushing Blackfoot attackers.

Her rifle boomed, and as she knelt to reload, Clay scrambled back to his feet and peered over the lip of the cut. More men were fleeing from the nearby woods, Piegan warriors in hot pursuit. Clay pulled the pistols from his belt, primed and loaded them, then let loose with both shots. One ball smashed the breastbone of a charging Blackfoot, while the other left a bloody crease on a raider's head, sending him tumbling to the ground.

Clay turned to Shining Moon, and she thrust her reloaded rifle into his hands, taking the empty pistols from him. While she could handle a gun quite well, in a case like this she could do more good reloading for him. Clay looked at her just long enough to make sure she was not wounded, then turned his attention to the Blackfoot.

Smoothly he brought the rifle to his shoulder, settled the sights on the chest of another Piegan, and squeezed the trigger. The flintlock kicked hard against his shoulder as its charge of black powder exploded. Through the smoky haze,

Clay saw his target jerk, the .56 caliber rifle ball knocking him backward.

Shining Moon had not quite reloaded both pistols, so Clay had a few seconds to glance around. Aaron and Proud Wolf were in the gully with Professor Franklin, Lucy, and Rupert von Metz. The young woman and the Prussian artist, both terrified, were crouched low, their hands over their ears. Franklin knelt beside Lucy, one hand on her shoulder, the other holding a small pistol. Five other men from the group had reached the comparative safety of the cut, and two others were almost there. The rest had fallen, either in the woods or trying to escape. Bodies were sprawled here and there, and a red rage burned inside Clay at the sight.

He took the reloaded pistols from Shining Moon and fired another volley, cutting down two more Blackfoot and giving the fleeing men time to reach the gully. They vaulted into it just as arrows slashed through the air where they had been an instant earlier. One of them was bleeding heavily from an arm wound, but the other seemed to be unhurt, just scared half out of his wits.

As any sane man would be, Clay thought. The Blackfoot outnumbered them more than two to one. Here in the gully, he and his companions might be able to fight off a direct assault, at least for a while, but they would be hopelessly pinned down in a cross fire if the Blackfoot got behind them and attacked from the river at the same time.

"We've got to get out of here," Clay said in a low voice as their attackers loosed more arrows, then pulled back toward the trees.

"Looks like they're leaving," Aaron said.

"It might look that way, but they'll regroup and hit us again," he said grimly. "There's still a lot more of them than us. They're not giving up, not by a long shot."

"What—what do we do, Mr. Holt?" the professor said.

"Remember when they had you pinned down on that island in the Yellowstone? This is a lot like that. We're not on an island, but we're backed up against this river, so we might as well be. If they ford the stream and get behind us, they can pick us off however they damn well please. And there aren't enough of us to guard all directions at once."

"So what can we do?"

Clay turned his head and looked across the stream toward the far bank. There were trees and higher ground over there. It would be a lot easier to defend than this rock-strewn gully.

"We're going to get the hell out of here," Clay said.

He glanced at the trees again. The Blackfoot had disappeared, but he knew they were there, just waiting, letting their intended victims stew awhile in their own fear. In two minutes, or five, or ten, the warriors would burst out of concealment again and charge toward the river and the small group trapped there.

"Shining Moon," Clay snapped. "Take Proud Wolf and Aaron and get the professor, Lucy, and von Metz across the river. Fort up in those trees over there. The rest of us will cover you until you're across. Then you can lay some fire for us. Understand?"

The raven-haired woman nodded. She handed Clay his rifle, then picked up her own. Proud Wolf and Aaron had heard the orders, too, and were ready to go.

"I can't swim," Lucy said nervously. "And that river looks fast and deep."

"Hang on to me," Proud Wolf told her. "I will get you across."

"How about you, von Metz? Can you swim?" Aaron asked.

"Of course I can swim," the Prussian said. "But what about my paints and my canvases?"

"Leave them here," Clay said curtly. "Now get moving, all of you, before those Blackfoot start in again."

While Clay and the remaining men lined the edges of the cut, their rifles half cocked, Shining Moon, Proud Wolf, and Aaron herded their charges into the water. The Flathead was some forty feet wide at this point and like most mountain streams carried a swift current. It would have been better if the swimmers could have shed some of their clothing, but there was no time for that. Shining Moon swam next to Professor Franklin, ready to help him if need be. She carried her rifle and powder horn high above

470

her head to keep them dry. Aaron and Proud Wolf did likewise. Proud Wolf had a more difficult time of it because Lucy Franklin clung to him, but like most of the young men in his tribe, he had learned to swim almost before he could walk, and he managed to get across with Lucy and dry powder and rifle.

Clay watched their progress while keeping an eye on the trees where the Blackfoot lurked. Just as the swimmers reached the far bank safely and pulled themselves out of the water, the war party attacked again. Several trade muskets boomed, but the old weapons were so inaccurate that Clay did not particularly worry about the fire from them. The Blackfoot were much more deadly with arrows and lances.

As the warriors came boiling out of the trees, Clay spoke calmly to his men. "Hold your fire just a little bit longer, boys. . . . Now!"

Rifle balls slashed through the charging men, knocking a couple of them off their feet. But others were still approaching. Clay hoped Shining Moon and her companions across the river were ready to rejoin the battle.

"Go!" he yelled, waving the other men toward the river. He hung back long enough to fire both pistols one last time, dropped them in the gully, then turned and plunged into the stream, careful to keep his rifle and powder horn above the water. He hoped he would have a chance to recover his pistols.

As he swam for his life, arrows splashed around

him, but when shots rang out from the opposite bank, the Blackfoot fell back again. Shining Moon, Aaron, and Proud Wolf were laying down an effective covering fire, yet with the amount of time required to reload between shots, there was only so much they could do. Soon Blackfoot were darting forward again to throw lances after Clay and the other fugitives.

Abruptly the guns in the trees on the far bank fell silent. Fear, not for himself but for his wife, surged through Clay. Something must have happened to Shining Moon and the others, but he could do nothing except keep swimming.

The men with him reached the shore first and scrambled into the trees. Clay thought they would load and fire, but the eerie silence continued.

He was the last one to reach the other side of the river, and as he climbed out of the shallow water, a white man stepped from the trees on the bank and stood over him. Clay froze as the man, a total stranger, pointed a pistol at his head. Beyond him, at the edge of the trees, Clay saw other men herding his friends back into sight at gunpoint.

"Well, you've led my redskinned friends and I on a merry chase, my good man," the stranger said in a cheerful voice as he aimed the pistol at Clay. "But we've got you now."

Clay blinked water out of his eyes and glared up at the man. "You're working with those Black-foot?"

"They're working for me," the man replied. "And you and all your companions are my prisoners. My name is Simon Brown." Though he smiled broadly, Brown's eyes remained as icy as the stream in which Clay still stood. "Welcome to my kingdom."

XXII

For the first time since leaving Ohio on his quest to find Melissa, Jeff Holt's mind was at ease, or at least as much at ease as was possible these days. His wife was still missing, and her loss was like an empty spot in his soul, but the long days of riding and hard work had returned to him other things that had been missing: a sense of purpose over and above finding Melissa, a feeling of duty and responsibility to someone else, and a change from concentrating on his problems.

He was on the move again, and it felt damned good.

The wagon train had left Wilmington on an overcast summer day with clouds scudding in from the ocean. Ned and India had gone to the camp to see Jeff off, as had Dermot Hawley. Jeff had been glad to see Ned and India but disappointed in what Hawley had to tell him.

"I'm afraid I didn't have any luck at the courthouse, Holt," Hawley had said in a low voice after drawing Jeff aside. "There's no record of a Charles Merrivale buying or selling any property in the area, nor paying any taxes. In fact, there were no Merrivales listed at all. So it seems that your wife's family never visited this part of the country. I'm sorry to have to tell you this."

Dejectedly Jeff had said, "I appreciate your checking on that for me, Mr. Hawley. By the way, I posted a letter this morning to a fellow named Washington Irving, up in New York. He's the editor of a magazine up there, and I put a notice in it asking for information about Melissa or her family. I gave Mr. Irving the address of your office, just in case he ever gets a reply. I hope you won't mind holding them for me."

"Not at all," Hawley said heartily.

The man had been friendly and helpful, Jeff had to give him that. But for some reason, Jeff did not particularly like Dermot Hawley. He had not been able to put his finger on the reason, and he did not spend a great deal of time worrying about the matter.

He liked Ned and India, though, and he was going to miss them. Ned had shaken his hand, then grabbed him in a bear hug.

"I don't know how to thank you for everything you've done for me, Jeff," Ned said solemnly, or at least as solemnly as Ned Holt ever managed to get. "If it weren't for you, I'd be back in Pittsburgh, getting into trouble and worrying my folks to death."

"And now you're on the high seas getting into trouble," Jeff kidded gently.

"Maybe, but at least Ma and Pa don't know about it." He had lowered his voice conspiratorially. "Anyway, I reckon India'll keep me in line. She's something, isn't she?"

"You be careful," Jeff had advised his cousin. "I'm afraid you're going to have your hands full with her."

Ned grinned. "I hope so."

After that, Jeff had shaken India's hand and told her to look after Ned for him.

"Oh, I shall keep an eye on young Mr. Ned Holt," she had said. "I can assure you of that." Then she'd thrown her arms around Jeff's neck for a brief hug.

A few minutes later, Amos Tharp had ridden to the head of the column of wagons and bellowed out the command to start the teams of oxen moving as he lifted his arm and swept it forward. They were on their way to Tennessee.

The caravan followed the Cape Fear River inland, making good time across the coastal plains. After a few days the terrain became more rolling, gradually climbing onto the Piedmont Plateau. The going was easy there, too, and enough settlers had followed this route into Tennessee to beat down a good path. The land became more wooded, and after several days on the plateau, Jeff had spotted mountains rising to the north and south.

"Those're the South Mountains and the Brushy

Mountains," Tharp told Jeff as the two of them rode side by side at the head of the wagon train. "There's a valley between them where the Catawba River runs, and that'll take us on into the Blue Ridge. Once we get across there, we cut west between the Bald Mountains and the Smokies, and the trail's straight on into Tennessee. Pretty country up there."

"I'm looking forward to seeing it," Jeff said. "You don't think about how much you miss mountains until you get away from them for a while."

Tharp leaned over in the saddle and spat onto the ground. "I know what you mean. Ain't nothing uglier'n flatland. I'm not overly fond of flatlanders, either."

Jeff said nothing. It was true he missed the rough-and-tumble company of mountain men, but he had nothing against flatlanders, as Tharp called them.

It was good to be back in a saddle again. Jeff rode alongside the wagons most of the time, on a mouse-colored gelding with a stripe of darker hair down the center of its back. The horse was part of Hawley's outfit, but Jeff would have the use of it as long as he was with the wagon train. From time to time, he relieved one of the drivers, and although it had been awhile since he had handled a team of oxen, the knack came back to him quickly. One of the most important qualities of a driver, Jeff soon remembered, was the ability to curse a blue streak, and that came

476

back to him as well, although he shuddered to think what his mother would say if she were to hear him bellowing such profanities. Norah Holt had always been a God-fearing woman, and she had tried to instill that same feeling in her children.

Maybe it hadn't taken with him, Jeff thought as he cracked the whip and kept the oxen moving during his turn on a wagon. He hardly ever prayed, and he had not been inside a church in years—unless you counted those mornings when he awoke in the high country and saw eagles soaring majestically over snow-topped peaks and wooded valleys still partially obscured by morning mist. Places like that were the most magnificent cathedrals of all, Jeff had heard Clay say once, and while he was surprised to hear such a sentiment coming from his brother, Jeff understood completely.

He wanted Melissa to see those mountains, and one day, he vowed, she would.

As Amos Tharp had promised, the valley of the Catawba River provided a fairly easy route. Jeff and the other outriders ranged farther from the wagons most of the time now. Tharp had said that the Cherokee would not pose much of a threat until the caravan had crossed the Blue Ridge Mountains into Tennessee. Bandits and highwaymen could strike anywhere, however, so Jeff remained alert.

But trouble stayed away, and the miles rolled

on. The only problem occurred when Jeff was relieving a wagon driver and was perched on the high seat, guiding the heavy vehicle along the trail, which was bordered to the right by a steep slope leading down to the river. Suddenly he heard a cracking sound, and the wagon lurched to the right. He felt it tipping over. He stayed on the seat as long as he dared, hoping the wagon would right itself, but after a couple of perilous seconds he gave up. Leaning forward, he yanked the pin that connected the wagon tongue with its double-tree, single-trees, and oxen to the body of the vehicle, then dove to the left as the wagon tumbled down the slope.

Jeff landed hard on his shoulder and rolled over, hearing the cries of alarm from the other drivers. He got to his feet and hurried over to the edge of the trail. The rolling wagon came to a stop short of the river, landing upright against a good-sized outcropping of rock. It had not fallen completely apart, but it was sagging at the seams.

Tharp galloped up, having been summoned from his position at the front of the train by the shouts from the other drivers.

"What the hell happened?" he called as Jeff gathered up the reins of the team. Once they had been cut loose from the wagon, the oxen had stayed stolidly in the trail.

"Front axle snapped near the right wheel," Jeff explained. "Threw the load to the side and unbalanced the wagon. If the trail hadn't been so narrow, all we would've needed to do was replace the broken axle."

"Never seen anything like it," the driver of the wagon immediately behind him said. "Holt had to've knowed that wagon was gonna tip over the edge, but he stayed on the seat long enough to unhook the tongue. Saved them oxen from a bad mess."

Tharp let out a low whistle of admiration. "Thanks, Jeff," he said sincerely. "We can repair that wagon, but we'd have been in bad shape if we'd lost the oxen. Not to mention that if you hadn't gotten off the seat in time, the wagon might've rolled right over you. If it'd taken the oxen down with it, they'd have landed on you, too."

"Reckon I'd be mashed pretty flat if that'd happened."

Tharp directed the salvage operation on the damaged wagon. After it had been unloaded of its cargo and carefully blocked up enough for the broken axle to be replaced, Jeff took a heavy rope down the slope and attached it to the ring on the front of the vehicle, where the tongue was normally fastened. Then he took the rope and dallied it around a tree on the other side of the trail. Tharp attached it to the harness of the team, then got them moving with a few shouts and some cuts from the braided rawhide quirt he carried. The oxen lurched into motion and pulled the wagon to the trail. Then several men got busy with hammers and nails, knocking the loosened boards back into place. The cargo was loaded again, and when the wagons were ready to roll, Tharp told Jeff to reclaim his spot as one of the outriders.

"I reckon you've spent enough time on a wagon today," he said. "I'd be pretty shook up, if I was you. You came damn close to getting killed."

"Not the first time," Jeff said casually.

Despite what he said, however, he still felt uneasy. A man never really got used to flirting with death.

The wagon train pressed on, and as if the incident of the broken axle had used up all their bad luck, everything went smoothly again for a time. Soon the Catawba River played out, forcing the caravan to swing south before picking up another river that would take it to the pass through the Blue Ridge.

One evening, after the wagon train had halted for the night in a grassy meadow, Jeff was walking behind a parked wagon, heading toward the rope corral where the saddle horses were kept to make sure his mount was settled down for the night. This particular wagon, unlike most of the others in the caravan, had no canvas top and was piled high with kegs of nails. As Jeff passed it he heard a sudden pop as one of the ropes securing the load gave way. The heavy kegs shifted, then began to roll—straight toward Jeff at the rear of the wagon.

480

For the second time on this journey, only Jeff's frontier-honed reflexes saved his life. Had he tried to step back, he would have been too slow, and the kegs would have crushed him. Instead, he dove without hesitation in the same direction he had been going, and although one of the kegs clipped him on the shoulder as it fell, he landed clear of the others, which crashed to the ground where he had been walking seconds earlier.

Amos Tharp ran up from the gathering shadows, followed soon by the other men.

"What's happened now, blast it?" Tharp bellowed. He looked at the pile of nail kegs that had fallen from the wagon and muttered, "Lord, I hope nobody's under them!"

"Nobody is," Jeff said, picking himself up from the ground on the far side of the wagon and brushing himself off. "Seems like things keep trying to fall on me, but I got out of the way in time again."

Tharp turned angrily to the men who had come up behind him. "Who in blazes secured the load on this wagon?" he demanded.

"Guess that'd be me," one of the freighters answered, his voice a little surly because he knew what was coming. "But I don't know how come this happened, Mr. Tharp. I swear them ropes was good and tight, and they hadn't been frayin' any."

"Well, one of them had to snap for those kegs to fall like that," Tharp growled. "Next time you tie down a load, Miller, you better make damn sure you do a good job of it. And keep an eye on the ropes in the future!"

"Sure, Mr. Tharp," the man muttered. "Sure."

Jeff went back to the campfire, his intention to check on the horses forgotten for the moment. As he poured himself a cup of coffee from the pot resting in the embers on the edge of the blaze, he looked over at Tharp, who had followed him.

"I'm not what you'd call a superstitious man," Jeff said, "but it's starting to look like I'm some sort of Jonah. Trouble seems to follow me around no matter where I go."

"I don't believe in no jinxes," Tharp said. "Accidents happen, Holt. Tonight's no different from the time that axle snapped and wrecked that wagon you were driving."

"Maybe you're right," Jeff said, but he did not sound convinced. Looking back on the last few years of his life, a lot of things that did not make sense—the feud with the Garwoods, the death of his parents, the disappearance of his wife—could be explained a little easier if there was indeed such a thing as a jinx.

And if that was the case, maybe it meant he would never find Melissa. . . .

Jeff tried not to think about that over the next few days as the wagon train climbed higher into the Blue Ridge Mountains. While the peaks were considerably lower and less rugged than the Rockies, the craggy, wooded elevations were still impressive. Jeff took advantage of the opportunity to ride out ahead of the wagons, and as the trail followed a winding path through the mountains, he was often out of sight of the others. At times like that, as he looked up at the deep blue summer sky and the mountaintops thrusting into it, he felt again as he sometimes had in the Rockies: as if he were the only man in a pristine wilderness, put there to appreciate its rugged, solitary beauty.

Of course, not all days were like that. Some started pretty but turned ugly before they were over.

One such day occurred a week after the the nail kegs incident. The morning dawned clear and bright, but the sky had a brassy tinge to it that made Jeff uneasy, even though he was uncertain why he felt that way. He was not the only one affected, however. An air of tension hung over the camp, and men snapped at one another as they prepared for the days journey. The oxen were balkier than usual, too.

"Don't much like the looks of the sky," Tharp muttered as he paused beside Jeff while riding toward his customary place at the head of the caravan. "Could be we'll be in for a storm later."

"Maybe," Jeff said. "The air's awful still."

"That's what I don't like about it," Tharp said darkly.

Jeff had seen some bad spring storms on the plains around the upper Missouri, as well as in the Ohio Valley, and he remembered the motionless, oppressive air that had been in evidence before such storms broke. Just about everything in North Carolina had seemed rather placid to him, however, including the climate.

"I guess we can stop if it gets bad," he said to Tharp.

"We may have to. For now, we'd best put some miles behind us." He stood in his stirrups, waved the wagons into motion, and shouted at the drivers. The call was repeated on down the train.

The weather did not change much during the morning. The air grew hotter and stayed as stale as it had been when the men rolled out of their blankets. Jeff ranged ahead of the wagons, following the road where it climbed steadily to a high pass. From there he looked to the west. On the far horizon was a dark blue line, and as he watched, he could almost see it move closer by the second. Soon it had resolved itself into a low, thick bank of clouds.

He turned his horse and rode back quickly to the wagons. A storm was coming, all right, and while he was no judge of such things, he figured it might be a bad one, just as Tharp had suspected.

Tharp spotted Jeff and must have recognized the urgency on his face. Reining in, Tharp waited until Jeff had ridden up to him.

"What's wrong?" he asked.

"There's a storm on the way, just like you figured. From up ahead there, I could see the clouds off to the west. I thought you might want to get the wagons off the road. Looks like it might become a cloudburst, and we'll need some shelter."

Tharp frowned. "You're right. Damn! This'll set us back some."

Scowling, he turned around in the saddle and motioned the wagons on at a greater pace. There was no shelter in the immediate vicinity; they would have to keep moving until they found a better place to wait out the storm.

Jeff rode alongside Tharp and watched the sky as the clouds loomed over the mountains ahead of them. A cool breeze suddenly was blowing, and after a long morning of breathing hot, torpid air, it was refreshing. As the wind increased, Jeff caught the tang of distant rain.

"Smells good, don't it?" asked Tharp. "Too bad we didn't really need it right now, or it might've been pleasant to hole up and watch it rain for a while."

"Those clouds look mighty dark."

"Sun shining on them makes them look that way."

It was not long before the clouds had swallowed up the sun, plunging the landscape into gloom. The wind, which had been cool and refreshing at first, quickly became dank and unpleasant.

The wagons finally arrived at an open stretch of road bordered by a thick stand of trees. As Tharp directed the drivers to pull the heavy vehicles off to the side, drops of rain began to fall, big drops that splattered onto the dusty surface of the road with thuds almost like those of fallen rocks.

Jeff expected the rain to become heavier. From the looks of the clouds, they were in for a real deluge. Instead, it remained intermittent. Maybe the worst of it was going to blow over and miss them, he thought, and the road would not become impassable after all. Lightning flickered in the sky and thunder rolled, making the horses and oxen nervous. Jeff stood beside his mount under one of the trees, stroking the animal's neck and talking softly to it.

Amos Tharp came over to join him a few minutes later. "Don't look like its going to be as bad as we thought," Tharp said, confirming Jeff's impression. "Might be able to move on in a little while."

No sooner were the words out of Tharp's mouth than a low rumbling began, unlike anything Jeff had ever heard before. He was about to ask what it was when a frightened cry came from one of the other men.

"Tornado!"

Jeff felt his blood run cold. He had heard plenty about tornadoes back in Ohio, but he had never actually seen one. Now he did. An ominous black funnel dipped down out of the rapidly scudding clouds. It was hard to judge just how big the cylinder of whirling winds really was as long as it stayed aloft, but with a darting motion like a snake, its tail licked down to the ground and began laying a swath of destruction at least a hundred yards wide. The monster touched down at the base of a hill about a mile away from the spot where the wagons had taken cover and roared straight toward them.

The men gave frantic cries as they hurried around the grove of trees, but they could not outrun the tornado and had little chance of hiding from it.

"Get under the wagons! Hug the ground, boys!" Tharp called out.

He ran toward one of the wagons with Jeff close behind him. The tornado was covering ground with dizzying speed, and Jeff saw they were not going to reach the shelter of the wagon in time. Besides, crouching under a heavy wagon suddenly did not seem the wisest course of action.

"No, Amos!" he cried. He had spotted a slight depression in the ground, and without waiting to explain what he was doing, he launched himself into a dive, tackling Tharp around the waist. The big frontiersman fell with a surprised grunt. Jeff hung on tightly to him and rolled both of them into the little gully.

The roaring of the tornado grew even louder, a hellish sound that slammed against the ears. For an instant, Jeff felt himself lifted slightly, as if by a gigantic hand, and he knew that in that moment the tornado was passing directly over them. The wind tore at them, strong enough to pull them upward and suck out their souls. Then the unholy grip eased, letting Jeff and Tharp slump back to the wet ground.

Nearby was a crashing noise that seemed to go on forever, even though in reality it probably lasted only seconds. Then, with a startling suddenness, calm settled over the land again. Jeff lifted his head, blinked raindrops out of his eyes, and saw that with the capriciousness of nature, the tornado had abruptly disappeared. The threat was over.

Tharp pushed himself up onto his knees, looked around, and exclaimed, "Goddamn! Look at that wagon!"

Jeff saw the wreckage not far off and realized it was the same wagon under which Tharp had intended to take shelter. It was smashed to kindling, some of its cargo scattered around the grove, the rest of it plucked up and carried off by the tornado. The oxen that had been attached to the wagon were down, three of them dead, the remaining one badly injured. A couple of nearby trees were uprooted, as well.

But that seemed to be the extent of the damage. Evidently, the tornado had already been skipping, about to pull back up, when the edge of it struck the wagon.

Jeff got to his feet, brushed himself off as best he could, and offered a hand to Tharp.

"Looks like we were mighty lucky, especially me," Tharp said. He was looking at Jeff with a strange expression in his eyes. "If you hadn't tackled me, I'd have been under that wagon when it got hit. That tornado would've either crushed me or carried me off. Reckon you saved my life, Holt."

"I just did what seemed right at the time," Jeff said, checking his pistols for dirt. "I didn't stop to think about it or anything."

Tharp extended a hand to Jeff. "What you said earlier about being a Jonah . . . I reckon you proved today there wasn't anything to that."

"How do you figure?" Jeff asked, returning the handshake.

"Well, you were following me when you got the idea to dive in that ditch. You saved your own life as well as mine. Seems to me that if you think about it, you've been lucky all along. Most men would've got themselves killed in those accidents that happened to you. Somebody must be watching over you."

Jeff laughed. "I never believed in guardian angels."

"Neither did I." Tharp looked long and hard at the wreckage of the wagon where he had intended to seek shelter. He repeated quietly, "Neither did I."

Cracks appeared in the clouds overhead, letting stray shafts of sunlight come through. A few drops of rain still fell, and thunder continued to rumble in the distance as lightning flickered, but the storm was just about over.

"Let's get busy," Tharp said, clapping his hands together. "We got to gather up all the cargo we can find from that wrecked wagon and spread it out among the other wagons. Then we'll get back on the road. We've got some lost time to make up!"

Jeff followed him, ready to work. But as he did so, he was thinking. Maybe they were all luckier than he had thought—and maybe he was the luckiest of all.

XXIII

As soon as he looked into Simon Brown's cold eyes, Clay Holt knew instinctively that the man was the most evil person he had ever met. Duquesne had been ruthless and, yes, downright evil, but his depravity had been motivated by greed, at least at first. He had also been more than a little insane, Clay was convinced.

Simon Brown, however, was sane enough. It was just that he was possessed by a sheer love of killing.

Given that, they were lucky to be alive, Clay thought that night as the expedition and their captors camped near the river. Brown had ordered that everyone associated with the expedition be tied up, and he had spent the last few hours going through Professor Franklin's journals and specimens.

"Fascinating," Clay heard Brown mutter more than once.

Now Brown walked over to the professor and

said in his cultured British accent, "So you're a naturalist and a botanist, eh, Professor Franklin."

"That's right," Franklin replied, and Clay could tell he was making a great effort to keep his voice calm and steady. "Are you an educated man?"

"I spent four years at Oxford," Brown murmured.

"Then—then for God's sake, man, why are you doing this to us?" Franklin asked in astonishment.

"My reasons are my own." Brown reached over and stroked Lucy's hair. The young woman was sitting beside her father, and she flinched from Brown's touch. He did not seem bothered by her reaction.

"Be thankful I didn't have you killed out of hand," Brown said. "That's what the Blackfoot would like to do, you know. They hate all white men, but they hate Americans the most. That's why they were willing to help me track you down and capture you."

"But why?" Franklin asked again. "We weren't bothering you. We left you alone and continued our journey."

"You know of our existence," Brown replied. "You know about our fort. The company won't like that."

For the first time Clay spoke up. "The company?"

Brown cast a languid glance toward him. "The

491

London and Northwestern Enterprise. I see no harm in telling you."

That simple statement sent a cold chill through Clay, and he could see that Shining Moon, Proud Wolf, and Aaron shared his feeling.

It had taken the expedition five days to reach the Flathead River after leaving the meadow where they had been camped when Aaron was captured by the British trappers. Now, as prisoners, they returned to that vicinity in only three days, because Brown set a brutal pace for them. Even Brown's men were exhausted by the journey, but no one complained. That told Clay a great deal about the fear with which they regarded Brown, and rightly so, he decided. Only the Blackfoot, accustomed to great hardships and grueling journeys, seemed unaffected by the trip.

Brown said little to the prisoners during the three days, preferring to wait until they had reached the London and Northwestern's fort before conducting any sort of interrogation. Clay saw the way Brown looked at Lucy from time to time, and he had to repress a shudder of revulsion and outrage. Brown had plans for her that extended beyond merely satisfying his curiosity.

Although Clay constantly kept alert for a chance to escape or turn the tables on Brown, no such opportunity presented itself. Several of the Blackfoot and three or four of the trappers, all holding loaded rifles, watched them at all times. Knowing Simon Brown as he already did, Clay figured it would mean the life of any guard who was careless. Terror had a way of sharpening a man's senses.

The group crossed the dividing ridge again, heading east this time, and late in the afternoon of the third day of their captivity, Brown called a halt atop a peak and waved expansively toward the sprawling log structure in the valley below them.

"Welcome to Fort Tarrant," he declared. "It'll be your new home—at least for a few days."

The prisoners were prodded down the slope, and the small force of men Brown had left at the fort opened the stockade gate. His step jaunty, Brown led them through the opening, the captives walking reluctantly behind him.

Clay looked at Aaron, who had suffered the most on the return trip. The young man's injuries had left him with less strength than the others, and now he was pale and exhausted. Even Rupert von Metz, who had been too petrified with fear to talk during the past three days, seemed in better shape than Aaron. Shining Moon and Proud Wolf had held up well during the journey, as had Clay himself, but Professor Franklin and Lucy looked almost as exhausted as Aaron.

The band of Blackfoot warriors balked at entering the fort, and Brown went back to talk with them in their own language. As the Indians turned and left, Brown returned to the others.

"The savages don't fully trust us, so they're

493

going to camp nearby," he explained. "Their war chief says that we're to turn over at least half of the prisoners to them to be tortured and killed. Otherwise, they will be our enemies in the future."

The British trappers looked uneasy at that announcement, and after a moment one of them said, "You're goin' to give the bloody aborigines what they want, ain't you, Mr. Brown? I ain't fond of the idea of torture, but I don't want them savages goin' after *us* next time!"

A general muttering of agreement went through the group.

Brown said, "Don't worry. I'm sure our friends' bloodlust will be more than satisfied. In the meantime, let's make our guests comfortable in one of the storehouses."

Clay and his companions were taken to one of the windowless, sturdy log structures where the beaver pelts were stored. The one Brown chose was only half full, so there was room for all the prisoners, and once the small log that was used as a bar was dropped into place, it would be escape-proof.

The prisoners were silent as the door of the building was closed and the bar dropped into place outside it.

Then, into the blackness, Shining Moon said quietly, "Clay?"

"We wait," he declared. "We wait until the time's right. And then we'll make Simon Brown wish he'd left well enough alone."

An unknowable time after the door had been closed, Clay heard the bar being lifted from its brackets outside. Night had fallen, Clay was sure of that; the few chinks between the logs of the storehouse had allowed light to filter through, but he had seen nothing but blackness for what seemed like hours.

As the door was swung open, the flickering yellow light from a torch spilled into the building. Most of the prisoners flinched away from it, the darkness having made them sensitive to the torch's glare. The only ones who had quickly averted their eyes before the door opened were Clay, Shining Moon, Proud Wolf, and Aaron. Now, as they turned slowly to face the light, they could at least make out the shapes of the men who stood there, rifles in hand. Brown was the one who held the torch. He was behind the guards, but they stepped aside to let him pass. He stopped just inside the entrance to the storehouse.

"I do hope you're enjoying your stay here at Fort Tarrant," he said in mock politeness. "One's last night on earth should be a memorable one, much like one's last meal. And I've come to make you aware that this is, indeed, your last night."

Shining Moon's hand was on Clay's arm, and her fingers tightened at Brown's taunting words. Clay wanted to reassure her that everything would be all right, but he had no way of knowing if it would.

"Although I've decided to keep your papers and specimens to study, I've also decided I no longer have any need of you. In the morning, you'll be turned over to our Blackfoot friends, for them to do with as they will."

Clay had heard men say that their blood ran cold when they were in bad trouble, but until now he had never experienced that particular sensation. He had faced death many times, but always on relatively equal footing, with a fighting chance for survival. To be given to the Blackfoot for a long, slow, agonizing death by torture . . . It might be better to jump Brown now and be shot by the guards.

Only Clay's stubbornness kept him from doing just that. He was still alive, and as long as there was breath in his body, he was not going to give up. He would not give Simon Brown the satisfaction of seeing him panic.

"If you're not giving us to the Blackfoot until the morning," Clay said coolly, "why don't you get the hell out of here so that we can get some sleep?"

"You're a very annoying man," Brown said to Clay, examining him as he walked around him. "I'll leave you alone, but not before I give you one more bit of information to ponder. The young white woman will remain at the fort. I will enjoy her company. Also, a community of men such as this one can always use a woman to help with the cooking and cleaning, and when I tire of her . . . well, I'm sure the rest of the men can find other uses for her as well."

"You—you—" the professor sputtered. Even a man such as he, with an almost limitless vocabulary, was unable to find words to describe Brown's villainy. Aaron and Proud Wolf each grabbed an arm to hold him back.

"The Indian woman will also go to the Blackfoot," Brown added. "I'm certain they know how to deal with a woman of their enemies."

The verbal thrust went into Clay like a knife. The Blackfoot would turn Shining Moon into a slave and eventually kill her.

"Remember," Brown said as he backed out of the building with the guards. "First thing tomorrow morning."

Then he was gone, and the door was shut, cutting off the torchlight and plunging the fetid interior of the storehouse once more into darkness. Clay felt Shining Moon close beside him, felt a tremble go through her.

"This must not happen," she whispered, her voice strained.

"It hasn't happened yet," Clay told her. But he was damned if he could see any way to stop it.

Not surprisingly, none of the prisoners locked in the storehouse slept much that night, despite the comfort provided by the piles of beaver pelts. Clay curled up with Shining Moon beside him and tried to calm his racing mind long enough to drift off, but with little success. He could tell from Shining Moon's restlessness that she was having as much trouble sleeping as he was. Finally, along toward morning, exhaustion claimed them, and they fell into a light sleep that was easily broken when the bar on the door was removed at dawn.

The reddish glare of the rising sun shafted into the building as the door opened. As he sat up, blinking against the light, Clay saw guards armed with rifles. Simon Brown was with them.

"Rise and shine, my friends. Time to go," Brown called in a maddeningly cheerful voice.

Again Clay thought about jumping Brown, but all that would get him would be a rifle ball in the head. Then Shining Moon would be left on her own. He would wait awhile longer, he decided, and hope for a chance to turn the tables on their captors.

None of the prisoners were eager to walk to their own deaths, naturally enough, and several trappers had to go into the storehouse to prod them out at riflepoint. The men kept as much distance as possible between themselves and the captives, however, so again Clay had no chance to make a move. He stumbled out into the dawn with Shining Moon beside him and the others behind.

Rupert von Metz was the last one out of the storehouse. He had to be dragged out by a couple of men who handed their rifles to their companions so that von Metz could not grab one of the weapons. As they hauled him bodily from the building, he began to scream.

Clay felt a wave of disgust. He could understand being afraid—he was about as scared as he'd ever been—but he could not imagine letting his fear get the best of him like that. He might die—hell, everybody died sooner or later, he thought—but when the time came, he would die with dignity, and if at all possible, he would die fighting. But he would not go to his death kicking and screaming.

Von Metz seemed to be strengthened by his own terror, however, and as he was pulled into the morning light, he suddenly tore away from his guards and ran toward Simon Brown.

Brown let out a startled curse, and a couple of the trappers swung their rifles toward von Metz. The young Prussian dropped to his knees and flung his arms around Brown's legs in supplication.

"Please don't let them kill me!" he pleaded. "You said you didn't have to give all of us to the Blackfoot, Herr Brown. Please, for God's sake, spare me!"

Brown looked down at the quivering man. "Why the hell should I?"

"I can help you!" von Metz cried. "I have been making maps ever since we left St. Louis! I can show you where the Americans are and how you can avoid them. I can help you find new places to trap beaver. I will do anything!"

Brown's forehead wrinkled in thought. "A

mapmaker, eh?" he mused. "And I suppose it's you who painted all those pictures we found back where we caught you."

"That's right! I am an artist, too! I have painted all the crowned heads of Europe. Surely you would like a portrait of yourself, Herr Brown!"

Clay had to give credit to von Metz. The Prussian knew how to reach Brown. He went straight for the Englishman's vanity, and the plea fell on receptive ears.

"All right," Brown said abruptly. "You can stay here at the fort—for now. But I'll want to see that portrait before I decide if you live or die, my friend. You'll understand if I don't trust you fully just yet. Get back in there."

Blubbering in relief, von Metz scrambled back through the door of the storehouse. He giggled as he flung himself down on a pile of pelts. One of Brown's men shut the door behind him.

"As long as you're sparing people," Clay said coolly to Brown, "what about my wife and the professor and his daughter?"

"I'm afraid not," Brown said. "Although keeping the professor alive is tempting. It would be good to have another educated man to talk to out here in this godforsaken wilderness. But I'm afraid I could never trust him. Better to make a clean sweep of things now, eh? No offense, Professor."

Franklin regarded him through eyes narrowed with hate. "I'll see you in hell, you devil."

Brown threw back his head and laughed. "Quite possibly."

"What do you intend to do with Shining Moon?" Clay asked.

"Ah, yes. I do believe that the Blackfoot will appreciate her much more than I. I do believe that young Lucy will keep me well enough occupied for a while." Brown reached out and grasped Lucy Franklin's arm, plucking her out of the group.

Lucy screamed, "No!" and in fear and desperation flailed at him.

Her father uttered a heartfelt oath, then leapt toward Brown and Lucy with surprising speed. But he was not fast enough for Brown, who nonchalantly whipped a pistol from his belt and clubbed the professor over the head. Franklin staggered and went down, stunned, as Lucy screamed again.

Every fiber of Clay's being wanted to lunge forward and launch an attack of his own, but he knew that if he did, Brown's men would shoot him down like a dog. He controlled himself with an effort of will, telling himself that he could do more good in the long run by waiting for a better time to strike.

"Get him on his feet," Brown told a couple of his men, indicating the half-conscious professor. He turned to Lucy and slapped her, a hard forehand and backhand that rocked her head from side to side. She subsided into stunned silence.

"That's better," Brown said.

Professor Franklin was lifted to his feet and shoved along with the others.

Brown gestured curtly to his men. "Now get them out of here. The Blackfoot will be waiting outside the stockade. I'm taking the fair Lucy back to my cabin. After she's tied up, I'll return to enjoy the festivities we've planned for today."

The gate was swung open, and as Brown had said, the Blackfoot were there to take charge of the prisoners. Clay scanned the paint-streaked faces of the warriors and saw grim anticipation of the joy they would take in torturing the helpless men to death. All three bands of the Blackfoot tribe—the Blood, the Northern Blackfoot, and the Piegan—were brutal and bloodthirsty, but the Piegan were the worst of the lot.

And now Clay and his friends were in their hands.

XXIV

The weather had been clear since the storm. Jeff Holt looked up at the towering peak of Mount Mitchell from below, where the wagon train was traveling in a pass of the Blue Ridge Mountains. Again he was reminded of the Rockies. True, these mountains were more heavily wooded and lacked the stark majesty of the Rockies, but being here felt almost like being back home.

As that thought went through Jeff's head, he realized for the first time the Rockies were home to him now. No longer did he think of Ohio and the farm near Marietta as his home, although he would always have a soft spot in his heart for that place. Home now was far to the west, the wild, high country where he and his brother and men like them were carrying the banner of civilization—and at the same time, perhaps, mourning it a bit because the land they found would be irrevocably changed by their coming.

Jeff heeled his horse into a faster trot alongside the line of wagons. Right now, he had to concentrate on getting these wagons and their cargoes safely to Tennessee. After that . . .

Well, he had to admit, after that he was not quite sure what he would do.

Amos Tharp had changed since the tornado that had nearly taken his life. He had been friendly to Jeff all along, but now the feeling seemed more genuine. Most of the time the two men rode together, Tharp pointing out landmarks and spinning yarns about the adventures he'd had in this country when he had first come over the Blue Ridge. He had hunted, guided settlers, and fought Indians, and as Jeff listened to Tharp's stories, his liking for the man grew. They were a lot alike, and that feeling was confirmed by the look in Tharp's eyes whenever Jeff talked about the Rockies and his experiences out West. Jeff recognized a yearning in Tharp's expression: the wanderlust of the pioneer, the need to see what was on the other side of the next hill or mountain or river. Many times Jeff had seen the same look on Clay's face, and he had felt the same thing in his own heart.

As the wagons went through a pass Tharp called Newfound Gap between the Bald Mountains to the northeast and the Smokies to the southwest, Tharp declared, "Well, we're in Tennessee now. Ought to start seeing some farms before too much longer."

"Think we could stop at one of them, maybe trade a few goods for a home-cooked meal?" Jeff asked.

Tharp grinned. "Sounds like a good idea to me."

Two more days had passed before the trail took them near a homestead, however. Jeff had ridden about a quarter of a mile ahead of the train, and when he spotted a thin column of smoke climbing into the sky, he followed it to the chimney of a good-sized log cabin a short distance from the road. Behind the cabin were plowed fields, a barn for milk cows, and a pigpen made of saplings. Two small children were playing in the dirt in front of the cabin while their mother sat beside the open door churning butter. Perched on a nearby stump was a young man in buckskins, using a rag and a long stick to clean the barrel of an old flintlock. He looked up with a friendly expression as Jeff rode into the small yard.

"Howdy," the farmer called in a deep voice. "Light and set awhile, stranger."

"Thanks." Jeff swung down from the saddle. "How're you folks doing?"

"Fine and dandy," the young man replied as he stood up. He was a tall, well-built man, and his jovial demeanor took any sting from his words as he asked, "Mind if I ask what you're doin' in this part of the country?"

"Outrider for a wagon train bringing in supplies from North Carolina," Jeff answered, pitching his voice loud enough so that the woman could also hear. The children had stopped playing and run to their mother, and now they shyly regarded Jeff from behind the chair on which she was sitting.

"Wagon train, eh?" the young farmer said. He turned to his wife. "Hear that, Polly?"

"I heard." The pretty young woman smiled at Jeff. "Would you and your friends like to stay to supper, Mr. . . . ?"

"Holt," Jeff supplied. "Jeff Holt."

The farmer stuck out his hand. "I'm Davy, and this is Polly. These are our young'uns. Pleased to meet you, Mr. Holt."

"Same here," Jeff said as he returned the firm handshake. "And we'd be honored to stay for supper, ma'am, but there're quite a few of us."

"Don't worry, Mr. Holt. We have plenty," Polly assured him. "Our garden produced well this year, and we always have more than enough meat on hand. I can't seem to keep Davy from going

505

out hunting, even when we don't really need any more food."

Davy let loose with a rumbling laugh, then said, "I do like to hunt." He patted the gleaming stock of his rifle. "I wouldn't want ol' Betsy here to feel neglected."

"I swear, Davy, sometimes I think you're married to ol' Betsy instead of me."

"Glad I ain't," Davy said with a twinkle in his eye. "This here gun's never let me down, but it ain't much for keepin' a man warm at night."

"Davy!" Polly, with a look of mock sternness, stood up from her butter churn and turned to Jeff. "Go fetch your friends, Mr. Holt. We'll be glad to have you all stay for supper."

The young homesteaders welcomed the other members of the wagon train, and true to her word, Polly fed them all. After weeks of eating on the trail, the meal of roast venison, potatoes, greens, cornbread, and fresh apple pie was like a taste of heaven to Jeff. And seeing the obvious love between Davy and Polly was a poignant reminder of his own relationship with Melissa. They had dreamed of just such an existence as this—a comfortable cabin, a good farm, youngsters running around underfoot. . . .

Jeff ached inside as he thought about what he had missed so far in his young life. True, he had seen and done things that few men had ever experienced, but he had been denied the commonplace pleasures of everyday life.

Davy talked a blue streak, and when he was

not spinning a tale of his own, he was asking questions. When he found out that Jeff had spent time trapping in the Rocky Mountains, the young farmer's eyes lit up.

"Lordy, I've always wanted to go west," he said fervently. "I reckon there's more sights to see out there than a man could fit into a whole lifetime."

"It's pretty country," Jeff said. "Good country. But don't let that wanderlust get too strong a hold on you, Davy. You've got good things to live for right here in Tennessee."

"Yep, I reckon you're right. Still, I'd sure like to see more of the country one of these days."

Amos Tharp joined them and said, "I surely do appreciate the hospitality, mister. You mind if we camp here overnight? I promise we'll keep our animals out of your garden and not bother you."

"You're welcome to stay, Mr. Tharp. Make yourself to home. We're glad for the company, ain't we, Polly?"

The young woman nodded as she carried another platter of potatoes to the table. She seemed genuinely pleased to have so many visitors.

Jeff sat up late that night, talking to Davy, who smoked his pipe and asked questions about the West. When Jeff finally turned in, he slept well, rolled in his blankets under one of the wagons, and the next morning, the smell of bacon and biscuits cooking woke him and made his mouth water in anticipation.

Polly fed her guests as cheerfully as she had the night before, and Jeff was not the only one feeling regretful when the wagons were ready to roll again. They would miss the good food and pleasant company.

As he sat on his horse near the head of the train, Jeff leaned over to shake hands with Davy, who was walking along the line of wagons saying farewell to the drivers and outriders.

"You boys take care of yourself," he told Jeff sincerely. "And if you ever come back through this neck of the woods, Jeff, you be sure and stop."

"I'll do that," Jeff promised. "So long, Davy."

"So long," the farmer said, and Jeff knew it would be a long time before he forgot Davy's sheer zest for life.

As Jeff joined Tharp at the head of the train and the wagons began to roll, Tharp said in a low voice, "That boy sure can talk, can't he? Ought to be a politician with that gift of gab he's got."

"Maybe he will be," Jeff said, turning in the saddle to look back at Davy and Polly Crockett and lift a hand in farewell to them.

"We're heading for a settlement called Knoxville," Tharp said to Jeff later that day. "It's getting to be a pretty good-sized place, and I figure we can sell the whole load of supplies there. It's about two or three days from here." He turned to Jeff. "Looks like your luck's turned around since that twister, just like I said. Haven't been any more accidents."

"Reckon that's true enough," Jeff said. "I just hope the luck holds for all of us. Davy told me that the Cherokees west of here have been raising a ruckus from time to time."

"Yep, that's right," Tharp said. "The Chicka-saws have mostly made peace with the govern-ment, but the Cherokees are still holding out. We'll have to pass through their land before we get to Knoxville."

Jeff shot his companion a sharp glance. "You think they'll attack the wagons?"

"Could happen," Tharp said with a shrug. "We'd best keep our eyes open. Why don't you pass the word along to everybody else to do the same?"

Jeff wheeled his horse around to convey Tharp's warning to the other men. An air of tension settled over the train as everyone got ready for the possibility of an Indian attack. Jeff, returning to the head of the line of wagons, rode alongside Tharp, his rifle poised in his hands.

The trip through the wooded Tennessee hills proceeded peacefully, however, and when they camped that night in a swale between two hills, they saw no sign of hostile Cherokee. Maybe Tharp was right, Jeff thought. Maybe their luck had turned for the better and would stay that way for the rest of the journey.

The next morning dawned hot and clear,

and again the sun had a brassy tint to it as it began its long climb through the sky. By the time Jeff had gotten up, seen to his horse, and eaten breakfast, his homespun shirt was wet with sweat. The weather was similar to the morning the tornado had struck, and Jeff felt edgy because of it. But a hot, dry breeze was blowing that he hoped would keep any such storms from developing.

He finished his coffee, scrubbed out his cup and plate with sand, and was headed back to the rope corral to saddle his horse when he heard a startled cry from a sentry Tharp had posted the night before. The yell was cut off abruptly.

A second later someone shouted, "Let 'em have it!"

Gunfire erupted all around the camp. Rifle balls plowed up dirt near Jeff's feet, and as he spun around in shock, he saw several wagon drivers knocked off their feet by the shots. He dove for the shelter of one of the nearby wagons, landed hard on the ground, and rolled under the vehicle as he gasped for the air that the impact had knocked out of him.

Jeff bellied over to the far side of the wagon and peered out past the spokes of the big rear wheel. He saw men rising from concealment on one of the hillsides overlooking the camp. Bandits! The grass was tall there, and the men must have crawled up close to the wagons during the night and then lain there quietly until given the word to attack. Now some of them were firing toward the wagons while others ran forward to carry the fighting closer.

Quickly Jeff loaded and primed his flintlock, then settled the butt of the Harper's Ferry rifle against his shoulder. Lining the sights on the chest of a raider, he squeezed the trigger. The weapon blasted and bucked hard against his shoulder, and the bandit running toward the wagons was flipped backward by the heavy lead ball driving into his chest.

Jeff twisted around, pulled his powder horn and shot pouch around his body where he could reach them more easily, then took a patch from the patchbox on the stock of his rifle. As he started the reloading process, he heard balls thud into the wagon above him. From the sound of it, one hell of a lot of lead was flying through the air up there, and he was glad he was below the level of most of the shots. He wondered where Amos Tharp was. Tharp was the closest thing he had to a friend in this bunch.

From the sound of the shooting, Jeff realized that the bandits had surrounded the camp. He and the others were going to have a hard time fighting their way out.

When the rifle was reloaded, he picked out another target, this time one of the gunners crouched on the hillside, and let fly with another shot. The ball knocked the man on his backside in a bloody, inelegant sprawl.

The stench of burned powder was heavy in the

air, stinging the nose and making the eyes water. The constant crashing of guns blended into a constant, ear-numbing roar. But even that noise was not enough to drown out the cries of wounded and dying men. Jeff blinked to clear his eyes and did not waste time wondering if they were watering because of the smoke—or because once again violence and death had dogged his trail.

Some of the bandits had reached the wagons and were engaged in hand-to-hand fighting. The men on the hillsides, unable to continue firing for fear of hitting their friends, abandoned their positions and charged down toward the wagons, yelling stridently as they came. Pistols barked and knives flashed in the early-morning sunlight. The timing of the attack had been good; while most of the men in the camp were awake, not all had been fully alert when the shooting started. The defenders were in danger of being overrun, even though from what Jeff had seen so far, the men with the wagon train outnumbered the bandits.

Heavy feet ran past the wagon where Jeff had taken cover. He laid the rifle aside, then waited for a chance to emerge from under the vehicle. When the opportunity came, he pulled his pistol, made sure it was ready to fire, then rolled out and jumped to his feet.

A bandit who was coming toward him stopped in shock at Jeff's sudden appearance. The man was ugly, with a large nose that had been broken more than once and a bushy black beard. He growled an oath and lifted a brass-barrel flintlock pistol in his hand.

Jeff reacted fast, firing almost from the hip, and the ball took the bandit high on the left side of the chest, spinning him around with its impact. As he staggered, he nearly dropped his unfired pistol, but Jeff sprang forward to snatch it from his fingers. As the man toppled to the ground, Jeff whirled in search of another target, the raider's pistol gripped in his left hand.

He saw a man about to plunge a long, heavy-bladed knife into the back of an unsuspecting wagon driver. Jeff snapped up the pistol he had taken and hoped it fired accurately as he squeezed the trigger. The pistol's recoil was stronger than what Jeff was used to. It must have had a heavier charge in it, Jeff thought. But the shot had been on target, and the ball propelled by the heavy load of black powder tore through the body of the man with the knife, killing him instantly.

Something smashed into Jeff's back, sending him stumbling forward and nearly knocking him down. He felt an arm loop around his neck and then jerk up hard under his chin, exposing his throat for a killing slash with a knife. He drove his elbow back as hard as he could into the midsection of the man grappling with him and lifted his shoulder to block the knife. The blow with his elbow had done the job, knocking him loose from the man's grip. Jeff pivoted smoothly, ducking even lower, and left his feet in a dive that sent his shoulder smashing into the bandit's belly. Both men slammed to the ground, but Jeff landed on top. He caught the wildly flailing wrist of the man's knife hand and wrenched it around with all his strength as he shoved down at the same time. The would-be robber's own blade buried itself in his chest.

Jeff rolled off the dead man, sprang to his feet, and bent over long enough to yank the knife from the man's body. He straightened just in time to meet the charge of another bandit, this one clubbing at Jeff's head with an empty pistol. Acting instinctively, Jeff flung his arm up to block the blow, and the blade of the knife in his hand sliced neatly across the bandit's wrist, grating on bone. Blood spurted from the severed veins and arteries, and the suddenly nerveless fingers released the pistol, which fell harmlessly at Jeff's feet. The bandit shrieked, clutched his wrist in an effort to stem the spouting blood, and stumbled away. Jeff let him go.

In the chaos that surrounded him, Jeff could not judge how the battle was going. Men ran and shouted through a haze of gunsmoke tinted red by the rising sun. He managed to reload both pistols during a lull in the frenzy, and that was all that saved his life when two raiders jumped him at the same time, one brandishing a knife and the other wielding a club. Jeff did not hesitate. He shot them down, one after the other.

"Tharp!" Jeff shouted over the din of battle. "Amos! Where are you?"

For a moment, no one answered. Then he heard someone call, "Holt! Over here!"

Jeff spun around in time to see Tharp lifting a pistol about twenty feet away. The muzzle of the gun looked like the mouth of a cannon; it was trained on Jeff.

Jeff's eyes widened in amazement. Bright orange flame bloomed from the barrel of the gun, and for one crazy instant, Jeff almost thought he could *see* the ball emerge from the barrel to speed toward him.

Then it whistled past his ear, and behind him someone grunted. Jeff jerked his head around and saw a man crumple to the ground, an ugly round hole in the center of his forehead where Tharp's shot had caught him. A bloodstained hatchet slipped from the man's fingers.

Jeff turned back to Tharp, remembering the way he had saved the man's life by knocking him off his feet during the tornado. He saw the broad grin on Tharp's rugged face and knew Tharp was thinking about the same thing.

Then one of the bandits loomed out of the smoke next to Tharp and sank the foot-long blade of a knife into his side. Tharp staggered, and the bandit ripped the knife free only to plunge it into him again.

"No!"

Jeff was not even aware of the ragged shout that came from his throat as he flung himself

515

forward, covering the ground between him and Tharp in a flash—but not before the robber had stabbed Tharp a third time. The man tried to meet Jeff's rush, but he was too late. Jeff swung the empty pistol in his right hand in a roundhouse blow that crashed into the bandit's head. The man staggered and thrust weakly at Jeff with the knife. The blade ripped the sleeve of Jeff's shirt and drew a fiery line across the skin of his arm, but Jeff ignored the pain. He slammed the pistol into the man's head again, driving him to the ground. Even then, Jeff did not stop. He landed on top of the bandit and battered his skull until it was barely recognizable as something human. Only then did Jeff regain control of himself; he felt a sickening wrench deep in his belly as he saw what he had done.

He crawled away from the dead man, then pushed himself upright. Gradually he became aware that less fighting was going on around him. Lifting his head, he wiped the back of his hand across his eyes, leaving a streak in the powder-smoke grime that had settled on his skin. He saw that the wagon train's defenders were finally routing the rest of the bandits. Their superior numbers and the fighting ability of the men Tharp had recruited had finally won out.

But not in time to save Amos Tharp himself. Jeff went to his knees beside Tharp's sprawled, bloodstained form. Tharp's mutilated chest rose and fell in a ragged rhythm as he fought to breathe. Jeff got a hand under his head and lifted it, and Tharp's eyes opened.

"Looks like . . . my luck changed, too," Tharp gasped out.

"Hang on, Amos," Jeff told him. "The fight's over. We'll take care of you. You'll be all right."

"Hell! Don't . . . lie to me, Jeff." Tharp's hand came up and clutched feebly at Jeff's arm. "Just listen. . . . Got something mighty important to tell you."

"I'm listening, Amos," Jeff said grimly. It was about all he could do for his friend now, and both of them knew it.

"Glad I could . . . even the score."

"You saved my life," Jeff told him.

"Fair enough. I tried to . . . to end it a couple of times."

Jeff leaned closer to Tharp and frowned, not sure he had heard the man right. "What are you talking about, Amos?"

"Those accidents back on the trail. . . . They weren't accidents. . . . Was trying to . . . to kill you."

The hubbub of the battle's aftermath faded away for Jeff. He was sure now that he had heard Tharp correctly, but he still could not understand what Tharp was trying to tell him.

"Why would you want to kill me?"

"Hawley paid me to . . . to make sure you didn't come back alive." A shudder ran through Tharp's body as he forced the words out.

"Hawley," Jeff repeated in amazement. He had

never even met Dermot Hawley until he arrived in North Carolina. Why in the world would Hawley want him dead?

Tharp's fingers tightened on Jeff's arm again. "You got to . . . to promise me something," he rasped. "These wagons . . . you get 'em through, Jeff." His voice seemed to strengthen for a moment. "Get 'em to Knoxville and take care of things. Whatever money you get, take it back to Hawley . . . and his partner."

"Partner? What partner?" The revelations were coming almost too fast for Jeff to keep up with them.

Tharp chuckled. "Hawley figured I didn't know nothin' about it . . . but I kept my ears open, knew more than he thought I did. Don't know why he wanted you dead, Jeff. Just promise me . . . you'll take the money back."

"I will, Amos," Jeff vowed. "You can count on it."

"Good. When you get there, you can . . . ask him yourself." Tharp's voice faded away, and his eyes closed. Jeff could almost feel the life slipping from him.

Leaning closer again, Jeff said urgently, "Ask *who*, Amos? Hawley?"

Tharp's eyelids fluttered. In a hoarse voice little more than a whisper, he said, "Ask . . . Hawley's partner. Man named . . . Merrivale. . . . Could be he's the one . . . you been look—"

Stunned almost beyond belief by what he had just heard, Jeff stared down into Tharp's open,

518

sightless eyes for a long moment before he realized the man was dead. Then, moving slowly and awkwardly as if all his senses had been numbed, he gently lowered Tharp's head to the grass and stood up. Looking down at the knees of his buckskin trousers, he saw crimson stains from the blood that had leaked from Tharp's body and pooled where Jeff had been kneeling.

Merrivale. Dermot Hawley had a partner named Merrivale, and Hawley wanted Jeff dead. There had to be a connection with Melissa.

"I'll get the wagons through, Amos," Jeff whispered, even though Tharp could no longer hear him. "And I'll go back to North Carolina, all right. Because if Charles Merrivale is Hawley's partner, I want to see the expression on his face when I hand him his blood money!"

XXV

Screams filled the mountain air as the men who had joined the ill-fated botanical expedition in St. Louis were systematically tortured to death. Clay Holt's wrists were tied behind his back. He was bound shoulder to shoulder with Proud Wolf, both of them lashed to a stout tree trunk facing away from the gory arena where the torture was taking place. They could not see what was being done to the others. That was part of the fiendish Blackfoot plan: let them hear what was going on but not see it, so that their imaginations could furnish all the horrible details.

Clay knew all too well what was happening— and so far, he had not been able to do a damned thing to stop it.

Already three men had been dragged to their deaths, and their cries of agony had torn at Clay's soul. As he listened to the hideous sounds and smelled the stench of burning flesh and freshly spilled blood, he blamed himself for what was happening. He had undertaken to get these people through the mountains and safely to the Pacific, and he had failed.

Of course, he had never dreamed they would encounter such a monster as Simon Brown.

Professor Franklin and Aaron Garwood were tied to the tree next to Clay and Proud Wolf, and beyond them were the other four men left from the original party put together by Harry Lawton. The Blackfoot were working their way down the line of trees, saving Clay and Proud Wolf for last; Clay because they knew that Brown wanted him to suffer the longest, and Proud Wolf because the youngster was a Sioux, a hated enemy of the Piegan.

Shining Moon was lying on the ground in front of the tree where Clay and her brother were bound. Her wrists and ankles were lashed together with rawhide. So far, she had not been hurt, only tied up and shoved onto the ground. From where she lay, she was able to see what was going on behind the other captives, but she had quickly averted her eyes when the torture started. Clay knew that his wife was the strongest, bravest woman he had ever met, but even Shining Moon had her limits.

Two Blackfoot men strode past Clay and into his line of sight. Clay saw something he had been afraid of: They were carrying earthen jugs, occasionally lifting them to their lips to take long swallows from them. The British trappers had provided the liquor, Clay guessed, and whatever it was, rum or whiskey, the stuff was doing its work. The Indians were well on their way to being drunk—and that meant they would become meaner and more inventive in their torture.

One of them bent and took hold of Shining Moon's arm, jerking her roughly to her feet. He cut her ankles loose from the rawhide binding.

"Come," he grunted.

The other was more fluent in English. "We are tired of killing," he said to Shining Moon. "Now we take woman."

Shining Moon tried to pull away from them, and both Clay and Proud Wolf strained futilely at the ropes that held them.

"Leave her alone, you bastards!" Clay bellowed at the two Blackfoot men, knowing it would do no good but unable to contain his rage.

One of them released Shining Moon and stepped over to Clay. Casually, he backhanded the captive, driving his head against the tree.

"Shut up, or we make you watch," he growled. "Or maybe white man would like that?"

Shining Moon tore herself from the grip of the Blackfoot and flung herself toward Clay. With her wrists tied in front of her, she could not throw her arms around him, but she pressed tightly against him anyway, moaning and sobbing. She slid her arms past his side and behind his back, hunching against him as if she were trying to hide behind him. She looked up at him, and her desperate eyes met his for an instant.

Then one of her captors grabbed the shoulder of her buckskin dress and jerked her away from Clay. She cried out as the Blackfoot lifted a knife and cut away the dress. The other man held her as the first one slit the dress most of the way down the front and peeled it away from Shining Moon, leaving her nude except for her leggings and moccasins.

Clay watched, his face stony as they shoved her past him, out of sight. They were laughing, and he heard the slap of brutal fists on her flesh as they beat her to the ground. Then came the awful grunting as they took turns mounting her.

Clay's head dropped forward, and his chest heaved. He knew the significance of what he was hearing. He also knew that Shining Moon had perhaps given him what he needed to take revenge.

In that instant when their gazes had met, he had seen that her eyes were clear and cold and

522

calm, despite the hysterics she was demonstrating. Then she had shoved something into his hand, and his fingers had closed tightly on it. Now, as he tried not to think about what he was hearing, he explored what she had slipped to him.

It was one of the stones from her necklace, he realized, and even though he could not see it, he knew which one it was. She had taken it from the bottom of a clear stream, a beautiful piece of translucent crystal that had been slightly rounded by the action of the water. Now, though, it had a sharper edge on it, and Clay knew that for the past few hours, as men were being tortured behind them, she must have been surreptitiously rubbing the crystal against the stones under her, putting an edge on it.

An edge that could fray rope? Maybe, Clay decided, carefully testing its sharpness.

If the Blackfoot had used rawhide thongs to bind all the prisoners, there would have been no hope of cutting through them. But these bonds were rope, no doubt provided by Simon Brown as part of his payment to his Blackfoot henchmen.

Well, that bit of bribery might just backfire on Brown, Clay thought.

Still trying not to think about what was going on behind him, he maneuvered the stone, fraction of an inch by fraction of an inch, maddeningly slowly, until the edge rested against a rope around his other wrist. He and Proud Wolf were tied with the same ropes, and if he could loosen the right ones, they could slip out of the bonds.

With a deep breath and a prayer that none of the Blackfoot would notice what he was doing, Clay got to work.

The next few hours were the most agonizing of his life. His fingers, already partially numb from his wrists being tied so tightly, refused to work some of the time, and it took a supreme effort of will to keep rubbing the stone against the ropes. From time to time he shifted the stone in his hand and tried to explore the bonds to see how much damage he had done to them, but his blunt fingertips were too deadened to sense much.

The sounds of Shining Moon being beaten and raped accompanied his efforts. The first two Blackfoot had finished with her, but others had taken their place. Clay knew what kind of hellish ordeal his proud young wife was suffering, and while he would not allow himself to dwell on that knowledge, it nevertheless made the fires of hate burn more brightly, adding to his determination to free himself.

Proud Wolf knew what Clay was doing and occasionally gave him a glance of encouragement. Clay also saw the pain in Proud Wolf's eyes, caused by what was happening to his sister.

The other four men from the expedition had been untied from the trees and hauled off, kicking and screaming and flailing, but it had done them no good. Their screams and shrieks sliced through the air like knives, the sounds fading one by one into pitiful, bubbling whimpers before fading completely into silence—a silence even more awful than the screams.

By late afternoon the only prisoners left were Clay, Proud Wolf, Aaron Garwood, and Professor Franklin. The Blackfoot were no longer molesting Shining Moon, and Clay could hear the rasp of her breathing and knew she was still alive behind him, probably unconscious. Considering what had been done to her during this endless day of agony, perhaps that unconsciousness was merciful.

He strained against his bonds, and this time he felt a sudden give to them. One of the strands of rope had parted.

But it was not enough, he realized. His hands were looser now, and the ropes had more play, but he still could not get free. There was hope, though, and that propelled him to keep working. Soon his fingers began to tingle and burn as blood returned to them. The pain of restored circulation was greater than he would have imagined, but he gritted his teeth against it and forced himself to continue as the sun touched the mountaintops to the west.

He froze as the sound of footsteps told him the Blackfoot were approaching again. Their last victim had died several minutes earlier; they were probably ready for some new thrills. To Clay's surprise, about a dozen of them stumbled drunkenly past the prisoners and continued on toward the fort.

One of the warriors stepped in front of the tree where Clay and Proud Wolf were tied.

"My brothers go to get more white man's water from the British chief," he said. Three more Blackfoot came into view, and the spokesman waved a shaky hand toward them. "But the rest of us will stay here and take care of you." The man leaned over and spat into Clay's face. "Waaugh! Killer of Blackfoot! You will cry and beg for your life while we take your eyes and your skin and your tongue from your body."

One of the other men said worriedly, "The British chief told us to save this one for last."

The first Blackfoot shook his head. "We take him now. He has suffered long enough, endured the torments of hearing what we have done to his wife and friends. Let him die now—so that I can drink more of the white man's water and go to sleep."

"I say!" Professor Franklin exclaimed. "You filthy heathen savages! I've never seen a more cowardly lot of dogs!"

"Better shut up, Professor," Aaron advised him quickly.

It was too late. The four captors stumbled over to the tree where Franklin and Aaron were tied.

"What is this you say, fat white man?" the leader demanded.

"I said you're cowards, each and every one of

you," the professor declared, sneering in contempt. "You attack helpless women, and you do the dirty work of an even more cowardly white man. And for what? A few jugs of liquor! You're disgusting."

The Blackfoot put his face up close to Franklin's and warned, "You shut up, or we take you next." Then he brought his knife up and placed the tip against the professor's cheek. As he drew the point down, a bright red line of blood appeared. "We cut you open like a fat buffalo cow."

"Go—go ahead," Franklin jeered through his pain. "I'm not afraid of you."

The man moved his knife to the other side of Franklin's face and slit that cheek as well. A shudder ran through Franklin's body, but he did not cry out. Clay never would have expected such a display of bravery from him.

"Maybe you are a man of courage. We will see." To his companions, the Blackfoot snapped, "Cut him loose!"

Professor Franklin looked over at Clay then and said calmly, "I imagine you've been praying, my friend. I implore you—keep doing what you've been doing."

Understanding blossomed in Clay's brain. The professor must have seen what he was doing with the stone, must have known that Clay was in the process of loosening his bonds. He had taunted the Blackfoot and goaded them into taking him for torture next so that Clay would have more time to free himself. *He is sacrificing himself for the rest of us.*

Clay wanted to say something to the professor, but no words came to his lips before the Blackfoot slashed Franklin's bonds and jerked him out of sight. Beside Clay, Proud Wolf breathed some words in the Sioux tongue; Clay recognized them as a prayer.

Almost ten minutes passed before the professor surrendered to his first scream. Clay shut his ears to the sound and concentrated on severing the ropes. He was not going to give up. The ropes were fraying more. It was just a matter of time—time that Professor Franklin had bought with his life.

As the professor's cries finally became whimpers and moans, Clay bunched his shoulders and prepared for one more attempt to break the ropes. He strained with all his might, and Proud Wolf did the same, until suddenly, almost surprising them, the ropes parted.

Clay pressed back against the tree behind him so the Blackfoot would not notice. They were free!

"Wait!" Clay whispered urgently to Proud Wolf. "Just wait."

Proud Wolf understood. The time had to be right.

After Professor Franklin had finally fallen silent, the four Blackfoot returned to the tree. The leader pointed his bloodstained knife at Clay.

"Now you," he said. "No one will stop us this time."

"Just me," Clay said.

And then he moved.

He was glad he had worked some feeling back into his hands and arms, for it allowed him to move quickly. Like a striking snake, his left hand darted out and grabbed the leader's knife wrist while his right fist whipped through the air and crashed into the man's jaw. Taken totally by surprise, the Blackfoot was knocked backward into his companions by the blow. Clay followed like a deadly whirlwind, plucking the man's knife from his hand and flicking the blade across his throat. Blood spurted, and Clay felt its hot spatter on his face. His lips drew back in a savage snarl as he threw himself into the midst of the remaining captors.

Proud Wolf was right behind him, picking up one of the heavy branches that had fallen from the trees and swinging it through the air like a war club. The branch crushed the skull of one Blackfoot.

Clay plunged his knife into the belly of another, ripping the blade from one side to the other, spilling the screaming man's entrails on the ground. Clay shoved him aside and went for the fourth and final Blackfoot, who managed to dart aside, avoiding Clay's lunge. He was carrying a lance, and as Proud Wolf leapt at him, the man whipped the lance around and cracked the weapon's shaft against Proud Wolf's skull. Stunned, Proud Wolf stumbled and went down.

As Clay recovered his balance and turned to face the Blackfoot again, the man tossed aside his lance and pulled a pistol from the waist of his trousers.

"White man!" he howled at Clay, making the words sound like a curse. "I will kill you with your own weapon."

He pointed the gun at Clay and pulled the trigger. A grin split Clay's blood-streaked face as nothing happened.

"Should've cocked it first, you damned fool," he said.

Then he bolted forward, crashing into the man. The pistol sailed off into the gathering twilight.

Clay and the Blackfoot went down hard, rolling over and over as Clay tried to sink his knife into the man's body. A knee slammed into Clay's groin, causing a red haze of agony to wash through his brain. Vaguely, he heard Aaron shouting encouragement. If there had been time to cut Aaron loose, he could have dealt with this last man. As it was, Clay had to finish him off.

But that seemed doubtful. As they rolled on the ground, one of the Blackfoot's hands caught hold of Clay's hair, and he used the grip to smash Clay's head against the hard, rocky earth. Combined with the knee to the groin a moment earlier, this blow was enough to send Clay spinning into blackness. He hung desperately on to consciousness, fighting his way back toward the light, but he felt the Blackfoot slam his hand down against the ground and knock the knife loose from his fingers. Perched on Clay's chest, the Blackfoot snatched up the knife and raised it high over his head, poised to bring it down in a killing strike.

A gun boomed, and the Indian's head jerked back, a hole appearing between his eyes and a much larger opening erupting in the back of his head as the pistol ball blew away most of his brain and skull. Dead instantly, he rolled limply off Clay and fell to the side.

Shocked back to full consciousness by the shot, Clay turned onto his side, then pushed himself onto his hands and knees. He lifted his head, and by the light of the fire that had been built by the Blackfoot earlier, he saw Shining Moon's recumbent form. In her hand, smoke curling from its muzzle, was the pistol with which the last warrior had tried to kill Clay. Nude and battered, she had pushed herself off the ground enough to aim and fire the weapon just in time to save her husband's life.

"I knew to cock it," she said, smiling wearily at Clay.

The gun slipped from her fingers, and she slumped down again, either dead or out cold.

The sight of his wife renewed his strength, and Clay jumped up and ran to her side. As he knelt beside her and rolled her onto her back, he saw her bosom rising and falling. She was alive!

He put his hand on her neck and felt a pulse, erratic but strong. Shining Moon was alive, and somehow Clay knew that she would be all right.

Proud Wolf, having regained his senses, hurried over to them. "My sister! Is she—"

"She's alive." Clay gestured toward the remaining prisoner. "Cut Aaron loose and gather up any guns you can find. The rest of those Blackfoot may come back here any minute."

If they did, Clay vowed, they would get a hell of a different reception from what they expected!

But no one seemed to have heard the shot. Either that, or the men at the fort were ignoring it on the assumption that a Blackfoot had used a pistol to finish off one of the prisoners.

Clay felt better after Proud Wolf, Aaron, and he had found enough rifles and pistols to arm themselves. As they divided the weapons, Clay avoided looking at the mutilated bodies of their companions, especially the professor. But then a moan came from the slumped, bloody form of the naturalist.

Proud Wolf jumped in surprise and exclaimed, "Clay!"

"I heard," Clay said. He hurried over to Franklin and knelt beside him. "Professor! Can you hear me?"

Franklin turned his head toward the sound of Clay's voice. His eyes were gone, and his face was a mask of blood. He lifted a hand, and Clay clasped it gently and said, "I'm right here, Professor."

"M-Mister . . . Holt," Franklin rasped.

The Indians had not cut out his tongue, as they had threatened. He had probably passed out from the pain before they got that far, Clay guessed.

"You just take it easy, Professor," Clay told him. "Everything's going to be all right now."

"L-Lucy."

"We'll take care of her. You have my word on that."

Franklin's hand tightened slightly on Clay's. "Take her home. . . . Promise me you will."

"I promise," Clay said quietly. It was a pledge he meant to keep.

"I knew you would free yourself . . . if you had the chance. Thank you . . . Mr. Holt."

"Thank you, Professor," Clay said, making an effort to control his voice. "We couldn't have done it without what you did. You gave us the time."

"Knew you were . . . Lucy's best chance. Never should have brought her."

"She'll be all right, Professor. She'll be all right." Clay hoped that was true, hoped that Lucy was not already dead.

"My journals—" Franklin arched slightly off the ground as a spasm seized his mutilated body. Then he eased back down, and his next words were spoken in a clear voice from which all the pain had vanished. "My, these mountains are a beautiful place, aren't they? So many plants, so many trees . . ."

After almost a full minute of silence, Clay knew that Franklin was dead. He pulled out a bandanna and covered the man's face. Then he stood up slowly and turned to Aaron and Proud Wolf.

"Tie the bodies of all four of those Blackfoot on the trees, so it'll look like we're still there."

"What are we going to do, Clay?" Aaron asked, his voice shaky.

"We've got to get into the fort. Lucy's still there, and so's von Metz." Clay's grip tightened on the rifle in his hands. "And Brown. He's got a little surprise coming to him."

It was less than an hour before dawn, and the grayness of approaching day tinged the sky to the east. Fort Tarrant slept under the fading stars. One man dozed fitfully in the guard tower beside the gate, fighting to stay awake. He knew that if he went to sleep at his post, Simon Brown would have his hide.

Inside the stockade the dozen or so Blackfoot —whose distrust of the white man had disappeared after a couple of jugs of rum—were curled up next to the barracks, sleeping off their binge.

The guard in the tower shook himself awake, stumbled to the edge of the small platform, and peered blearily into the night. He thought he had heard something; probably just a small animal, he told himself.

The arrow flew out of the darkness. The arrowhead pierced his throat, scraped past his upper spine, and emerged from the back of his neck. He dropped his rifle and for a moment pawed feebly at the shaft, then tumbled lifelessly over the railing to the ground outside the fort. The soft thump his body made as it hit the grassy earth was not loud enough to disturb anyone inside.

"Good shot," Clay said to Proud Wolf as they crouched, along with Aaron, at the edge of the woods near the fort. "He never had a chance to make a sound."

Continued silence was crucial if they hoped to get into the fort, rescue Lucy and von Metz, and have their vengeance on Simon Brown and the other trappers.

The night had been an eventful one. As Clay wrapped Shining Moon in robes from the Blackfoot camp, she had regained consciousness, and he gave her the remaining rum from one of the jugs the Indians had tossed aside as empty. The liquor had been enough to blunt her pain.

"I am all right," she had told Clay, her voice surprisingly firm. He explained what had happened—the professor's sacrifice, the battle with the remaining Blackfoot, the promise he had made to Franklin—and Shining Moon had said, "You must go to the fort and save Lucy. I will wait here."

"I can leave Proud Wolf or Aaron with you."

Shining Moon had shaken her head. "No. It may take all three of you to rescue her—and von Metz, even though he is a craven dog."

Clay had to grin at that. "I reckon we feel the same way about him. But I'm not going to leave him there."

"No, you must help him, too, if you can. I ask only one thing of you, my husband: Leave a pistol with me so that I can fight my enemies this time if they come for me."

"Nobody's coming for you except me," Clay promised. But he had left the pistol and a powder horn and shot pouch there with her anyway.

He, Proud Wolf, and Aaron had scouted around the fort in a wide circle, looking for any sign of the Blackfoot who had left the camp earlier. They were nowhere to be found, so Clay had concluded that they were inside, probably passed out from drinking. He hoped so, anyway. That would mean their enemies were concentrated in one place. By this time the rum had probably put them into a deep sleep.

Now, with the guard dead, Clay and his two companions were ready to make their move. He thought of Jeff for the first time in a while. He wished his brother were here. With Jeff at his side, Clay thought, he would not hesitate to charge straight into the jaws of hell itself. But Proud Wolf and Aaron Garwood were valiant allies, too. The odds were against them, of course, but then Holts had a habit of overcoming odds.

"Let's go," Clay said in a whisper.

Little more than shadows in the gloom, they

flitted forward. When they reached the wall, Clay and Aaron boosted Proud Wolf over it, since he was the lightest of the three. A few minutes later he tossed one end of a rope back over, having secured it on the other side, and Clay and Aaron used it to climb into the stockade. They had discussed having Proud Wolf open the gate but decided against it because of the noise involved and the possible difficulty.

As they dropped lightly to the ground inside the fort, Clay motioned for Proud Wolf and Aaron to come closer to him.

"I'm going to find Brown's cabin," he breathed, the words too faint to be heard more than a couple of feet away. "Proud Wolf, see about getting von Metz out of that storehouse. Aaron, take a look around and see if you can find their powder magazine."

Both young men faded off into the darkness while Clay catfooted toward the buildings to find Brown's cabin.

Aaron's pulse raced as he stole among the crude log buildings of the fort. He had survived more dangers in the past few months than he would have thought possible. He had stared death in the face, and so far, luck had been on his side. But anybody's luck was bound to run out eventually. Would this be the day for him?

He put that thought out of his mind. Clay had given him a job to do, and by God, he was going to do it. The British trappers had to have stored their supply of black powder somewhere inside the fort, and he was going to find it. He checked the other storehouses. Their doors were latched, but the bars were not in place except on the one where von Metz was being kept, and Proud Wolf was tending to the Prussian. Aaron looked in each of the other buildings he came to, carefully opening the doors to avoid making any noise. The sky was lightening enough now for him to see inside the buildings once his eyes had adjusted.

The powder was in the fourth one he checked, half a dozen large barrels of the stuff.

Proud Wolf slowly lifted the bar that closed the door of the storehouse where von Metz was being held. He hoped the Prussian would not be awakened and call out; that could alert the enemy.

He had already noticed the sleeping figures near the trappers' barracks. The Blackfoot were sleeping peacefully only a few feet from their grudging allies. Under other circumstances, the Blackfoot and trappers would be doing their best to kill each other. Politics, and liquor, did strange things to men, Proud Wolf reflected. He would just as soon have nothing to do with either.

Quietly he set the bar aside, then unfastened the rawhide thong that served as a latch. After swinging the door open, he stepped into the darkness of the storehouse. With the light filtering in from the fading stars and the approaching sunrise, Proud Wolf was able to see the sleeping form of Rupert von Metz. He was curled up on a pile of beaver plews and was snoring softly. Proud Wolf crept over to him, knelt beside the pelts, and closed his hand over von Metz's nose and mouth.

Shocked out of sleep by Proud Wolf's touch, von Metz jerked wildly until the Hunkpapa leaned close to his ear and hissed, "Be still! It is Proud Wolf. I have come to take you from here. If I take my hand away, will you be quiet?"

Von Metz's head went up and down in a nod, and Proud Wolf released him.

Von Metz whispered, "What . . . how did you—"

"Never mind about that now. Come." Proud Wolf rose and led him to the door. Von Metz was trembling and stumbling, and Proud Wolf hoped he would not make so much noise that their erstwhile captors would be roused.

Clay stepped up onto the porch of the cabin and walked across to the door with all the skill he had learned from his years on the frontier. His passage was as close to soundless as possible. Unlike the storehouses, the cabin had a window, and it was open. Clay bent slightly to the side to peer through it. He could barely make out a bunk and a chair. Lucy was still tied in the chair, he realized, and Brown was on the bunk, flung across it, wearing his clothes and boots. One of his hands hung over the bed, and near it was an overturned liquor bottle. Lucy's dress was torn off one shoulder. Perhaps Brown had become too besotted to harm her, Clay thought. It was the first glimmer of brightness he had seen for some time.

He walked to the door and silently let himself into the cabin.

Proud Wolf and von Metz emerged from the storehouse just as Aaron stepped out of the building that served as the fort's powder magazine, leaving the door open behind him. Proud Wolf lifted a hand to get his friend's attention, and at that moment Rupert von Metz did something totally unexpected.

He grabbed the rifle from Proud Wolf and shouted at the top of his lungs, "Help! Help me! Everyone wake up!"

Proud Wolf whirled around and lunged at von Metz, but the Prussian darted nimbly out of the way.

"Shut up, you fool!" Proud Wolf said, though he knew it was much too late for such a warning.

Von Metz cocked the flintlock as he lifted it. "I will show Herr Brown he was right to spare me!"

Proud Wolf twisted aside as the rifle blasted and the ball lashed past him. Aaron was running toward them now.

The Blackfoot warriors roused themselves groggily from their drunken slumber, but the

British trappers were more alert. Several of them hurried out of the barracks, rifles in hand, awakened by the shouts and gunshot.

"Over there!" a trapper yelled as he spotted Proud Wolf, Aaron, and von Metz in the shadowy light.

Proud Wolf saw muzzles swing toward them, and he called to "Aaron, Get down!"

Both men dropped to the ground. Von Metz, however, whirled around to face the trappers, the empty rifle still in his hands. His eyes widened in shock as he saw what was about to happen, and he just had time to cry, "No, wait!" before thunder and flame volleyed from the guns of the British trappers.

Three of the heavy lead balls caught him in the chest, lifting him off his feet and driving him backward in a loose-limbed sprawl. He landed on his back and was dead in a matter of seconds.

Von Metz had served as a valuable distraction. As the Prussian was dying, Proud Wolf and Aaron dove behind a stack of logs left over from the construction of the fort. The trappers had left them there to use as firewood during the next winter, but right now they functioned quite well as cover for Aaron and Proud Wolf. More rifle balls thudded into the logs.

Inside Brown's cabin, the Englishman rolled over and sat up sharply at the sound of the first shot. He looked at Lucy in the chair and murmured something to her, and when she did not respond, he backhanded her across the face. Even in this bad light, Clay could tell that her face was swollen and covered with bruises. He lifted his rifle, ready to bound across the room and smash Brown's skull with the butt.

Brown's hand came up holding a small pistol, which he had cocked and trained on Clay before the tall frontiersman could move.

"Hold it!" he snapped, and Clay froze, knowing that Brown would not hesitate to kill him. More shots rang out, and a smile stretched across Brown's face.

"So, you've come back to haunt me like a ghost. Well, we'll soon put a stop to that."

Outside, Proud Wolf and Aaron crouched behind the logs.

"Rush 'em!" they heard one of the trappers yell. "The little bastards can't reload fast enough to get all of us!"

Proud Wolf turned to Aaron and said, "It has been good to know you, my friend. Now we will sell our lives for as high a price as we can."

"I wouldn't count on that," Aaron said.

The trappers charged toward the makeshift barricade, shouting as they came. Their route took them beside the storehouse where the barrels of powder were kept, and as they passed the open doorway, Aaron popped up from behind the logs, the butt of his rifle socketed firmly against his shoulder and a prayer on his lips as he squeezed the trigger.

The flintlock cracked, and the ball sped past

the running men, going through the open door and smacking into a powder barrel.

The whole world blew up. At least that was what it sounded like to Aaron as he dived behind the logs again, hoping they would shield him and Proud Wolf from the force of the explosion. In the brief instant before he had taken cover, he had seen flame and debris erupt from the exploding storehouse and engulf the trappers.

The blast shook the entire fort, including Simon Brown's cabin.

"What the hell—!" Brown yelled.

Clay lunged forward and to the side as Brown fired the pistol. The ball clipped Clay on the right shoulder, making his arm go numb. He dropped the rifle.

Brown jumped up from the bed and reached for the blackhawk ax lying on a nearby table.

Clay hit him just before his fingers closed around the ax handle. The collision drove both of them away from the table. Clay tried to reach the pistol in his belt with his left hand, but Brown grabbed his arm and wrenched it away from the gun. Grappling desperately with each other, the two men fell to the floor and rolled over and over.

That brought them bumping up against the legs of the table, overturning it. The ax fell, and Brown snatched it up and whipped it toward Clay's head. Clay jerked aside just in time, and the ax blade bit deep into the puncheons of the floor. Brown tried to pull it free, but while he was doing that, Clay smashed his left fist into the Englishman's face.

Brown shrugged off the blow and pulled the ax free, however, and Clay jumped frantically backward to avoid another swing of the razor-sharp blade. He was near the open door of the cabin as he scrambled to his feet. Brown flung himself forward, tackling Clay and knocking him out of the cabin.

Clay got hold of the ax handle with one hand as he and Brown tumbled across the porch and into the dirt in front of the cabin. The sun was peeking above the tops of the trees to the east, but Clay had no time to notice it. He was holding off the ax with all his strength. His right arm was still numb, and fighting one-handed put him at a definite disadvantage, especially since Brown seemed possessed by a demon that gave him the strength of ten men. Clay brought his leg up between them and tried a trick he had learned from the Sioux. He flipped Brown up and over his head. The Englishman sailed through the air and came down hard on his back. Both men had lost their grip on the ax, which skittered away in the dust.

Brown recovered first, and Clay was barely on his feet in time to meet his charge. Brown's fists battered Clay, forcing him back. Clay managed to block a few of the blows, but with only one good arm, he could not throw any punches of his own. He tripped on something and fell backward.

The ax! He reached for it, but Brown got there first, snatched up the blackhawk, and slashed at Clay's head. Clay rolled aside, but Brown came after him, flailing the deadly instrument. Clay kicked out with his foot and caught Brown in the knee, spilling him, and as Brown fell, Clay grabbed the ax, jerking it out of Brown's hands. He swung it wildly, and both men came to their feet for the final time.

With an impact that shivered throughout Clay's arm, the blackhawk's blade met the side of Simon Brown's neck. The keen steel sliced through flesh, sinew, and bone with a grating sound, then came free in a shower of blood. His chest heaving from exhaustion, Clay stood there, facing Brown. The head of the self-styled king of the Rockies had toppled from his shoulders—and hit the ground before his body crumpled.

Letting the ax slip from his fingers, Clay looked around. On one side of the fort was a crater, put there by the explosion. The barracks was on fire, and the other storehouses had been flattened by the blast. Dead men littered the open area inside the stockade. Any trappers or Blackfoot warriors who had survived the explosion had fled into the woods.

Proud Wolf and Aaron hurried toward Clay, both of them unhurt. Proud Wolf grasped his brother-in-law's arm.

"Clay?" he said anxiously.

"I'm all right. Where's von Metz?"

"Dead," Proud Wolf replied flatly. "He was the one who tried to warn the trappers."

Clay's grimy features were bleak.

"Lucy's in the cabin," he said. "Let's get her, and then let's get the hell out of here."

The three men went inside to where Lucy was tied to the chair. As Aaron freed her, Clay spotted a dispatch case lying next to the table. He picked it up and read Brown's name, and beneath it were the words *London and Northwestern Enterprise*. Clay opened the case quickly and pulled out a piece of foolscap, folded into thirds and originally sealed with wax imprinted with the letter *M*. The seal had been broken. Clay opened the documents. It was from a man named Fletcher McKendrick, the North American manager of the London and Northwestern Enterprise, and the only address given was Fort Dunadeen in Canada. The body of the letter informed Brown of the supplies that were being sent to him at the fort, a long, detailed list against which Brown could check the delivery to ascertain the reliability and integrity of the men hired to transport the goods.

Clay was intrigued. His speculations about the British incursion into American territory had just been confirmed. But it was the last sentence of the letter that caused all the elements of the theory to fall into place: "I expect a shipment of furs to arrive within a month, since I do not anticipate that you will have failed to accomplish your mission, as the Frenchman Duquesne did."

"Fletcher McKendrick," Clay said. "I reckon I'll have to pay your Fort Dunadeen a visit. We've got some scores to settle."

"Where's my father?" Lucy said. She was wrapped in blankets.

"Let's go outside," Clay said. He knew this was not going to be easy.

Aaron supported Lucy after she had heard the news. A couple of pouches were slung over his shoulder, and Clay recognized them as the ones that held Professor Franklin's journals.

"She wouldn't leave without them," Aaron explained.

"That's fine," Clay said. His face was grim as he remembered the professor's courageous death. "In fact, it's just right. Let's go."

Clay opened the gate, and then the four of them walked out of the stockade, leaving the blazing ruins of Fort Tarrant behind them. The black smoke climbed high into the clear morning sky.

XXVI

Lucy Franklin was asleep, and Clay was grateful for that. She needed the rest after the ordeal she had been through. But Shining Moon had been passed out when Clay and the others returned for her, and now, hours later, she was still unconscious. Clay stared broodingly at her motionless form as he sat by the campfire Proud Wolf and Aaron had made.

With the British trappers and their Blackfoot henchmen dead, they did not have to worry much about being discovered by enemies, so Proud Wolf and Aaron had built the fire high, and the flames danced merrily, casting a large circle of flickering light around the clearing. The ruins of Simon Brown's fort were half a mile away. Once the fires started by the explosion had died out, Proud Wolf and Aaron had spent some time in the late afternoon poking through the rubble. The flames had not reached Brown's cabin, and inside they found all the rock and plant samples Professor Franklin had gathered during the expedition. They had salvaged the specimens to go along with the professor's journals.

In the meantime, Clay had already begun keeping a vigil over his unconscious wife, a vigil he had continued into the night after gently carrying her limp form to this spot.

Proud Wolf and Aaron were sitting nearby, and not far away was the blanket-swathed shape of the sleeping Lucy Franklin. She had been battered by Simon Brown and then devastated by the news of her father's death, but overall, she seemed to be holding up well. Lucy was stronger than even she knew, Clay suspected.

"When will Shining Moon awaken?" Proud Wolf asked, sounding as though he was talking as much to himself as to anyone else.

"I don't know," Clay answered. "She's hurt bad."

"But she will be all right. She *must* be all right."

They had had this conversation before, earlier in the evening. Clay made no reply now. There was nothing left to say, nothing to do but wait.

"What are we going to do about Lucy?" Aaron asked, looking at the sleeping woman.

"I don't see that we have much choice," Clay said. "We promised her pa we'd take her back to civilization. That means St. Louis. From there, she can head back East. We've got the professor's journals and his specimens. Reckon Lucy'll know what to do with them."

"We cannot leave until Shining Moon is better," Proud Wolf pointed out.

Clay agreed. That went without saying. He would never leave his wife.

Aaron wearily got to his feet. "Think I'll try to get some sleep."

"That's a good idea," Clay said. "Proud Wolf, you might as well do the same."

Proud Wolf shook his head stubbornly. "As long as Shining Moon—"

"As long as Shining Moon's unconscious, there's nothing you can do for her," Clay cut in sharply. In gentler tones, he added, "Get some sleep, son. I'll stand the first watch."

And all the ones after that if I have to, he added silently.

Reluctantly Proud Wolf followed Aaron's example and rolled up in his blankets. Despite his vow that he was not tired, his breathing soon became heavy and regular, and Clay knew he was asleep. Aaron was resting easily, too, and silence settled over the camp, broken only by the crackling of the fire and an occasional rustling noise as a small animal moved in the nearby brush.

Clay felt a pang deep inside as he looked at Shining Moon's face, so still in the firelight. He knew she was breathing, was alive, but that was all he could tell about her. He did not know if she would ever recover.

But one thing he did know. When they returned after taking Lucy to St. Louis, the three of them were heading north, toward Canada.

Two names were burned into Clay Holt's brain: the London and Northwestern Enterprise, and Fletcher McKendrick. The company, and the man, that had been responsible for everything the renegade called Duquesne and then the monster known as Simon Brown had done.

It was time for a showdown, and Clay would not rest until McKendrick had paid for all the evil he had set in motion.

A sudden snap made Clay jolt in alarm. He blinked his eyes, realizing that he had made one of the worst greenhorn mistakes a man could make on the frontier. In his brooding he had looked too long at the fire, and the flames had hypnotized him, at the same time stealing his night vision. He could not see—

A shadowy form stepped into the ring of light. Clay spotted it and surged to his feet, clutching his rifle. He had cocked the weapon, and his finger was on the trigger, ready to fire, before his vision cleared enough for him to recognize that the shape belonged to an old Indian woman, her bent, twisted body wrapped in a tattered blanket.

Clay relaxed, but only a little. How in the hell had an old woman come to wander into their camp? Were there other Indians around?

Easing off on the flintlock's trigger, he said, "Greetings, grandmother. Why have you come here?" He was not sure if the old woman was Sioux or not, but that was the tongue he used.

The bent figure made no reply, although he sensed that she understood his words. Instead, she slowly lifted her arm and pointed with a gnarled finger. Clay realized with a shock that she was pointing at Shining Moon.

He frowned. "I don't understand. Are you a medicine woman? Have you come to help?"

The old woman just smiled, a hideous, toothless grin that stretched her weathered, lined face into something only vaguely human.

Clays heart pounded, and a coldness settled deep in his belly. He lifted his rifle a little.

"I think you'd better get out of here," he said.

She kept pointing at Shining Moon, unafraid of his rifle. In the black pits of her eyes was a look that seemed to say she considered him no threat at all. She shuffled forward, and even though her gait was slow and halting, she moved as if supremely confident that he could not stop her.

Clay moved quickly, putting himself between Shining Moon and the old woman.

"You've come for her, haven't you?" he asked, knowing that his voice had risen and become ragged with tension and emotion. "Well, you can't have her, damn it! You hear me? You can't have her!"

The woman continued to move toward him.

Clay wondered fleetingly why Proud Wolf and Aaron and Lucy did not wake up and help him. They all seemed to be sleeping so soundly. He was alone, alone to face the strangest menace he had ever encountered.

But he would not give up. Not with something so precious to him at stake.

"Take me," he said suddenly, not sure where the words came from but knowing somehow that they were right. "If you've got to take somebody, then take me!"

The old woman pointed past him, pointed at Shining Moon.

"No," Clay whispered. "You can't have her. Not unless you take me, too."

The old woman stopped, and a heavy sigh shook her frail body. She pointed one more time at Shining Moon, but Clay stood firm.

Something glittered in the old woman's eyes,

and Clay could hear her words in his mind as clearly if she had spoken: *We will meet again someday, Clay Holt. We will meet again, you and I.*

"That's fine," Clay said out loud. "But not here and not now."

She inclined her head just a little, as if acknowledging his point. Then she turned, and in the same halting gait with which she had approached, she walked out of the camp and vanished into the surrounding woods.

It was strange, Clay thought as beads of sweat broke out on his face, but he could not hear the sound of her going.

"Clay?"

He heard the whispered name and whirled around, falling to his knees beside Shining Moon. Her eyes were open, and she looked up at him with an expression of wonderment.

"Shining Moon?" he said.

"Was there . . . someone else here just now? I was waking, and I thought I saw . . . something—"

"No," Clay said firmly. "There was no one here. Nobody but me and Proud Wolf and Aaron and Lucy." He leaned closer to her and brushed his lips across her forehead. "How do you feel?"

"Better. Rested. I think I will be all right."

"You will be. I know you will."

She held out her hands to him, and he lifted her into a sitting position and settled down beside her so that he could put his arms around her and hold her close. She leaned against his shoulder and made a sound of contentment.

"I love you, Clay Holt," she murmured. "I will always love you."

"And I love you. But that's enough talking. You still need some rest. Just take it easy, lean on me, and close your eyes."

"Yes. I will do that."

This time, as her eyes closed and her breathing became deeper, Clay knew she was only asleep. Shining Moon was going to need a lot of healing, but tonight she had taken the first step on that journey.

Strange things were said to happen in these mountains. Clay supposed staring into the fire could have disoriented him until his imagination had played a trick on him. But he was not going to worry about what he had seen, was not going to concern himself about whether it had been real or only a product of exhaustion and worry. He had the only reality he needed right here in his arms.

The roll of money in Jeff's pocket seemed to be on fire as he rode through the streets of Wilmington, North Carolina. He supposed he should have gone to Dermot Hawley's office first, but he did not trust himself to face the man, not yet. And he had to see if what he suspected was true. He had to find out if Hawley's partner was none other than Charles Merrivale.

554

The wagons had reached Knoxville without further trouble, and as Amos Tharp had predicted, it had not been difficult to sell the supplies once they got there. Jeff did not consider himself much of a businessman, but he thought he had gotten a fair price for the goods. He had even sold the wagons, which had not been part of the plan, but he was long past worrying about doing anything to upset Hawley. After all, the man had tried to have him killed.

Some of the drivers were going to stay on in Tennessee and settle there, while others were returning to North Carolina. Jeff had paid them off and left all of them behind, retracing the route across the mountains and the Piedmont in much shorter time than the westbound journey had taken. He had ridden long and hard to get back.

And now the real payoff was about to take place.

It had not been difficult to find someone who could tell him how to find the Merrivale Mercantile Company. If Hawley had not hustled him out of town practically as soon as he arrived on the *Fair Wind* weeks earlier, he would have no doubt stumbled onto Merrivale then. Hawley had done his best to prevent that, just as he had lied to Jeff about checking the records at the courthouse.

He still did not know the reason why, but he would soon, he vowed.

Spotting the sign he was looking for, he reined

in and studied the big building in front of him. Merrivale's business took up damn near a whole city block, with the big double-doored main entrance on the corner. Jeff swung down from the saddle, looped the horse's reins over a long hitch rack, and stepped up onto the store's porch.

He opened the doors and stepped inside, then strode toward the rear of the building. That was where he would find Merrivale, he knew. He ignored the long aisles bordered with shelves stacked high with all sorts of goods, just as he ignored the clerks who asked him if he needed help. He pushed past them, his eyes fixed on a door behind the rear counter. Somehow, he knew that door led to an office.

"You can't go—" one of the white-aproned clerks started to say, edging over in front of Jeff, but he stopped short as he saw the expression on Jeff's face and the look in his eyes. Hastily, he backed out of Jeff's path.

Jeff put his hand on the knob, turned it, and thrust the door open. As he stepped into the room, he saw that it was indeed an office, with two large windows in the wall to the left. In the center of the airy, well-lit room was a big desk, and behind it a man with white hair and stern, craggy features looked up in annoyance from the ledger book open before him.

"What's all this?" he demanded. "Who—"

Then Charles Merrivale saw who had barged into his office without knocking, and his lined features turned almost as white as his hair.

Acting calmer than he felt, Jeff took the roll of bills from his pocket and tossed it onto the desk in front of Merrivale.

"There's the money from the wagon train," Jeff said. "You can split it up with your partner, Hawley."

Merrivale's mouth opened and closed two times, but nothing came out except a croaking sound. He swallowed hard.

"What are you doing here, Holt?" he said in a low voice.

Jeff kicked the office door closed with his heel.

"Surprised to see me, aren't you, Merrivale? You figured I was dead by now. That was some plan you and Hawley came up with, hiring Tharp to kill me like that. But it didn't work."

"Tharp?" Merrivale repeated. A look of genuine confusion appeared on his face. "I don't know what the hell you're talking about. But yes, I did think you were dead. I believed some red savage had probably killed you by now."

"You don't know anything about Hawley arranging to have me killed?" Jeff sounded skeptical.

Merrivale pushed himself to his feet. "That's insane," he said brusquely. Some of the color had come back into his face as he recovered from the shock of seeing his son-in-law again. "It's true I've had some business dealings with Dermot Hawley, but I don't know anything about hiring someone to kill you." He hesitated, then added, "Although perhaps it might not be a bad idea."

"You sorry old son of a bitch," Jeff grated. His fists clenched, and it took every ounce of his self-control to keep from leaping across the desk and battering that smug look off Merrivale's face.

"I don't know what you're doing here in North Carolina, Holt," Merrivale went on, "but you're neither needed or wanted here. Melissa has forgotten about you and made a new life for herself. If you have the least bit of common decency left in you, you'll leave town without bothering her and go back to whichever little squaw you've been living with for the past few years."

"You're lying," Jeff said stubbornly. "I've been true to Melissa. I promised her I'd come back, and now I have. Where is she, Merrivale?"

The older man drew himself up and glared across the desk.

"I won't tell you. And if you don't get out of here and leave Wilmington immediately, I'll have you arrested! I'm a man of some influence in this town, you know."

"I'll just bet you are," Jeff said softly. He reached across his body and let his fingers curl around the smooth wooden grip of the pistol at his waist. If he could not make Merrivale talk one way, there were always others. . . .

As Merrivale's eyes widened in fear, a voice came from the other side of the door. Jeff recognized it as belonging to the clerk who had tried to stop him.

"Wait!" the man was saying urgently. "You can't

go in there, Miss Melissa! There's a crazy man in there with your father—"

Jeff whirled around and threw the door open.

"Melissa!" The cry was torn from the core of his soul.

She was there, only a few feet away from him, after all these years. And as she turned to face him, he saw that she was just as lovely as ever, though her face was ashen with shock at the moment. Then, as he stepped forward to meet her, she threw herself into his arms. All the old familiar sensations—her warmth, the scent of her hair, the taste of her mouth—came flooding back to him as he kissed her.

The long search was over, and none of it mattered, Jeff realized now. He and Melissa were together again.

"Mama?"

The little voice made Jeff stiffen. He took his lips away from Melissa's and looked down to see a child tugging at her skirts. The boy was a sturdy youngster, with blond hair and clear blue eyes, almost the color of the high country skies.

"Ours?" Jeff whispered.

Melissa nodded.

"My God," Charles Merrivale said. "My God."

Jeff glanced back at him long enough to see the look of defeat on his father-in-law's face. Then he forgot about Merrivale and turned his attention to the child, kneeling in front of the boy to smile tenderly at him.

"Jeff," Melissa said, "I want you to meet Michael."

Jefferson Holt looked into the eyes of his son and knew that nothing in his life would ever be the same again.